The Tenderness of Wolves

STEF PENNEY

SIMON & SCHUSTER

New York London Toronto Sydney

SIMON & SCHUSTER
A Division of Simon & Schuster, Inc.
1230 Avenue of the Americas
New York, NY 10020

Originally published in Great Britain in 2006 by Quercus Publishing, PLC
Published by arrangement with Quercus Publishing, PLC

SIMON & SCHUSTER and colophon are registered
trademarks of Simon & Schuster, Inc.

Designed by Jaime Putorti

Manufactured in the United States of America

ISBN-13: 978-0-7394-9165-2

For my parents

Disappearance

THE LAST TIME I SAW Laurent Jammet, he was in Scott's store with a dead wolf over his shoulder. I had gone to get needles, and he had come in for the bounty. Scott insisted on the whole carcass, having once been bamboozled by a Yankee who brought in a pair of ears one day and claimed his bounty, then some time later brought in the paws for another dollar, and finally the tail. It was winter and the parts looked fairly fresh, but the con became common knowledge, to Scott's disgust. So the wolf's face was the first thing I saw when I walked in. The tongue lolled out of the mouth, which was pulled back in a grimace. I flinched, despite myself. Scott yelled and Jammet apologized profusely; it was impossible to be angry with him, what with his charm and his limp. The carcass was removed out back somewhere, and as I was browsing, they began to argue about the moth-eaten pelt that hangs over the door. I think Jammet suggested jokingly that Scott replace it with a new one. The sign under it reads, "Canis lupus (male), the first wolf to be caught in the town of Caulfield, 11th February, 1860." The sign tells you a lot about John Scott, demonstrating his pretensions to learning, his self-importance, and the craven respect for authority over truth. It certainly wasn't the first wolf to be caught around here, and there is no such thing as the town of Caulfield, strictly speaking, although he would like there to be, because then there would be a council, and he could be its mayor.

"Anyway, that is a female. Males have a darker collar, and are bigger. This one is very small."

Jammet knew what he was talking about, as he had caught more wolves than anyone else I know. He smiled, to show he meant no offense, but Scott takes offense like it is going out of fashion, and bristled.

"I suppose you remember better than I do, Mr. Jammet?"

Jammet shrugged. Since he wasn't here in 1860, and since he was French, unlike the rest of us, he had to watch his step.

At this point I stepped up to the counter. "I think it was a female, Mr.

Scott. The man who brought it in said her cubs howled all night. I remember it distinctly."

And the way Scott strung up the carcass by its back legs outside the store for everyone to gawp at. I had never seen a wolf before, and I was surprised at its smallness. It hung with its nose pointing at the ground, eyes closed as if ashamed. Men mocked the carcass, and children laughed, daring each other to put their hands in its mouth. They posed with it for each other's amusement.

Scott turned tiny, bright blue eyes on me, either affronted that I should side with a foreigner, or just affronted, it was hard to tell.

"And look what happened to him." Doc Wade, the man who brought in the bounty, drowned the following spring—as though that threw his judgment into question.

"Ah, well . . ." Jammet shrugged and winked at me, the cheek.

Somehow—I think Scott mentioned it first—we got talking about those poor girls, as people usually do when the subject of wolves is raised. Although there are any number of unfortunate females in the world (plenty in my experience alone), around here "those poor girls" always refers to only two—the Seton sisters, who vanished all those years ago. There were a few minutes' pleasant and pointless exchange of views that broke off suddenly when the bell rang and Mrs. Knox came in. We pretended to be very interested in the buttons on the counter. Laurent Jammet took his dollar, bowed to me and Mrs. Knox, and left. The bell jangled on its metal spring for a long time after he walked out.

That was all, nothing significant about it. The last time I saw him.

Laurent Jammet was our closest neighbor. Despite this, his life was a mystery to us. I used to wonder how he hunted wolves with his bad leg, and then someone told me that he baited deer meat with strychnine. The skill came in following the trail to the resulting corpse. I don't know, though; that is not hunting as I see it. I know wolves have learned to stay out of range of a Winchester rifle, so they cannot be entirely stupid, but they are not so clever that they have learned to distrust a free gift of food, and where is the merit in following a doomed creature to its end? There were other unusual things about him: long trips away from home in parts unknown; visits from dark, taciturn strangers; and brief displays of startling generosity, in sharp counterpoint to his dilapidated cabin. We knew that he was from Quebec. We knew that he was Catholic, although he did not often go to church or to confession (though he may have indulged in both during his long absences). He was polite and cheerful, although he did not have particular friends, and kept a certain distance. And he was, I daresay, handsome, with almost-black hair and eyes, and features that gave the impression of having just finished smiling, or being just about to start. He treated all women with the same respectful charm, but managed not to irritate either them or their husbands. He was not married and showed no inclination to do so, but I have noticed that some men are happier on their own, especially if they are rather slovenly and irregular in their habits.

Some people attract an idle and entirely unmalicious envy. Jammet was one of those, lazy and good-natured, who seem to slide through life without toil or effort. I thought him lucky, because he did not seem to worry about those things that turn the rest of us gray. He had no gray hairs, but he had a past, which he kept mostly to himself. He imagined himself to have a future, too, I suppose, but he did not. He was perhaps forty. It was as old as he would ever get.

It is a Thursday morning in mid-November, about two weeks after that meeting in the store. I walk down the road from our house in a dreadful temper, planning my lecture carefully. More than likely I rehearse it aloud— one of many strange habits that are all too easy to pick up in the backwoods. The road—actually little more than a series of ruts worn by hooves and wheels—follows the river where it plunges down a series of shallow falls. Under the birches patches of moss gleam emerald in the sunlight. Fallen leaves, crystallized by the night's frost, crackle under my feet, whispering of the coming winter. The sky is an achingly clear blue. I walk quickly in my anger, head high. It probably makes me look cheerful.

Jammet's cabin sits away from the riverbank in a patch of weeds that passes for a garden. The unpeeled log walls have faded over the years until the whole thing looks gray and woolly, more like a living growth than a building. It is something from a bygone age: the door is buckskin stretched over a wooden frame, the windows glazed with oiled parchment. In winter he must freeze. It's not a place where the women of Dove River often call, and I haven't been here myself for months, but right now I have run out of places to look.

There is no smoke signal of life inside, but the door stands ajar; the buckskin stained from earthy hands. I call out, then knock on the wall. There is no reply, so I peer inside, and when my eyes have adjusted to the dimness I see Jammet, at home and, true to form, asleep on his bed at this time in the morning. I nearly walk away then, thinking there is no point waking him, but frustration makes me persevere. I haven't come all this way for nothing.

"Mr. Jammet?" I start off, sounding, to my mind, irritatingly bright. "Mr. Jammet, I am sorry to disturb you, but I must ask . . ."

Laurent Jammet sleeps peacefully. Around his neck is the red neckerchief he wears for hunting, so that other hunters will not mistake him for a bear and shoot him. One foot protrudes off the side of the bed, in a dirty sock. His red neckerchief is on the table . . . I have grasped the side of the door. Suddenly, from being normal, everything has changed completely: flies hover around their late autumn feast; the red neckerchief is not around his neck, it cannot be, because it is on the table, and that means . . .

"Oh," I say, and the sound shocks me in the silent cabin. "No."

I cling on to the door, trying not to run away, although I realize a second later I couldn't move if my life depended on it.

The redness around his neck has leaked into the mattress from a gash. A gash. I'm panting, as though I've been running. The door frame is the most important thing in the world right now. Without it, I don't know what I would do.

The neckerchief has not done its duty. It has failed to prevent his untimely death.

I don't pretend to be particularly brave, and, in fact, long ago gave up the notion that I have any remarkable qualities, but I am surprised at the calmness with which I look around the cabin. My first thought is that Jammet has destroyed himself, but Jammet's hands are empty, and there is no sign of a weapon near him. One hand dangles off the side of the bed. It does not occur to me to be afraid. I know with absolute certainty that whoever did this is nowhere near—the cabin proclaims its emptiness. Even the body on the bed is empty. There are no attributes to it now—the cheerfulness and slovenliness and skill at shooting, the generosity and callousness—they have all gone.

There is one other thing I can't help but notice, as his face is turned slightly away from me. I don't want to see it, but it's there, and it confirms what I have already unwillingly accepted—that among all the things in the world that can never be known, Laurent Jammet's fate is not one of them. This is no accident, nor is it self-destruction. He has been scalped.

At length, although it is probably only a few seconds later, I pull the door closed behind me, and when I can't see him anymore, I feel better. Although for the rest of that day, and for days after, my right hand aches from the violence with which I gripped the door frame, as though I had been trying to knead the wood between my fingers, like dough.

WE LIVE IN DOVE RIVER, on the north shore of Georgian Bay. My husband and I emigrated from the Highlands of Scotland a dozen years ago, driven out like so many others. A million and a half people arrived in North America in just a few years, but despite the numbers involved, despite being so crammed into the hold of a ship that you thought there couldn't possibly be room in the New World for all these people, we fanned out from the landing stages at Halifax and Montreal like the tributaries of a river, and disappeared, every one, into the wilderness. The land swallowed us up and was hungry for more. Hacking land out of the forest, we gave our places names that sprang from things we saw—a bird, an animal—or the names of old hometowns: sentimental reminders of places that had no sentiment for us. It just goes to show you can't leave anything behind. You bring it all with you, whether you want to or not.

A dozen years ago there was nothing here but trees. The country to the north of here is a mean land that is either bog or stones, where even the willows and tamaracks cannot take hold. But near the river the soil is soft and deep, the forest around it so dark green it is almost black, and the sharp-scented silence feels as deep and endless as the sky. My first reaction, when I saw it, was to burst into tears. The carriage that brought us rattled away, and the thought that, however loudly I screamed, only the wind would answer, could not be pushed away. Still, if the idea was to find peace and quiet, we had succeeded. My husband waited calmly for my fit of hysteria to subside, then said, with a grim sort of smile:

"Out here, there is nothing greater than God."

Assuming you believe in that sort of thing, it seemed a safe bet.

In time I got used to the silence, and the thinness of the air that made everything seem brighter and sharper than it had back home. I even grew to like it. And I named it, since it had no name that anyone knew of: Dove River.

I'm not immune to sentimentality myself.

* * *

Others came. Then John Scott built the flour mill near the river mouth, and having spent so much money on it, and it having such a nice view of the bay, decided he might as well live in it. Somehow this started a fashion for living near the shore, inexplicable to those of us who had gone upriver precisely to escape the howling storms when the bay seems to turn into an angry ocean intent on clawing back the land you have so presumptuously settled. But Caulfield (sentiment again; Scott is from Dumfriesshire) took in a way that Dove River never could—because of the abundance of level land and relative sparseness of the forest, and because Scott opened a dry-goods store that made backwoods life a lot easier. Now there is a community of over a hundred—a strange mix of Scots and Yankees. And Laurent Jammet. He hasn't—hadn't—been here long, and probably would never have moved here at all had he not taken the piece of land that no one else would touch.

Four years ago he bought the farm downstream from ours. It had been lying empty for some time, on account of the previous owner, an elderly Scot. Doc Wade arrived in Dove River seeking cheap land where he would not be so much under the noses of those who judged him—he had a wealthy sister and brother-in-law in Toronto. People called him Doc, although it turned out he was not a doctor at all, just a man of culture who had not found a place in the New World that appreciated his varied but nebulous talents. Unfortunately Dove River was not the exception he was looking for. As many men have found, farming is a slow, sure way to lose your fortune, destroy your health, and break your spirit. The work was too heavy for a man of his age, and his heart was not in it. His crops failed, his pigs ran wild in the forest, his cabin roof caught fire. One evening he slipped on the rock that forms a natural jetty in front of his cabin, and was later found in the deep eddy below Horsehead Bluff (so named, with that refreshing Canadian lack of imagination, because it resembles a horse's head). It was a merciful release after his troubles, said some. Others called it a tragedy—the sort of small, domestic tragedy the bush is littered with. I suppose I imagined it differently. Wade drank, like most men. One night, when his money was gone and the whisky finished, when there was nothing left for him to do in this world, he went down to the river and watched the cold black water rushing past. I imagine he looked up at the sky, heard the mocking, indifferent voice of the forest one last time, felt the tug of the swollen river, and cast himself onto its infinite mercy.

Afterward, local gossip said that the land was unlucky, but it was cheap and Jammet was not one to take note of superstitious rumors, although perhaps he should have. He had been a voyageur for the Company, and had fallen under a canoe while hauling it up some rapids. The accident lamed him, and they gave him compensation. He seemed grateful rather than otherwise for his accident, which gave him enough money to buy his own land. He was fond of saying how lazy he was, and certainly he did not do the farmwork that most men cannot avoid. He sold off most of Wade's land and made his living from the wolf bounty and a little trading. Every spring a succession of dark, long-distance men would come from the Northwest with their canoes and packs. They found him a congenial person to do business with.

And now he is dead. Half an hour later I am knocking on the door of the biggest house in Caulfield. I flex the fingers of my right hand as I wait for an answer—they seem to have seized up into a sort of claw.

Mr. Knox has a poor, grayish complexion that makes me think of liver salts, and is tall and thin, with a hatchet profile that seems permanently poised to strike down the unworthy—useful attributes for a magistrate. I suddenly feel as empty as if I had not eaten for a week.

"Ah, Mrs. Ross . . . an unexpected pleasure . . ."

To tell the truth he looks, more than anything, alarmed at the sight of me. Perhaps he looks at everyone this way, but it gives the impression he knows slightly more about me than I would like, and thus knows I am not the sort of person he would want his daughters to associate with.

"Mr. Knox . . . I'm afraid it is not a pleasure. There has been a . . . a terrible accident."

Scenting gossip of the richest sort, Mrs. Knox comes in a minute later, and I tell them both what is in the cabin by the river. Mrs. Knox clutches at the little gold cross at her throat. Knox receives the news calmly, but he turns away at one point, and turns back, having, I can't help feeling, composed his features into a suitable cast—grim, stern, resolute, and so on. Mrs. Knox sits beside me stroking my hand while I try not to snatch it away.

"And to think, the last time I saw him was in the store that time. He looked so . . ."

I nod in agreement, thinking how we had fallen into a guilty silence on her approach. After many protestations of shocked sympathy and advice for shattered nerves, she rushes off to inform their two daughters in a suitable way (in other words, with far more detail than if their father were present). Knox dispatches a messenger to Fort Edgar to summon some Company men. He leaves me to admire the view, then returns to say he has summoned John Scott (who, in addition to owning the store and flour mill, has several warehouses and a great deal of land) to go with him to examine the cabin and secure it against "intrusion" until the Company representatives arrive. That is the word he uses, and I feel a certain criticism. Not that he can blame me for finding the body, but I am sure he regrets that a mere farmer's wife has sullied the scene before he has had a chance to exercise his superior faculties. But I sense something else in him, too, other than his disapproval—excitement. He sees a chance for himself to shine in a drama far more urgent than most that occur in the backwoods—he is going to investigate. I presume he takes Scott so that it looks official and there is a witness to his genius, and because Scott's age and wealth give him a sort of status. It can be nothing to do with intelligence—Scott is living proof that the wealthy are not necessarily better or cleverer than the rest of us.

We head upriver in Knox's trap. Since Jammet's cabin is close to our house, they cannot avoid my accompanying them, and since we reach his cabin first, I offer to come in with them. Knox wrinkles his brow with avuncular concern.

"You must be exhausted after your terrible shock. I insist that you go home and rest."

"We will be able to see whatever you saw," Scott adds. And more, is the implication.

I turn away from Scott—there is no point arguing with some people—and address the hatchet profile. He is affronted, I realize, that my feminine nature can bear the thought of confronting such horror again. But something inside me hardens stubbornly against his assumption that he and only he will draw the right conclusions. Or perhaps it is just that I don't like being told what to do. I say I can tell them if anything has been disturbed, which they cannot deny, and anyway, short of manhandling me down the track and locking me in my house, there is little they can do.

The autumn weather is being kind, but there is the faint tang of decay when Knox pulls open the door. I didn't notice it before. Knox steps forward, breathing through his mouth, and puts his fingers on Jammet's hand—I see him hover, wondering where to touch him—before pronouncing him quite cold. The two men speak in low voices, almost whispering. I understand—to speak louder would be rude. Scott takes out a notebook and writes down what Knox says as he observes the position of the body, the temperature of the stove, the arrangement of items in the room. Then Knox stands for a while doing nothing, but still manages to look purposeful—an accident of anatomy I observe with interest. There is a scuff of footprints on the dusty floor, but no strange objects, no weapon of any sort. The only clue is that awful round wound on Jammet's head. It must have been an Indian outlaw, Knox says. Scott agrees: no white man could do something so barbaric. I picture his wife's face last winter, when it was swollen black and blue and she claimed she had slipped on a patch of ice, although everybody knew the truth.

The men go upstairs to the other room. I can tell where they go by the creak of their feet pressing on floorboards and the dust that falls between them and catches the light. It trickles onto Jammet's corpse, falling softly on his cheek, like snowflakes. Little flecks land, unbearably, on his open eyes, and I can't take my gaze off them. I have an urge to go and brush them off, tell the men sharply to stop disturbing things, but I don't do either. I can't make myself touch him.

"No one has been up there for days—the dust was quite undisturbed," says Knox when they are down again, flicking dirt off their trousers with pocket handkerchiefs. Knox has brought a clean sheet from upstairs, and he shakes it out, sending more dust motes whirling around the room like a swarm of sunlit bees. He places the sheet over the body on the bed.

"There, that should keep the flies off," he says with an air of self-congratulation, though any fool can see that it will do no such thing.

It is decided that we—or rather they—can do no more, and on leaving, Knox closes and secures the door with a length of wire and a blob of sealing wax. A detail that, though I hate to admit it, impresses me.

WHEN THE WEATHER TURNS COLD Andrew Knox is made painfully aware of his age. Every autumn for some years now his joints have started to hurt, and go on hurting all winter no matter how many layers of flannel and wool he wraps them in. He has to walk gingerly, to accommodate the shooting pains in each hip. Each autumn the pains start a little earlier.

But today weariness spreads through his entire soul. He tells himself that it is understandable—a violent event like murder is bound to shake anyone. But it is more than that. No one has been murdered in the history of the two villages. We came here to get away from all that, he thinks; we were supposed to leave that behind when we left the cities. And yet the strangeness of it . . . a brutal barbarian killing, like something that would happen in the southern states. In the past few years several people have died of old age, of course, of fever or accident, not to mention those poor girls . . . But no one has been slaughtered, defenseless in their stockinged feet. He is upset by the victim's shoelessness.

He reads through Scott's notes after dinner, and tries not to lose his patience: "The stove is three feet high and one foot eight inches deep, faintly warm to the touch." He supposes this might be useful. Assuming the fire was going strongly at the time of death, it could take thirty-six hours to become cold. So the murder could have happened the day before. Unless the fire had already started to die down when Jammet met his end, in which case it could have happened during the night. But it is not inconceivable that it took place the previous night. In their search today they found little. There were no clear signs of a struggle; no blood other than on the bed, where he must have been attacked. They wondered aloud whether the place had been searched, but his belongings were scattered so haphazardly—their usual state, according to Mrs. Ross—that it was impossible to be certain. Scott protested loudly that it must be a native: no white man could do something so barbaric. Knox is less sure. Some years ago Knox was called to a farm near Coppermine, after a particularly regrettable incident. There is a practice popular in some communities whereby a groom is ritually humiliated on his wedding night. It is known as a "charivari" and is meant as a genial show of disapproval at, say, an old man taking a much younger wife. In this case the elderly bridegroom had been tarred and feathered and strung up by his feet from a tree outside his own house, while local youths paraded in masks, banging kettles and blowing whistles.

A prank. Youthful high spirits.

But somehow the man had died. Knox knew of at least one youth who was unquestionably involved in the business, but no one, despite their regret, would speak out. A prank gone wrong? Scott had not seen the man's suffused face; the wires cutting savagely into bloated ankles. Andrew Knox feels unable to exempt a whole race from suspicion on the grounds that they are incapable of cruelty.

He has become aware of the sounds beyond the window. Outside his walls there may be a force of evil. Perhaps the sort of cunning that would think to scalp a man to throw suspicion onto those of a different color. Please God, not a Caulfield man. And what motive can there have been for this death? Surely not the theft of Jammet's old and ill-used possessions. Did he have a secret cache of wealth? Did he have enemies among the men he traded with—perhaps an unpaid debt?

He sighs, dissatisfied with his thoughts. He had been so sure that seeing the cabin would provide him with clues, if not answers, but he is left with less certainty than before. It hurts his vanity to admit that he could not read the signs, especially in front of Mrs. Ross—a provoking woman who always makes him feel uncomfortable. Her sardonic gaze never softened, even when describing her appalling discovery, or confronting it for the second time. She is not popular in the town, for she gives the impression of looking down her nose at people, although by all accounts (and he has heard some pretty hair-raising gossip), she has nothing to be conceited about. However, to look at her and to recall some of these lurid stories is to find them incredible: she has a regal bearing, and an admittedly handsome face, although her prickly manner is not compatible with true beauty. He had been aware of her eyes on him when he stepped up to the corpse to feel for warmth. He could barely keep his hand from trembling—there seemed to be no flesh free from blood to touch. He took a deep breath (which only made him feel nauseous) and placed his fingers on the dead man's wrist.

The skin was cold, but felt otherwise human, normal—like his own skin. He tried to keep his eyes off the terrible wound but, like the flies, they seemed unable to stay away. Jammet's eyes stared up at him, and it occurred to Knox that he was standing where the killer must have stood. He hadn't been asleep, not at the end. He felt he ought to close the eyes but knew he wouldn't be able to do so. Shortly afterward he fetched a sheet from upstairs and covered the body. The blood was dry and wouldn't stain, he said—as if it mattered. He tried to cover his confusion with another practical remark, hating the hearty sound of his own voice as he did so. At least tomorrow it will not be his sole responsibility any more—the Company men will arrive and, probably, they will know what to do. Probably, something will become apparent, someone will have seen something, and by evening it will have been solved.

And with this spurious hope, Knox tidily rearranges the papers into a pile and blows out the lamp.

IT IS PAST MIDNIGHT, BUT I sit up with a lamp and a book I am unable to read, waiting for a footstep, for the door to open and cold air to fill the kitchen. I find myself thinking yet again about those poor girls. Everyone in Dove River and Caulfield knows the story, and it is recounted to anyone who comes here, or repeated over and again with subtle variations on winter evenings in front of the fire. Like all the best stories, it is a tragedy.

The Setons were a respectable family from St. Pierre La Roche. Charles Seton was a doctor, and his wife, Maria, a recent Scottish immigrant. They had two daughters who were their pride and joy (as they say, though when are children ever not?). On a mild day in September Amy, who was fifteen, and Eve, thirteen, set off with a friend called Cathy Sloan to gather berries and picnic by the banks of a lake. They knew the way, and all three girls had been brought up in the bush, were familiar with its dangers and respected its code: never stray from the paths, never stay out after dusk. Cathy was exceptionally pretty, famous in the town for her looks. This detail is always added, as though it makes what happened even more tragic, although I cannot personally see that it matters.

The girls set off with a basket of food and drink at nine in the morning. At four, the time by which they should have returned, there was no sign of them. Their parents waited a further hour, then the two fathers set out to trace their daughters' footsteps. After zigzagging around the path, calling constantly, they arrived at the lake and searched, still calling, until after dark, but found no sign of them. Then they returned, thinking it possible that their daughters had taken another route and had by now arrived home, but the girls were not there.

A massive search was got up, and everyone in the town turned out to help look for the children. Mrs. Seton took to fainting fits. On the evening of the second day, Cathy Sloan walked back into St. Pierre. She was weak, and her clothes were filthy. She had lost her jacket and one of her shoes, but was still holding the basket that had contained their lunch; apparently now (grotesque detail and probably untrue) it was full of leaves. The searchers redoubled their efforts, but they never found a thing. Not a shoe, not a scrap of clothing, not even a footprint. It was as though a hole had opened in the ground and swallowed them up.

Cathy Sloan was put to bed, although whether she was actually ill was a moot point. She said that she had had some sort of argument with Eve shortly after setting off, and had dawdled behind the other two until losing them from sight. She walked to the lake and called for them, thinking they were mean to have hidden from her. She became lost in the woods and could not find the path. She never saw the Seton sisters again.

The townspeople went on searching, sending delegations to the nearby Indian villages, for suspicion fell on them as naturally as rain falls on the ground. But not only did they swear their innocence on the Bible, there was not a scrap of evidence of a kidnapping. The Setons looked further and further afield. Charles Seton hired men to help him look, including an Indian tracker and then, after Mrs. Seton had died, seemingly of a broken heart, a man from the States who was a professional searcher. The searcher traveled to Indian bands all over Upper Canada and beyond, but found nothing.

Months became years. At the age of fifty-two Charles Seton died, exhausted, penniless, and at a loss. Cathy Sloan was never quite the beauty she had been; she seemed dull and stupid—or had she always been that way? No one could any longer remember. The story of the case spread far and wide, and then passed into legend, recounted by schoolchildren with wild inconsistencies, told by frazzled mothers to curb their children's wandering. Wilder and wilder theories grew up as to what had happened to the two girls; people wrote from far-flung addresses claiming to have seen them, or married them, or to be them, but none ever proved well founded. In the end, no explanation could possibly fill the void left by the disappearance of Amy and Eve Seton.

All that was fifteen years ago or more. The Setons are both dead now; first the mother died of grief, then the father, bankrupt and exhausted by his relentless quest. But the story of the girls belongs to us because Mrs. Seton's sister is married to Mr. Knox, and that is why we fell into a guilty silence when she came into the store that day. I do not know her particularly well, but I do know that she never speaks of it. Presumably, on winter evenings in front of the fire, she talks of something else.

* * *

People disappear. I'm trying not to assume the worst, but all the lurid theories about the girls' disappearance are haunting me now. My husband has gone to bed. Either he isn't worried, or he is indifferent—it is years since I could tell what he was thinking. I suppose that is the nature of marriage, or perhaps it just goes to show that I am not very good at it. My neighbor Ann Pretty would probably incline toward the latter; she has a thousand ways of implying that I am deficient in my wifely duties—when you think of it, an astonishing feat for a woman of such little sophistication. She holds my lack of living natural children as a sign of failure to do my immigrant duty, which is, apparently, to raise a workforce large enough to run a farm without hiring outside help. A common enough response in such a vast, under-populated country. I sometimes think that the settlers reproduce so heroically as a terrified response to the size and emptiness of the land, as though they could hope to fill it with their offspring. Or maybe they are afraid that a child can slip away so easily, they must always have more. Maybe they are right.

When I got back to the house this afternoon Angus was back. I told him about Jammet's death, and he examined his pipe for a long time, as he does when he is deep in thought. I found myself close to tears, although I did not know Jammet well. Angus knew him better, had gone hunting with him on occasion. But I could not read the currents moving under his skin. Later we sat in the kitchen at our usual places, eating in silence. Between us, on the south side of the table, another place was set. Neither of us referred to it.

Many years ago, my husband took a trip back east. He was gone for three weeks, after which he sent a telegram saying to expect him back on the Sunday. We had not spent a night apart in four years, and I looked forward keenly to his return. When I heard the rumble of wheels on the road, I ran to meet him, then saw, puzzled, that there were two people in the cart. As the cart came closer I saw that it was a child of about five years, a girl. Angus pulled up the pony and I ran toward them, my heart beating thickly in my throat. The girl was asleep, long lashes lying on her sallow cheeks. Her hair was black. Her eyebrows were black. Purple veins showed through her eyelids. She was beautiful. And I couldn't speak. I just stared.

"The French Sisters had them. Their parents died of plague. I heard about it and went to the convent. There were all these children. I tried to get one who would be the right age, but . . ." He trailed off. Our infant daughter had died the year before. "But she was the bonniest." He took a deep breath. "We could call her Olivia. I don't know if you'd want to, or—"

I threw my arms around his neck and suddenly found that my face was wet. He held me tight, and then the child opened her eyes.

"My name is Frances," she said in a noticeable Irish brogue. She had a sharp look about her with her eyes open—alert.

"Hello, Frances," I said, nervous. What if she didn't like us?

"Are you going to be my mama?" she asked.

I felt my face go hot as I nodded. She went quiet after that. We took her inside and I made the nicest dinner I could muster—whitefish and vegetables and tea with lots of sugar, although she didn't eat much, and stared at the fish as though she wasn't sure what it was. She didn't say another word, her dark blue eyes flickering from one of us to the other. She was exhausted. I picked her up in my arms and carried her upstairs. The sensation of holding this hot, limp body made me tremble with feeling. Her bones felt fragile under my hands, and she smelled stale, like an unaired room. Since she was almost asleep I just took off the dress, shoes, and socks, and tucked a blanket around her. I watched as she twitched in her sleep.

Frances's parents had arrived at Belle Isle aboard a packet ship called the *Sarah*. The steerage was packed with Irish from County Mayo, which was still suffering after the potato famine. Like those people who catch on to a fad long after it has gone out of fashion, they developed typhus fever on board, although the worst of the epidemics had subsided. Nearly a hundred men, women, and children died on that ship, which sank on its return journey to Liverpool. Several children were orphaned and had been taken to the nunnery until they could be found homes.

The next morning I went to the spare room to find Frances still asleep, although when I touched her shoulder gently I had the impression that she was pretending. I realized she was scared; perhaps she had heard terrible stories about Canadian farmers and thought we were going to treat her as a slave. Smiling at her, I took her hand and led her downstairs to where I'd prepared a tub of hot water in front of the stove. She kept her eyes on the floor as she lifted her arms for me to peel off the long petticoat.

I ran out of the house, looking for Angus, who was splitting wood at the corner of the house.

"Angus," I hissed, feeling angry and stupid at the same time.

He turned around, axe in hand, frowning at me, puzzled. "Is something wrong? Is she all right?"

I shook my head to the first question. It occurred to me that he knew, yet I instantly dismissed the idea. Used to me, he turned back to the log; down came the axe; neat halves span into the log basket.

"Angus, you got a boy."

He put the axe down. He didn't know. We went back inside to where the child was playing idly with the soap in the bathtub, letting it pop up through his fingers. His eyes were large and wary. He wasn't surprised to see us staring at him.

"Do you want me to go back?" he asked.

"No, of course not." I knelt beside him and took the soap from his hands. The shoulder blades stuck out like wing stumps on his skeletal back.

"Let me." I took the soap and began to wash him, hoping my hands would tell him more than words that it didn't matter. Angus went back to the woodpile and let the door bang behind him.

Francis never seemed surprised that he had come to us dressed as a girl. We pondered for hours over the French Sisters' motives—did they think a girl would find a home more easily than a boy? Yet there had been boys in the group of orphans. Had they simply not noticed, been blinded by the beauty of his face, and dressed him in the clothes that seemed to suit it best? Francis himself didn't offer an explanation, or express any shame; nor did he offer resistance when I made him some trousers and shirts and cut off his long hair.

He thinks we never forgave him for it, but that's not so with me. With my husband, though, I'm not sure. A Highlander through and through, he doesn't like to be made a fool of, and I don't know that he ever recovered from the shock. It was all right when Francis was a child. He could be very funny, clowning and mimicking. But we all got older, and things changed, as they always seem to, for the worse. He grew into a youth who never seemed to fit with the others. I watched him try to be stoic and tough, to cultivate a foolhardy courage and that casual disrespect for danger that is common currency in the backwoods. To be a man you have to be brave and enduring, to make light of pain and hardship. Never complain. Never falter. I saw him fail. We should have lived in Toronto, or New York, then maybe it wouldn't have mattered. But what pass for heroics in a softer world are daily chores here. He stopped trying to be like the others; he became surly and taciturn, no longer responded to affection, wouldn't touch me.

Now he is seventeen. His Irish accent is quite gone, but in some ways he is as much a stranger as ever. He looks like the changeling he is; they say there is Spanish blood in some Irish, and to look at Francis you would believe it—he is as dark as Angus and I are fair. Ann Pretty once made a labored joke that he had come to us from a plague, and had become our own personal plague. I was furious with her (she laughed at me, of course), but the words stuck and barge out of my memory whenever Francis is storming through the house, slamming doors and grunting as if he were barely able to speak. I have to remind myself of my own youth and bite my tongue. My husband is less tolerant. They can go for days on end without a good word passing between them.

That is why I was afraid to tell Angus that I have not seen Francis since the day before. Still, I resent him for not asking. Soon it will be morning and our son has not been home for forty-eight hours. He has done this before—he will go on solitary fishing trips that last for two or three days, and return, usually without fish and with barely a word about what he has done. I suspect that he hates to kill anything; the fishing is just a cloak for his desire to be alone.

I must have fallen asleep in the chair, because I wake when it is nearly light, stiff and cold. Francis has not returned. Much as I try to tell myself it is a coincidence, just another extended fishing-for-nothing trip, the thought keeps coming back to me that my son has disappeared on the day of the only murder that Dove River has ever known.

FIRST LIGHT FALLS ON THREE riders making their way from the West. They have been traveling for hours already, and daylight comes as a relief, especially to the man at the rear. Donald Moody finds the half-light a particular strain on his weak eyes; no matter how he rams his spectacles up against his nose, this monochrome world is full of uncertain distances and subtle, shifting shapes. It is also freezing. Even wrapped in layers of wool and a skin coat with the fur on the inside, his limbs are numb and long past aching. Donald breathes in the thin, sweet air, so different from that of his native Glasgow, sooty and raw at this time of year. The air is so clear that the unhindered sunlight seems to travel farther; when the sun has just broken the horizon, like now, their shadows reach behind them forever.

His horse, which has been crowding the mount ahead, stumbles and rams its nose into the gray's hindquarters, earning a warning swish of the tail.

"Curse you, Moody," says the man in front of him. Donald's brute of a mount is continually either lagging behind or bumping into the quarters of Mackinley's beast.

"Sorry, sir." Donald tugs at the reins and the horse flattens its ears. It was bought from a Frenchman and seems to have inherited some of his anti-British prejudice.

Mackinley's back radiates disapproval. His mount is perfectly behaved, like the horse in front of him. But then Donald is continually being re-minded of his greenness—he has been in Canada just over a year and still makes huge blunders with Company etiquette. No one ever warns him in advance, because almost their sole entertainment is to watch him struggle along, falling into bogs and offending locals. Not that the other men are exactly unkind, but it is clearly the way here: the most junior member of staff must serve his apprenticeship as figure of fun. Most of the Company men have education, courage, and a spirit of adventure, and they find their lives in the big country sorely lacking in incident. There is danger (as advertised), but it is the danger of frostbite or exposure rather than unarmed combat with wild animals or war with hostile natives. Their daily lives are made up of petty endurances—of cold, darkness, screaming boredom, and the overconsumption of bad liquor. Joining the Company, Donald realized early on, was like being sent to a labor camp, only with more paperwork.

The man in front, Mackinley, is the factor of Fort Edgar, and leading them is a native employee, Jacob, who insists on accompanying Donald everywhere, rather to his embarrassment. Donald does not much care for Mackinley, who is sarcastic and bluff by turns—a two-pronged method of deflecting the criticism he seems to expect from every quarter. He guesses that Mackinley is so touchy because he feels socially inferior to some of the men beneath him, Donald included, and is constantly on the lookout for signs of disrespect. Donald knows somehow that if Mackinley were less concerned about such things, he would be more respected, but the man is not likely to change now. As for himself, he is aware that Mackinley and the others regard him as a rather effete bean counter—useful enough, but hardly a real backwoods adventurer in the old style.

When he got off the ship from Glasgow, he meant to be himself and let the men take him as they found him. But he has, in fact, made valiant attempts to improve his image in their eyes. For one thing, he steadily increased his tolerance of the rough alcohol that is the lifeblood of the fort, although it does not agree with him. When he first arrived, he would sip politely at the rum they decanted from vast smelly barrels, thinking he had never tasted anything so disgusting. The other men noted his abstinence and left him marooned as they journeyed into the realms of drunkenness, telling long, boring stories and laughing repeatedly at the same jokes. Donald put up with this for as long as he could, but the loneliness weighed on him until he could no longer bear it. The first time he got spectacularly drunk the men cheered, slapping him on the back when he vomited onto his knees. Through the nausea and acrid dampness Donald felt a kernel of warmth: he belonged—finally they would accept him as one of them. But, although the rum no longer tasted as bad as it once did, he was aware that the others treated him with a sort of amused tolerance. He was still just the junior accountant.

The other bright idea he had to prove himself had been to organize a rugby football match. Overall this was disastrous, but out of it had come one small ray of light, which causes him to pull himself straighter in the saddle.

Fort Edgar is a civilized posting compared to most of the Company's forts. It lies near the shore of the Great Lake, a huddle of wooden buildings inside a palisade—the whole obstinately sheltering from a stunning prospect of islands and bay behind a belt of spruce. But what makes Fort Edgar civilized is the proximity of settlers, and the nearest are at Caulfield on Dove River. The residents of Caulfield are happy to live near the trading post, as it is stocked with imported English goods and upstanding Company men. The traders are equally happy to be near Caulfield, as it is stocked with English-speaking white women, who can occasionally be persuaded to decorate the fort's dances and other social events—like rugby matches.

On the morning of the match, he found that he was nervous. The men were sullen and bleary-eyed after a marathon drinking session, and Donald was unnerved to see a party of visitors arrive. He was even more unnerved when he met them—a tall, stern-looking man who was the image of a hell-fire preacher, and his two daughters, who were excited to be surrounded by so many youngish, unattached men.

The Knox sisters watched the proceedings politely, utterly mystified. Their father had attempted to explain the rules, as he knew them, on the journey to Fort Edgar, but his grasp of the game was rusty, and he had only confused them more. The players moved around the meadow in a large ragged knot, the ball (a weighty lump stitched by a voyageur's wife) generally invisible.

As the game progressed, the mood darkened. Donald's team seemed to have reached a consensus to keep him out of the game, and they ignored his shouts to pass to him. He ran up and down, hoping the girls could not tell that he was superfluous, when the ball came rolling toward him, leaking bits of furry stuffing. He picked it up and ran up the pitch, determined to make his mark, when he found himself on the ground, winded. A short half-breed, Jacob, grabbed the ball and ran, and Donald gave chase, determined not to let his opportunity slip. He hurled himself at Jacob, slicing the man's legs from under him in a severe but fair tackle. A giant steersman scooped up the ball and scored.

As he lay on the ground, Donald's triumphant cheer gurgled in his throat. He lifted his hands from his stomach to see them dark and warm, and Jacob standing over him with a knife in his hand, his features slowly animating into an expression of horror.

The spectators eventually realized something was amiss and rushed the pitch. The players gathered around Donald, whose first recognizable emotion was embarrassment. He saw the magistrate bending over him with an expression of avuncular concern.

"... barely injured. Accident ... heat of the moment."

Jacob was distraught, tears running down his face. Knox peered at the wound. "Maria, pass your shawl."

Maria, the less pretty daughter, tore off her shawl, but it was Susannah's upside-down face that Donald fixed on as the shawl was pressed to his wound.

He began to feel a dull ache in his gut, and to notice how cold he was. The game forgotten, the players stood around awkwardly, lighting their pipes. But Donald met Susannah's eyes, which were full of concern, and found that he no longer cared about the outcome of the match, or whether he had displayed rugged and manly qualities, or even that his lifeblood was now seeping through his capote, turning it brown. He was in love.

The wound had the strange outcome of making Jacob his undying friend. He had come to Donald's bedside the day after the match, in tears, expressing his deep and terrible regret. It was drink that had made him do it; he had been possessed by the bad spirit, and he would atone for the injury by personally looking after Donald for as long as he remained in the country. Donald was touched, and when he smiled his forgiveness and held out his hand, Jacob smiled back. It was perhaps the first real smile of friendship he had seen in this country.

Donald staggers when he slides off his horse and tries to stamp some circulation back into his limbs. He is unwillingly impressed by the size and elegance of the house they have come to, especially thinking of Susannah, and how much more unattainable it makes her. But Knox smiles warmly at them when he comes out, then looks with ill-concealed alarm at Jacob.

"Is this your guide?" he asks.

"This is Jacob," Donald says, feeling heat rise in his cheeks, but Jacob doesn't seem offended.

"A great friend of Moody's," puts in Mackinley waspishly.

The magistrate is puzzled, since he is almost certain the last time he saw

the man he was sticking a knife into Donald's guts. He assumes he is mistaken.

Knox tells them what he knows, and Donald takes notes. It doesn't take
long to write down the known facts. Tacitly they know there is no hope of
finding the perpetrator unless someone saw something, but someone always
sees something in a community like this; gossip is the lifeblood of small
country places. Donald stacks fresh paper on top of his notes and straightens it with an efficient tap as they get up to visit the scene of the crime. He
is not looking forward to this part and hopes he won't disgrace himself by
becoming nauseous, or—he tortures himself by imagining the worst possible outcome—what if he were to burst into tears? He has never seen a dead
body before, not even his grandfather. Though this is unlikely, he imagines
with an almost pleasurable horror the teasing he would endure. He would
never live it down; he would have to return to Glasgow incognito, probably
live under another name . . .

Thus engaged, the journey to the cabin passes in a flash.

NEWS TRAVELS FAST THESE DAYS, thinks Thomas Sturrock. Even where there are no roads or railways, news, or its nebulous cousin rumor, travels like lightning over vast distances. It is a strange phenomenon, and one that might benefit from the attention of a diligent mind such as his. A short monograph, perhaps? The *Globe* or the *Star* might be interested in such an item, if it were amusing.

He has allowed himself to think, on occasion over the past few years, that he has become even more prepossessing with age. His hair is silver, swept back from a high and elegant forehead, worn slightly long and curling around his ears. His coat is old-fashioned but well cut and rather rakish, of a dark blue that echoes his eyes, no dimmer now than thirty years ago. His trousers are natty. His face is finely made and hawklike, agreeably honed with outdoor living. There is a spotted and cloudy mirror hanging on the wall opposite, and it reminds him that, even in these straitened circumstances, he is a rare figure of a man. This secret vanity, which he grants himself rarely as a small (and, more important, free) pleasure, makes him smile at himself. "You are undoubtedly a ridiculous old man," he silently tells his reflection, sipping cold coffee.

Thomas Sturrock is engaged in his usual occupation—that of sitting in slightly shabby coffeehouses (this one is called the Rising Sun), making one cup of coffee last an hour or two. The musing about news and rumor have come from somewhere, he realizes, when he finds that he is listening to a conversation being carried on behind him. Not eavesdropping—he would never stoop to such a thing—but something has caught his wandering mind, and now he tries to work out what it was that hooked him . . . Caulfield, that was it, someone mentioned the name Caulfield. Sturrock, whose mind as well as his dress sense is as sharp as it ever was, knows someone who lives there, although he has not seen him for a while.

"They said you'd never seen anything like it. Drenched in blood, all up the walls and everything . . . must have been Indian raiders . . ."

(Well, no one can be blamed for listening to a conversation like that.)

"Left to rot in his cabin . . . had been there for days. Flies crawling over him, thick as a blanket. Imagine the smell."

The companion agrees.

"No reason for it, nothing was stolen. Killed in his sleep."

"Christ, we'll be getting as bad as the States next. Wars and revolutions every five minutes."

"Could have been one of those deserters, couldn't it?"

"Traders ask for trouble, dealing with all sorts . . . Foreign, apparently, so you never know . . ."

"What are we coming to . . ."

Etc. Etc.

At this point, Sturrock's attention, already keen, sharpens still further. After a few more minutes of desultory doom-mongering, he can hold out no longer.

"Excuse me, gentlemen . . ."

There are looks that he chooses to ignore as he turns to the two men: commercial travelers, judging from their cheap but ostentatious dress and generally low-class demeanor.

"I do apologize. I know what a terrible bore it is when strangers butt in on one's conversation, but I have a personal interest in what you have just been discussing. You see, I have some business with a trader who lives near Caulfield, and I couldn't help noticing you describing—very graphically—a particularly shocking and tragic occurrence. Obviously I could not help but become concerned at such a story, and I only hope that it doesn't involve my acquaintance . . ."

The two commercial travelers, both dull-witted men, are rather set on the back foot by such eloquence, not often heard within the walls of the Rising Sun. The storyteller recovers first, and he glances down at Sturrock's cuff, which is dangling over the back of his chair. Sturrock instantly recognizes the look, combined with a downward tilt of the head, a short meditative pause, and then back to Sturrock's face. The man has just calculated the likelihood of financial gain from selling what information he has to this man—not great, from the state of the cuff, although the East Coast Yankee voice might be good for something. He sighs, but the natural delight in passing on bad news wins out.

"Near Caulfield?"

"Yes, I believe he lives on a small farm or something, the place is called something River . . . a bird or an animal, some such name."

Sturrock remembers the name perfectly well, but he wants to hear it from them.

"Dove River."

"Yes, that's it. Dove River."

The man glances at his companion. "This trader. Is he a Frenchie?"

Sturrock feels the coldness of shock clench his spine. The two men see it in his face. Nothing more needs to be said.

"A Frenchie trader in Dove River was murdered. I don't know if there's more than one such there."

"I don't think there is. You didn't . . . hear a name by any chance?"

"Not that I remember off the top of my head—something French, is all I recall."

"The name of my acquaintance is Laurent Jammet."

The man's eyes light up with pleasure. "Well, I'm sorry, I truly am, but I think that was the name that was mentioned."

Sturrock falls uncharacteristically silent. He has had to deal with many shocks in his long career, and his mind is already working out the repercussions of this news. Tragic, obviously, for Jammet. Worrying, at the least, for him. For there is unfinished business there that he has been very keen to conclude, awaiting only the financial means to do so. Now that Jammet is dead, the business must be concluded as soon as possible; otherwise, the chance may slip out of his reach for good.

He must have looked very shocked indeed, because the next time he looks down there is a cup of coffee and a chaser of bourbon standing on his table. The commercial travelers are looking at him with great and genuine interest—a violent and dreadful piece of news is exciting enough, but to stumble across someone directly affected by the tragedy—what could be better? It is worth several dinners in cold currency. Sturrock accordingly reaches out with a trembling hand for the liquor.

"You look like someone walked over your grave all right," remarks one of them.

Realizing what is required of him, Sturrock hesitatingly tells a sad tale of a present promised to his sick wife, and a debt unpaid. He is not, in fact, married, but the travelers do not seem to mind. At one point he leans on the table, his eyes following a plate of chops on their way past, and two minutes later a hot roast dinner lands in front of him. Really, he thinks (not for the first time), he missed his vocation—he should have been a writer of romances, the ease with which he conjures the consumptive wife. When at last he feels he has given them their money's worth (no one could accuse him of not being generous with his imagination), he shakes them both by the hand and leaves the coffeehouse.

It is late afternoon, and the day is fleeing over the western horizon. He walks slowly back to his lodgings, his mind working out how he is going to find the cash for a trip to Caulfield, for that is what he will have to do, to keep his dream alive.

There is probably one person left in Toronto whose patience he has not entirely exhausted, and if he approaches her in the right way, she might be good for a loan of twenty dollars or so. Accordingly, he turns his footsteps right at the end of Water Street and heads toward the more salubrious districts along the lake shore.

W HEN I COULD NO LONGER pretend it was night—long after the sun came up—I gave in to exhaustion and climbed upstairs to bed. Now it must be midday, but I can't get up. My body refuses orders, or rather my mind has given up issuing them. I stare at the ceiling, mired in the certainty that all human endeavor, but especially mine, is futile. Francis has not come home, thus adding weight to the argument that I am utterly without talent, courage, or use. I am anxious for him, but my concern is overwhelmed by the inability to make a decision to do anything. I am not surprised he has run away from such a mother.

Angus got up just as I was coming upstairs, and not a word was said. We have had difficult conversations about Francis before, although not under such dramatic circumstances. Angus tends to repeat that he is seventeen and can look after himself; it is normal for boys of his age to take off for days on end. But he is not like normal boys, I try not to say, but in the end always do. The unspoken words press on me in the small room: Francis is gone; a man is dead. Of course there can be no connection.

A voice in my head wonders if Angus would not grieve too much if Francis did not come back. Sometimes they look at each other with such venom, like sworn enemies. A week ago Francis came in late and refused to do one of his chores. He would do it in the morning, he said, treading on thin ice as Angus had just had a fruitless argument with James Pretty over the boundary fence. Angus took a breath and told him just what a selfish, ungrateful youth he was. When he said the word "ungrateful," I knew what was coming. Francis exploded: Angus expected him to be grateful for giving him a home; he treated him as an indentured servant; he hated him and always had . . . Angus withdrew into himself, betraying nothing but a thin glimmer of contempt that chilled me. I shouted at Francis then, my voice trembling. I wasn't sure how much he included me in his anger; it was so long since he had looked me in the eye.

* * *

How could I have prevented it coming to this? Probably Ann is right to deride me; I am incapable of raising a family, even though I used to despise women who thought it was all that mattered. Not that I have produced anything else of worth.

A sort of waking dream haunted me through my vigil; I had been reading a gothic story about an artificial man who hated the world because his appearance inspired terror and loathing. At the end of the novel the creature ran away to the Arctic, where no one could see him. In night-induced delirium I saw Francis being pursued, like the monster, who is a murderer . . . In daylight I can see how silly this was; Francis can't even kill a trout. At the same time, he has been gone for two days and nights.

Something occurs to me in the tangle of sheets, and eventually forces me to go into Francis's room and pick through the chaos. It is hard to tell what is there and what is gone, so it takes me some time to find what I am looking for. When I do, I go into a frenzy, pulling things out of cupboards, scrabbling under the bed, and then tearing through the rest of the house in a desperate search. But it is no good—because I am praying for things not to be there when they irrefutably are. I find his two fishing rods and the spare rod Angus made for him when they were still on speaking terms. I find tinderboxes and sleeping blankets. I find all the things he would have taken on a fishing trip. The only things missing are a set of clothes and his knife. Without thinking I take his favorite fishing rod out the back and break it in two, and bury the halves in the woodpile. When I have done that I am breathing heavily. I feel guilty and dirty, as if I have accused Francis myself, so I go inside and boil pans of water for a bath. Luckily I don't get into the tub straightaway, for Ann Pretty marches into the kitchen without even a knock.

"Ah, Mrs. Ross, what a life of leisure you lead! Bathing in the middle of the day . . . You ought to be careful with hot baths at your age. My sister-in-law had a seizure in her bath, you know."

I do know, as she has told me at least twenty times. Ann likes to remind me that she is three years younger than I, as though this were a whole generation. For my part I refrain from pointing out that she looks older than her years and is shaped like a bear, whereas I have kept my figure and was thought, in my youth at least, something of a beauty. She wouldn't care anyway.

"Did you hear they are investigating? They have brought in Company men. A whole troop. They are asking questions up and down the river."

I nod, noncommittal.

"Horace came up from the MacLarens' and said they'd been there talk-ing to everyone. I expect they'll be here soon." She looks around her in a predatory fashion. "He said Francis hasn't been around since yesterday morn."

I don't bother to correct her and say it was longer than that. "He'll get a shock when he comes back," I say.

"Didn't he hunt with Jammet?" She looks sly, her eyes raking the room like a bird of prey, a rosy-faced, broad-beamed buzzard, looking for car-rion.

"A few times. He'll be sad when he finds out. They weren't great friends, though."

"What a business. What are we all coming to? Still, he was a foreigner. They're hot-blooded, Frenchies, aren't they? I know when I lived in the Sault they were always at each other's throats. I expect it was one of them come to do business."

She is not going to accuse Francis to my face, but I can imagine her doing so elsewhere. She has always thought of him as a foreigner, too, with his dark hair and skin. She considers herself a well-traveled woman, and from each place she has been to, she has brought away a prejudice as a sou-venir.

"So when's he coming back? Aren't you worried, with a murderer run-ning around?"

"He's fishing. Probably not till tomorrow."

I suddenly want her to leave, and she takes the hint and asks me for a loan of tea—a sign that she thinks there is nothing else to be had from me. I give her the tea more willingly than usual, and add some coffee beans in a fit of generosity that ensures she won't be back soon, as backwoods eti-quette dictates you bring an equal offering with each visit.

"Well . . . Best be getting on."

And yet she still doesn't go, looking at me with an expression I don't think I have seen on her face before. It disturbs me somehow.

Hot water has a beneficial effect on me. Bathing is not de rigueur in No-vember, but I see it as a more civilized alternative to the shock baths they used to give us in the asylum. I experienced the douche only twice, in the early days, and although excruciating in anticipation and duration, it left you feeling remarkably calm and clear-headed, even exhilarated. It was a simple device whereby the patient (in this case, me) would be strapped to a wooden chair in a thin cotton shift while a large bucket of cold water was raised above your head. An attendant pulled a lever and the bucket tipped over, drenching you in icy water. That was before Paul—Dr. Watson—took over as superintendent and instigated a gentler regime for the mad, which meant (for the women at least) sewing, flower arranging, and all sorts of nonsense. I only agreed to go into the hospital in the first place to get away from that sort of thing.

Thinking about my time in the asylum always cheers me—the advantage, I suppose, of a miserable youth. I must remember to share this pearl of wisdom with Francis when he comes home.

He introduces himself as Mr. Mackinley, factor of Fort Edgar. He is a slight man, his thick hair cut short so that it looks, appropriately, like fur. Something about me surprises him—I think my accent, which is more cultured than his and probably seems out of place here. His manner becomes slightly obsequious at this, although I can see him fighting it. All in all, not a happy man. Not that I've got anything to shout about.

"Is your husband in?" he asks stiffly. As a woman I'm obviously not supposed to know anything.

"He is out on business. And our son is on a fishing trip. I am Mrs. Ross. I found the body."

"Ah. I see."

He's a fascinating case—one of those rare Scotsmen whose expression reveals his mind. Assimilating all this information, his face changes yet again, and on top of the surprise and deference and courtesy and mild contempt is a keen interest. I could watch him all day, but he has his job to do. And I have mine.

He gets out a notebook, and I tell him that Angus will be back later but was in the Sault until yesterday afternoon, and Francis left yesterday morning. This is a lie, but I have thought about what to say, and no one knows any different. He seems interested in Francis. I say he has gone up to Swallow Lake, but may move on if the fish aren't biting.

I say they were friendly. He takes notes.

I thought hard about what to say about Francis and Jammet and their friendship. It has occurred to me that Jammet was perhaps his only friend, even though Jammet was so much older, and French. Jammet persuaded Francis to go hunting, something Angus had never managed. There was also that time earlier this summer when I was walking to the Maclaren place and passed his cabin. I heard a violin playing—a bright, infectious sound, totally unlike Scottish fiddle music—some French folk tune, I suppose. It was so attractive that I veered toward the cabin in my urge to listen. Then the door burst open and a figure spilled out, limbs flailing, then dashed back inside, in some sort of game. The music, which had stopped, started up again, and I walked on. It had taken me a couple of moments to realize that the figure was Francis. I hardly recognized him, perhaps because he was laughing.

He's not stupid, this one, despite his revealing face. But perhaps it is all an act—it throws you off the scent. Now, strangely, his expression is quite different—he looks at me almost kindly, as if he has established that I am a poor creature who can be no threat to him. I am not sure what I have done to give him this idea, but it annoys me.

Through the window I watch him walking up the road to the Prettys' farm and think of Ann. I wonder whether the expression I saw on her face was pity.

DONALD QUICKLY LEARNS SOME FACTS about Caulfield. For one thing, when he knocks on the door of a house, the occupants panic—no one knocks in the normal run of things. When they have established that no members of their immediate family are dead, injured, or under arrest, they drag him in to ply him with tea and pump him for information. His notes are a chaos of cross-references: the first family have seen nothing but send for a cousin, who turns out to be the husband of another woman, whom he awaits for an hour before realizing he has already met him. People surge in and out of their houses swapping stories, theories, and excited, doom-laden prophecies about the state of the country. Trying to make sense of it is like trying to gather the river in his arms.

It is dark by the time he has completed his allotted round of questioning. He waits in the parlor at Knox's house and tries to draw conclusions from what he has heard. His notes reveal that no one he spoke to saw anything unusual—he discounts the atypical squirrel behavior seen that morning by George Addamont. Donald hopes that he hasn't let the others down by missing something obvious. He is tired and has been fed a great deal of tea and, latterly, whisky; has made promises to revisit several households; but he has not, he is fairly certain, met a murderer.

He is wondering how to ask for directions to the bathroom when the door opens and the plainer Knox daughter looks in. Donald immediately stands up and drops some sheets of paper, which Maria hands back to him with a sly smile. Donald blushes, but is thankful that it is Maria and not Susannah who witnesses his clumsiness.

"Father has roped you in to play detective then?"

Donald immediately feels that she has sensed his insecurity about the afternoon and is making fun of him.

"Surely someone must attempt to find the villain?"

"Well of course, I didn't mean . . ." She trails off, looking annoyed. She was only making small talk, he realizes, too late. He should have agreed lightheartedly, or made some sort of quip.

"Do you know when your father is to return?"

"No." She looks at him with that calculating look. "I have no way of knowing that." Then she smiles, not kindly. "Shall I ask Susannah? Perhaps she knows. I'll go and find her."

Maria leaves Donald to wonder what he has done to incur such sharpness. He imagines the sisters giggling over his lack of social graces, and feels a surge of affection for his ledgers at the fort, full of neat figures that, with a little manipulation, he can always make come out right. He prides himself on his ability to account for vague items like the cleaning done by the native women, or the food brought in by the hunters, so that they balance the "hospitality" the Company extends to the voyageurs' families. If only people were as easy to manage.

A polite cough alerts him to Susannah's presence just before she opens the door.

"Mr. Moody? Oh, you have been quite abandoned; shall I send for some tea?"

She smiles gracefully, so different from her sister, but still has the effect of making him jump to his feet, though this time he holds on to his notes.

"No, thank you, I have been . . . Well, yes, perhaps, that would be very . . . Thank you." He tries not to think about the gallons of tea he has drunk.

When the tea has arrived, Susannah sits down to keep him company.

"This is a terrible business, Miss Knox. I wish we were meeting again under happier circumstances."

"I know. It is awful. But the last time was awful, too—you were . . . attacked. Are you quite recovered? It looked dreadful!"

"Quite recovered, thank you." Donald smiles, eager to please with good news, though, in fact, the scar tissue is soft and tender and often aches.

"Has the man been punished?"

Donald had not even thought about Jacob being punished. "No, he was very contrite and has become my sworn protector. I think that is the Indian way of making amends for a wrong. More useful than punishment, don't you think?"

Susannah's eyes widen in surprise, and Donald notices that they are a peculiarly attractive shade of hazel, flecked with gold.

"Do you trust him?"

Donald laughs. "Yes! I think he is quite sincere. He is here now."

"Goodness! He looked so frightening."

"I think that the real culprit was drink, and he has forsworn it forever. He is really very gentle—he has two tiny daughters whom he adores. You know, I am helping him with his reading, and he told me he finds reading and writing quite as fascinating as hunting for deer."

"Really?" She laughs, too, and then they fall silent.

"Do you think you will find whoever killed the poor man?"

Donald glances at his notes, which certainly aren't going to help. But Susannah has a way of looking at him with such warmth and trust that he wishes to solve not just this murder, but all the wrongs there are.

"I think someone must have seen a stranger in a place like this—it seems people generally know what everyone is doing."

"Yes, they do," she says with a grimace.

"Something as abominable as this . . . we will not rest until we have brought the man to justice. You shall not have to live in fear."

"Oh, I am not afraid." Susannah tilts her head defiantly. She leans toward him a little and lowers her voice. "We have lived through tragedy, you know."

It is such an extraordinary statement that Donald stares, as he was intended to do. "Oh, I didn't know . . . I'm terribly sorry . . ."

Susannah looks pleased. As the youngest member of the family it is rare that she gets to be the one to relate the Great Story—everyone in Caulfield knows it already, and strangers are not usually left to her mercy. She draws a breath, reveling in her moment.

"It was quite a long time ago, and we were very little when it happened so I can't remember, and it was Mama's sister you see . . ."

The door opens so suddenly that Donald is sure Maria must have been listening behind it.

"Susannah! You can't tell him that!" Her face is white and taut with emotion, though from the emphasis of her words it is hard to tell whether she is more upset that Susannah is the teller, or that Donald is the audience. She turns to Donald. "You had better come; my father has returned."

Knox and Mackinley are in the dining room, piles of notes stacked on the table. To Donald's dismay, they both seem to have written far more than him. Donald looks around for Jacob.

"Where is Jacob? Will he be dining with us?"

"Jacob is all right. He has been taking care of the, er, body."

"What was his opinion of the mutilation?"

Mackinley stares at him in mild outrage. "I am sure his opinion is the same as ours."

Knox coughs, to draw them back to the matter in hand, but Donald notices that he has receded somehow, while Mackinley has come forward, assuming the lead in their discussion. He is the one in charge. The Company has taken over.

Each man summarizes his findings, which amount to the conclusion that no one saw much at all. A trader by the name of Gros André passed through a few days ago. And a peddler called Daniel Swan, familiar to everyone, was in Caulfield the day before, and has moved on toward St. Pierre. Knox has sent a message to the magistrate there. Mackinley found a young boy who saw Francis Ross go to Jammet's cabin one evening—he can't remember which one—and now Francis is absent.

"The mother says she doesn't know when he'll be back. I spoke to some of the neighbors about him, and he sounds a queer fish. Keeps himself to himself."

"Which doesn't mean that he did it," puts in Knox.

"We have to look at every possibility. We don't know whether either of the other two visited Jammet."

"Surely the trader would have? He sounds French. You said before that it was probably a disagreement over trade."

Mackinley turns his eyes on Donald. "I propose to follow him, and find out."

"Well, shall I follow this Swan fellow?"

Knox shakes his head. "That won't be necessary. I have sent a messenger, and he will be detained at St. Pierre. I have to go there myself, so I will question him. We were going to suggest that you wait here with Jacob and question the Ross boy on his return."

Donald is momentarily disappointed, and then, realizing what opportunities it affords him, can't believe his luck.

Mackinley frowns. "Perhaps they would do better to follow him. If he has run, there is no point waiting until the trail gets cold."

"But where would they look? He may not have gone to Swallow Lake at all. We have only the mother's word for it. And he's only a lad. He had no motive, as far as we know. Quite the reverse; it seems they were friends."

"We have to keep an open mind." Mackinley glares.

"Of course. But I think Mr. Moody would be wasting his time rushing up to this lake." He turns to Donald. "Perhaps you could wait a day or two, and if he hasn't returned by then, you can go after him. A day will make no difference to Jacob; the boy is no Indian, and he'll be easy to track."

Jacob is a Christian, but he still felt a deep unease at the thought of contact with a dead body, and one butchered in this way held a particular kind of uncleanness. He and two paid volunteers, one a midwife practiced in laying out, were dispatched to bring the body to Caulfield, and she was the only one not stopped in her tracks by the smell. The midwife merely tutted in valediction and began to sponge the dried blood away. The body had relaxed, so they straightened him and closed his eyes and placed a coin in his mouth. The midwife tied a cloth around his head to keep his jaw closed and cover up the wounds, and then they wrapped him in sheets, until only the smell remained. The road back to Caulfield was so rough Jacob had to keep a hand on the body to keep it from rolling off the cart.

Now it lay on a table behind hastily rigged curtains in Scott's dry-goods warehouse, surrounded by crates of cloth and nails. The three of them and Scott's janitor stood around the table in an impromptu silence before turning away. All of them commented on the weather—how lucky that it was cold.

Donald follows the smell of tobacco to the stables, where Jacob smokes his pipe in a nest of straw, and sits beside him in silence. Jacob fiddles with the tobacco in the bowl. To talk about the dead man will be unlucky, he feels sure. But he knows that this is what Donald wants to do.

"Tell me what you think."

Jacob is getting used to Donald's peculiar questions. He is constantly asking what he thinks of this and that. Of course it is normal to be asked what you think of the weather, or the prospects for hunting, say, or a journey time, but Donald prefers to talk about things that are vague and unimportant, like a story he has just read, or a remark that someone made two days ago. Jacob tries to think what it is that Donald wants to know.

"You know he was scalped. It was quick, clean. His throat was cut as he lay down, perhaps sleeping."

"Could a white man have done it?"

Jacob grins, his teeth gleaming in the lamplight. "Any man can do it, if that is what he wants to do."

"Did you get a feeling—about who might have done it, or why? You were there."

"Who did it? I don't know. Someone who felt nothing for him. Why did he kill him? Perhaps he had done something a long time ago. Perhaps he hurt someone . . ." Jacob pauses, his eyes following the trail of smoke up to the rafters. "No. If you want to do that, you want him to be awake, to know you have won."

Donald nods, encouraging him.

"Perhaps he was killed for what he was going to do, to stop him. I don't know. But I think whoever did it has probably done it before."

Donald tells him about waiting for the Ross boy, and following him if necessary. Mackinley is going after the trader, obviously the most likely suspect, cornering the potential glory of capturing the murderer for himself.

"Maybe he shouldn't go alone if this man is so tough." Jacob grins. "Maybe he will do him, too."

He draws his finger across his neck. Donald tries not to smile. Since befriending Jacob he has become aware of Mackinley's universal unpopularity.

"Don't you think it odd that no one has seen any . . . er, Indians, in the last few days? If it was an Indian who killed him, I mean."

"If an Indian doesn't want to be seen, he won't be. At least for our people this is true. For others . . ." He sniffs disparagingly. "Chippewa, I don't know, maybe they no good trackers." He is careful to smile, to show Donald he is joking.

Sometimes Donald feels like a child next to this young man, who is barely older than himself. After he recovered from his wound, he started to help Jacob with his reading and writing, but theirs is not a relationship of teacher and pupil. Donald has a suspicion that the book-learned knowledge he imparts to Jacob is not really his to give; he just happens to know how to tap into it, whereas when Jacob tells him something, he seems to own it entirely, as if it comes from inside himself. But perhaps Jacob feels the same way; after all, the world around him is just a series of signs that he happens to understand, in the same way that Donald can discern the meaning of words on paper without thinking. Donald would like to know what Jacob thinks about this, but he cannot imagine how he would begin to ask him.

MARIA KNOX IS OBSERVING A phenomenon she has seen many times before: the effect of her sister on a young man. She is used to it, since from the time she was fourteen and her sister twelve boys clustered around Susannah, and altered their behavior in her presence, becoming gruff and shy or loud and boastful, depending on their nature. Maria they ignored; plain and sarcastic, she was either a playmate or, later, someone to copy homework from. But Susannah was of a peculiarly sunny disposition, and as they got older it became apparent that she was also a beauty. She was never precious; she was adept at most games; and if she was aware of her looks (which, of course, she was), she was modest, even resentful of the attentions they brought. As members of a family (and of society as well, presumably) carve, or are pushed into, roles for themselves, and then become imprisoned by them, so Susannah became everyone's darling: spoiled but slightly patronized, in need of protection from unpleasant facts of life like blocked sanitary closets and taxation. Meanwhile, Maria became an argumentative bluestocking, reading ferociously through her adolescent years, taking an interest in Expansionism, the war to the South, and other subjects generally thought unsuitable for young ladies. For the past three years she has had her own subscriptions to a number of Canadian and foreign journals. She is publicly a Reformer (but secretly favors the Clear Grits), admires Tupper, and argues with her father about his liking for George Brown. All this in a town where reading a newspaper while wearing a dress marks one out as something of a freak. But Maria is aware that the difference between the mental capacities of Susannah and herself is not so very great. If Susannah had been plain and therefore left to her own devices, she was probably just as capable of making herself an intellectual. And she is honest enough to admit that if she herself had been more aesthetically favored, she would have been lazier in the pursuit of knowledge. It is really such small differences that determine the course of a life.

Every so often Maria brings up the subject of college—she is twenty years old and beginning to feel that if she does not go soon it will become embarrassing. But her family proclaims that she is indispensable, and proves it by involving her in everything that goes on. Her mother consults her about every aspect of the household, claiming that she cannot cope ("So what did you do when I was a child?" Maria asks, rhetorically). Her father often discusses his cases with her. As for Susannah, she throws her arms around her and wails that she could not live without her. Of course, it may be that she lacks the courage to make the break from Caulfield. (Perhaps, even, she would not make the grade in the city?) She has wondered about this, but thinking about it too often depresses her, so whenever the possibility occurs, she picks up another newspaper and pushes the thought aside. Besides, if she had gone to college this fall, she would not have been here to support her family during this trying time. Her mother puts on a brave face, but her eyes reveal her worry—on the surface about accommodating two strangers in her house, but deeper down there is a well-hidden terror of the wilderness.

For two days Maria has attempted to get her father alone to ask him about the case, which has been impossible until this evening. She is confident that he will share his thoughts with her, and she is keen to discuss her own theories. But after the Company men have gone to bed, his face, never a good color, is almost gray with fatigue. His eyes are sunken, and his nose appears more prominent than ever. She goes and puts her arms around him instead.

"Don't worry, Papa; very soon this will be solved, and it will become a memory."

"I hope so, Mamie."

She secretly likes being called this—a nickname from her childhood that absolutely no one else is allowed to use.

"How long are they going to stay?"

"As long as it takes for them to question everyone they want to question, I suppose. They mean to wait until Francis Ross comes back."

"Francis Ross? Really?" Francis is three years younger than she is, and therefore she still thinks of him as a sullen, handsome boy who was much giggled over by the girls in senior school. "Well, they don't need to stay with us. They could go to the Scotts'. I'm sure the Company can afford it."

"I'm sure it can. How are your mother and Susannah coping with it all?"

Maria pauses to give this serious thought. "Mama would be happier without the guests."

"Mm."

"And Susannah is fine. It's an exciting diversion from the usual run of things. Although I found her today on the point of telling Mr. Moody about our cousins, and I almost lost my temper. I'm not sure why. It's none of his business, is it?" After a pause she adds, though slightly ashamed of it, "I think she was trying to impress him. Not that she needs to try."

Her father smiles. "I expect she was. It's not often that she gets looked up to."

Maria laughs shortly. "What are you saying? She is nothing but looked up to, as far as I can tell."

"Admired in one sense, yes. But not regarded in the way people regard you, Mamie, with a certain awe."

He gives her a look. Maria smiles, feeling a blush flare over her cheeks. She likes the thought of being regarded with awe.

"I didn't mean to flatter you."

"Don't worry, I am not at all flattered by being compared to Niagara Falls or the Heights of Abraham."

"Well, just as long as you're not . . ."

Maria watches her father climb the stairs—stiffly, which means he is suffering with his joints. It is awful to watch your parents age and know that pains and frailties are only going to accumulate in the body, building up until it fails completely. Maria has already developed a rather cynical outlook on life, probably another by-product of having a beautiful sister.

Not that Maria is at all interested in Mr. Moody for herself. Not at all. But, just occasionally, it would be nice to think that she stood a chance.

AFTER MACKINLEY LEAVES I PACE the kitchen until Angus returns, and I don't have to tell him that Francis has still not come back. I tell him the fishing rods are all here, and that I hid one. Now he, too, looks uneasy.

"You must go and look for him."

"It's been less than three days. He's not a child."

"He could have had an accident. It's cold. He hasn't taken any blankets."

Angus thinks, then says he will go up to Swallow Lake tomorrow. I am so relieved I go and embrace him, only to meet with a stiff and unyielding response. He simply waits for me to detach myself, and then turns away as though nothing has happened.

Our marriage seemed to work as long as I didn't think about it. Now, I don't know, the more I worry about other people the less they seem to like it. When I thought of nothing but myself, I only had to snap my fingers and men did whatever I wanted. Then I try to become a better person and look where it's got me: my own husband turning away and refusing to meet my eyes. Or maybe it is none of those things, and is simply to do with age—as a woman gets older she loses the ability to charm and persuade, and there is nothing that can be done about it.

"I could come with you."

"Don't be silly."

"I can't stand this waiting. What if something's . . . happened?"

Angus sighs, his shoulders hunched like an old man's. "Rhu . . ." he breathes out the old endearment, which causes a small tremor inside me. "I'm sure he is all right. He will be back soon."

I nod, touched by the endearment. In fact, I seize at it like a lifebelt—although, I think afterward, if I am really still his "rhu," his dear, why does he not look at me when he says it?

As the light fades, I go for a walk, skirt pockets bulging. At least that is what I tell Angus; whether he believes me is anyone's guess. At this time of day everyone in Dove River sits down to eat, as predictable as a herd of cattle, so no one will be outside or anywhere they shouldn't be. Nobody but me.

I thought about this most of the day, and decided that evening was the best time. I could have waited till dawn, but I don't want to leave it any longer. The river is fast and high—there have been rains to the north. But the rock from where Doc Wade took his leave is dry—it is only the spring floods that cover it.

And yet there is a footprint on it. A dark, wet mark. Even in the dusk I see it. Perhaps Knox has arranged for a guardian after all. Who got bored and went for a paddle. I don't believe it for a minute, so I creep softly down the side of the cabin, out of sight of the front door. All is silent. Perhaps I imagined it—I can no longer see the rock. I have brought a knife in my pocket, which I am now holding, rather more tightly than is necessary. It's not really that I think for a moment the murderer would come back—for what?—but I creep on, one hand on the cabin wall, until I can listen by the window for sounds within. I stand there so long my leg goes to sleep, and I have not heard so much as a fly's breath. I step up to the door, which is wired shut, take out the pliers, and unpick the fastening. Inside is dim, but I still pull the door closed, just in case.

The cabin looks exactly as I remember it, except that the bed is now empty. There is still an awful smell coming from the mattress and blankets, stacked up against the wall. I wonder who is going to wash them—or will they simply be burned?

I start upstairs. It doesn't look as though Jammet came up here very much—there are boxes and crates stacked against the walls, and dust blankets everything, showing where the men went yesterday, their feet rubbing little clearings where they stopped and peered at something. I put down the lamp and start to go through the nearest box, which contains his best clothes—an old-fashioned black coat and trousers, which I would say were too small for him. Did they belong to him when younger, or to his father? I sift through the other boxes: more clothes, some papers from the Hudson Bay Company, mainly relating to his retirement after "an accident incurred in the line of duty."

Several items open doors that lead to Jammet's other lives, before he came to Dove River. I try not to think about some of them too much: a pressed silk flower, for instance, faded with age—a token of love from a woman, or one he meant to give but didn't? I wonder about the invisible women in his life. And here is a rare thing—a photograph that shows

Jammet as a younger man, grinning his infectious smile. He is with several men I take to be voyageurs, all wearing neckerchiefs and capotes and squinting to varying degrees in the bright sunlight, clustered around a mountain of boxes and canoes, but he is the only one who could keep up a smile for that long. What occasion could have merited a photograph? Perhaps they had just beaten the record for a particularly grueling portage. Voyageurs take pride in such things.

Having searched the boxes I pull them away from the wall. I am not sure what I think I might find there, but there is nothing other than dust and mouse droppings, the desiccated husks of wasps.

I go downstairs disheartened. I don't even know what I am looking for, other than something that will confirm that Francis has nothing to do with this, which of course I already know. I cannot imagine what that might be.

I become aware that I am breathing thickly through my mouth as I go through his foodstuffs. The smell inhabits the whole building, worse than when he was still here. For the sake of thoroughness, so I will not be tormented in the night and have to come back, I stick my hand into the bins of grain and flour, and that's when I find it. In the flour bin my hand brushes against something, and I jerk backward with a sort of yelp before I can stop myself, throwing flour everywhere. It's a slip of paper torn from a larger piece, with numbers and letters written on it: 61HBKW. Nothing else. I can't really imagine anything less useful. Why hide a piece of paper in a flour bin if it has nonsensical letters on it, particularly if, like Jammet, you can't read? I put it in my pocket before it occurs to me that it could have fallen into the flour bin by accident. Come to that, it could have fallen into the flour anywhere; in Scott's warehouse, for instance. Even if Jammet did hide it, it seems hardly likely to give me the identity of his killer.

I have so far avoided the area around the bed, and am unwilling, to say the least, to put my hands on it. I should have brought gloves, but that is one thing I did not think of. I peer around inside the empty firebox while I think about it. Then something happens that very nearly causes me to faint from shock: there is a knock at the door.

I stand stock-still for several seconds, but it is foolish to pretend I am not here, what with the lantern shining through the translucent windows. I stand for several more seconds, while I try to concoct a good reason for being there, but I still haven't thought of one when the door opens and I am confronted with a man I have never seen before.

SHORTLY AFTER HE EMERGED FROM the bright fog of childhood, Donald had to acknowledge that he had difficulty seeing objects at any distance. Anything beyond the range of his outstretched hand became indistinct; small objects escaped him; people became anonymous. He could no longer recognize friends, or even his own family, and he stopped hailing people at a distance, as he had no idea who they were. He developed a reputation for coldness. He confided his unease to his mother and was provided with a pair of uncomfortable wire-framed spectacles. This was the first miracle of his life—the way the spectacles brought him back into the world.

The second, related miracle occurred one evening soon after. It was November, a rare clear night, and he was walking home from school when he looked up and stopped dead in astonishment. The full moon hung low and heavy in front of him, casting his shadow along the road. But what made his jaw drop was its clarity. He had assumed (without ever thinking about it much) that the moon was a fuzzy disc to everyone. How could it be otherwise, when it was so far away? But here it was, in sharp, exquisite detail—the wrinkled, pocked surface, the bright plains and dark craters. His new, augmented vision reached not just to the far side of the street and the hymn board in church, but countless leagues into space. Breathless, he took the glasses off—the moon was softer, larger, somehow nearer. His surroundings closed in, appearing both more intimate and more threatening. He put the glasses back on and distance, clarity, was restored.

That night he walked home filled with a huge, brimming delight. He laughed out loud, to the surprise of passersby. He wanted to shout to them and tell them of his discovery. He knew it would mean nothing to them, they who had seen it all along. But he felt sorry for them, not to know what it was to appreciate a gift like eyesight, having lost it, and been granted it again.

How often, since then, has he felt that perfect, overwhelming delight? In truth, not once.

* * *

Donald lies in the narrow, uncomfortable bed staring at the moon over Caulfield. He takes his spectacles off and puts them on again, reliving that ecstatic moment of revelation. He remembers being sure he had been afforded a glimpse of something portentous, although not certain what it meant. Now it doesn't seem that it meant anything much. But he became accustomed to looking at things from a distance, in order to keep them in focus. Perhaps that is why he gravitated toward numbers, attracted by their mute simplicity. Numbers are only ever themselves. If things can be reduced to numbers, they can be ordered and balanced. Take the community of native families that live beyond the palisade of Fort Edgar, and cause constant headaches to the factors. The voyageurs breed at an alarming rate, producing ever more mouths for the Company to feed. There has been much grumbling about the food they consume and the medical attention they demand, so Donald set to enumerating the work that the women do for the fort. He listed the washing and vegetable tending, the tanning of hides, the making of snowshoes . . . and attributed a value to each task, until he could show that the Company was benefiting at least as much from the association as the families were. He was proud of this achievement, even more so since getting to know Jacob's wife and children—two girls who stare at their father's pale friend with huge, liquid brown eyes. These children with their trusting gaze and incomprehensible secret names are set against the furs that the Company lives on, although, to be honest, no one is in any doubt which are more important.

When Donald first arrived at Fort Edgar, the clerk in depot, a man called Bell, had shown him around the post. Donald saw the offices, the crowded sleeping quarters, the trading counter, the Indian village beyond the palisade (at a suitable distance), the log church, the graveyard . . . and finally the huge cold storerooms where the furs were stacked, waiting to start on their epic journey to London, where they would be converted into hard cash. Bell glanced furtively around him before breaking open a bale, and the glossy pelts slithered out onto the dirt floor.

"Well, this is what it's all about," he said in his Edinburgh accent. "This lot will be worth several guineas in London. Let's see . . ." He stirred the pelts with his hand. "Here's a marten. You can see why we don't want them to shoot the beasties—the traps barely leave a mark, look!"

He waved the flattened leg of a weasel-like animal at Donald. The head was still attached to it—a small, pointed face with its eyes squeezed shut, as though it couldn't bear to remember what had happened to it.

He laid the marten down and plunged his hand back into the skins, offering them to Donald in quick succession, like a magician. "These are the least valuable; beaver, wolf, and bear, though they are useful enough—good wrappings for the other furs. Feel how coarse it is . . ."

The glossy pelts rippled under his hands, vestigial legs folding under them. Donald took the pelts as he was handed them and was surprised at their touch. He had felt rather disgusted at this vast warehouse of death, but as he pushed his hands into the cool, silky luxuriance, he experienced an urge to put the soft fur to his lips. He resisted, of course, but understood how a woman could want such a thing draped around her neck, where she could, with just a small tilt of the head, brush the fur against her cheek.

Bell was still talking, almost to himself. "But the most valuable . . . ah, this is silver fox—this is worth more than its weight in gold." His eyes shone in the dirty light.

Donald reached out a hand to touch, and Bell almost flinched. The fur was gray and white and black, blended together into a silvery sheen, thick and soft, with a heavy, watery flow. He withdrew his hand, as Bell seemed unable to let go of it.

"The only one more valuable is black fox—that comes from the far north, too, but you hardly see one from one year's end to the next. That would cost you a hundred guineas in London."

Donald shook his head in wonder. As Bell started to press the furs into a wooden packing mold, tenderly laying the silver fox in the middle, Donald felt uncomfortable, as if, despite Bell's best efforts to hide it, he was in the presence of some secretive act of pleasure.

Donald wrenches his mind back to the present. He wants to think about his conversation with Jacob, to balance the facts until he comes up with a brilliant solution that makes everything come out right, but there aren't enough facts. A man is dead, but no one knows why, let alone who did it. If they could trace Jammet's life back from its end point, if they could know everything about him, would it lead to the truth? It is, he feels, an idle thought; he cannot imagine the Company committing the men and the time to find out. Not for a free trader.

His mind turns again toward Susannah. He had sat with her in the parlor for several minutes without any awkward silences, and she seemed to find him interesting; she wanted to tell him things, and to hear what he had to say. He was too anxious to feel delight, but there was something like happiness there, unfurling like buds after a Canadian winter. He folds his spectacles and puts them, for want of a bedside table, on the floor beside him, where, he hopes, he won't stand on them in the morning.

AFTER THE INITIAL SHOCK, I realize I am not in imminent danger. The man in the doorway is at least sixty years old, his bearing is bookish, and, most important, he isn't armed. He looks distinguished more than anything, with smooth white hair brushed off a high forehead, a thin face, and aquiline nose. His expression strikes me as kind. In fact, for a man of his age, he is (the word surprises me but it is right) beautiful.

I have got into the reprehensible habit, common here where accent is no longer a reliable guide, of checking off a list of items in a stranger. Whenever I encounter someone new I glance at cuffs, shoes, fingernails, and so on, to establish station in life and financial security. This man is dressed in a flamboyant coat that is well cut but has seen better days, and though he is neat and clean-shaven, his shoes are disgracefully worn. In the moment it takes to reach these conclusions, I notice he has been taking much the same sort of inventory of me, and so presumably has concluded that I am the wife of a reasonably prosperous farmer. Whether he goes any further and decides that I am a faded and probably bitter former beauty, I really could not say.

"Excuse me . . ." His voice is pleasant, with a Yankee twang. My heart slows its frantic hammering.

"You gave me a shock," I say severely, aware that there is flour on my dress and probably in my hair. "Are you looking for Mr. Jammet?"

"No. I heard . . ." He gestures toward the bed and bloody blankets. "A terrible thing . . . a terrible waste. Excuse me, ma'am, I don't know your name."

He smiles gravely, and I find myself warming to him. I do appreciate nice manners, especially when someone is questioning my presence at a scene of crime.

"I am Mrs. Ross. His neighbor. I came to sort out his things." I smile regretfully, indicating the unpleasantness of the task. Is it my imagination, or has he quickened at the mention of Jammet's things?

"Ah, Mrs. Ross, I apologize for disturbing you. My name is Thomas Sturrock, from Toronto. Lawyer."

He extends his hand, and I take it. He bows his head.

"You are here to see to his estate?" Lawyers, in my experience, don't turn up on their own, snooping around after dark, getting their hands dirty. Nor do they tend to have frayed cuffs and holes in their shoes.

"No, I'm not here on business."

Honest. Not a typical lawyer at all.

"It is a personal matter. I'm not sure who I should apply to in this, but, you see, the fact is, Monsieur Jammet had an object which is of some importance to my research. He was going to send it to me."

He pauses, assessing my reaction, which is one of bemusement. Having searched the cabin from top to bottom, I can think of nothing that could be of any interest to anyone, especially a man like this. If Jammet had had such a thing, I assume he would have sold it.

"It's not something of value," he adds, "just of academic interest."

I continue to say nothing.

"I suppose I must place myself in your hands," he says with a diffident smile. "You can have no way of knowing whether what I say is true, so I will tell you everything. Monsieur Jammet had acquired a piece of bone or ivory, about so big . . ." He indicates the palm of his hand. "With markings on it. It may be that this object is of archaeological significance."

"You said you were a lawyer . . . ?"

"A lawyer by profession. An archaeologist by inclination."

He spreads his hands wide. I'm puzzled, but he seems sincere. "I must admit, I did not know him particularly well, though I am sorry for his death. I believe that it was . . . sudden."

I suppose sudden is one way of putting it.

"It must seem rather grasping of me to come for this object so soon after his death, but I really think it could be important. It is nothing to look at, and it would be a terrible pity if it were thrown away out of ignorance. So there you are—that is why I am here."

He has a way of looking at me that I find disarming—open and rather unsure of himself. Even if he is lying, I can't think what harm he could mean.

"Well, Mr. Sturrock," I begin, "I haven't—"

I break off suddenly, for I hear something else—a rattle of pebbles on the path behind the cabin. Instantly I seize the lantern from the stove.

"Mr. Sturrock, I will help you, if you will help me and do as I say. Go outside and hide yourself in the bushes by the river. Say nothing. If you do this, and are not discovered, I will tell you what I know."

His mouth opens in amazement, but he moves with impressive speed for a man his age: he is out the door the second I finish speaking. I blow out the lantern and pull the door to, giving the wire a twist to hold it closed before slipping into the bushes of Jammet's overgrown garden. I silently thank Jammet for his lack of horticultural pride; the place could hide a dozen of us.

I try to melt into the bushes, aware that one of my feet is sinking into something soft and wet. The footsteps come closer, and a lantern light, swinging in the hand of a dark figure.

To my eternal shock, it is my husband.

He holds up the lantern, opens the door, and goes inside. I wait for an appreciable time, getting colder by the moment, my shoe soaking up water, wondering when Sturrock is going to get fed up and reappear to talk to the newcomer instead of the insane woman. Then Angus comes out again, fixing the door behind him. He barely looks around before disappearing up the path, and soon even his light is hidden from view.

It is now quite dark. I stand up stiffly, my joints cracking, and pull my foot out of the soft muck. The stocking is soaked. I find matches and manage with difficulty to relight the lamp.

"Mr. Sturrock," I call, and a few moments later he comes into the circle of my lantern, brushing leaves off his shabby coat.

"Well, that was rather an adventure." He smiles at me. "Who was the gentleman from whom we had to hide?"

"I don't know. It was too dark to see. Mr. Sturrock, I apologize for my behavior, you must think me very peculiar. I am going to be frank, as you have been with me, and perhaps we can help each other."

I unfasten the door as I speak, and the smell hits me afresh. If Sturrock notices, he does a good job of hiding it.

Most men, when their wives disappear at twilight and come back after dark with a male stranger, would not be as gracious as Angus is. It is one of the reasons I married him. In the beginning it was because he trusted me: now, I don't know, perhaps he no longer believes me capable of arousing impure feelings, or simply no longer cares. Total strangers are rare in Dove River; usually they are cause for celebration, but Angus just looks up and nods calmly. Then again, perhaps he saw him at the cabin.

Sturrock talks little about himself, but as we eat I form a picture. A picture of a man with holes in his shoes and a taste for fine tobacco. A man who eats pork and potatoes as if he hadn't seen a decent meal in a week. A man of delicacy and intelligence, and disappointment, perhaps. And something else—ambition. For he wants that little piece of bone, whatever it is, very much.

We tell him about Francis. Children do get lost in the bush. It has been known. We discuss, inevitably, the Seton girls. Like everyone else above the border, he knows of them. Sturrock points out the differences between the Seton girls and Francis, and I agree that Francis is not a defenseless young girl, but I have to say it's not exactly reassuring.

Sometimes, you find yourself looking at the forest in a different way. Sometimes it's no more than the trees that provide houses and warmth, and hide the earth's nakedness, and you're glad of it. And then sometimes, like tonight, it is a vast dark presence that you can never see the end of; it might, for all you know, have not just length and breadth to lose yourself in, but also an immeasurable depth, or something else altogether.

And sometimes, you find yourself looking at your husband and wondering: is he the straightforward man you think you know—provider, friend, teller of poor jokes that nonetheless make you smile—or does he, too, have depths that you have never seen? What might he not be capable of?

DURING THE NIGHT, THE TEMPERATURE plummets. A light dusting of snow greets Donald when he rubs frost off the inside of his window and looks outside. He wonders if Jacob spent the night in the stables. Jacob is used to the cold. Last winter—Donald's first in the country—was relatively mild, but still a shock to him. This bone-aching morning is just a foretaste.

Knox has arranged for a local man to accompany Mackinley on his pursuit of the Frenchman. Someone sufficiently lowly that Mackinley will not have to share the glory with him . . . Then Donald dismisses the thought as uncharitable. More and more of his thoughts seem to be uncharitable nowadays. This is not what he had expected before he left Scotland—the great lone land had seemed like a promise of purity, where the harsh climate and simple life would hone a man's courage and scour off petty faults. But it isn't like that at all—or perhaps it is he who is at fault, and isn't up to the scouring. Perhaps he didn't have enough moral fiber in the first place.

After Mackinley has gone, terse and prickly to the last, Donald lingers over his coffee in the hope of seeing Susannah. Of course it is also a pleasure to sit at a table covered with white linen and look at the paintings on the wall, to be served by a white woman—albeit a rough Irish one—and to stare pensively into the fire without crude jokes being aimed in his direction. Finally his patience is rewarded, and both girls come in and take their seats.

"Well, Mr. Moody," Maria says, "so you are guarding our safety while the others pursue the suspects."

It is extraordinary how in one sentence Maria can make him feel like a coward. He tries not to sound defensive. "We are waiting for Francis Ross. If he doesn't return today, then we will go after him."

"You don't think he could have done it?" Susannah frowns at him charmingly.

"I know nothing about him. What do you think?"

"I think he's a seventeen-year-old boy. A rather good-looking one." With this, Maria looks slyly at him.

"He's sweet," Susannah says, looking at the table. "Shy. He doesn't have many friends."

Maria snorts sarcastically. Donald thinks that it would be hard for any youth to appear other than shy and awkward in the face of Maria's acidity and Susannah's beauty.

Maria adds, "We don't know him that well. I don't know who does. It's just that he always seems rather a sissy. He doesn't hunt or do the things most of the boys do."

"What do the other boys do?" Donald tries to assume a great distance between now and his seventeen-year-old self, when he did not hunt and would undoubtedly have been called a sissy by these young women.

"Oh, you know, they go around together, play practical jokes, get drunk . . . Stupid things like that."

"You think someone who doesn't do those things couldn't commit murder?"

"No . . ." Maria looks reflective for a moment. "He always seems moody and . . . well, as though there are things going on under the surface."

"There was once, I remember, at school," Susannah says, her face brightening. "He was about fourteen, I think, and another boy, was it George Pretty . . . ? No, no, it was Matthew Fox. Or . . ." She trails off, frowning. Her sister gives her a look.

"Well, Matthew, or whoever, tried to crib his task, and was showing off about it, you know, making sure his friends saw . . . and suddenly Francis realized and went into the most frightful rage. I'd never seen anyone's face go white with anger before, but he did—he went paper-white, and his skin is normally sort of golden, you know . . . ? Um, anyway, he started hitting Matthew as if he wanted to kill him. He was in a sort of frenzy; he had to be dragged off by Mr. Clarke and another boy. It was quite frightening."

She looks at Donald, hazel eyes wide. "I hadn't thought of that for ages. Do you suppose . . . ?"

"It wasn't a frenzied attack, was it, Mr. Moody?" Maria has remained calm while Susannah worked herself up into a state of excitement.

"We can't rule anything out."

"Mr. Mackinley thinks it was the French trader, doesn't he? That's why he's gone after him. Or perhaps he just wants it to be the French trader. You don't like free traders, do you, Mr. Moody, in the Company?"

"The Company tries to protect its interests, of course, but it is generally of benefit if trappers can get a fixed price for their skins; and the Company looks after a lot of people—the trappers know where to go, and the situation is . . . stable. Where there is competition, prices go up or down, and the free traders don't look after their families. It is the difference between . . . order and anarchy." Donald hears the patronizing tone in his voice and winces inwardly.

"But if a free trader offers a higher price for a fur than the Company, surely a trapper is entitled to take it? Then he can look after his family himself."

"Of course, he is free to do so. But then he must take the risk that that trader will not be there the next year—he cannot rely on him in the way he can rely on the Company."

"But isn't it true," she persists, "that the Company encourages the Indians they trade with to become dependent on liquor, and makes sure that it is the only supplier of liquor so that they always come back?"

Donald feels a warm flush rising above his collar. "The Company does not encourage anything of the sort. The trappers do what they want, they are not coerced into anything."

He sounds quite angry. Susannah turns on her sister. "That is a horrible accusation. Besides, it is hardly Mr. Moody's fault if things like that go on."

Maria shrugs, unconvinced.

Donald walks outside, letting the air cool his face. He will have to try to find Susannah alone later—it is impossible to have a conversation with the rebarbative Maria around. He lights his pipe to calm himself, and finds Jacob in the stables, talking to his horse in the nonsense language he uses with them.

"Morning, Mr. Moody."

"Good morning. Did you sleep well?"

Jacob looks puzzled, as he usually is by this question. He slept—what else is there to say? He also lay awake, thinking about the dead man and the warrior's death he met at home, on his bed. He nods, though, to humor Donald.

"Jacob, do you like working for the Company?"

Another bizarre question. "Yes."

"You wouldn't prefer to work for someone else—like a free trader?"

Jacob shrugs. "Not now—with my family. When I am away, I know they are safe and won't starve. And Company goods are cheap—much cheaper than outside."

"So it's good that you work for the Company?"

"I guess so. Why, you want to leave?"

Donald laughs and shakes his head, and then wonders why this has never occurred to him. Because there is nowhere else for him to go? Perhaps there is nowhere for Jacob either—his father was a Company man, a voyageur, and Jacob started working when he was fourteen. His father died young. He wonders now if he was involved in an accident, but as with so many other aspects of Jacob's life, he cannot think of an appropriate time to ask.

The reason Donald became so agitated was because Maria was right to say the Company jealously guards its monopoly—but it has good reason to fear competition. Tired of its centuries of supremacy in the wilderness, a number of independent fur traders—mainly French and Yankee—are attempting to break the Company's hold on the fur trade. There have been rival outfits in the past, but the Company subsumed or quashed them all. But this new alliance, the one known as the North America Company, has the mandarins worried. There are deep pockets behind it, and a disregard for the rules (rules laid down by the Company, that is). Traders offer trappers high prices for furs and extract promises that they will avoid the Company in the future. It is likely that bribery and threats are being used—more than probable, in fact, since the Company uses them itself. Trade, and consequently profits, are suffering.

Mackinley has had several terse discussions with Donald on the devious nature of free traders, and the necessity of binding the natives to the Company with liquor, guns, and food. That was what brought the blood to Donald's cheeks—Maria's accusation was quite accurate. But it is no worse than what the Yankees do, for heaven's sake. He should have told Maria about the Indian village that depends on the fort for food and protection. He should have told her about Jacob's wife and the two little girls with trusting eyes, but, as usual, he did not think of these things at the right moment.

It was during one of these conversations with Mackinley that something occurred to Donald: perhaps the problem of falling profits stemmed from a more fundamental source than Yankee greed. The trapping has gone on for over two hundred years, and it has taken its toll. When the Company set up the first trading posts, the animals were neighborly and trusting, but the quest for profit thrust a murderous desire deep into the wilderness, driving the animals before it. Since that day in the depot with Bell, Donald has not seen another silver fox, has never seen a black fox. None have arrived there.

Donald spurs on his pony to catch up with Jacob. They are riding through a stretch of woodland where the last leaves have turned even brighter colors, with the rime of frost on the leaf fall. If Susannah does not concern herself with the Company's methods, why should he? After all, when it comes down to it, the fact remains that order is better than anarchy. That is what he has to remember.

They leave the ponies grazing on the riverbank as they walk up to the cabin. Donald is relieved to think that it is empty now. He managed not to embarrass himself when confronted with the body, but it was not an experience he is in a hurry to repeat. In the patch of weeds that surrounds the house Jacob stops and studies the ground. Even Donald can see the muddled footprints.

"These are from last night. Look, someone hid here." Jacob indicates the ground under a bush.

"Maybe village boys?"

There seem to be several different sets of footprints. Jacob points them out.

"Look, here . . . a man's boot, and under it, another, but a different shape—so there were two men. The man with the larger foot was here first. But the last person to leave the house was this one—smaller still, perhaps a boy . . . or a woman."

"A woman? Are you sure these aren't the prints from yesterday? That could be the laying-out woman?"

Jacob shakes his head.

Donald is triumphant when he discovers the loose floorboard with the hollowed-out space underneath, but it is Jacob who finds the cache under some rocks. The mystery of Jammet's missing wealth is solved—in a lead-lined case are three American rifles, some gold, and a packet of dollars wrapped in oiled cotton. Jacob lets out a cry of astonishment when he sees them. Donald ponders what to do with it, and decides to rebury it until they can come back with a cart. They replace the stones, and Jacob scatters fallen leaves on the smoothed earth to make the spot look undisturbed. Donald looks at Jacob as he gets out his pipe. A flicker of mistrust crosses his mind and he chides himself for thinking that Jacob might be tempted by what is in the case, which is more than he could earn in ten years. Donald is aware that he cannot read Jacob's face as he believes he could another white man's. He hopes that Jacob finds his own visage as opaque, and so does not see his lack of faith.

Ann PRETTY IS SURPRISED TO see me so soon after the loan of the coffee, and her expression becomes guarded, although for once I have not come to reclaim my possessions. Ida is sitting by the stove, sulkily turning sheets. She looks up with a pale, haunted face. She is fifteen, and I find her interesting, perhaps because she is the age Olivia would have been now. Also because she fits into the Pretty family like a crow in a chicken run— she is skinny, dark, and introverted, and rumored to be clever. She has recently been crying.

"Mrs. Ross!" Ann bellows from three feet away. "Have you had any news of your boy?"

"Angus has gone to look for him."

Now I'm here I'm not sure I can keep up the appearance of lighthearted unconcern. And if Angus won't talk to me, who else can I turn to?

"Ah, children are such a cross." She shoots a harsh glance at the silent Ida. Ida keeps her head bowed to the sheet, sewing with small, tight stitches.

"He was in such a mood when he left, I didn't ask where he was going. And when he comes back, he'll be upset about Jammet. Whatever else you can say about him, he was a kind man. He was good to Francis."

"What a time. God knows what we're all coming to."

Ida lets out the smallest of sighs. Her head is bent, so I cannot see her face, but she is weeping again. Ann sighs, too, sharply.

"My girl, I don't know what you're crying about. It's not as though you knew him to speak of."

Ida sniffs and says nothing. Ann turns to me, shaking her head.

"It's his mother I feel for. She's got no one else, from what I hear. You know he was in Chicago only two months ago? What does a man like him go to Chicago for, I ask you?"

"I wish they'd go to Chicago and stop bothering about Francis, it's absurd to keep on after him."

"It is that."

Ida makes another small noise—and now her shoulders are trembling.

"Ida, will you give over? Go upstairs if you can't sit there without snivelling. My Lord . . ."

Ida gets up and goes without a look at us.

"She'll drive me crazy, that one. You should be glad you don't have girls . . ." Just as it comes out of her mouth she remembers Olivia, and I believe it crosses her mind to apologize, before she banishes such a silly notion from her head. "But you've had your trials with that one."

I acknowledge this to be true.

"It's the blood in them, coming out. You can't help it. You never knew his parents, did you? Who's to know they weren't thieves and tinkers? That's the Irish in him. They can't be trusted. When I was in Kitchener, we had a crowd of Irish—steal the clothes off your back soon as look at you. Not that I'm saying that about your Francis, mind, but it's in them. It's in them and you've got to watch for it."

Despite the insults, I know she is trying to be kind; she just has no other way of showing it.

"What's the matter with Ida, then? You shouldn't be too hard on her; you remember what it's like when you're that age."

Ann snorts. "I was never that age. I was keeping house from the age of ten, didn't have the time to sit and moon about." She shoots me a look, the slyly humorous one that's usually followed by a joke at my expense. "You know what I think? I think she's sweet on your Francis. She won't say so, but I reckon I know."

I'm so surprised I nearly laugh out loud. "Ida?" It's hard to think of her as anything other than a skinny child. And I never thought any of the Pretty family had much time for Francis. There had been a disastrous camping trip that Angus and Jimmy had bullied the boys into, when Francis had gone off with George and Emlyn. They came back after two days, and Francis never said a word about it. I gave up urging him to go and play with them after that.

"They were tight at school, before he left."

"Let me go and talk to her. I know what I was like at that age. You know, I've always thought that she reminds me of myself when I was young." I smile at Ann, enjoying the thought that the prospect of her daughter turning out like me is probably her worst nightmare.

I follow the sound of sniffing to find Ida in her tiny bedroom, staring out of the window. At least, I'm sure she was staring out of the window, although she is bent over the sheet when I look in.

"Your mother says you're enjoying school at the moment."

Ida looks up with reddened eyes and a mutinous mouth. "Enjoy it? Not hardly."

"Francis is always saying how clever you are."

"Really?" Her face softens for a moment. So perhaps Ann was right.

"Said you were quite the scholar. Maybe you could go on to the school at Coppermine—have you thought of that?"

"Mm. Don't know that Ma and Pa would let me."

"Well, they've got enough boys to look after the place, haven't they?"

"I guess."

I smile at her, and she almost smiles back. She has a peaky little bony face with smudges under the eyes. No one will ever accuse her of being beautiful.

"Mrs. Ross? Did you go on with your schooling?"

"Yes, I did. It's well worth doing."

It's almost true. I certainly might have done, if I hadn't been in an asylum at the time. Now she's looking at me with a shy sort of admiration, and I am filled with a desire to be what she thinks I am. Maybe I could be a sort of mentor to her—I've never thought like this before, but it's a pleasing thought. Perhaps it is one of the compensations of getting older.

"Francis should go on with school. He's really smart." She blushes with the unaccustomed effort of expressing a personal opinion.

"Well, maybe. He won't talk to me at the moment. You'll find out: when you're someone's mother they don't listen to you."

"I'm not going to get married. Ever."

Her face has changed again—the dark shadow is back.

"Do you know, I can remember saying the same thing? But things don't always turn out the way you think."

For some reason I am losing her. The tears well up in her eyes.

"Ida . . . I don't suppose Francis talked to you before he went on this trip? About where he was going, or anything like that?"

The girl shakes her head. When she lifts her face again, I am stunned by the raw pain in her eyes. Sorrow and something else—is it anger? Something about Francis.

"No, he didn't."

* * *

I go home feeling worse than when I started. I don't really expect Angus to come back with Francis, and when, long after dark, he arrives home alone, I feel no surprise. His skin is slack with weariness, and he talks without looking at me.

"I got to Swallow Lake. Saw traces of someone going—more than one person, clear as day. But he's not there. And no one fished there, I'd swear to it. Went straight through. If that was Francis, he was running."

And you came back, I think to myself. You turned your back and walked away. I stand up. I've already decided; I don't have to think anymore.

"Then I'll go after him."

To give him credit, he doesn't laugh like most husbands would. I don't know if I secretly want him to stop me, at least to argue and beg me not to leave, not to do something so foolish and brave and dangerous. Anyway, he doesn't. I think about the Company men at Caulfield—they'll be up at the farm first thing, to see if Francis is here. Looking with sly eyes at our faces to see how afraid we are. Well, I haven't the energy to pretend anymore. I will look them in the eye and show them I am scared.

I am scared to death.

DONALD AND JACOB ARRIVE BACK in Caulfield late in the morning, and Donald arranges for a cart to collect Jammet's stashed wealth. Ashamed of his earlier suspicion, he sends Jacob alone to bring back the chest, which makes him feel better, and has the added benefit of making him available for lunch with Mrs. Knox and her daughters. But they have barely started on the pork before he puts his foot in it.

"I was wondering if I might meet Mr. Sturrock here when I came back," he begins conversationally. "I believe he is an old acquaintance of your husband's."

Mrs. Knox looks at Donald with a start of alarm. "Mr. Sturrock . . . ? Thomas Sturrock?" The girls exchange rapid, meaningful glances.

"Well, I don't know his first name, but . . . I was told he knows your husband . . . I'm sorry, did I say something . . . ?"

Mrs. Knox has gone decidedly pale, but she sets her mouth into a firm line. "It's quite all right, Mr. Moody. I am surprised, that is all. I have not heard that name in a long time."

Donald looks at his plate, abashed and confused. Susannah is glaring at her sister. Maria clears her throat.

"The explanation, Mr. Moody, is that we had two cousins, Amy and Eve, who went for a walk in the woods, and never returned. Uncle Charles brought in several people to try and find them, and Mr. Sturrock was one of them. He had a reputation as a searcher—you know, for finding children who had been kidnapped by Indians. He looked for a long time but never found them."

"He spent all of Uncle Charles's money, and he died of a broken heart," says Susannah quickly.

"He had a stroke," says Maria to Donald.

Mrs. Knox tuts quietly.

Donald is stunned. From Susannah's face he understands that this is what she began to tell him the day before, stripped of embellishments. And that she is annoyed at having her story taken from her.

"I'm so sorry," he finally remembers to say. "What a terrible thing."

"It was," says Mrs. Knox. "Neither my sister nor her husband ever recovered. Maria is correct in saying that he suffered a stroke, but he was only fifty-two. It broke him."

Susannah gives her sister a triumphant look.

In the ensuing silence, the only sound is Donald's fork clashing against his plate, and suddenly feeling boorish for continuing to eat, he suspends his fork hand uncertainly in midair. Even his chewing sounds horribly loud, but now that his mouth is full, there is not much he can do about it.

"I hope the pork is to your liking," says Mrs. Knox with a firm smile; she is not a hostess to be knocked off her stride by anything.

"Delicious," mutters Donald, acutely aware that, to his left, Susannah has put down her fork.

"It was a long time ago," says Maria. "Seventeen or eighteen years. But you haven't said, has Francis Ross returned? Or will you be setting off into the bush tomorrow?"

Donald feels a rush of gratitude to her. "The latter, at the moment—he has not come back. His parents are worried about him."

"Do they think he has disappeared, like . . ." Susannah stops before she finishes.

"Francis Ross is always running off into the woods. He's quite the native. He must know them like the back of his hand."

"Either way, we will clear up the matter by finding him. Jacob is an excellent tracker. A few days' delay makes no odds to him."

Now, after lunch, Donald sits in the study, going over his notes from yesterday and adding the events of the morning. He has just decided to go and find this man Sturrock and question him, when Susannah comes in without knocking. He jumps to his feet and manages, unbelievably, to knock over his chair in his haste.

"Damn! I'm sorry, I—"

"Oh, dear me . . ."

Susannah comes to help him pick it up, and they end up standing very close, both laughing, their faces only inches apart. Donald backs away, suddenly terrified that she will sense the hammering of his heart.

"I came in to apologize," she says. "We have been such miserable company for you, and you know, I had hoped it would be different, the next time we saw you."

Her face is quite serious, but there is a faint pinkness in her cheek. Donald is hit by the utterly amazing conviction that this beautiful girl likes him, and this awareness washes over him like the aftershock of strong brandy. He hopes he isn't grinning like an idiot.

"You have nothing to apologize for, Miss Knox."

"Please, call me Susannah."

"Susannah."

It is the first time he has said her name to her face, and it makes him smile. The feel of her name in his mouth, and the sight of her face looking up at him, sears onto his heart like a fiery brand.

"You have been the most charming company, and a welcome diversion from all this . . . business. I am . . . glad I came—I mean, glad that Mackinley chose me."

"But I suppose you will go tomorrow, and then we will not see you again."

"Well . . . I expect the Company will need to keep an eye on things here, so . . . Who knows, I may be back sooner than you think."

"Oh. I see."

She looks so forlorn that he is emboldened to add, "But, you know, what would be wonderful . . . is if you would write to me, and, and . . . let me know how things are here."

"You mean, like a report?"

"Well . . . yes, although, I would also like to know . . . how things are with you. I would like to write to you, if that would be agreeable."

"You would like to write to me?" She sounds charmingly surprised.

"I would like that very much."

There is a moment when they are breathless in the knowledge of what they are saying, and then Susannah smiles in response.

"I would like that, too."

Donald is insanely elated, full of a power and energy he had forgotten existed. He gives thanks, urgently and silently, as, hardly knowing what he does, he rushes out of the house, finding paradoxically that he wants to be alone to celebrate his newfound happiness fully. He walks to Scott's store, assuming that whatever goes on in Caulfield, John Scott will know about it.

He bursts in through the door, trying to keep the foolish grin from his face—a man has died, after all—to see a slender, round-faced woman behind the counter. She looks up at the sound of the door, and her first expression is one of fear, quickly masked by a blank neutrality.

John Scott is not there, but Mrs. Scott proves nearly as helpful. Donald notices her distracted air and tries to concentrate as she tells him that Mr. Sturrock is staying in their house, and may be there now, she can't say.

"You're welcome to call and see. The maid is there . . ." Mrs. Scott breaks off, as if she has just remembered something. "No, I will send a message, that would be better."

She disappears through a door at the back. Donald stares out of the window at a sky that looks like curds and remembers Susannah's soft mouth.

Thomas Sturrock has a way about him that Donald warms to—when told the man was a searcher, he assumed he would be an old woodsman with coarse manners and the sort of tangy humor he has to endure at the fort, and he is pleasantly surprised at the refined gentleman he encounters instead.

"I wonder if I could ask, how did you end up in such a line of work?"

They are drinking Scott's bitter coffee, in two chairs that Mrs. Scott has placed by the stove. Sturrock stares into his cup with disappointment before replying.

"I've done a few things in my time, and I'd written about the Indian way of life. I've always been a friend to the Indian, and someone knew this and asked me to help in a case where a boy had been taken. And that worked out, so other people asked me. I never set out to do it, it just came my way. Too old for it now."

"And the item you have come to look for, do you have any written proof that Jammet wanted you to have it?"

"No. He wasn't planning on getting killed last time I saw him."

"And you weren't aware of any enemies he might have had?"

"No. He would drive a hard bargain, but that's no reason to kill a man."

"No, indeed."

"When he first showed me the bit of bone, I asked him if I could copy down the markings on it, and he could tell I was interested, so he refused, and said he would sell it to me."

"But you didn't buy it then?"

"No. I was, you see, temporarily out of funds. But he agreed to keep it until I could pay him. I have the money now, but, of course"—he spreads his hands helplessly—"I don't know where it is."

"I will talk to Mr. Knox about it. We haven't found a will. If Mr. Knox is agreeable, I daresay he could sell it to you. That is, assuming we find it."

It suddenly occurs to Donald to wonder if Sturrock has already looked for this piece of bone. He remembers the footprints by the cabin. Three sets. Three people who came to look at the cabin last night.

"That's generous of you, Mr. Moody. I appreciate that."

"What sort of thing is it? Is it something from Rome or Egypt?"

"I'm not altogether sure what it is. It doesn't seem to be anything like that, but that's why I need it—I intend to take it to some museum men who know about such things."

Donald nods, still unsure as to why Sturrock is so interested in this thing. One thing he is certain of, though, is that if someone is keenly interested in a thing, it is as well to tread warily. Could it be that Sturrock had arrived earlier and Jammet had refused to sell him the bone, so Sturrock killed him? Or had Jammet already sold it to someone else? Whichever way he adds it up, Sturrock doesn't seem a likely killer. But it is also true that there has been no sign of this object, which clearly has a value. So who has it now?

Donald leaves the store with Sturrock's assurance that he will stay in Caulfield for the next few days. He wonders why it did not occur to him to ask about the Seton girls—perhaps because he finds it impossible to believe this gracious-mannered man is the grasping fraud portrayed by the Knoxes. He wonders—not for the first time—whether his inexperience leads him to form favorable impressions too easily. Should he be more suspicious, like Mackinley, who takes against people on principle, assuming that sooner or later they will disappoint him—and is usually proved right?

On his way down the road he sees Maria carrying a basket. He raises his hat, and she smiles slightly. She seems decidedly less hostile since this morning, but he still wouldn't have risked speaking to her had she not spoken first.

"Mr. Moody. How is the investigation proceeding?"

"Er, slowly, thank you."

She pauses, as if waiting for him to say something, so he finds himself saying, "I have just been talking to Mr. Sturrock."

She doesn't betray surprise, nodding as if she expected it. "And?"

"I thought he was charming. Educated, sensitive . . . not at all what I expected."

"I suppose he had to be charming to swindle my uncle out of all his money—there was quite a lot, I believe."

Donald must have frowned, because she goes on: "I know my uncle was desperate enough to do anything, but a man of honor would have told him it was pointless to keep looking for the girls and refused his money. It would have been kinder in the long run. In the end he had neither his daughters nor anything to live on, and he . . . well, as good as destroyed himself. This was after my aunt died. I know it sounds terrible to say this, but . . . I've always supposed they must have been eaten by wolves. Other people say so, and I think they are right. Aunt and Uncle could never accept that, though."

"How could anyone?"

"Is that so much worse than what they did think?"

"I would have thought life, at any cost . . . is better than death."

Maria looks at him with those appraising eyes—like a farmer assessing a horse for broken wind. She'll never find a husband if she looks at all men like that, he thinks, irritated.

"Perhaps the wolves saved them from a fate worse than death." The cliché sounds, in her mouth, like a bad joke.

"You don't really think so." He is surprised at his boldness in contradicting her.

Maria shrugs. "A few years ago, two children here were drowned in the bay. It was a terrible accident. Their parents grieved, of course, but they are still alive. They seem happy enough now—as happy as any of us are."

"Perhaps it is lack of certainty that is so hard to bear."

"Which enables the unscrupulous to prey upon your hope, until you are sucked dry."

Donald is surprised again by the things she says. He dimly hears his father's voice, saying in that lecturing tone of his, "The desire to shock is an infantile trait that should disappear with maturity." Yet Maria seems anything but immature. He reminds himself that he doesn't need to agree with his father anymore; they are on different continents.

"Mr. Sturrock does not appear to be a rich man," Donald says, in a sort of defense.

Maria looks past Donald down the street, then looks at him with a smile. Her eyes, unlike Susannah's, are blue. "Just because you like someone doesn't mean that you can trust them." And with a bob of the head—almost a mockery of a curtsy—she walks away from him.

Donald spends the rest of the afternoon and evening combing through Jammet's possessions, but, like others before him, he can find nothing that seems of relevance to his death. The Frenchman's worldly possessions are stacked in a dry part of the stables, and he and Jacob, who supervised the emptying of the cabin in the interests of security, have sorted them into boxes and piles. It all adds up to surprisingly little. Donald tries not to think about how little his colleagues would be sifting through if he were suddenly swept off this mortal coil. There would be nothing at all to indicate these new but enormously significant feelings for Susannah, for instance. He vows to himself to write to her the instant he leaves Caulfield—absurdly, since they are still in the same house, and since Donald has made the decision to wait until Mackinley and Knox have returned before setting out on what is probably a wild-goose chase, he could be here for another day or two.

He will ask for a picture of her, or a keepsake. Not that he is planning on getting himself killed, of course. Just in case.

W HEN I WAS A GIRL, while my parents still lived, I was troubled by what were termed "difficulties." I was seized with paralyzing fears that rendered me incapable of movement, even of speech. I felt that the earth was sliding away from under me, and that I could not trust the ground beneath my feet—a terrifying feeling. Doctors took my pulse and stared into my eyes before saying that whatever it was, it would probably disappear with the onset of adulthood (by which I think they meant marriage). However, before this theory could be tested, my mother died in unclear circumstances. I believe she took her own life, although my father denied it. She had been taking laudanum, and an overdose killed her, whether intended or not. I was increasingly plagued by fears until my father could stand it no longer and had me placed in a—not to put too fine a point on it—mental asylum, although it had a fancy name to do with exhausted gentlefolk. Then he, too, died, leaving me at the mercy of the unscrupulous superintendent, and I ended up in a public asylum, which was at least honest enough to call itself what it was.

In the public asylum laudanum was freely available. First prescribed for the crippling panics, it became the thing I relied on, taking the place of parents or friends. It was widely applied to quiet troublesome patients, but I soon realized that I preferred to be in charge of administering it myself, and had to resort to guile to get it. I found it easy to persuade male members of staff to do things for me, and the superintendent—an idealistic young man called Watson—I could wrap around my little finger. Once you become accustomed to a thing, you forget why you wanted it in the first place.

Later, when my husband decided that my habit was a barrier to real intimacy, I gave it up. Or rather, he took my supply of laudanum and threw it away, leaving me no choice but to do without. He was the only person who thought this a trouble worth taking. It was like being sober again after a prolonged period of drunkenness, and that sobriety seemed wonderful for a while. But sobriety makes you remember things you had forgotten—for example, why you felt the need to take the drug in the first place. When, in years since, times have been hard, I know exactly why I became habituated, and in the past few days I have thought about laudanum almost as much as I have thought about Francis. I know that I could go to the store and buy some. I know that every minute of the day and half the night. The only thing that stops me is that I am the one person in the world Francis can rely on for help. And so far I am not being any help at all.

It is five days since Francis left, and I am walking down the path to Jammet's cabin when I hear a noise up ahead. A dog runs across my path and whines: a dog I don't know, large, shaggy and wild-looking—a sled dog. I pause: there is someone at the cabin.

On the rise behind the building, I creep behind a bush with the stealth of practice and wait. A disgruntled insect sinks its jaws into my wrist. Eventually a man comes out of the cabin and whistles. Two dogs run up to him, including the one that was on the path earlier. In my hiding place I hold my breath, and as his face turns toward me I feel a cold tremor down my spine. He is tall for an Indian, strongly built, and dressed in blue capote and skin trousers. But it is his face that makes me think of the story of the artificial man. He has a low, broad forehead, high cheekbones, and a nose and mouth that turn downward like a raptor's beak and give a powerful impression of wildness and cruelty. Deep lines are incised in the copper skin on either side of the mouth. His hair is black and tangled. I have never seen anyone quite so ugly in my life—a face that could have been hacked out of wood with a blunt axe. If Miss Shelley had needed a pattern for her terrifying monster, this man would have been perfect inspiration.

I wait, hardly daring to breathe, until he has gone back inside the cabin, then I ease backward out of my hiding place. I debate for a moment the best course of action—find Angus on the farm and tell him, or ride straight down to Caulfield and tell Knox? Today I decide not to confront the man myself, because, I reason, he is clearly dangerous. Despite myself, I find it hard to believe that anyone could have a face like that and not have a fierce and cruel disposition. In the end I go and find Angus. He listens to me in silence, then takes his rifle and walks down the path.

I found out later that he walked up to the cabin and went straight in. The stranger was surprised while searching the room upstairs. Angus called to him, and told him, very politely I'm sure, that he would have to escort him down to Caulfield, since this was the scene of a crime and he had no right to be there. The man hesitated but put up no resistance. He picked up his rifle and walked ahead of him the three miles down to the bay. Angus marched him up to the Knoxes' back door. While they waited, the stranger stared at the bay with a proud, distant look, as though he didn't care what anyone might do to him. By the time Angus left to come home, the stranger had been arrested and imprisoned. Angus took pity on the two dogs, which Knox refused to let into his yard, and brought them home, claiming they would be no bother. I thought he must have found something to like in the stranger, to go to the trouble.

ANDREW KNOX SITS ACROSS FROM Mackinley and smokes his pipe. The firelight turns their faces a warm shade of orange—even the whey-faced Mackinley loses his sallowness. Knox cannot share the other's blatant satisfaction. They questioned the man for over an hour and had discovered nothing concrete other than his name, William Parker, and that he was a trapper who had traded with Jammet before. He claimed he had not known Jammet was dead, but had called on him in passing and found the cabin empty. He had searched the house to find some clue as to what had happened.

"You say a murderer wouldn't come back to the scene of his crime," Mackinley breaks the silence. "But if he had wanted the guns and so on, and didn't find them the first time, he could have waited until things died down, and come back to search again."

Knox acknowledges the truth of this.

"Or perhaps he thought he had left something behind and came back to retrieve it."

"We didn't find anything that didn't belong there."

"Perhaps we missed it."

Knox fixes his teeth in the groove worn in the pipe stem; it is a pleasurable feeling—teeth and stem fit together perfectly after long use. Mackinley is too hasty to condemn the trapper, allowing his desire for a solution to shape the facts rather than the other way around. Knox wants to point this out but without offending his pride—after all, Mackinley is officially in charge.

"It is possible that he is simply what he says, a trapper who has traded with him in the past, who did not know he was dead."

"And who goes snooping through an empty house?"

"That is not a crime—or even unusual."

"It isn't a crime, but it is suspicious. We have to infer what is most likely from what we have."

"We don't have anything. I'm not sure we have any grounds for holding him at all."

Knox has insisted that the man is not a prisoner and must be treated well. He has had Adam take a tray of food to the warehouse where he is being kept, and light a fire. He hated having to ask Scott for another favor, but he could not countenance keeping the man in a room, even a locked room, in the same house as his daughters and wife. Despite his words, there is something about the stranger's face that evokes dark and terrifying thoughts. It reminds him of faces in engravings of the Indian wars: painted faces, twisted in fury, blasphemous, alien.

They unlock the door of the warehouse for the second time, and hold up their lanterns, to see the prisoner sitting immobile near the fire. He does not turn his head as the door opens.

"Mr. Parker," calls Knox. "We would like to talk some more."

They sit on chairs brought earlier for this purpose. Parker does not speak or turn to face them. Only his breath, condensing in pale clouds by his face, indicates a living man.

"How did you come by the name Parker?" asks Mackinley. His tone is insulting, as if he's accusing the man of lying about his identity.

"My father was an English native. Samuel Parker. His father came from England."

"Was your father a Company man?"

"He worked for the Company all his life."

"But you don't."

"No."

Mackinley is leaning forward, mention of the Company drawing him like a magnet. "You used to work for them?"

"I served an apprenticeship. I am a trapper now."

"And you traded with Jammet?"

"Yes."

"For how long?"

"Many years."

"Why did you leave the Company?"

"To be beholden to no one."

"Did you know that Laurent Jammet was a member of the North America Company?"

The man looks at him, half amused. Knox casts a glance at Mackinley—did he find this out from the other Frenchman?

"I didn't trade with a company, I traded with him."

"Are you a member of the North America Company?"

Now Parker laughs harshly. "I am a member of no company. I trap furs and sell them; that's all."

"But you have no furs at the moment."

"It is fall."

Knox puts a warning hand on Mackinley's arm. He tries to make his tone friendly and reasonable. "You understand why we have to ask these questions—Mr. Jammet died a brutal death. We need to find out what we can about him so that we can bring the perpetrator to justice."

"He was my friend."

Knox sighs. Before he can say anything else, Mackinley speaks again:

"Where were you on the day and night of November fourteenth—six days ago?"

"I told you, I was traveling south from Sydney House."

"Did anyone see you?"

"I travel alone."

"When did you leave Sydney House?"

The man hesitates, for the first time. "I wasn't at Sydney House itself, just in that direction."

"But you said you were coming from Sydney House."

"I said Sydney House so you would know where I was. That was the direction I came from. I was in the bush."

"And what were you doing there?"

"Hunting."

"But you said it isn't the season for furs."

"Hunting for meat."

Mackinley looks at Knox and raises his eyebrows. "Is that normal for this time of year?"

Parker shrugs. "It is normal any time of year."

Knox clears his throat. "Thank you, Mr. Parker. Well . . . that will be all for now."

He is embarrassed by his voice, which sounds like that of an old man, fussy and womanish. They get up to go, then Mackinley turns back to the man by the fire. He picks up his mug of water from the tray and pours it on the fire, extinguishing it.

"Give me your firebag."

Parker looks at Mackinley, who holds his eye. Parker's eyes are opaque in the lamplight. He looks as if he wants to kill Mackinley right there. Slowly he takes the leather bag from around his neck, and hands it to Mackinley. Mackinley takes it, but Parker does not let go.

"How do I know I'll get it back?"

Knox steps closer, anxious to defuse the tension in the air. "You'll get it back. I'll see to it myself."

Parker lets go and the two men walk out, taking the only lanterns and leaving the prisoner in darkness and cold. Knox peers back in as he pulls the door closed, seeing—or does he only imagine it?—the half-breed as a concentration of darkness in the dark space.

"Why did you do that?" Knox asks as they return through the quiet town.

"You want him to set fire to the place and escape? I know these people. They have no scruples. Did you see the way he looked at me? Like he wanted to take my scalp then and there."

He holds the bag up in front of the lantern—a leather pouch, beautifully decorated with embroidery. Inside is the man's equipment for survival—flints, tinder, tobacco, and some dried and unappetizing strips of nameless meat. Without it, in the wilderness, he would probably die.

Mackinley is jubilant. "Well, how did you like that? He changed his story so that we can't prove he was where he said he was. He could have been in Dove River a week ago and no one any the wiser."

Knox can think of nothing to say to this. He, too, had felt a tremor of doubt as Parker hesitated—a gap opened in the man's confident demeanor; he had not known quite what to say.

"It's not proof," he says at last.

"It is circumstantial. Would you rather believe the boy did it?"

Knox sighs, feeling very tired, but not yet tired enough to rise to it. "What is all this about the North America Company? I've never heard of it."

"It's not an official company, but it might become one. André told me Jammet was involved. He is, too. French Canadian traders have been talking about setting up a company in opposition to us. They have backing from the States, and there is interest even among some of the British here."

Mackinley's jaw is taut. He is a man of simple loyalties; the thought of any Canadian of British extraction siding against the Company is hurtful to him. To Knox it is less surprising. The Company has always been run by wealthy men in London, sending their representatives (they refer to them as servants) out to the colony to extract its riches. To those who were born here, it is a foreign power, stripping their land of its wealth, scattering crumbs in return.

He chooses his words carefully. "So Jammet could have been seen as an enemy of the Hudson Bay Company?"

"If you are implying that a Company man would have done that to him . . . I assure you, that is quite unthinkable."

"I'm not implying anything. But if it is a fact, then we cannot ignore it. How great was his involvement with this North America Company?"

"The man didn't know. Just that Jammet had mentioned it in the past."

"And it is certain that André was in the Sault when Jammet died?"

"Lying in a corner of a bar, insensible, according to the landlord. It would not have been possible for him to be killing Jammet in Dove River at the same time."

Knox feels a wave of irritation at the events of this evening. At Mackinley's officiousness and certainty, at the prisoner's raw and powerful presence, even at the unfortunate Jammet and his messy death. In its short life Caulfield has always been a peaceful community that has no jail and never needed one. Now, for the last few days, wherever he looks there is violence and bitterness.

His wife is still awake when he goes upstairs. Even when the man Parker is out of sight, he is in everyone's mind. There may be a murderer in their town, separated from them by thin wooden walls. There is something about the man that makes it easy to believe in his guilt. A man cannot help his face, of course, and should not be judged by it. Is that what he is doing?

"Some people don't make it easy for you to like them," he observes as he undresses.

"Are you talking about the prisoner, or Mr. Mackinley?"

Knox allows himself a suppressed smile. He looks at her face and thinks she looks tired. "Are you all right?"

He loves the way her hair waves when she lets it down, just as lustrously brown as when they married. She is proud of it and brushes it for five minutes every night until it crackles and clings to the hairbrush.

"I was going to ask you the same question."

"Quite all right. I'm looking forward to all this being over. I prefer Caulfield when it is quiet and dull."

She shifts over as he climbs between the sheets. "Have you heard the other news?"

He can tell by her voice that it is not good. "Other news? What is it?"

She sighs. "Sturrock is here."

"Sturrock the searcher? In Caulfield?"

"Yes. Mr. Moody has met him. He knew Jammet, apparently."

"Good God." He never ceases to be amazed by what his wife can pick up on the rumor circuit. "Good God," he repeats quietly. He lies down, doubts crowding into his mind. Who would have thought Jammet had so many unseen connections? Some peculiar power extends from the empty cabin, drawing the unlikely and the undesirable to Caulfield, in pursuit of who knows what. He has not seen Thomas Sturrock for ten years, not since shortly before Charles died. He has tried to forget that meeting. Now try as he may, he cannot think of an innocent reason for Sturrock's presence.

"Do you think he did it?"

"Who?" For a moment he can't remember what it is she is talking about.

"Who! The prisoner, of course. Do you think he did it?"

"Go to sleep," says Knox, and kisses her.

THE DAY BEFORE THEY LEFT, Donald spent valuable time combing Scott's store for a present for Susannah. He considered buying her a fountain pen; although it would be an apt present on parting, she might find it too heavy-handed a reminder of her promise to write to him. There was a limited choice of items, and in the end he settled for an embroidered handkerchief, ignoring the potential implication that he might be expecting her to cry in his absence—she probably wouldn't think of that.

That afternoon Susannah loitered for hours in the library of their house, waiting for Donald to find her by chance, leafing through a book. She had the opportunity to read one right through by the time he finally realized what was going on, but had not; the novels in the library were mostly dull, having been chosen by her father when young, or by Maria, who had strange tastes. Donald heard her cough, and timidly opened the door holding one hand behind his back.

"We are leaving tomorrow. Before dawn, so we won't see you."

She hastily put down the treatise on fishing and glanced at Donald with her irresistible sideways look. "It will be very dull without you."

Donald smiled, his heart rioting inside his rib cage. "I hope you don't think it a liberty, but I bought you this. I wanted to give you something before I left."

He held out the little parcel, wrapped in the store's brown paper and tied with a piece of ribbon. Susannah smiled and opened it, unfolding the handkerchief.

"Oh, it's so pretty! You are too kind, Mr. Moody."

"Please, call me Donald."

"Oh . . . Donald. Thank you so much. I will keep it with me always."

"I can think of no greater honor."

He wavered on the brink of saying how he envied the handkerchief, but lost confidence, perhaps fortunately. He was not to know that Susannah had another just like it, bought from the same store and presented to her less than a year ago by a smitten local youth. But now Susannah was blushing; the faint wash of color in her cheeks made her seem to glow from within.

"Now I am embarrassed I have nothing to give you in return."

"I don't want anything in return." Again, he hovered on the brink of daring to ask for a kiss, but again his courage failed him. "Only that you will write to me now and again, if you are not too busy."

"Oh yes, I will write to you. And perhaps, if you are not too busy, you may write to me occasionally."

"Every day!" he said recklessly.

"Oh, I think you will be too occupied to do that. I do hope it won't be . . . dangerous."

The remaining few minutes in the library passed in a sweet daze. Donald didn't know what to say next, but he felt that the ball was in his court and eventually plucked up the courage to take one of her hands in his. Then someone banged the Sumatran gong that stood in the hall—the signal for dinner—and she withdrew her hand, otherwise who knows what might have ensued. It makes him dizzy to think about it.

There are only two ways to leave Dove River: south to the bay, or north, following the river's course through the forest. Jacob picks up the trail beyond the Price homestead. Angus Ross told them he found signs that Francis had passed Swallow Lake, and Jacob pauses only to assess the tracks and determine whether they were likely to have been made by the boy. The path is clear and they walk at a fair pace, passing the lake in early afternoon. Jacob kneels to take a closer look.

"It has been some days, but more than one person came through here."

"At the same time?"

Jacob shrugs.

"It could be that French trader. He came this way, didn't he?"

"More than one person went in this direction: two footprints, different sizes."

They follow the trail for several miles. Where a tributary joins the Dove the trail turns westward and follows that, over stony ground that shows no traces. Donald follows Jacob, assuming he knows what he is doing, but is relieved to see a patch of ground near the stream where footprints have pressed leaves and moss into the mud.

"Say he has been traveling on foot for six, seven days. And he is tired and hungry. I think we go faster. We catch him."

"But where is he going? Where does this lead?"

Jacob doesn't know. The trail goes on, winding through the forest alongside the river, always climbing, but there is no sign that it leads anywhere other than into boundless wilderness.

After they have built a shelter and made a fire and Jacob has cooked a mush of meat and corn, Donald hunches by the fire and takes out pen and paper to write to Susannah. He hadn't thought how the letters are going to get to her, but presumably there will be some form of habitation along the way from where delivery is possible. He writes, "Dear Susannah," and then pauses. Should he describe the trek today, the forest with its dark greens and flaming yellows, the purplish rocks that rear through brilliant moss, the sleeping arrangements? He rejects those as being potentially tedious to her, and writes, "It has been a most interesting . . ." before somehow succumbing to the heat of the fire and losing consciousness, so that Jacob has to jolt him awake and push him under their shelter's birch roof, where he collapses onto fir branches. Exhaustion hits him like a sledgehammer, and he is too tired to notice the moon cast ethereal shadows among the trees, certainly too tired to see Jacob observe the halo of ice crystals that surrounds it, and frown.

I HAVE, OVER THE YEARS, BUILT up a fine, if eclectic, collection of books, and have just lent some of them to Ida. Unlike her mother she is grateful, and she seems genuinely touched that I would trust her with something so valuable. I wouldn't have done it before last week, but now even my most precious possessions don't seem that important. One of the books I lend her is my dictionary, a book I have treasured for twenty years. I kept it with me throughout my asylum career, making up for my lost education, but Ida particularly requested it, as the Pretty household has never seen such a thing.

My mother gave it to me shortly before she died, as if to make up for the lack I would soon have of her. I hated coming across words in books that I did not know and doggedly looked them up: "limpid," "termagant," "intimated." I looked up "suicide" after her death. I thought it might help me understand why she had done it. "The act of self-destruction" sounded purposeful and violent, whereas my mother was dreamy and gentle, often absentminded. I asked my father, to see if he could explain—I assumed he knew her better than I did. He blustered and ranted that it was nonsense— she would never have done such a thing; it was a sin even to think it. Then, to my acute embarrassment, he cried. I put my arms around him, trying to comfort him as he sobbed. After a minute or two of our standing in a simulacrum of father-daughter togetherness that made no difference whatsoever—a minute or two that seemed to last an hour—I let go of him and left the room. He didn't seem to notice.

I don't think either of us knew her at all.

I realized later that he was angry because I had guessed the truth. I think he blamed himself, and I believe he sent me to the asylum because he was afraid he had depressed my mother, and was doing the same to me. He was not an inspiring sort of person, and I suspect he was right.

I have spent my life trying not to be like either of my parents. Now that I am approaching the age my mother was when she died, I don't know how

successful I have been: my only child has run away in these terrible circumstances, and clearly I can't blame it all on his Irish blood. I have played a
part, I don't yet know how damaging, in his fate.

It gives me some relief to talk to Ida, who is more cheerful today, and
there is the added spice of gossip about the man locked in the warehouse in
Caulfield. Ida does a good imitation of Scott puffing his cheeks with indig-
nation at being asked to give over his precious real estate for such a purpose. And she adds something interesting—her brothers found signs that
the man had come past their farm on his way to Jammet's, which means he
came from the North. Which means it is possible he saw Francis. Which
means that, even if he is a villain, I have to go and ask him. And just before
she leaves she mentions Thomas Sturrock, who is staying at the Scott house.
Did I know he was the famous Indian searcher who failed to find the Seton
girls? The whole town is talking about it. I nod, vaguely, and say I've heard
something about it. I wonder why he failed to mention it when we dis-
cussed the case.

Predictably, Knox kicks up a fuss about my talking to the prisoner. He
argues that I will not get anything out of him, that they have already asked
him, that it might be prejudicial, that it would be unsuitable, and finally
that it will be dangerous. I remain reasonable. I know that if I stay there
long enough and refuse to go away, he will eventually give in, and he does,
with much headshaking and gloomy sighing. I assure him I am not scared
of the man, however fearsome he looks—he has everything to lose if he be-
haves badly (unless he is convicted, when I suppose it makes no difference
how many murders he is hanged for, but I don't say so). In any case, Knox
insists on sending his servant with me, with instructions to sit by the warehouse door and keep an eye on things.

Adam unlocks the door to the warehouse, which has been cleared of
enough dry goods that the prisoner is marooned in an ocean of space.
There are two windows near the roof, presenting scant escape opportunities, but in any case he is slumped on a pallet and takes no notice when the
door opens. He may have been asleep—he stirs only when Adam calls out,
whereupon he sits up slowly, pulling a thin blanket around him. There is no
fire, and the cold seems even harsher and more insidious than outside.

I turn to Adam. "Are you trying to freeze the man to death?"

Adam mumbles—something about burning us all to the ground—and I order him to fetch some hot stones for our feet, and some coffee. Adam looks at me in astonishment. "I am not to leave you."

"Fetch them this instant. Don't be ridiculous, we can't sit here talking in this cold. I'm sure I shall be quite all right until you get back." I fix him with my most imperious stare until he goes, disconcertingly locking the door behind him.

The prisoner does not look at me, but sits like a statue. I move a chair over to a spot a few feet from the pallet and sit down. I am nervous but determined not to show it. If I want his help, I have to try to look as though I trust him.

"Mr. Parker." I have considered how to put this at length. "My name is Mrs. Ross. I come to you asking for help. I apologize for taking advantage of your . . . detainment."

He doesn't look at me or acknowledge that I am there in any way. It occurs to me that perhaps he is a little deaf.

"Mr. Parker," I go on, louder, "I believe you came from the North, past Swallow Lake?"

After a long pause, he speaks, quietly. "What is it to you?"

"It is this: I have a son, Francis. Seven days ago he went away. I think he went north. He knows no one up there. I am worried. I wondered whether you had seen any sign . . . ? He is only seventeen. He has . . . dark hair. A slight build."

Well, that's it. There's no other way of saying it, and anyway I find my throat has constricted so fiercely I'm not sure I could get more words out.

Parker seems to be thinking; his face has lost that blank cast, and his black eyes are fixed on mine.

"Seven days ago?"

I could kick myself. I should have said eight. Or nine. I nod.

"And Jammet was found six days ago."

"My son didn't kill him, Mr. Parker."

"How do you know?"

I feel a surge of anger at his question. Of course I know. I'm his mother. "He was his friend."

Parker does something very unexpected then: he laughs. Like his voice, it is low and harsh, but not unpleasant.

"I, too, was his friend. Yet Mr. Knox and Mr. Mackinley seem to think I killed him."

"Well . . ." I am taken aback by this turn of events. "I suppose they don't know you. But I think an innocent man would surely do his utmost to help a woman in my situation. That would establish him as a man of good character."

Am I imagining it, or is he actually smiling? The downturned mouth twists a little.

"So if I help you, you think Mr. Mackinley will release me?"

I cannot tell if he is being sarcastic. "That will depend on circumstances I know nothing about, Mr. Parker, such as whether you are guilty or not."

"I am not. Are you?"

"I . . ." I hardly know what to say. "I found him. I saw what had been done to him!"

Now he looks genuinely surprised. And I have the overriding impression that he wants to know what I saw. And, it occurs to me in a rush, if he wants to know, then it stands to reason that he cannot have done it.

"You saw him? They did not tell me what had been done."

If he is lying, he makes a convincing show. He leans forward. I try not to lean away from him, but his face is terrifying. I can almost feel the anger radiating from him.

"Tell me what you saw. And I may be able to help."

"I can't do that. I can't make a deal with you."

"Then why should I help you?"

"Why would you not?"

Suddenly he stands up and strides to the wall of the warehouse—just a few paces, but I flinch before I can stop myself. He sighs. Perhaps he is used to people being afraid of him. I wonder where Adam is with the coffee—he seems to have been gone at least an hour.

"I am a half-breed, accused of killing a white man. Do you think they care if he was my friend? Do you think they believe anything I say?"

Parker is standing in a particularly shadowy patch of the warehouse, and I cannot see his expression. Then he turns back to his pallet bed.

"I am tired. I will have to try and remember. Ask me tomorrow."

He lies on the bed and pulls the blanket over him, his back to me.

"Mr. Parker, I beg you to think on this." I'm not at all certain that I can argue my way back in here. "Mr. Parker . . . ?"

* * *

When Adam returns, I am waiting inside the door. He looks at me in astonishment, the pot of coffee steaming like a miniature volcano in the dank
air.

"Mr. Parker and I are finished for the time being," I tell him. "But why
don't you leave the coffee here."

Adam looks unhappy but does as I suggest, placing the pot and a cup a
cautious distance from the pallet.

And that, it would seem, is that.

ANDREW KNOX SOMETIMES WISHES HE were not the upstanding community elder he has become. When he retired from the law, it was to get away from all those people who begged him to instill order into their tangled, messy lives. People who lied and cheated but still thought the world was conspiring against them and that whatever iniquities they had committed, none of their troubles were of their own making. As if it is not enough to have the whole town in an uproar because a potential murderer is in their midst, John Scott was in his study this morning, complaining that he must have his warehouse back, or substantial compensation for giving his building over for the town's benefit, as he put it, or else he will have to take up the matter with the government. Knox wished him luck. Other inhabitants have stopped him in the street to ask why the culprit has not been moved to a proper jail—no one seems to entertain the possibility that he is innocent. And Mackinley is in no hurry to leave—Knox suspects him of wanting to extract a confession in person so that he can parade the conviction like a trophy. Knox is caught between the hungers of ambitious men and wants no more to do with any of it.

And then there is the business of Sturrock, which he can't ignore.

Mary taps on the door and says that Mrs. Ross is here to see him—again. The woman won't leave him alone. He nods and sighs inwardly—he has a sinking feeling that if he said no she would wait outside in the hall—or even, God forbid, in the street.

"Mr. Knox . . ." she starts speaking before the door is closed.

"Mrs. Ross, I trust your talk was helpful?"

"He wouldn't talk. But he knows something. I have to come back tomorrow."

"I can't let you do that, you see—"

"He didn't do it."

She sounds so certain he stares at her with his mouth open, until he remembers to close it. "What makes you so sure? Feminine intuition?"

She smiles sarcastically—an unpleasant trait in a woman. "He wanted to know how Jammet died. He didn't know. And I am sure he knows something about Francis. But he doesn't trust Mr. Mackinley to be fair on a . . . half-breed."

Knox suspects that Parker doesn't trust him either, but she is being diplomatic.

"Perhaps you also know what he was doing in Jammet's cabin?"

"I'll ask him."

Knox frowns. The whole thing is getting out of hand. He forgets that a few moments ago he was wishing himself free of his responsibilities—the prospect of a farmer's wife taking them from him is preposterous.

"I'm sorry, it's quite out of the question. We are going to move the prisoner as soon as possible. I cannot let anyone who feels like it walk in and talk to him."

"Mr. Knox." She takes a step toward him, almost as if (were she a man) to threaten him. "My son is in the bush, and the Company men may not find him. He may be lost. He may be injured. He is a boy, and if you stop me finding out whatever I can, you may be responsible for his death."

Knox has to make an effort not to step backward. There is something about her—or perhaps it is that sense of inadequacy that tall, handsome women tend to provoke in him. Looking into her flinty eyes—eyes of a peculiar gray and mineral hardness—he is aware of the fierceness of her will.

"I would have thought that you, of all people, would understand what it is to lose a child. Would you deny me help if it is possible?"

He tells her to come back in the morning, very early, impressing on her the need for discretion, and sighs with relief as she goes. He supposes it is only natural for a mother to act so in protection of her child; it is just that it would be more natural (and he would find it easier to sympathize) if she cried or showed some softness in the doing.

"Mr. Knox!" Mackinley barges into his study without knocking. Really the man is becoming more and more unbearable; he saunters through the house as though he owns it. "I think one more day should do it, don't you?"

Knox looks at him wearily. "Do what, Mr. Mackinley?"

"Get the fellow to confess. No point stringing things out."

"What if he doesn't confess?"

"Och, I don't think that will be a problem." Mackinley smiles cunningly. "Deprive these fellows of their freedom and you soon have them groveling. Can't stand the confinement, like animals."

Knox looks at him with hatred. Mackinley doesn't notice.

"I thought I'd have another go before dinner."

"I have urgent paperwork. Can it wait?"

"I don't see why you should trouble yourself, Mr. Knox. I am quite prepared to question him alone."

"I think it would be . . . sounder if both of us were present."

"I don't think I'll be in any danger." He pulls back his jacket to reveal a revolver in his waistband. Knox feels a flush of anger.

"It wasn't your safety I was thinking of, Mr. Mackinley. Rather the need to have more than one witness to whatever is said."

"Then I will take Adam, if that is your concern. The key, if you please."

Knox bites his tongue and opens the drawer where the two keys to the warehouse lie in his custody. He wonders whether he should change his plans and go with him. He has started to think of Mackinley as a criminal, and of course he is nothing of the sort, but a respected servant of the Company. He gives him one of the keys and forces a smile.

"Adam should be in the kitchen."

After Mackinley has gone, Knox hears raised voices from the drawing room. His daughters are quarreling. He briefly considers intervening, as he used to when they were younger, but cannot raise the energy. Besides, they are grown women now. He listens to the familiar sounds: Susannah's voice dissolving into tears; Maria's lecturing tone, which makes him wince; a door slam; and then footsteps running up the stairs. Grown women is what they are.

KNOX FINDS STURROCK IN RESIDENCE at the Scotts'. He announces himself to the maid, and Scott comes to greet him. He looks at him with raw curiosity, but Knox says nothing about why he has come. Let them all gossip (they will anyway, whether he allows it or not); it is none of their concern. Perhaps they will think Sturrock another murder suspect.

He is shown to the room at the back of the house that the Scotts let out to traveling salesmen. The servant knocks on the door, and when Sturrock answers, Knox goes in.

Thomas Sturrock has aged since Knox last saw him. But then it must be ten years—and the ten years between fifty and sixty can mark the difference between a man in the prime of life and his dotage. Knox wonders if he himself is as changed. Sturrock is as straight and elegant as ever, but seems thinner, drier, more fragile. He stands up when Knox comes in, masking his surprise, or whatever he feels, with an easy smile.

"Mr. Knox. I suppose I should not be surprised."

"Mr. Sturrock." They shake hands. "I hope you are keeping well."

"I manage to find things to occupy me in my retirement."

"Good. I expect you know why I've come."

Sturrock shrugs extravagantly. Even with frayed cuffs and slightly stained trousers he gives the impression of being foppish. It has counted against him.

Knox feels awkward. He had forgotten the effect of Sturrock's presence and had almost managed to persuade himself that the accepted story going around Caulfield was true.

"I'm sorry about . . . well, you know. I know how people talk. It can't be pleasant."

Sturrock smiles. "I am not tempted to contradict them, if that's what's worrying you."

Knox nods, relieved. "It's my wife I'm worried about. It would be a cause of such anguish to her, and my daughters . . . I'm sure you understand."

"Yes, of course."

He doesn't agree, Knox realizes; he can't trust him. He wants his reputation back.

"Anyway, what brings you to Caulfield? I have heard all sorts of strange stories."

"I expect they are true," Sturrock says with a smile.

Just then Knox hears a creak outside the room. He gets up noiselessly and goes to open the door. John Scott is standing there with a tray, trying to look as if he has only just arrived.

"I thought you might like a wee dram," he says, with unconvincing heartiness.

"Thank you." Knox takes the tray with a stern look. "Most thoughtful of you. I believe you need me to write in support of your application for compensation?"

Scott's face goes sullen and then, in an attempt to salvage the situation, conspiratorial. "He's an interesting man," he whispers, jerking his head in the direction of Sturrock.

Scott's face is disturbingly pink and shiny in the lamplight. Knox is suddenly reminded of a pig on his parents' land that used to snuffle coquettishly for tidbits, its snout poked through the hedge at the bottom of the garden. He is so surprised at this collision of images that he merely nods and pushes the door shut with his foot.

He puts the tray down on a table. "Mr. Scott is not only our grocer, miller, and entrepreneur, but also the local gazette." He pours a glass of whisky for Sturrock. "Can I be of any assistance to you, while you are here? Short of offering you a room in my house, which would be . . . inappropriate."

"Kind of you to ask." Sturrock appears to think the matter over, which he doesn't need to do. He tells Knox the reason for his presence, and Knox promises to do his best, though privately bewildered by the request. Half an hour later and several dollars lighter, he makes his way out of the house and finds his feet taking him toward the warehouse that looms, a large, windowless monolith, apart from the illuminated houses.

He pauses outside—the light has almost gone—listening for sounds from within. He can hear nothing, and he takes out the second key, confident that Mackinley will have gone.

Even before his eyes adjust to the darkness inside, he realizes something has changed. The prisoner does not turn to face him.

"Mr. Parker? It is Mr. Knox."

Now the man moves and reveals his face. For a moment Knox's eyes do not understand what he sees—the face appears, as before, like a rough carving of a face, only one that has been left unfinished, or spoiled by an unfortunate slip of the knife. With a shiver of recognition, Knox sees the swelling of brow and cheek, the blood darkening the skin.

"Good God, what has happened?" he cries out, before his brain catches up with his mouth and he bites his tongue.

"Is it your turn?" The man's voice is harsh, but without obvious emotion.

"What did he do?" He should have insisted on accompanying Mackinley. He should have listened to his doubts. Damn the man! He has ruined everything.

"He thought he could encourage me to confess. But I cannot confess to what I did not do."

Knox is pacing up and down in his agitation. He remembers Mrs. Ross's assurance that Parker was innocent, and is inclined to agree with her. Knox experiences the rising panic of a juggler who has suddenly found he has too many balls in the air, and realizes that disaster, and attendant humiliation, are imminent.

"I will . . . find you something for that."

"Nothing is broken."

"I . . . I apologize. This should never have happened."

"I will tell you something I would not tell the other."

Knox stares at the man in wild hope.

"Laurent had enemies. And the worst of his enemies were in the Company. He was a threat to them, alive. Dead he is no threat."

"What sort of threat?"

"He was a founder of the North America Company. But more than that, he was formerly one of them, as I was. The Company do not like those who turn against them."

"Who in the Company?"

A long pause.

"I don't know."

Knox feels a trickle of sweat making its way down his breastbone, despite the cold of the warehouse. Something has occurred to him, something stupid and reckless and insistent, something quite unlike anything he has ever done before—and he knows what he is about to do.

* * *

All through dinner that evening, he watches Mackinley wax jovial under the influence of wine and female attention. His voice rises with his color, and he expounds the virtues of great Company men he has known. He discusses a Company factor who famously defused a quarrel between two Indian tribes, to the detriment of both, and then a particularly admired outdoorsman, who would think nothing of trekking hundreds of miles in the depths of winter. Apparently even the native guides admired his prowess at navigation and survival, thus proving that there is nothing innately superior about the natives' wilderness craft—nothing that, given the right circumstances, the white man (especially a Scottish white man) will not excel at.

Knox watches Mackinley talk, and if he does not take part in the conversation, he manages to hide his repulsion for the other man. Afterward, his wife will ask him if he is quite well, and he will smile and say that he is tired, but that there is no need to worry.

From now on he will be talked about; rumors will travel vast distances, telling of his incompetence, his unfitness. Fortunately he is retired. If his reputation is the price to pay for justice, then so be it.

He has shut his mouth on the truth before. He can do it again.

The Fields
of Heaven

HE HAS FAILED. HE HAS lain in silence in this room for some days now, with barely the strength to move. His left leg throbs intermittently, waking him at night. From the narrow bed he has studied the whitewashed walls, the painted wooden chairs, the curtainless window that shows only sky. If he lifts himself up on his elbows he can see a small church spire, painted dull red. Mostly, the sky has been gray, or white. Or black.

The shaking has subsided. He knows now that he must have developed a fever after falling into the bog. He had crossed a still, peaty stream—the water so quiet it had oily rainbows on its surface—when on the far side he slipped and plunged into the quagmire. He was horrified by the speed with which he sank, grabbed at handfuls of reeds, spreading his upper body flat on the mud in an attempt to halt the slide. He could clearly see himself being sucked under the surface, the mud filling his mouth and nose, clotting his throat. He yelled out, more a statement of intent than a cry for help—there was no point in that, it was painfully clear. It took him what seemed like hours to haul himself out, and subsequently to crawl up the liver-colored bank onto a patch of blueberry scrub. Blueberry was good, safe; its roots in firm and stony soil. He lay exhausted. Something bad had happened to his left leg; when he tried to stand, it buckled under him and the pain in his knee made him retch, although nothing came up. He hadn't eaten properly for three days—or was it more? He can't remember. He doesn't remember being found either, or brought here, wherever here is. He woke up in the white room and wondered whether this was what death looked like: a featureless white room where angels drifted to and fro, speaking in tongues.

Then his fever lessened and he realized the room was not featureless, and the angels were earthbound and quite ordinary, although he still could not understand them.

There are two women who tend to him, feeding him soup and doing things that he blushes to think about. Still, they must be his mother's age, and he is being treated like one of their own children. They are brisk and no-nonsense: sponging him down, straightening sheets, stroking his hair. Yesterday—he thinks it was yesterday—a man came in, spoke with one of the women, and came to look down on him from what felt like a great height. The man was his father's age; he had a fair, full beard, very unfashionable, and prominent goaty eyes.

"*Êtes-vous Français?*" he asked in a peculiar accent. Francis was alarmed that the man knew his name before he recognized the French words. He wondered what to say. There is so much he doesn't know. The man then turned to the woman and spoke in their guttural tongue for a moment.

"Enk-lish?"

Francis stared at the man and decided then that he would say nothing at all. It was probably best.

The man and woman looked at each other. The man shrugged, and after a moment he folded his hands together and began to talk. After a minute Francis realized he was praying. The woman prayed, too, but by listening to the man. Their clothing was very plain—rough materials in black and white and gray, like their sky.

Just recently—in the last hour or so—he has started to remember things: he remembers trudging mile after mile along the banks of the river as it cut through the forest, farther than he had ever gone in his life, following the trail of the man. He hadn't seen him again since that night at the cabin, and it had stretched his skills as a tracker to their limit to follow the signs. But the land had been kind to him. Every time he thought he must have gone wrong—after walking for hours, scanning and searching and finding nothing printed on the ground, just when he thought he must have missed the man's turning—he would come across another signal: the blunt press of a moccasin in leaves, piss-melted frost in a hollow. He saw the man's spoor and the scanty trace of his fires, hurriedly swept over. He did not know when he ate. He had never known anyone move so fast.

Francis had dared light a fire only once, and had failed to sleep afterward, terrified the man was going to realize he was being followed, and find him. But nothing happened. He had taken care not to get too close, always looking ahead in case of a trap. In the end, his caution was his undoing. On the fourth day he lost the trail. It left the forest for higher ground and swung northwest into a desolate, treeless landscape—a scrubby, swampy plateau where bogs slowed him down and a north wind knifed through his wolf-skin coat. He went slowly, grown used to the shelter of trees, nervous of being seen in the open. After several hours of this he had almost fallen into another, smaller river that carved itself a channel through oily mudbanks. The water was opaque, and he could find no signs of passage. Then he floundered, trapped. This was where he became, for the first time, truly scared. He had been scared all along, of course, but now he realized that the country had him in its grip, and was going to let him die, never to be found. His bones would lie under the sky, bleached and scoured like the skeletons of deer that lay scattered around him. He struggled, waist-deep, until after dark. He even called out, in case the man was nearby—at least death at his hands would be swift. At least it would be human. But somehow, somehow, he had got himself out. This was where his strength failed him altogether.

In the end it was all the same: he had passed out by that river, exhausted, weak, and frozen. He has failed.

He thinks it is afternoon: he ate some soup an hour ago, and then had to suffer the embarrassment of using a bedpan with one of the women, the dark-haired one. He turned his eyes from her, and she laughed as though she found him really amusing, and she seemed not embarrassed at all.

He cannot see his clothes anywhere, but is unsure whether to ask about them, and if so, how. The prospect of not speaking is appealing. If he doesn't speak, then maybe no one will ask him anything. He regrets his failure, but at a distance—he did what he could. His reasons for leaving now seem very far away, from a different world. A painful world, and not one he is eager to go back to. Of more immediate concern is the whereabouts of the bone tablet.

One evening, months ago, Laurent had taken the piece of bone out of his hiding place (he was drunk at the time) and showed it to Francis, and together they had studied the little stick figures and the angular marks that looked like writing. Laurent thought Francis might know what it was. Francis thought back to school and Egyptian hieroglyphics, ancient Greek, the pictures in his mother's books, but could not remember anything that corresponded to these marks. The only way you could establish which way they went was from the stick men who trooped around the edge. Laurent said he had got it from a trader in the States, said he had met a gentleman in Toronto who would pay a lot of money for it. They laughed at the folly of rich men. Then, later, he had said Francis could have it. Francis refused, nervous in part of something he could not understand. Who knew—maybe it was a curse? But Laurent had offered it to him, so when he took it, it wasn't really stealing. As for the other things, he had to take them to survive. He would have taken the gun, too, if he had seen it. Another part of him—the part that echoes the boys he endured through the long years at the village school—says, what would you have done with it if you had? You can't even bring yourself to shoot a rabbit.

When he opens his eyes again, the bearded man is sitting by his bed. He puts down a book—he has been waiting for him to wake up. Francis sees the title of the book, but the words seem to be a weird jumble of consonants. The man smiles at him. His teeth are discolored, which is all the more noticeable because of the redness of his lips. Francis stares back, but something in his face must have softened, because the man beams with pleasure and pats him on the shoulder. He speaks, and asks him again if he is French or English. It has occurred to Francis that the people who found him might have seen the man he was following. Who knows, perhaps he even came here? He could give up the idea of speech, but with it he would have to give up his hope. He finds, to his surprise, that he is not ready to give up yet.

He moistens his mouth, which feels rusty and foul. "English," he croaks.

"English! Good." The man is overjoyed. "Do you know your name?"

Francis hesitates for a fraction of a second, and then it comes out without thinking. "Laurent."

"Laurent? Ah. Laurent. Yes. Good. I am Per." He turns his head and shouts, "Britta! Kom."

The fair woman appears from somewhere nearby, and smiles at Francis. Per speaks to her in their language, explaining.

"Laurent," she says. "Welcome."

"She doesn't speak English a lot. Mine is best. Do you know where you are?"

Francis shakes his head.

"You are at Himmelvanger. It means the Fields of Heaven. Good name, yes?"

Francis nods. He has never heard of it. "What river . . . ?" His voice still sounds strange and weak.

"River? Ah, we found you . . . yes. Ahh, a river without a name. Jens was hunting . . . and saw you there. Very surprised!" Per mimes the surprise of the man looking for hares but finding instead a bedraggled youth.

Francis smiles, as much as he can. His mouth finds it an effort. "Can I talk to Jens?"

Per looks surprised. "Yes, I am sure. But now . . . you are sick. Sleep and eat. Get better. Britta and Line care for you good, yes?"

Francis nods. He smiles at Britta, who giggles unexpectedly.

Per leans down and picks up Francis's clothes. "All clean, yes? And this . . ." He produces Laurent's bag, and Francis takes it.

"Thank you, very much. And thank . . . Jens for finding me. I hope I can speak to him soon."

The others smile and nod.

Britta speaks to Per, who scrapes the chair back as he stands up with a satisfied grunt.

"Now you sleep, Britta tells me. Yes?"

Francis nods.

He allows himself to think of his parents at the homestead. He supposes they will be worried about him, although whether they will worry enough to come after him is another matter. People must have found Laurent by now. What will they think? Will they think he did it?

The thought almost makes him smile.

LINE IS OUTSIDE WITH TORBIN and Anna when Britta comes out to tell her that the youth has spoken. Line thinks it is odd that an English youth is called Laurent. She knew a Frenchman called Laurent in her previous life, when Janni was alive. Her English is better than anyone's, even Per's, so she is secretly pleased. She has felt protective of him ever since Jens brought him in, slung over the back of a pony, and now she feels justified—she can be the link between him and the others.

Torbin and Anna run up to her, amid a squawking of chickens, ears flapping.

"Can we see him now?" asks Torbin, his face flushed from cold.

"No, not yet. He is very weak. You would exhaust him."

"We wouldn't. We'd be like little mice. Tiny little mice." Anna makes little squeaking mouse noises.

"Soon," says Line. "When he can get up and walk about."

"Like Lazarus," prompts Anna, keen to fit the stranger into her Himmelvanger-shaped worldview.

"Not quite like Lazarus. He wasn't dead."

"Nearly dead! Wasn't he?" Torbin is hopeful of more drama.

"Yes, nearly dead. He was unconscious."

"Yeah, like this. Mama—look!" Torbin throws himself down in the snow and feigns unconsciousness, which involves, in his interpretation, the tongue lolling from the side of his mouth. Line smiles. Torbin can always make her smile. He's irrepressible, indestructible, like a dense rubber ball. He doesn't remind her so much of Janni, whereas Anna is like Janni reincarnated—broad cheekbones, brown hair, fjord-deep blue eyes. A smile of terrible sweetness, which comes out only a few times a year and is all the more devastating for its rarity.

The children climb out of the chicken run and head across the yard. Line is supposed to be feeding the chickens, and then helping Britta with quilt making. She doesn't have a lot of time to herself, but that's not what she came for. She likes being in the chicken shelter, stoutly built against winter winds with a steeply raked roof to repel the snow. There is a pleasingly sturdy quality to all the buildings at Himmelvanger. Everything had to be built well, because it was being built for God: dove-tailed joints; double-walled construction; the sweeping lines of roofs, neatly shingled with cedar tiles, each one nearly heart-shaped. The spire on the small chapel, with its painted cross. For ten years it has withstood the worst wind and weather the Canadian winter could muster. God has protected them.

And the people here have accepted her with kindness and grace, even if it is mixed with advice. You should pray more, Line; you should put your trust in God; you should infuse your work with faith and that will give your life meaning. You should stop mourning for Janni, because he is with God now, so he is happy. She has tried to do those things, because she owes them her life. When Janni disappeared—she still finds it hard to say "died," even to herself—she had two tiny children and no money. She was evicted from her lodgings and had nowhere to go. Had contemplated going back to Norway but could not raise the fares. Had contemplated throwing herself and her children into the St. Lawrence. And then a friend had told her about Himmelvanger. The prospect of her going to live in a model religious community was so far-fetched as to be comical. But they were Norwegians, and they wanted hard workers. More important, they didn't ask for money.

Ironically, she had set off in the same direction Janni had taken on his final journey. Or, if not his final journey, then the last time she had seen him. He was looking for work and had met another Norwegian who was going to work for the Hudson Bay Company. They were promised high wages for a season's work, but it was a long way, up in the Northwest, in Rupert's Land. He would not see Line or the children for over a year, but then, he said, they would have enough money to buy a house. It would be a short-cut to the life they wanted: their own home and some land. Line would not have to wash and mend other people's soiled clothes; he would not have to bite his tongue and work for fools.

She got only one letter after he left. Janni wasn't much of a writer, so she hadn't expected passionate love letters, but still, one letter in six months hurt her feelings a little. He had written that things were not quite as he had expected—he and his friend were billeted with a group of Norwegian convicts whom the Company had imported. The men were rough and violent, and formed a clique that was left alone by the other employees. Janni felt

uncomfortable being lumped in with these men, but the divisions of na-
tionality were stronger than those of legality. But some of them were all
right, he wrote, and he was looking forward to seeing Line and the children
the following summer and choosing a site for their house. No messages of
love; no endearments; it was a letter he could have written to an aunt. And
after that, nothing.

When the next summer came, she waited without patience, asking
people for news. Toronto was hot and humid; the black flies tormented
the children, and their cramped, cheap lodgings reeked of sewage. At
night she dreamed of wide-open landscapes empty of people, covered in
cold, pure white snow, only to wake up sweating and scratching at fresh
insect bites. She became bad-tempered and peevish. Then, in July she received a letter addressed to "Family of Jan Fjelstad." It had been sent to
the wrong address, and had been opened and the envelope readdressed in
childish handwriting. Its stiff phrases regretted to inform her that her
husband was one of a party of Norwegians who had mutinied and deserted from the post the previous January, stealing valuable Company
property. They had vanished into the wilderness, undoubtedly perishing
in the blizzards that swept the country that month. However (the letter
took care to note), if by some strange chance they hadn't perished, they
were fugitives from justice.

At first Line simply did not believe it. She kept waiting for her husband
to turn up, thinking they must have mistaken him for someone else. The
English found Norwegian names confusing, she told herself. She could not
believe Janni would have stolen anything. It wasn't in his nature.

She went to the Toronto office of the Company and demanded to see
someone, and a sandy-haired English youth received her in his small office.
He was polite and apologetic, but he said there was no reason to doubt the
letter. There had been a desertion, and although he personally had no
knowledge of the people involved, he was sure it was accurate. Line shouted
at the youth, who looked angry. He didn't seem to appreciate that he was
talking about the death of her husband and her hopes. She ran out of the
office and went on waiting.

But weeks crawled past, and he didn't come back, and she ran out of
money. In the end it didn't really matter what she believed; whether it was
true or not, she had to make a decision, so one morning in September she
set off with the children on a three-week journey to the ridiculously named

Himmelvanger, traveling almost as far as Janni had on his penultimate journey, to the equally ridiculously named Moose Factory.

That was three years ago, and she has become used to her new life. At first she was sure Janni would find her; before they left Toronto she told everyone where they were going. One day he would ride into the yard on a large horse, and call her name; and she would drop whatever she was doing and come running. At first, she thought about that every day. Then, gradually, she stopped indulging in that fantasy. She grew listless and depressed, until Sigi Jordal had urged her to confide in her. Line wept, for the only time since arriving, and confessed to Sigi that sometimes she wanted to die. This was a mistake. She was besieged by members of the community, each in turn coming to her to urge her to repent of the great sin of hopelessness, to accept the Lord into her heart and let him cast out despair. She quickly assured them that she had (suddenly) accepted God, and he was leading her out of the dark vale of sorrow. Somehow the pretense comforted her; occasionally she wondered if she didn't half believe it. She would go and sit in church and stare at the sun coming in, following an individual mote of dust until her eyes ached. Her mind wandered pleasantly. She didn't pray, exactly, but neither did she feel alone.

It was about then that Espen Moland had started paying her particular attention. He was a married man (the community was intended only for families), and his children played with Torbin and Anna, but his interest in her was more than purely spiritual. She was wary at first, knowing that this was utterly proscribed. But secretly she liked it. Espen made her feel beautiful again. He said that she was the best-looking woman in Himmelvanger and that she was driving him crazy. Line tutted but privately agreed. Espen wasn't exactly handsome, not like Janni, but he was quick and funny, and always had the last word in an argument or exchange. It was peculiarly sweet to hear words of passion from a man who never stopped joking, and it proved to be more than her flesh could stand. Eventually, some months ago, they had started to sin. That was how she thought of it, although she did not feel guilty. Just cautious and careful. She cannot afford another disaster.

Line hears him coming now, whistling one of his made-up tunes. Is he coming to the henhouse? Yes—the door opens.

"Line! I haven't seen you all day!"

"I have work to do, you know that."

"Of course, but if I don't see you, I am sad."

"Oh yeah, sure."

"I've come to mend the hole in the roof."

He is wearing his tool belt—he is their carpenter—and Line glances upward to scan the roof.

"There is no hole."

"Well, there might be. It's best to be on the safe side. We don't want our eggs getting wet, do we?"

She giggles. Espen is always making her laugh, even when he says the stupidest things. He slides his arm around her waist and presses himself against her, and she experiences the familiar melting sensation that overcomes her in his presence.

"Britta's waiting for me."

"So? She won't notice a few minutes."

How hard it is to behave properly, even in a strict religious community like this one. He is kissing her neck, his lips hot on her skin. If she doesn't leave now, she is done for.

"It's not a good time." She wriggles out of his grasp, breathing heavily.

"My God, you look beautiful today. I could—"

"Stop!"

She loves the beseeching look in his eyes. It is nice to know she has it in her power to make someone so happy, just by touching him. But if she doesn't walk out of the henhouse right now, he might start using those words that send the blood rushing around her skull, obliterating her reason. Dirty, obscene words that she could never speak, but that have an extraordinary, almost magical power over her. It's not something Janni would ever have done, but he wasn't much of a talker. In fact, the way she feels around Espen is not something she has ever experienced before; she seems to be changing in ways that sometimes alarm her, as though she is riding a flood tide in a paper-light canoe—buoyed up, exhilarated, but not at all sure she is in control.

She forces herself to back away, the inside of her body clamoring for him, and smiles, just at the last minute, so that he won't think—God forbid!—that she has lost interest.

Outside the henhouse she wipes the smile off her face, trying to think about something else—something repellent, like the smell of pigs, not

Espen and his sweet, dirty mouth. She will have to sit with Britta over the needlework, and she has been getting too many sharp and questioning looks from Britta lately. She can't possibly know, but perhaps something about her has betrayed them. She makes herself think about the sick boy, to sober herself, but somehow that doesn't have the desired effect now. Instead, she imagines lifting up the sheets and looking at his naked body. She has seen what he has, his appealingly golden skin, and has felt its smoothness . . .

God! Espen has poisoned her whole mind. Perhaps she should slip into the church for a few minutes and pray, try to conjure up some suitably becoming shame.

IT IS FREEZING: THE COLDEST of the five days they have been following the trail. A wind screams down from the Arctic and scours their faces with hail. It makes Donald's eyes water, and the tears freeze on his cheeks, making them chapped and raw. Water from somewhere also freezes in his mustache, so he started wrapping his muffler across the lower part of his face, until it froze solid with the moisture from his breath, and he had to tear it painfully free before he suffocated. He is cold and exhausted even though Jacob has the lion's share of the load, since Donald cannot keep up if he carries half.

After the second day, Donald found every movement brought a pain somewhere in his body. He had become accustomed, previously, to thinking of himself as a fairly strong, fit young man, but now he finds that he is just beginning to learn about endurance. Jacob tramps ahead of him, shoulders the heavy load, makes detours to scout the trail, and when they stop in the late afternoon, it is Jacob who gathers wood, builds a fire, and cuts branches for their sleeping shelter. At first Donald protested that he was going to do his share, but he was simply too tired and clumsy to be of any use, and their camp was set up much quicker if he left it all to Jacob. Jacob kindly but firmly told him to sit down and concentrate on boiling some water.

Early this morning they left the forest and began to cross a barren, hummocky plateau where nothing seems to stand between them and the wind blowing off the frozen Hudson Bay. Despite heavy clothing, it finds its way into his tender places with sharp, prying jabs. Very quickly it emerges that the plateau is one enormous bog. Pools of black water ooze from the ground, skimmed with ice. Reeds and ground willow catch the blowing snow and hold it in tangled skeins. It is impossible to find more than a couple of firm footholds in a row, and Jacob has given up trying to keep his feet dry; he plods from hummock to hollow with a grimly monotonous tread. No matter how determined he is to keep up, Donald has had to call out to him to slow down on three occasions, and now Jacob pauses every so often, waiting for him to catch up. He manages to do this without making Donald feel inadequate, but instead makes it seem as though he has stopped to update Donald on the state of the trail. It is clear that Donald is finding it harder to follow in this landscape, but he listens with mounting indifference. Yesterday he found it hard to care whether they ever found the boy; today it has occurred to him that he might not even return from this journey. He is not sure he cares about that either.

Increasingly, they pass the corpses of animals. Now they plod past the skeleton of a deer, which must have been here some time, since it is picked clean but a dark yellowish brown. The skull faces them, within shouting distance of its scattered bones, watching Donald through empty eye sockets, silently reminding him of the futility of their endeavor.

Donald tries to turn his thoughts to Susannah, to shut a door between what his body is enduring and what he is feeling. Disappointingly he hears his father, instead, lecturing him: "Mind over matter, Donnie. Mind over matter. Rise above it! We all have to do things we don't want to do." He feels the old irritation bubble to the surface like marsh gas. His father—an accountant in Bearsden—never had to march through an endless bog in the Canadian winter.

Tucked inside his shirt, close to his heart, lie three letters to Susannah. He is disappointed by his lack of eloquence, but it is, he consoles himself, hard to write witty prose while trying to get close enough to the fire to see without igniting one's hair. He fears the letters are rather smudged and grimy, and probably smell of smoke, if not worse. Perhaps, if they ever find civilization again, he can copy them out on clean paper, or even start all over again, in an improved literary style. That would probably be best.

At four in the afternoon, Jacob is confused. He makes Donald wait while he scouts around in a circle, then signals for Donald to join him. They retrace their steps for some time. Donald silently curses the wasted effort, but he is too exhausted to ask questions. A thin snow is falling, and visibility is poor. The air feels both wet and sharp. Jacob breathes out slowly, a habit with him when he is thinking hard.

"I think they went different ways here."

Donald peers at the ground but can see nothing to indicate that anyone has been here before, ever.

"They both left the forest at the same place. The trail was clear until then, but I think the second man was getting slower. Now one goes off that way, because there is a footprint frozen into the mud pointing in that direction. But it's some distance away and a trail is hard to follow in the bog. I think the second one lost him, and went on this way . . ." He points to where the ground dips to form a shallow incline. "There are signs here that someone got stuck, and went on. I should have seen it earlier."

Donald inwardly agrees. "And you think Ross was the second trail?"

"The first trail is a fast traveler, used to going long distances. He knows where to go without having to stop and look. So yes, the second is the boy, and he is tired."

"But where the hell are they going? I mean, the forest is one thing, but this . . . My God, look at it! No one can live here!"

As far as they can see, there is nothing, just scrub and these infernal pools of water. There are no elements of landscape that are generally felt to be attractive (rightly so, Donald feels)—no contrast of mountain and valley, no lakes, no forest. If this land has a character, it is sullen, indifferent, hostile.

"I don't know this place very well," Jacob is saying, "but there are posts in this part, farther north."

"God. Pity the poor bastards who have to live in them."

Jacob smiles. They have fallen into the roles of novice and tutor with some relief. It makes it easy to know what to say, for one thing. Easy to know how the other will react. Over the past few days, they have established a familiar routine.

"People live everywhere. But they call this Starvation Country."

Donald blasphemes. "Then we'd better find him as soon as possible." He doesn't need to describe the alternative.

"Perhaps the first man was going to one of the posts up there." Jacob points into the howling wind in a direction that looks as unpromising as all the others.

"And the second?"

"I don't know. Perhaps he was lost."

Donald feels awed at the thought of finding only a body, which must now be a strong possibility. How long could anyone survive in this, lost and alone? He tries to tell himself that they are not far behind him, but he is seized with the morbid thought that Jacob might leave him, inadvertently, behind, and then he, Donald, would be alone just like the boy. How long would he survive? He struggles after the dark figure up ahead, determined that he will not let that happen. By some ironic twist of physiology, the recently healed wound under his ribs has started throbbing again, reminding him of his frailty—or is it reminding him that Jacob, on whom he depends for his survival, recently stabbed him?

At length the two men come to a river that worms invisibly through the landscape. Black as oil between iced banks. Jacob stops him and points to a turmoil of mud, frozen into peaks and troughs.

"There were people here. And a horse. I would say he joined them."

Jacob smiles, and Donald tries to feel pleased. But mainly he feels he can't go on much longer. He nurtures a growing hatred for this landscape that is quite unlike anything he has encountered before. People aren't meant to be here. The thought of a man on a horse picking up the boy is potentially horrifying—God knows how much farther they will have to walk now. He cannot understand why Jacob wouldn't let them bring the horses; he entertains the possibility that the whole thing is an elaborate attempt to finish off what the knife wound failed to achieve.

Jacob leads them away from the river, and Donald struggles in his wake, his eyes doggedly fixed on the treacherous ground, numb to their progress.

Suddenly Jacob has stopped, and Donald walks straight into the back of him, so dulled is he to his surroundings. Jacob takes his arm and laughs into his face.

"Mr. Moody, look! Look!"

He's pointing into the snow and the dusk, which has crept up on them imperceptibly. And in the swirling grayness, Donald sees points of light. He grins hugely, and feels something warm run down his chin—his lip has split. But nothing can quench this ferocious joy. There will be houses, people, warmth . . . there will be fires, and even better, walls! Walls that will come between him and the elements. In a moment of fiery elation he relives the excitement of seeing the moon's surface, he feels the undiluted pleasure of the fourteen-year-old boy, and he experiences such a pure happiness that all the past days' toil, in fact, all the privations of the past year and a half, seem worth it. He claps Jacob clumsily on the shoulder, convinced he is the best, the finest fellow he has ever met in his life.

Forty minutes later they walk into a large courtyard surrounded by neat wooden buildings. There are barns with livestock penned, steaming, inside; a small church with a stubby spire, topped by a cross painted a dull red. Lights are on, spilling out of windows onto the icy yard, looking like the promised land. Donald chokes back tears of gratitude as they make for the largest of these buildings, and knock on the door.

I USED TO THINK, WHEN I was a girl, and even later when I was in the asylum, that when people married they never felt alone again. At the time I doubted I ever would marry; I assumed I was destined to be an outcast from society, or worse, a spinster. I had friends in the asylum, even, in Dr. Watson, a special kind of friend; but being the muse of a mad doctor did not make me feel as though I belonged to the normal world, nor that I was safe. My husband gave me something I never expected: a feeling of legitimacy. And the feeling that here was someone I did not have to hide anything from. I didn't have to pretend. I suppose what I'm saying is, I loved him. I know that he loved me, I'm just not sure when that stopped being true.

It is late, and I am sleepless again, thinking about my next meeting with the prisoner; Knox has agreed that I can go back, as long as I am very discreet. I think he was hurt by my using his wife's tragedy against him, and it is to his credit that he agreed. He fears the Company man. He fears, too, being thought too soft. I lie beside my husband for a time, and Angus, in his sleep, turns and folds himself over me, something he has not done for a long time. I don't dare move, wondering if he knows, or dreams of, what he is doing. After a while he grunts and turns over, his back to me again. And I don't think, even in my darkest moments in the asylum after my father died, that I have ever felt so alone. If Olivia had lived, would things have been different? If Francis had never come to us?

Pointless questions. My favorite kind.

I despise this weakness in myself—this endless one-sided conversation that takes the place of action, and I wish at certain times (usually late at night), that I was more like Ann Pretty. Her surname may be unfortunate, but sometimes I think she is the perfect model of a backwoods pioneer, being an inveterate survivor, tough, unimaginative, and unscrupulous. She would not lie awake at night wondering what her husband, or anyone else, was thinking of her. She would not lose her child to the wilderness.

I get out of bed and, for something to do, start to assemble a pack for the journey I maintain I am planning. Truth to tell, I don't have much heart for it; I am very nearly face-to-face with my fear of the wilderness, my lack of courage. Who knows, perhaps Moody and the other man will be here tomorrow, with Francis. I don't care if they have to arrest him, as long as they find him and he is all right. Then perhaps it will be him in the warehouse in Caulfield, shivering in the dim cavernous space, but safe. Telling myself this, I assemble my warmest clothes and a selection of hardy, indestructible foods. It is a bit like planning a winter picnic; if I think of it like that, it doesn't seem so bad.

The softest of knocks on the door doesn't surprise me as much as it might have: I'm thinking of Francis, so perhaps it seems inevitable that my longing should at last be answered. I pull the door open with a gasp of joy, words gathered to tumble out at him, along with tears, when the darkness yawns at me. I look around, whispering his name—it is strange that I whisper, as though I have a sort of premonition.

He is standing in the darkness—to alleviate the shock, I suppose, so that my eyes have to find him and only gradually realize who it is.

The prisoner holds up his hand in a placatory gesture. "Please, don't scream."

I stare at him. I wasn't going to scream. I pride myself on not screaming, even under trying circumstances.

"I'm sorry to startle you. Knox has released me. I am going to follow your son, because I think he saw the killer. But I need provisions, and my rifle is impounded. And I believe you have my dogs."

I stare at him in total disbelief, barely understanding what he is saying.

"Mrs. Ross, I need your help, and you need mine."

So that's how it happens: mutual need is what makes people co-operate—nothing to do with trust or kindness or any such sentimental notion. I don't really take in what he says about Knox and why he released him in this underhand way, but looking at his violated face I can believe that Mackinley has done it. Parker wants a rifle and food and his dogs, and I want a guide to follow Francis, and maybe he thinks Francis will talk more readily if I am there—Francis has something he wants, too. And so while my husband sleeps upstairs we pack—and I prepare to go into the wilderness with a suspected killer. What's worse, a man I haven't been properly introduced to. I am too shocked to feel fear, too excited to care about the impropriety of it. I suppose if you have already lost what matters most, then little things like reputation and honor lose their luster. (Besides, if the worse comes to the worst, I can remind myself that I have sold my honor far more cheaply than this. I can remind myself of that, if I have to.)

A light snow falls as we walk out of Dove River, the two dogs padding silently beside Parker. An hour past the Pretty place, he goes to a cache among some tree roots and swiftly builds a sled from the materials he finds there—a light, slender structure of willow boughs with a sort of seat made from stiffened hide. I am about to express gratitude for his thoughtfulness when he ties the bundles of food and blankets to the seat. The dogs are excited by the snow and the sled, letting out a couple of whining barks. Throughout this operation, which takes about half an hour, Parker does not look at me, nor say a word. Somehow I do not think he is very interested in separating me from my honor. He gives the harness a final tug and sets off again, northward, along the course of the Dove, guided only by the sound of the river, and a dim, amorphous glow that seems to come from the snow itself.

I follow him, stumbling in the unfamiliar moccasins he insisted I wear, determined not to complain, ever, no matter what.

ALTHOUGH RARE, IT IS NOT unheard of for visitors to arrive at Himmelvanger out of the blue—usually Indians calling to trade goods and news. Per makes them welcome; they are neighbors, and one must live in peace with one's neighbors. And they are God's children, too, even if they live in squalor and ignorance like so many pigs. Sometimes they come when their relatives are sick and their remedies have failed them. They come with somber faces and desperate hopes, and watch while the Norwegians dole out tiny doses of laudanum or ipecac or camphor, or apply their own traditional remedies, which usually fail them also. Per hopes this is not going to be one of those times.

The white man extends a frozen hand. He wears spectacles whose metal frames are rimed with frost, giving him a startling appearance, like an owl.

"Excuse the intrusion. We are from the Hudson Bay Company, and we are on business here."

Per is even more surprised, wondering what on earth the Company could want with him. "Please, come in. You must be frozen. Your hand . . ." The hand he shakes is livid with cold, with no strength in it, like a pork chop.

Per backs away from the door, allowing them into the warm haven. "Do you have animals?"

"No. We are on foot."

Per raises his eyebrows, and leads them into a small room near the kitchen, where he calls for Sigi and Hilde and contrives hot stew and bread and coffee to be brought for the men. Sigi's eyes are round with curiosity at the sight of the two strangers.

"Good heavens, Per, the Lord is sending us all kinds of guests this winter!"

Per responds a little sharply—he doesn't want gossip and rumor spreading, not until he understands what's going on. Fortunately, the men don't seem to understand Norwegian. They smile the foolish grins of the hungry and weary, rubbing their hands and falling on the food with fervent cries of gratitude.

As warmth begins to creep back into his hands, Donald experiences sharp, tingling pains, and examining them in the firelight they look livid and puffy. A woman brings a bowl of snow and insists on rubbing his hands with it, gradually bringing them back to painful life. The woman smiles at him as she ministers to him, but doesn't speak—Per explains that they are Norwegians, and not all of them speak English.

"So what are two Company men doing here in November?"

"It is not Company business, exactly." Donald is finding it hard to keep the smile off his face—he can't believe their good fortune, not only at finding a habitation, but finding one of such civilization, and a cultivated man like Per Olsen to talk to.

"Are you on your way somewhere?"

His tone reflects the unlikelihood of this. Donald tries not to speak with his mouth full of almond cake. (Almonds! Truly, they are blessed here.)

"We are making this journey because we are following someone. We have followed his trail from Dove River on the bay, up to the river that cuts through the plateau, and then the trail led here." He looks at Jacob for confirmation, but Jacob seems shy in the others' presence, and merely inclines his head.

Per listens gravely, and then leaves the room for a while. Donald assumes he has gone off to consult with some of the others, because when he comes back, he is accompanied by another man, whom he introduces as Jens Andreassen.

"Jens has something to tell you," he says.

Jens, a shy, slow-moving man with a tongue that seems too large for his mouth, recounts how he found the boy on the riverbank, close to death. He brought him to Himmelvanger, where they have been caring for him. He says this in Norwegian, and Per translates, slowly, making an effort to get the words right.

Donald can feel the protectiveness in Per; Francis is the lamb who was lost, whom God has shepherded into his care.

"What do you suspect him of? What has happened?"

Donald doesn't want to reveal all the facts. If Per has taken an interest in the boy, he doesn't want to antagonize him. "Well, there was a serious attack."

Per looks up, his pale eyes bulging; when he translates for Jens, their eyes meet in shock.

"It is not certain that Francis is guilty, of course; but we had to find him. The boy's mother is extremely worried in any case."

Per frowns. "Who is Francis?"

"The boy. His name is Francis Ross."

Per considers for a moment. "This boy says his name is Laurent."

Donald and Jacob exchange looks. Donald feels a cold shiver of certainty travel down his spine.

"Perhaps it is not the same one," Per suggests.

Donald raises his voice in his excitement. "The trail leads here. It's quite unmistakable. He is an English youth with black hair. He doesn't look English, more . . . French or Spanish." That is how Maria described him.

Per purses girlishly red lips. "It sounds like him."

"What else has he said?"

"Just that . . . and that he was going to a new job, but his guide left him. He says he was going northwest with an Indian guide." Per's eyes flicker toward Jacob for an instant.

Per turns to Jens and explains this to him. Jens speaks again, in answer to some question.

"Jens says he thought it was strange to find him alone. This boy cannot . . . could not get here alone, in this weather."

"Why not?"

"The boy was so exhausted, so . . . worn. He could not have got so far unless he was helped or . . . forced."

Guilt is a strong spur, thinks Donald.

"I did think," Per goes on, "it was strange. He said he needed the job for money, but he had quite a lot of money on him, over forty dollars. He had this, too, and was very concerned to keep it with him."

Per picks something off the floor that Donald hasn't previously noticed; a skipertogan, a leather bag the Indians carry around their necks for tobacco and tinder. He opens it and shakes out a roll of paper money, and a slim, palm-sized tablet of bone or ivory, covered with scratched figures and dark little markings. It's very dirty. Donald stares at it, his throat constricting, and holds out his hand.

"This belonged to Laurent Jammet."

"Laurent Jammet?"

"The victim of the attack."

"You say 'belonged.'" Per stares at him. "I see."

Donald immediately understands Maria's description of Francis when they are shown into the sickroom. A dark, pretty young woman stands up as the door opens, gives them a suspicious look, and walks out, her skirt swishing insolently against his trouser legs. The boy watches them without speaking as they sit down, and Per introduces him. Against the white sheets his skin is sallow, almost Latin in appearance. His hair is black and rather long, his eyes a deep, striking blue. Maria also said that he was handsome, a handsome child. Donald has no idea whether Francis could be called handsome, but there is nothing childish about the hostility radiating from him. The blue eyes stare without blinking, making him feel ungainly and awkward. He takes out his notebook and then adjusts his chair, and the notebook slithers off his lap onto the floor. He curses inwardly and picks it up, trying to ignore the tide of warmth flooding his neck and face. He reminds himself who he is and what he is here to do. He meets those eyes again, which now slide away from his, and clears his throat.

"This man is Mr. Moody, of the Hudson Bay Company. He has come from Dove River. He says your mother and father are very worried about you." Per is trying to be reassuring.

"Hello, Francis."

Francis nods slightly, as if Donald is mostly beneath his notice.

"Do you know why I am here?"

Francis glares at him.

"Your name is Francis Ross?"

Francis drops his eyes, which he takes for assent. Donald looks at Per, who is staring at the boy, wounded.

"Um . . . in Dove River, did you know a man called Laurent Jammet?"

The boy swallows. His jaw muscles seem to tense, Donald notes, and then, to his surprise, the boy nods.

"When did you last see him?"

There is a long pause, and Donald starts to wonder whether he is going to speak at all.

"I saw him when he was dead. I saw the man who killed him, so I followed him north for four days, but then I lost him."

His voice, when at last he speaks, is flat and quiet. Donald stares at the boy, excited and incredulous in equal measure. He has to remind himself to go carefully, take things one step at a time; he must wait until one foothold is firm and steady before taking the next, like walking through the hellish bog. He settles the notebook more firmly on his lap.

"What . . . Um, tell me what you saw, exactly . . . and when this happened."

Francis sighs. "The night I left. It was . . . many days ago. I can't remember."

"You have been here five days," prompts Per gently. Donald frowns at him. Per returns his look with one of blameless mildness.

"So . . . five days before that, maybe? I was going to Laurent Jammet's cabin. It was late, and I thought he wasn't there. Then I saw a man come out and walk away. I went inside, and saw him."

"Saw who?"

"Jammet."

He swallows again, with apparent difficulty. Donald waits a long time for him to start again.

"He'd just . . . died. He was warm, the blood was wet. That's how I knew the other man was the killer."

Donald scribbles down what Francis says. "This . . . other man—did you know him?"

"No."

"Did you see what he looked like?"

"Only that he was native, with long hair. I caught a glimpse of his face, but it was too dark. I couldn't see much."

Donald writes, keeping his face neutral. "Would you recognize him if you saw him again?"

This one takes a long time. "Perhaps."

"What about his clothes—what was he wearing?"

Francis shakes his head. "It was dark. Dark clothes."

"Was he dressed like me? Or like a trapper? You must have formed some impression."

"Like a trapper."

"Why were you going to Jammet's cabin?"

"We were friends."

"And what time was this?"

"I don't know. Eleven. Midnight maybe."

Donald looks up, trying to watch the boy's face at the same time as writing down what he says. "Wasn't that rather late?"

Francis shrugs.

"Did you often visit him at this hour?"

"He didn't go to bed early. He wasn't a farmer."

"So . . . you saw the body. And then what did you do?"

"I followed the man."

"Did you go home . . . pack?"

"No. I took some of Jammet's things."

"You didn't think to tell your parents? Or ask anyone for help, someone better qualified to deal with such a thing?"

"There wasn't time. I didn't want to lose him."

"Didn't want to lose him. So what things did you take?"

"Just what I needed. A coat . . . Food."

"Anything else?"

"Why? What does it matter?" Francis lifts his eyes to look at Donald again. "Do you think I killed him?"

Donald looks back, calm. "Did you?"

"I just said—I saw the killer. Jammet was my friend. Why would I kill him?"

"I'm just trying to find out what happened."

Per shifts, warningly. Donald wonders whether to push the youth further, or to accuse him outright. He is probing in the dark like a novice surgeon, not knowing where to find the vital organ of truth.

"He is very tired." This from Per. The boy does look spent, his skin taut over his bones.

"Just a moment longer, if you please. So you say that you went to this man's—Mr. Jammet's—house at midnight, found him dead, and followed the man you thought was his killer, but you lost him."

"Yes." The boy closes his eyes.

"What is the piece of bone?"

Francis opens his eyes again, in surprise, this time.

"You know what I mean, don't you?"

"I don't know what it is."

"You brought it with you. You must have had a reason."

"He gave it to me."

"He gave it to you? It's valuable."

"Have you seen it? I don't think it's valuable."

"What about the money? Did he give you that, too?"

"No. But I needed help to find the . . . man. I might have had to . . . pay someone."

"I'm sorry, I don't understand. Pay someone for what?" Francis rolls his head away. "What did you have in mind?"

Per clears his throat and glares at Donald. He closes the notebook with a reluctant snap.

Outside, Per takes Donald by the arm. "I'm sorry, but I have to think of his health. He was close to death when Jens brought him in."

"That's quite all right." This is not what Donald actually thinks, but he is here as a guest, after all. "But I hope you'll understand that, under the circumstances, I have to place him under arrest. With the money in his possession, and so on."

Per has a habit of leaning slightly toward whomever he is talking to, which Donald realizes must be due to shortsightedness. Up close, with his prominent pale eyes, Per even seems to smell faintly of goat.

"That is your decision, of course."

"Yes. It is. So . . . I would like to arrange to have a guard outside the room."

"What for? He can hardly leave Himmelvanger, even if he could walk."

"Right. Well . . ." Donald feels foolish, suddenly aware of the snow falling outside the window. "As long as we can keep an eye on him."

"There are no secrets here," Per says gravely, with a coy glance at the ceiling.

ANDREW KNOX STARES OUT OF the window at the falling snow with mixed feelings. On the one hand, he is aware from a certain amount of sisterly teasing that Susannah has got herself involved with Donald Moody, and is therefore concerned in a fatherly sort of way about the young Company man out in the bush. On the other, he is relieved to think of the prisoner's tracks disappearing under a blanket of snow. It is dry snow, the true winter snow that once set in will hide the ground until spring. Of course, he bemoaned it with Mackinley and the rest, and helped organize volunteers into search parties to establish at least which direction the fugitive might have taken. After they set off, Knox took Adam into the study and gave him a long lecture on the seriousness of his error. Adam vehemently protested that he distinctly remembered chaining and locking the door, and Knox allowed that there might have been some other explanation for the escape, and for that reason Adam would not lose his position. Adam's expression was a mixture of righteous protest and resentful gratitude; they both know he is in the right, but they also know there is a limit to how much you can argue with your employer. Life is unfair.

As if this business wasn't complicated enough, an hour ago there came an extraordinary rumor from Dove River that Mrs. Ross has vanished, and gossip is rife that she has been kidnapped by the fugitive. Knox is horrified by this turn of events, and puzzles over his part in it. Did he somehow cause this by allowing her to speak to the man? Or are the two disappearances purely coincidental? This, he has to concede, is unlikely. On balance he has to hope that she has been kidnapped, for if she is on her own, her chances of survival in this weather are bleak.

When he broke the news to his wife and daughters, he was careful to stress his certainty that the prisoner would be putting as much distance between himself and Caulfield as possible. They reacted to the news of Mrs. Ross's disappearance with predictable horror. It is the nightmare of every white woman in a savage country, although he reminds them that it is as yet

only rumor. But in everyone's minds, his escape, and the disappearance of a
local woman, has sealed Parker's guilt.

Mackinley took the news with a sort of grim-faced satisfaction, even as
he swore at Adam's stupidity and railed at Caulfield's lack of proper facili-
ties. He is now out with one of the search parties, scouting for possible
tracks along the bay. After the encounter with Mackinley, when he told him
about the empty warehouse, Knox had to shut himself in his study for a
glass of brandy, where he succumbed to a fit of violent trembling. Fortunately it passed after a few moments, but he still cannot quite screw up the
courage to go out and face the world.

"Daddy?" Maria has not called him that for as long as he can remember.
"Are you all right?" She comes up behind him and puts her hands on his
shoulders. "This is terrible."

"It could be worse. It could always be worse."

Maria looks as if she has been crying—another childhood habit he assumed she had abandoned. He knows she is worried not for herself, but for
his reputation.

"I can't bear what people will say."

"Don't jump to conclusions. We have all assumed that we know what
happened, but it's all guess. If you want to know what I think . . ." He checks
himself. "Most escaped prisoners don't get very far. He'll probably be behind
bars again in the next day or two."

"I can't bear to think about that poor woman."

"No one has spoken to her husband yet. I will go and talk to him. There
may be nothing in it at all."

"Mackinley looked so angry I thought he was going to hit Adam."

"He's disappointed. He thinks a conviction will earn him promotion."

Maria makes a scornful noise in her throat. "I can't believe we can ever
go back to normal after this."

"Oh . . . in a few months' time we will barely remember any of it."

He glances out of the window and wonders if she finds this convincing.
He has, once again, the vertiginous sensation of impending disaster. When
he looks around (a few seconds later? a minute? He isn't sure) Maria has
gone. He had been mesmerized by the whiteness outside. The flakes settle
like feathers and trap a layer of air on the ground, each snowflake touching
the next only by the tips of its axes.

The perfect snow for covering tracks.

* * *

Susannah responds to the stresses of the day by trying on frocks in her room, flinging aside those that have become too démodé. This ritual takes place every few months, whenever Susannah feels the yoke of country life press too irksomely on her shoulders. Maria stands in the doorway watching her tug at the ribbons on a green moiré dress with determined scorn. She feels a flood of affection for her sister, for worrying about things like waistlines and sleeve widths at a time of crisis.

"That dress would trim up perfectly well, Susannah. Don't tear it."

Susannah looks up. "Well, I certainly can't wear it with these stupid things, they look quite ridiculous." She sighs and throws the dress down, defeated. The offending ribbons were sewn on by Maria herself, with tiny, firm stitches.

Maria picks it up. "We could put on new sleeves, lace perhaps, take these off, and change the shape of the neckline, so, and then it would be quite fashionable."

"I suppose. And what could we do with this one?" She holds up a sprigged cotton calico that has more than a hint of Marie Antoinette playing at milkmaids.

"Um . . . dishrags."

Susannah laughs—her private, at-home laugh, which is a substantial guffaw, as opposed to her simpering public laugh, which her mother tells her is more ladylike. "It is awful, isn't it? I don't know what I was thinking of."

"Matthew Fox, as far as I can remember."

Susannah flings the dress at her. "All the more reason for it to become a dishrag."

Maria sits on the bed, surrounded by the despised castoffs. "Have you written to Donald Moody yet?"

Susannah avoids her eye. "How can I? There's no way of delivering anything."

"I thought you promised?"

"Well, so did he, but I haven't received anything—and he knows where I am."

"Well, there's bound to be some news soon. I should imagine they'll hear about the prisoner somehow, and realize they're on a wild-goose chase." She lies down among the empty dresses. "I thought you liked him."

"He's all right." A blush rises in Susannah's cheeks, to her annoyance. Maria grins at her.

"Stop it! But what am I supposed to do?"

"Oh, I thought you might have written some long passionate letters and tied them with a pink ribbon, kept next to your heart."

Maria is pleased at Susannah's blush. She has seen plenty of young men conceive a passionate fondness for her sister and feel they have awoken some answering spark, only for Susannah to lose interest after a week or so, her eye fixing on something more appealing just around the corner. The drawers of her dressing table are stuffed with tokens of unrequited love. Maria's own dressing table is not so burdened, but this does not make her jealous of her sister—far from it. She sees how Susannah finds all the attention a great irritant, one which puts more pressure on her to behave like a young lady. All the men who find her face and figure so charming fail to realize a fundamental truth about Susannah—that she is a profoundly pragmatic girl who is fonder of swimming and fishing than elegant tea parties. She is bored by abstract talk and embarrassed by flowery professions of emotion. Because Maria knows this, she is not envious of the attention Susannah receives. And because Maria knew, when she became very fond of a young man who taught at the school last year, how sincerely Susannah hoped he would make her happy. It wasn't Susannah's fault that when Robert met her, he became confused about his feelings, and ended up stammering a confession of love to her, then slinking back to Sarnia on the next steamer, cowed by her horrified reaction. Susannah had not told Maria, but the rumor got around anyway, as everything does in Caulfield, sooner or later. Maria, after a period of silent agony, made a wax model of Robert Fisher and roasted it slowly over her bedroom fire. Strangely enough, it made her feel better.

Maria has more or less taken a vow of chastity since then, as she can't imagine meeting a man who would measure up to her ideal of manhood—her father.

But Donald seems a decent and intelligent man.

STURROCK, DRESSED IN A BORROWED winter coat, picks his way through the new snow, examining the ground for traces of flight. To his right a man called Edward Mackay is doing exactly the same. On his left, a youth with an alarming Adam's apple pokes the ground with a long stick. It is, Sturrock is aware, a hopeless task. Everything was done wrongly from the start. When the warehouse holding the prisoner was found empty, the news leaked out like quicksilver, simultaneously in every house in Caulfield, and people rushed out to stare and theorize, obliterating any tracks immediately outside. The powdery snow had started to fall in the night, probably covering all traces in any case, but the numbers of people involved made gleaning any information from the scene impossible.

By the time Sturrock arrived, the ground around the warehouse was a sea of mud and slush, and no one had any idea where to look. So the able-bodied men were divided into bands, and each took a different direction, scouring the ground in lines ten abreast. In this way they swept across the land around Caulfield, destroying any message the ground might have held for them. Sturrock protested mildly that this was the likely outcome, but since he was an outsider he was listened to politely and ignored. There have been several false alarms, as people shout that they have found a footprint or some sign of passage, but it always turns out to be a naturally occurring kink in the ground, or the trace of animals, or each other.

Sturrock's mind wanders back to the Scott house, where he has papers stashed under the mattress (he first checked for pests that might breakfast on them). He is prepared to stay as long as it takes, confident in the belief that he can ask Knox for more money, waiting for the reappearance of Mrs. Ross's son and the bone tablet. No one here has, he is certain, any idea of what it might be. He himself does not know, and it is a rare mind, like his, that can conceive of something so extraordinary.

* * *

When Sturrock first met Laurent Jammet, it was a dull, gusty day in Toronto a year before. Sturrock had, as usual, allowed his obligations to out-
strip his resources, and had been harangued at length by his landlady,
Mrs. Pratt. She was one of those people—sadly numerous—who did not
recognize that Sturrock was a man meant for the finer things in life, and
that he was favoring her by gracing her shabby premises. To recover from
the galling experience, and think about how he was going to remedy the
situation, he had entered one of the coffeehouses where he was still
confident of squeezing some credit. He was spinning out his cup of coffee
when he caught snatches of conversation from the men in the booth next
to his.

One of them, French by his accent, was saying he had traded with a man
from Thunder Bay and been given a peculiar and probably worthless object
that he didn't notice until much later. It was an ivory tablet with markings
on it, "like something from the Egyptians," he said.

"That's not Egyptians, they're pictures, like birds and such," said another,
from the sound of him another of those worthless Yanks who had taken advantage of the long border to escape the war. They were clearly passing the
thing around their table.

"I don't know what that is," said a third. "Perhaps it's Greek."

"Could be valuable, then," said the Frenchman.

At this point Sturrock stood up and made himself known to the men in
the next booth. It is his greatest skill, insinuating himself into all sorts of
company from miners to earls, and he is one of the few white men to have
earned the trust and liking of several Indian chiefs on both sides of the
border. It was why he had made such a good searcher, and the Yank had
heard of Sturrock, which helped in this instance.

He said he had made a study of archaeology, and could perhaps assist
them. The Yank regaled him with requests for stories, which Sturrock
gratified while examining the thing in his hand. He made a play of not
holding it of much account, and in truth he could not make heads or tails of
it. From the little he knew of Greek and Egyptian culture—his studies were
a slight exaggeration—it was neither. But he was intrigued by the tiny
figures surrounding the angular marks that seemed to be writing. They reminded him in style of the naive figures on Indian histories he had seen,
embroidered onto belts. Finally he handed the piece of ivory back to the
Frenchman, whose name was Jammet, and said he did not know it, but

knew that it was neither Egyptian, Latin, nor Greek, and therefore not one of the great old civilizations.

One of the other men commiserated with Jammet, saying, "Maybe it's ancient Indian then; that would be just your luck, eh?"

The men laughed loudly. Shortly after that they went their separate ways, and Sturrock stayed another hour, sipping the cup of coffee the Frenchman had stood him.

For the next couple of days the idea grew in his mind and would not be shaken out. Sturrock would be walking down the street (he could not afford to ride) when the sight of the tablet and its strange markings would swim up in front of his mind's eye. Of course, everyone knew that the Indians had no written culture. Had never had.

And yet. And yet.

Sturrock went back to the coffeehouse and asked for the Frenchman, and found him again, as if by chance, outside a lodging house—in a better district than his own, he was careful to note. They chatted for a while, and Sturrock said that he had spoken to a friend of his, a man who knew a lot of ancient languages and would be interested in seeing the tablet. If he borrowed it for a day or two, to show him, perhaps he could help settle the matter of its value. Jammet revealed himself then as the hard-nosed trader he was and refused to part with it, except for a considerable sum of money. Sturrock, who thought he had been careful to mask his interest, was wounded by the lack of trust, but Jammet laughed and slapped him on the shoulder and said he would keep it for him, until he came up with the money. Sturrock pretended indifference, then hummed and hawed and begged a chance to copy the markings, just to be sure the object was of interest. Jammet produced it, amused, and he scribbled them down on a scrap of paper.

Since then he had taken the transcribed copy to museums in Toronto and Chicago, to university professors and to men known for their scholarship, and had found no one who could disprove his theory. He didn't say what he thought it might be, just asked if it was one of the Indo-European languages. The scholars thought not. They eliminated, between them, all the languages of the Ancient World. It might have helped if he knew where it came from, but he was wary of alerting the trader to his interest. Somewhere in the intervening months, it ceased to be an interest. It became an obsession.

* * *

He fell into searching, as he told Moody, by chance. Sturrock had made a name for himself as a newspaperman, having previously tried his hand at the law, the theater, and the church. The last was the most successful of an unfortunate trio: his church developed a congregation of several hundred, drawn by his wit and eloquence, and he thrived—until his affair with the wife of a leading parishioner was exposed, and he was run out of town. Journalism suited his maverick tendencies better. It was varied, sociable, and allowed him to express his opinions in colorful language. But more than that, he discovered in himself a real campaigning spirit. Initially stirred by romantic ideas of noble savagery, he began to write about Indian affairs, and although he was quickly disabused of picturesque fancies, he was equally stirred by the reality he came to know. In particular he befriended a man called Joseph Lock, an octogenarian living in dire poverty near Ottawa, who told him stories of his tribe, the Pennacook, and how they had been forced off their land in Massachusetts. He was one of only a handful left, if not the very last remaining member of his tribe. Sturrock wrote brilliantly—he was often told, and he believed it—about Joseph's plight, and he found himself becoming a sought-after guest in fashionable drawing rooms of Toronto and Ottawa. He felt he had found his niche.

His fame led to introductions to more Indians, younger, angrier men than Joseph, and his articles, instead of vividly describing poverty and lamenting past injustices (there were only so many ways you could say it), became increasingly polemical. Suddenly Sturrock found that editors were reluctant to publish his work. He argued that people should be made aware of native feelings. The editors mumbled about affairs in England being more important, and shrugged. Doors closed to him.

It was around about then that he was contacted by an American family who had lost their son in an Indian raid. Though this was south of the Lakes, in Michigan, the father had been told about Sturrock and was intelligent and desperate enough to believe he could help. Sturrock was now close to fifty, but he threw himself into the task with imagination and vigor. Partly, perhaps, because of his outsider status, the Indians welcomed him, trusted him. After several months he found the boy living with a band of Huron in Wisconsin. The boy agreed to go back to his family.

After that first satisfactory outcome he took on several more cases of ab-

ducted children and was successful in two-thirds of them. Usually the problem lay not so much in locating the missing children as in persuading them
to return to their previous life. He was good at persuasion.

Then, after a couple of years, he received a letter from Charles Seton.
The Seton case was different from most he had known, seeing as it was
more than five years since the girls had vanished, and there was no evidence to say that they had been kidnapped by Indians in the first place.
Still, his confidence boosted by success, Sturrock was unwilling to turn
down what could, he felt, turn out to be the crowning glory of his career. He
was making a living, but no one was going to get rich by finding the children of poor settlers.

He had not noticed when it first began to get out of hand. Charles Seton
still, after five years, burned with grief. His wife had died of it, compound-
ing his loss. He no longer worked, and dedicated his remaining resources to
finding the girls. The search for his lost daughters had become the only
thing he had left. Sturrock should have recognized the signs of a man for
whom no explanation could suffice, no outcome recompense for all he had
suffered. Sturrock's hope that the girls would be found dwindled. Many believed that they must have perished instantly, their remains carried off by
wild animals. After a year of searching, Sturrock himself began to lean
toward this view, but Charles Seton would not hear of it. It was impossible
even to mention such a thing in his hearing.

During this time, when Sturrock was traveling frequently between Lake
Ontario and Georgian Bay, he met a young Indian called Kahon'wes, a mili-
tant journalist who was writing about the political plight of the natives.
Kahon'wes was eager to meet Sturrock and gather newspaper contacts, and
though Sturrock felt he could not help him much, having drifted out of
those circles, they became good friends. Kahon'wes called him Sakota:tis,
meaning Preacher, and Sturrock was flattered by the attention, and by the
way the young man idealized him. They had long talks into the night about
the wars south of the border, and about the politicians in Ottawa. They
talked about culture, the perception of Indians as a Stone Age people, and
the prejudice a written culture holds against an oral one. Kahon'wes told
him of excavations on the Ohio River that uncovered giant earthworks and
artifacts dating from before Christ. On finding such things, the white ar-
chaeologists refused to believe that Indians could be the same people as this
civilization of builders and carvers (and, therefore, the Indians could be

ruthlessly supplanted by the whites, just as the Indians had, supposedly, supplanted these others).

It was these conversations, a decade on, that came back to Sturrock as he trod the streets of Toronto and made his inquiries into the bone tablet. He started to imagine the monograph that he would write on the subject, and the shock wave that would sweep through North America on its reception. Publishing such a monograph could give incalculable help to the cause of his Indian friends and, incidentally, would make him famous. Sadly, he could no longer seek out Kahon'wes for his opinion, as the man had succumbed to drink and drifted across the border. Such a fate often befalls men who step off the path they are born onto.

So, as Sturrock plods through the snow, he ignores the stunning, somber landscape, and his blundering fellow searchers (amateurs, all of them), his thoughts turning again to Kahon'wes, and his own, long unrealized ambition. For such a prize, any amount of waiting, any amount of inconvenience, will be worth it.

OTHER THAN WITH MY HUSBAND, I have spent relatively little time alone with a man, so I find it hard to judge what's normal and what isn't. The third day out from Dove River I walk behind Parker and the sled and reflect that he's spoken all of five sentences to me, and wonder if I've done something wrong. Of course I know that the circumstances are unusual, and I am a more than normally reticent person, but even so, I find his silence unnerving. For two days I have not had the inclination to ask questions, and have needed all my strength to keep up with the punishing pace, but today it seems a little easier; we hit a stretch of path that is relatively smooth, where the cedars shelter us from the wind. We move through a permanent twilight under the trees, the only sound the creak of footsteps and the hiss of willow runners on snow.

Parker follows a course along the river without a moment's hesitation, and it occurs to me that he knows exactly where we are heading. When we stop for black tea and corn bread, I ask, "So this is the way Francis came?"

He nods. He is, to say the least, a man of few words.

"So . . . you saw this trail on your way to Dove River?"

"Yes. Two men came this way, at around the same time."

"Two? You mean he was with someone?"

"One was following the other."

"How can you tell?"

"One trail is always behind the other."

He seems to wait for a minute. I don't say anything.

"They made separate fires. If they were together, they would have one fire."

I feel a little foolish, not to have noticed that. Parker radiates a subtle satisfaction. Or perhaps I'm imagining it. We are standing over our own tiny fire, and the mug warms my frozen hands through my mittens—a painful comfort. I hold the cup so that it bathes my face with hot, moist steam, knowing it will hurt all the more when it's gone, but not enough of a winter veteran to forgo the fleeting pleasure.

One of the dogs barks. A gust of wind soughs through some snow-laden branches, and a curtain of white flakes drifts to the ground. I don't see how he will be able to follow the trail under the snow. As though reading my thoughts he says, "Four men leave a big trail."

"Four?"

"The Company men, who followed your son. They are easy to follow."

Am I imagining it, or do I see a ghost of a smile?

He tosses back the contents of his cup in one gulp and wanders off a few yards to relieve himself. He seems to have the facility I have noticed in other outdoorsmen, of swallowing boiling liquids without burning himself. His mouth must be made of leather. I turn away and watch the dogs, who have flopped down together in the snow for warmth. Strangely enough, one of them, the smaller, sandy-colored one, is called Lucie, which he pronounces Lucee, in the French way. As a result I feel a sentimental affinity with her—she seems friendly and trusting, as dogs are supposed to be, unlike her wolflike mate Sisco, with his unnerving blue eyes and menacing growl. It strikes me that there is a certain symmetry between the two dogs and the two humans on this trail. I wonder if this thought has occurred to Parker also, although of course I haven't told him my first name, and he isn't likely to ask.

In the icy air the tea cools so quickly that it is pleasant to drink within half a minute, and must then be swallowed quickly. A few moments later it is stone cold.

At night Parker makes camp and builds a small fire for me to sit next to, scorching my hands and face while my back freezes. Meanwhile, he cuts a stack of pine branches with the axe. (I suppose Angus will be cursing its loss, but that is too bad; he should have thought of that before abandoning his son.) The largest of the branches he strips, and with these he erects the skeleton of a shelter in the lee of a large trunk, or, if there is a suitable fallen tree, behind the plate of roots that have been torn out of the ground. He piles smaller leafy boughs on the ground, arranging them like the rays of the sun, leaves to the center. The first time I see it, I think it looks like a place of sacrifice, and then have to quash that thought before it goes any further. He then covers the whole with the tarred canvas sheets I took from the cellar. The canvas is anchored to the ground with more branches and with snow scooped up with a bark trowel, until the walls are banked high and keep the warmth in. Inside he rigs a smaller piece of canvas from the branch that forms the tent's spine, so that there is a sort of curtain dividing the space in half. This is his only gesture toward propriety, and I am grateful for it.

He builds this structure in the time it takes me to boil water and prepare a mash of oatmeal and pemmican, with a few shriveled berries thrown in. I forgot to bring any salt, so it tastes disgusting, but it's wonderful to eat something hot and solid and feel it burning its way down my throat. Then more tea, with sugar, to take away the taste of the hoosh, while I imagine the sparkling conversation I would be having if someone else were my guide—or is it my captor? Then, exhausted (in my case anyway), we crawl into the tent and the dogs worm their way in after us, before Parker seals the entrance with a rock.

The first night I crawled into the little dark tunnel with a hammering heart, curled up under my blankets, too scared to move, and awaited a fate worse than death. I held my breath, listening as Parker turned and shifted and breathed inches away from me. Lucie wriggled—or was pushed—under the curtain to curl up beside me, and I gratefully accommodated the small warm body next to mine. Then Parker seemed to stop moving, but some part of him, I realized with horror, was pressed up against the canvas curtain—and therefore against my back. I had no room to move away—my face was almost pressed against the snow-covered canvas where I lay. I kept waiting for something appalling to happen—sleep was, in any case, impossible—and then gradually, I felt a faint warmth emanating from him. My eyes were stretched sightlessly wide, my ears strained for the slightest sound, but nothing happened. I believe at some point I even dozed off. Finally, although I blush to think of it, I recognized the beauty of this system, which preserves a sort of privacy while allowing us to share the heat each of us generates.

The next morning I awoke to a faint light bleeding through the canvas. My cocoon was airless and stuffy, and reeked of dog. The tent was cold, but I was astonished, when I crawled backward into the daylight, how warm it was compared to the air outside. I am sure that Parker was watching as I wriggled gracelessly out on elbows and knees, my hair loosened and straggling all over my face, but thankfully he didn't smile or even stare much. He gravely handed me a mug of tea, and I stood up and tried to smooth my hair into a semblance of order, wishing I had brought along a pocket mirror. It is extraordinary how vanity clings to one in the least appropriate of circumstances. But then, I tell myself, vanity is one of the attributes that distinguish us from animals, so perhaps we should be proud of it.

This evening—our third—I am determined to make more of an effort with my silent companion. Over bowls of stew, I start to talk. I feel I have to prepare the ground, so to speak, and have been thinking about what to say for some hours.

"I must say, Mr. Parker, how grateful I am that you have taken me with you, and how I appreciate your efforts to make me comfortable."

In the orange firelight, his face is an impenetrable mask of shadows, although the darkness does have the effect of leaching out the bruising on his cheek, and softening the harshness of his features.

"I know that the circumstances are somewhat . . . unusual, but I hope that we can still be good companions." "Companions" sounds the right note, I think: cordial without implying overmuch personal warmth.

He looks up at me, chewing on a stubborn piece of gristle. I think he's going to go on not speaking, as though I don't exist or am a creature of no account, like a dung beetle, but then he swallows and says, "Did you ever hear him play the fiddle?"

It takes me several moments to realize he is talking about Laurent Jammet.

And then I am outside the cabin by the river at home, hearing that strange sweet tune and seeing Francis burst out of the door, his face transformed by laughter—and I am paralyzed by loss.

I haven't cried much in my life, considering. Any life has its share of hardship—if one gets to the age I am now and has crossed an ocean and lost parents and child—but I feel it is uncontroversial to state that mine has held more than most. And yet I have always felt that crying was pointless, as though it implies you think someone might see you and take pity on you, which in turn assumes they can do something to help—and early on I found that no one could. I haven't cried for Francis these last few days, because I was too busy lying and covering up and planning a way to help him, and it seemed like a waste of my scant powers. So I do not know what has changed now, to make tears spill down my cheeks, tracing warm paths on my skin. I close my eyes and turn my head away in embarrassment, hoping that perhaps Parker won't notice. It's not as though he can help, other than by guiding me through the forest as he is already doing. I am ashamed because it looks as though I am appealing to his humanity—throwing myself on his mercy, as it were, when for all I know he has none.

But all the while I weep I am aware of the sensuous pleasure of it, the tears stroking my face like warm fingers, offering comfort.

When I open my eyes again, Parker has made tea. He doesn't ask for an explanation.

"Please forgive me. My son liked his music."

He hands me a tin mug. I sip it and am surprised. He has given me extra sugar, the panacea for all ills. If only we could sweeten all our sorrows so easily.

"He used to play for us when we worked on a gang. The bosses allowed him to bring his fiddle with him on portages. They knew it was worth the extra weight."

"You worked with him? For the Company?"

I remember the photograph of Jammet with the group of voyageurs and examine it in my mind to see if Parker was one of them. I am sure I would have noticed a face like his, but I don't recall it.

"A long time ago."

"You don't seem like a . . . Company man." I smile quickly, in case that sounds like an insult.

"My grandfather was English. His name was William Parker, too. He came from a place called Hereford."

He is smoking a pipe now. One of my husband's, since his own was confiscated.

"Hereford? In England?"

"You know it?"

"No. I believe it has a very beautiful cathedral."

He nods, as if the presence of the cathedral were self-evident.

"Did you know him?"

"No. Like most, he didn't stay. He married my grandmother, who was a Cree, but he went back to England. They had a child, and that was my father. He worked for the Company all his life."

"And your mother?"

"Huh . . ." A spark of emotion animates his face. "He married a Mohawk woman from a French mission."

"Ah," I say, as if that explains something. And it does, the Iroquois being known for physical size and strength. And, supposedly (although of course I don't say so), their good looks. "You are Iroquois. That's why you're so tall."

"Mohawk, not Iroquois," he corrects me, but gently, without sounding annoyed.

"I thought they were the same thing."

"Do you know what "Iroquois" means?"

I shake my head.

"It means 'rattlesnakes.' It was a name given by their enemies."

"I'm sorry. I didn't know."

His mouth twists in what I am beginning to recognize as a smile. "She was supposed to be a good mission-educated Catholic, but she was always a Mohawk first."

There is warmth in his voice, humor. I smile across the flickering fire. It's always comforting to know that a suspected murderer loves his mother.

My tea is nearly finished—stone cold, of course. I want to ask about Jammet's death, but I fear it will upset the delicate rapport between us. Instead I gesture toward him.

"How is your face now?"

He touches it with two fingers. "Doesn't hurt so much."

"Good. The swelling has gone down." I think of Mackinley. He didn't seem like a man to give up easily. "I suppose someone will try and follow us."

Parker grunts. "Even if they do, with this snow, they will lose the trail. And it will make them slow."

"But will you be able to find the trail?"

I have become increasingly concerned about this. As the snow has fallen—deceptively light, pleasant snow, dry and powdery—I have convinced myself that Francis has taken shelter at a village somewhere. I believe this because I must.

"Yes."

I remind myself that he is a trapper and used to following subtle, light-footed creatures through the snow. But his confidence seems to stem from more than that. Once again, I have the sense that he already knows where the trail is going to lead.

We sit in silence for a while, with me envying the rhythm and ritual that is smoking a pipe, which makes a man look busy and deep in thought even while he's doing and thinking nothing. And yet I feel more at peace than I have done for some time. We are on our way. I am doing something to help Francis.

I am doing something to prove how much I love him, and that matters, because I'm afraid he has forgotten.

AT SOME POINT FRANCIS REALIZES that he is under arrest. No one has actually told him so, but something in the way Per looks at him, and at Moody, has made him assume that. Moody believes he is Laurent's killer. He feels irritated by this, rather than frightened or angry. Possibly, if he were in Moody's shoes, he would think the same.

"I don't understand," Moody is saying, pushing his spectacles up his nose for the hundredth time, "why you didn't tell someone what you saw. You could have told your father. He is a respected man in your village."

Francis bites his tongue on the obvious rejoinder. It seems a reasonable enough idea, now Moody suggests it. He wonders if Moody has met his father.

"I thought he would get too far ahead. I wasn't thinking clearly."

That is an understatement. Donald has his head on one side, looks as though he is trying to understand the concept of unclear thinking. He looks as though he fails.

This time, sitting silently beside Moody is a young half-breed, who has been introduced to Francis as Jacob. Francis has never heard him speak, but he supposes he is here as some sort of witness from the Hudson Bay Company. He has heard—from Jammet, among others—that in Prince Rupert's Land the Company will send out men to wield a rudimentary justice. If a murderer is known, Company officers quietly hunt him down and kill him. He wonders if Jacob is the designated executioner. His designated executioner. Mostly he sits with head cast down, but his eyes watch Francis intently. Maybe they think he is going to make a mistake and give himself away.

Moody turns and whispers something, and Jacob gets up and leaves the room. Moody pulls his chair closer to Francis and gives him a small smile, like a boy trying to make friends on his first day at school.

"I want to show you something."

Then he pulls up his shirt, tugging it out of his breeches until Francis sees the scar—tender shiny skin, red against white. "See that? The blade went in three inches. And the man who did that to me . . . was sitting right there."

He looks Francis in the eye. Despite himself, Francis feels his eyes widen with astonishment.

"Yet I don't think there's a man in this country who cares more for me than he does."

Francis forgets himself enough to half smile. Donald grins, encouraged. "You'll laugh when I tell you why. We were playing rugby, and I tackled him. Took the legs out from under him—classic sliding tackle. And he went for me on instinct. He'd never played rugby before. I didn't even know he was carrying a knife."

Donald laughs, and Francis feels a spark of warmth within him, responding. For a moment, it's almost as though they are friends.

Donald tucks the shirt back into his waistband.

"What I mean is, even with someone you are friends with, there can be a quarrel, and one man can lash out in a moment of anger. Without meaning anything. A moment later—and he would give his life not to have done it. Was that how it happened? You quarreled—maybe he was drunk . . . you were drunk . . . he made you angry, and you lashed out without thinking . . . ?"

Francis is staring at the ceiling. "If you care so much about justice, why aren't you following the other footprints, the ones the murderer left? You must have seen them. I could follow them. Even if you don't believe me, you must have seen them."

Something has given within him, and the words keep on coming, rising in volume.

"You could have followed the tracks just to make sure you got somewhere safely." Donald leans forward, as if he feels he's getting somewhere at last.

"If I were going to run away, I wouldn't run here! I'd go to Toronto, or get on a boat . . ." Francis rolls his eyes up to the ceiling with its familiar cracks and lines. Unreadable signs. "Where would I spend the money up here? It's crazy to think that I killed him, can't you see that? It's crazy even to think it . . ."

"Perhaps that's why you came here, because it's not obvious . . . You hide out up here and go where you want when things have died down—pretty smart, I'd say."

Francis stares at him—what's the point of talking to this idiot, who has already decided what happened? Is this the way it's going to be? If so, then so be it. Now his throat is tight, and the taste of sick is in his mouth. He wants to scream. If they knew the real truth, would they believe him then? If he told them what it was really like?

Instead, he opens his mouth and says, "Fuck you, fuck you! Fuck you all." Then he turns his face to the wall.

The moment he turns away, something comes to Donald's mind. He has at last remembered what has been nagging at him for the last few days—the thing about Francis that reminds him of a fellow he knew at school but, like everyone else, avoided. So perhaps that was the motive. Hardly surprising, really.

SOMETHING EXTRAORDINARY HAPPENS. AS THE weather continues utterly still and windless, and we carry on walking north through the forest, I realize I am enjoying myself. I am shocked and feel guilty, as I should be worrying about Francis, but I can't deny it: as long as I am not actually thinking about him lying hurt and frozen, I am happier than I have been for a long time.

I never thought I could stray so far into the wilderness without fear. What I always hated about the forest, although I never told anyone this, is its sameness. There are so few varieties of trees, especially now, when the snow makes them all cloaked, somber shapes and the forest a dim, twilit place. In our early years in Dove River I used to have a nightmare: I am in the middle of the forest, and turning around to look back the way I came, I find that every direction looks exactly alike. I panic, disoriented. I know that I am lost, that I will never get out.

Perhaps it is the extremity of my situation that makes it impossible—or just pointless—to be afraid. Nor am I afraid of my taciturn guide. Since he hasn't murdered me yet, despite plenty of opportunity, I have started to trust him. I wondered briefly if I had refused to go with him, what would have happened—would he have forced me? Then I stopped wondering. Walking for eight hours through fresh snow is a good way to still the mind's restlessness.

Angus's rifle is strapped to the dogsled and is unloaded, so offers little protection in the instance of sudden attack. When I ask Parker if this is wise, he laughs. He says there are no bears in this part of the country. What about wolves? I want to know. He gives me a pitying look.

"Wolves don't attack people. They might be curious, but they won't attack you."

I tell him about those poor girls who were eaten by wolves. He listens without interruption, and then says, "I've heard of them. There was no sign that the girls were attacked by wolves."

"But there was no proof that they were kidnapped, and nothing was ever found."

"Wolves will not eat all of a corpse. If wolves had attacked them, there would have been traces—splinters of bone, and the stomach and intestines would be left."

I don't know quite what to say to this. I wonder if he knows these macabre details because he has seen them.

"But," he goes on, "I have never known wolves to attack without being provoked. We have not been attacked, and there have been wolves watching us."

"Are you trying to frighten me, Mr. Parker?" I say, with a careless smile, even though he is ahead of me and cannot see my expression.

"There is no reason to be afraid. The dogs react as if there are wolves about, in the evening especially. And we are still here."

He tosses this over his shoulder as if it were a casual observation about the weather, but I keep glancing behind me, to see if anything is following us, and I am more anxious than before to stay close to the sled.

As the light fades I sense shadows moving and closing in around me. I wish I had not brought up the subject. I sit close to the fire, tiredness not overcoming my nerves, starting at every rustle of branches and flurry of snow. I collect snow from very near the fire and make supper with less attention than it deserves. While Parker is out of sight collecting branches, I strain after him with my eyes, and when the dogs start a round of excited barking, I nearly jump out of my skin.

Later, lying like a sausage in the tent, something wakes me. I can sense a faint grayness seeping through the canvas, so either it must be close to dawn, or there is a clear moon. Then, from right by me, making me start, comes Parker's voice:

"Mrs. Ross. Are you awake?"

"Yes," I whisper at last, my heart stuck in my throat, imagining all sorts of horrors beyond the canvas walls.

"If you can, move your head to the opening and look out. Do not be alarmed. There is nothing to fear. It may interest you."

It is easy to maneuver myself so as to look out, as after the first night I have slept with my head toward the opening. I find Parker has made a gap on my side of the curtain, and I peer out.

It is not yet dawn, but there is a cool, grayish light, perhaps from the unseen moon, that reflects off the snow and makes it possible to see, although among the trees it is dim and indistinct. In front of me is a black smudge that is the remnants of our fire, and beyond that, the two dogs are standing, bodies alert and tense, pointing away at something in the trees. One of them whines; perhaps it was this that woke me.

At first I can see nothing else, then after a minute or two I discern a flicker of movement in the shadows. With a sort of jolt I realize there is another doglike shape, gray against the lighter gray of the snow. The third animal is watching the dogs, eyes and muzzle faintly darker than its fur. They are watching each other, intensely interested, not apparently aggressive, but none seems to want to turn its back. Another whine comes, perhaps from the wolf. It looks small, smaller than Sisco. It seems to be alone. I watch as it approaches a few feet, then backs off again, like a shy child who wants to join in a game but isn't confident of a good reception.

For perhaps ten minutes I watch this almost silent communication between dogs and wolf, and in that time I forget to be afraid. I realize that Parker is right next to me watching them also. Although I do not turn my head toward him, he is so close that I can smell him. I become aware of this only gradually; normally the air is so cold it kills any scent. Something to be thankful for, I've always thought. But as I watch the animals, something smells of life—not the smell of dogs, or even of sweat, but something more like foliage, like the sharp, rich smell inside a greenhouse, damp and growing. I feel a sting like a nettle, and that is a memory: the memory of the greenhouse at the public asylum where we used to grow tomatoes, and how it smelled the same as Dr. Watson when I pressed my face into his shirtfront or against his skin. I had not known a man could smell like that, rather than of tobacco and cologne, like my father, or more unpleasantly of bodily exertions and unwashed clothes, like most of the attendants.

The only thing that can smell like Watson and the greenhouse in this frozen forest is Parker himself.

At this point I cannot stop myself turning my head a little toward him and inhaling, to get a stronger fix on that memory, which is tantalizing and not at all unpleasant. I try to do it imperceptibly, but I sense he notices, and have to raise my eyes to find out, and then I find him looking at me from a distance of a few inches. I start back, and then smile, to cover my embarrassment. I look back at the dogs, but the wolf has vanished like a gray ghost, and now I cannot say whether it has just gone, or whether it left some minutes ago.

"That was a wolf," I say, with true brilliance.

"And you are not afraid."

I glance at him again, to see if he is teasing me, but he is withdrawing into his side of the tent.

"Thank you," I say, and am then annoyed at myself. It is not as though he arranged the wolf's visit especially for me, so it is a silly thing to have said. I look at the two dogs again. Sisco is still staring intently into the trees after the intruder, but Lucie is looking at me with her mouth open and her tongue hanging out, as though she is laughing at me.

THE SEARCH PARTIES FOUND NO trace of the prisoner's flight, and the hysteria over Mrs. Ross's disappearance has been calmed by her husband's stoicism. It is assumed she will meet up with Moody and her son. Mackinley has not appeared to associate the two things, and broods in his room for most of the day. Almost three days after the disappearance, Mackinley still haunts the Knoxes' house like a vengeful spirit. He seethes with the impotent bitterness of a man who has had what he sought in his grasp only to lose it again.

The Knox family don't mention him by name, as if pretending he doesn't exist will make him go away. Knox suggests that he go back to Fort Edgar and await news from Moody. Mackinley refuses. He is determined to stay while messages are sent out with descriptions of the fugitive. He is obsessed with doing his duty, or that's what he claims he is doing; Knox is no longer sure.

Tonight after dinner, Mackinley starts talking about luck. He returns to one of his favorite subjects, Company heroes, and is regaling Knox with the already familiar story of one James Stewart, who pushed his men through the snow in winter to deliver some supplies to a trading post, accomplishing an astonishing journey in terrible weather. Mackinley is drunk. There is a mean glitter to his eyes that alarms Knox. If he is drunk, it is not on Knox's wine; he must be drinking in his room.

"But do you know what?" Mackinley is speaking to Knox, but his eyes are fixed on the soft, powdery snow outside, which he seems to take as a personal affront. His voice is soft, too; he is trying not to shout, trying not to be a little man. Oddly, although Knox recognizes that it is an affectation, the result is still chilling.

"Do you know what they did to him—a fine man like that? And all because of a bit of bad luck? He was one of the best. A fine Company servant who gave everything he had. He should be running the whole outfit now, but they pushed him aside to some godforsaken place in the middle of nowhere—no furs at all, a wasteland. All because of a bit of bad luck. And that's not right. It's not right, is it?"

"I'm sure it isn't." Nor is it right that he should have been landed with Mackinley for a houseguest, but there's no one he can complain to about that. If only Mackinley had gone after the Ross boy himself, and left Moody here. Susannah would have been happier, too.

"I won't let them push me aside. They won't do that to me."

"I'm sure that won't happen. It's not as though it was your fault."

"But how do I know they'll see it like that? I'm responsible for law and order at my fort and its surroundings. Perhaps, if you were to write a letter . . . setting out the facts, and so on . . ." Mackinley gazes at Knox with wide eyes as though this idea has only just occurred to him.

Knox stifles an in breath of disbelief. He had wondered whether Mackinley might make such a request, but thought it too shameless even for him. He gives himself several moments to frame his answer.

"If I were to write such a letter, Mr. Mackinley, it would be only fair if I set out all the facts as I know them, so as to avoid confusion." He turns his gaze to Mackinley, keeping his face blank and calm.

"Well, of course . . ." Mackinley begins and then stops, eyes bulging. "What do you mean? What did Adam say?"

"Adam did not say anything. I saw with my own eyes how your idea of justice is achieved."

Mackinley stares at him in fury, but doesn't say any more. Knox feels a guilty satisfaction at silencing him.

When Knox finally leaves the house, the snow and the clouds combine to produce a peculiar light, a pallor in the dusk that makes it seem colder. Although the days are short and the sun low, there is a compensatory feeling in the air—perhaps it augurs a show of the aurora borealis—that puts a lightness in his step. Strange, when he is courting disgrace in this way, to feel so carefree.

Thomas Sturrock opens his door and releases a rich, smoky fug into the corridor. Clearly he is a man who believes fresh air should stay out of doors.

"I think we will be undisturbed tonight. There has been some domestic strife, and my hosts are otherwise engaged."

Knox is not sure how to respond to this. But he is not prepared to face

John Scott when he has been drinking. Perhaps it is better that he takes his frustrations out on his wife and maintains the public face of a good citizen. Knox feels ashamed of this thought, and so pushes it out of his mind.

"I got your note, and I am curious as to what you have to say." He reminds himself to be on his guard, even with Sturrock.

"I was thinking about Jammet earlier, when we were searching the lakeshore." Sturrock pours two glasses of whisky and swirls the topaz liquid in his glass. "And I was thinking about a man I used to know, when I was a searcher. His name was Kahon'wes."

Knox waits.

"I wasn't sure whether to bring this up . . . I asked myself, why would a trader like Jammet be killed—for what purpose? And I suspect, although I have no certainty, of course—that it may have been because of the bone tablet."

"The bone tablet you spoke of before?"

"Yes. I told you I needed it for some research that I am undertaking at the moment, and it has probably occurred to you that if I am prepared to put myself out to obtain such a thing, others may be prepared to go to some lengths also. However . . . oh, hell, I don't even know if it is what I think it is." His face in the lamplight looks dry and old.

"What do you think it is?"

Sturrock swallows the contents of his glass and grimaces as if it were medicine.

"This will sound preposterous, but . . . well, I believe it may be evidence of an ancient written language of the Indians."

Knox's first desire is to laugh. It does sound preposterous—a boys' adventure story. He has never heard anything so ridiculous.

"What makes you believe that?" He has never thought Sturrock a fool, despite his shortcomings. Perhaps he has been wrong, and that is the man's flaw—the reason why, in his sixties, he wears an old-fashioned coat with frayed cuffs.

"I can see that you think it is preposterous. I have reasons. I have looked into the matter for over a year."

"But everyone knows there is no such thing!" Knox cannot stop himself. "There is not a scrap of evidence. If there had ever been such writing in existence, there would be traces . . . there would be some document or record, or anecdotal evidence . . . and yet there is nothing."

Sturrock regards him gravely. Knox puts on a conciliatory tone. "I'm sorry if I sound dismissive, but it is . . . fantastic."

"Perhaps. But the fact remains that some people think it possible. Do you concede that?"

"Yes. Yes, of course they may."

"And if I am looking for it, others might be looking for it also."

"That is also possible."

"Well, then, what I have been thinking is this: the man I mentioned, Kahon'wes, was a sort of journalist, a writer. An Indian, but a very gifted one. Educated, intelligent, able to weave a pretty phrase and so on. I always thought he might have some white blood in him, but I never asked. He was fanatically proud, obsessed with the notion of Indians having a great culture of their own, in every way equal to white culture. He was fervent in the way that some men of religion are. He thought me a sympathizer, and I was, up to a point . . . He was unstable, poor fellow—took to drink when he did not make the sort of splash he'd hoped for."

"What are you implying?"

"That he, or someone like him, who believed passionately in an Indian nation and culture, would do almost anything to get a piece of evidence like that."

"And did this man know Jammet?"

Sturrock looks slightly surprised. "I really don't know. But people get to hear of things, don't they—you wouldn't necessarily need to know someone to want what they had. I didn't know Jammet myself until I heard him talking about the piece in a Toronto coffeehouse. He wasn't closemouthed."

Knox shrugs. He's wondering if Sturrock really pulled him out of his house to tell him this bizarre story. "And where does this Kahon'wes live now?"

"That I can't tell you. The last time I saw him was years ago. I knew him when he was traveling around the peninsula, writing articles. As I said, he took to drink and dropped out of sight. I heard he went over the border, but that's all."

"And you are telling me this because you think he may be a suspect? Rather slim grounds, wouldn't you say?"

Sturrock looks at his empty glass. Already, dust has fallen onto the trails of liquid, thickening them.

"Kahon'wes talked to me once of an ancient written language. The possibility of one, I mean. I had never heard of such a thing." Sturrock smiles a wintry smile, tight at the corners of his mouth. "Of course, I thought he was crazy." He shrugs his shoulders in a gesture that Knox finds strangely pathetic.

"Then I came across the tablet. And I remembered what he'd said. It may be that I tell you this at some personal cost, but I felt you should know all the facts. It may not be important; I am merely telling you what I know. I do not want a man's death to go unpunished because I did not speak."

Knox drops his eyes, feeling that familiar sense of the absurd sweeping over him. "It is a pity you did not confide this information sooner, before the prisoner escaped. Perhaps you would have been able to identify him."

"Really? You think . . . ? Well, well."

Knox does not for an instant believe the look of dawning realization on Sturrock's face. In fact he is beginning to doubt the whole story. Perhaps Sturrock has some other motive for turning attention back onto the half-breed, to deflect attention from his own presence. In fact, the more he thinks about it, the more ludicrous the story becomes. Knox wonders whether there ever was a bone tablet; no one apart from Sturrock has mentioned it.

"Well, thank you for telling me, Mr. Sturrock. That . . . may be useful. I will discuss it with Mr. Mackinley."

Sturrock spreads his hands. "I merely want to help bring the murderer to justice."

"Of course."

"There was one other thing . . ."

Ah, now we come to the true matter, thinks Knox.

"I was wondering if you could possibly stand me a little more of the filthy lucre?"

On the short, cold walk back to his house, Knox suddenly remembers, with a hideous, piercing clarity, what he said to Mackinley earlier: "I saw with my own eyes how your idea of justice is achieved."

He had told Mackinley (or at least allowed him to form the impression) that he had not been back to see the prisoner after Mackinley's interrogation. He can only hope that Mackinley was too drunk or agitated to notice.

A forlorn hope, given the circumstances.

OVER BREAKFAST, PARKER TALKS ABOUT the nighttime visitor. The wolf we saw was a young female, probably about two years old and not yet fully mature. He thinks she had been following us for a couple of days, out of curiosity, staying out of sight. It is possible that she wanted to mate with Sisco, and may, in fact, have done so.

"Would she have followed us without the dogs?" I ask.

Parker shrugs. "Maybe."

"How did you know she'd be there last night?"

"I didn't know. It was possible."

"I'm glad you told me."

"A few years ago . . ." Parker pauses, as though surprised at himself for volunteering anything. I wait.

"A few years ago I found an abandoned wolf cub. I suppose its mother had been killed, or it may have been driven out of the pack. I tried to raise it like a dog. For a while it was happy. It was like a pet, you know . . . affectionate. It would lick my hand and roll over, wanting to play. But then it got older, and the playing stopped. It remembered it was a wolf, not a pet. It stared into the distance. Then one day it was gone. The Chippewa have a word for it—it means 'the sickness of long thinking.' You cannot tame a wild animal, because it will always remember where it is from, and yearn to go back."

Try as I may to imagine a younger Parker playing with a wolf cub, I cannot do it.

For four days the sky stays gray and low, the air wet as if we are walking through heavy cloud. We travel gradually but distinctly upward, all the time moving through forest, although the trees change; they become shorter, there are more pines and willows, fewer cedars. But now the forest thins out, the trees dwindle to sparse scrub, and we come, unbelievably, to the edge; the end of the forest that seemed to have no end.

We emerge onto a vast plain just as the sun burns through the cloud and floods the world with light. We are standing on the edge of a white sea on which waves of snow march to the horizon to north, east, and west. I haven't seen such distances since standing on the shores of Georgian Bay, and it makes me dizzy. Behind us, the forest; ahead, another country: one I have never seen before, glittering, white, and huge under the sun. The temperature has dropped several degrees; there is no wind, but the cold is like a hand that is laid with gentle but implacable force on the snow, telling it to stay.

I feel the mounting panic I felt when first confronted with the virgin forest of Dove River: this is too big, too empty for humans, and if we venture out onto that plain, we will be as vulnerable as ants on a dinner plate. There is truly, here, nowhere to hide. I try to stifle my desire to head back under the cover of the trees as I tread in Parker's footsteps away from the familiar, friendly forest. I feel a sudden kinship with those animals who burrow into the snow in winter, to live underground, in tunnels.

Actually the plateau is not flat, but full of mounds and cones of snow that hide bushes and hillocks and rocks. The whole plateau is a bog, Parker tells me, and hell to cross before it freezes. He points to a churned-up hollow where he claims someone sank in: one of the men we are following. We, apparently, have it easy. Even so, the ground is so rough that after two hours I can barely move my feet another step. I grit my teeth and concentrate on lifting one foot after the other, but I drop farther and farther behind. Parker stops and waits for me to catch up.

I'm angry. This is too difficult. My face and ears are frozen, but under my clothes I am sweating. I want shelter and rest. I am so thirsty my tongue feels like a dry sponge in my mouth.

"I can't!" I shout from where I am.

Parker treads back toward me.

"I can't go on. I need to rest."

"We haven't gone far enough to rest. This weather may change."

"I don't care. I can't move." I sink to my knees in the snow, as a protest. It feels so good to be off my feet I close my eyes in ecstasy.

"Then you'll have to stay there."

Parker's face and voice don't change at all, but he turns and walks away. He can't mean it, I think, as he reaches the sled and the dogs, who have been fidgeting and tangling themselves in their harness. He doesn't even look back. He flicks the dogs on, and they begin to move off.

I am outraged. He is prepared to walk away and leave me here. With tears of fury in my eyes, I struggle to my feet and begin forcing them painfully after the sled.

My anger drives me on for another hour, by which time I am so tired that I have no feelings at all. And then, at last, Parker stops. He makes tea and repacks the bags on the sled, then indicates that I should sit on it. He has arranged it so that the bags form a rough backrest. I am as touched now as I was angry before.

"Can the dogs manage?"

"We can manage," he says, but I don't understand what he means until he attaches another line to the sled to help the dogs. He places the loop of hide around his forehead, and leans into the pulling, shouting at the dogs, until the sled is torn free from where it has frozen into the snow. He tugs and strains and then finds the same metronomic stride as before. I am ashamed at being part of his burden, at making more difficult something that is already close to the limits of what is endurable. He doesn't complain. I have tried not to complain either, but I can't say I've been all that successful.

Clinging on to the sled as it bucks and plunges over mounds of snow, I realize that the plain is beautiful. The brightness makes my eyes water, and I am dazzled, not just physically, but awed by this enormous, empty purity. We pass bushes whose branches contain cobwebs of spun snow, and nodules of ice that catch the sunlight and split it into rainbows. The sky is a burnished, metallic blue; there is not a breath of wind, and there is no noise at all, of any kind. The silence is crushing.

Unlike some people, I have never felt free in the wilderness. The emptiness suffocates me. I recognize the symptoms of incipient hysteria and try to fend them off. I make myself think of the dark night, and relief from this blinding visibility. I make myself think of how tiny and unimportant I am, how far beneath notice. I have always found it comforting rather than otherwise to contemplate my own insignificance, for if I am negligible, why should anyone persecute me?

I once knew a man who had been spoken to by God. Of course there were many such men and women in the asylums I lived in—to the extent that I used to imagine that if a stranger from another land arrived at our door, he would think he had stumbled on the place where all the most holy of our society were gathered together. Matthew Smart was tormented by the conversation. He was an engineer who had conceived the idea that the power of steam was so great that it could save the world from sin. He himself had been charged by God with the task of building such an engine, and had sunk considerable resources into starting this project. When he ran out of money, his scheme, and his insanity, were uncovered, but being taken away from his engine was the most unbearable torture for him, because he thought that due to his enforced idleness, we were all going to Hell. He knew how important he was in the scheme of things, and would seize each of us in the grounds and beg us to help him escape, so he could continue his vital work. Among those tortured souls, almost all of them bewailing some private anguish, his beseechings were the most heartbreaking I ever heard. Once or twice I was even tempted to stick my loaded needle into him, to put him out of his misery (but not unbearably tempted, of course). Such is the torment of knowing your own significance.

Parker shouts to the dogs and we come to a bumpy halt. We are still nowhere, only now the forest has long been out of sight and I'm not sure I could any longer point to it.

He comes back toward me. "I think I know where they went."

I look around, to see nothing, of course. The plain stretches away in every direction. It is truly like being at sea. Without the sun, I would have no idea what direction we are traveling in.

"Over there"—he points in a direction away from the sun, now sinking to our left—"is a Company trading post called Hanover House. Several days away. Over this way the trail leads. There is a place called Himmelvanger—a religious village of some sort. Foreigners. Swedish, I think."

I follow his pointing finger and peer into the dazzling distance to the west, thinking of the asylum and its turbulently pious inmates.

"So, Francis . . . ?" I can hardly give voice to my hope, which is clutching me by the throat.

"We should be there by nightfall."

"Oh . . ."

I can't say anything more, in case I destroy this great gift of luck. In the sunlight I suddenly notice that Parker's hair is not black after all, but has hints of dark brown and chestnut in it, and no trace of white.

He shouts to the dogs again, a wild yell that rings around the empty plain like the cry of an animal, and with it launches himself into the harness, and the sled jerks away from its standstill. The breath is jolted out of my body, but I don't care.

I am giving thanks, in my own way.

E SPEN HAS DECIDED THAT HIS wife, Merete, suspects something. He suggests they stop meeting for a while, until things are calmer. Furious, Line carries out her chores, kicking the chickens when they get under her feet, stabbing her needle into the quilts, pulling the thread too tight and rucking the seams. The only thing she enjoys is attending to the boy. Of course everyone knows that he is under arrest for a terrible crime. Today he looks pale and listless as she changes the sheets on his bed.

"Aren't you afraid of me now?"

Line is looking out of the window. He's aware that she's loitering. She smiles.

"No, of course not. I don't believe it for a moment. In fact, I think they are all fools."

She says it with such vehemence that he looks shocked.

"I said so to the Scottish one, but he thinks he is doing his duty. He thinks the money is all the proof he needs."

"I suppose they'll take me back, and there will be a trial. So it won't be up to him."

Line finishes turning down the sheets, and he lies down again. She notices how thin his ankles and wrists are. Getting thinner. He seems so young and defenseless it makes her blood boil.

"I would leave here if I could. Believe me, it's a death of the soul to live in this place."

"I thought you were living good lives away from all temptation and sin."

"There's no such thing."

"Would you go back to Toronto?"

"I can't. I have no money. That's why I came in the first place. Life is hard for a woman alone with children."

"What if you had money? Would that make it possible?"

Line shrugs. "There's no point thinking about it. Unless my husband suddenly comes back, with a fortune in gold. But he isn't going to." She smiles bitterly.

"Line . . ." Francis takes her hand in his, which makes her stop smiling. He has a grave look about him, which makes her heart jump. When men get that look on their faces, it usually means only one thing.

"Line, I want you to take this money. There's nothing I can do with it. Per wouldn't let them take it away, so if you take it now, you could hide it, and then get away sometime—in the spring, maybe."

Line is watching him as he speaks, amazed. "No, you don't mean that. It's . . . no, I couldn't."

"I'm serious. Take it with you now. It's wasted otherwise. It was Laurent's—I know he would have wanted you to have it, rather than those men. Where would it end up then? In their pockets, most likely."

Her heart beats thickly in her throat. What a chance!

"You don't know what you are saying."

"I know exactly what I'm saying. You're not happy here. Use it to make yourself a new life. You're young, you're beautiful, you shouldn't be stuck here with all these married men . . . You should be happy." Francis trails off, a little out of his depth. Line puts her other hand on his.

"You think I'm beautiful?"

Francis smiles, a little embarrassed. "Of course. Everyone does."

"Do they?"

"You can see by the way they look at you."

She feels a flush of pleasure, and it is then that she bends down toward him and places her lips on his. His mouth is warm but immobile, and despite her closed eyes, she immediately knows she has made a terrible mistake. His mouth seems to recoil in disgust, as if it has been touched by a snail or an earthworm. She opens her eyes and pulls back a little, confused. He is looking away, an expression of appalled shock on his face. She tries to excuse herself.

"I . . ." She can't understand what she has done wrong. "I thought you said I was beautiful."

"You are. But I didn't mean . . . That's not why I want to give you the money. That's not what I meant."

He seems to be trying to get as far away from her as the bedclothes will allow.

"Oh . . . Ah Gott." Line feels hot and sick with shame. How could she have made things worse for herself? As though she had got up this morning and thought of all the really stupid things she could do today, and rejected shouting her feelings for Espen during morning prayers, and sticking her needle into Britta's fat behind (both tempting) in favor of kissing a young boy who has been arrested for murder. She starts to laugh, and then, just as suddenly, she is crying.

"Line, please don't cry. I'm sorry. I like you, I really do. And I do think you are beautiful. But I'm not . . . it's my fault. Don't cry."

Line wipes her eyes and nose on her sleeve, just like Anna would. One or two things have just become clear to her. She doesn't turn around again, but only because she couldn't bear it if he still looked disgusted.

"It's very kind of you. I'll take the money, if you really mean it, because I don't think I can stay here. In fact, I know I can't."

"Good. Take it."

And now she does turn around, and Francis is sitting up in the bed, holding the leather bag. She takes the roll of notes he holds out and resists the urge to count it, because that would look ungrateful. However, it seems to be at least forty dollars (forty dollars! Yankee dollars at that), and she tucks them inside her blouse.

After all, it doesn't matter if he sees this now.

Later she is in the kitchen, surreptitiously filling her mouth with cheese, when Jens bursts in, red with excitement.

"Guess what? There are more visitors!"

Jens and Sigi run outside, and Line follows sulkily to see the shapes of two figures and a dogsled. The Norwegians gather around and help the figure on the sled get to its feet. It staggers and has to be supported. Line catches a glimpse of a fierce dark face, and then fixes on the other person as she realizes it is a white woman. It is so unusual to see a woman like that— she has, even through the layers of clothing, an air of refinement—and with this villainous-looking native, that no one knows what to say or do first. The woman is clearly so exhausted that Per turns to the native. Line does not catch the first words spoken, but then she hears, in English, "We are looking for Francis Ross. This woman is his mother."

Line's first, shameful thought is that Francis will want the money back. She also feels a stab of jealousy. Even after the embarrassing events of this afternoon, she feels she has an exclusive bond with the boy; he is her friend and ally—the only one at Himmelvanger who does not patronize her. She doesn't want to be displaced, even in the affections of a potential killer.

Line presses her hand to her bosom over the roll of money and holds it there.

No one, she swears silently, no one will take this away from her now.

MEN AND WOMEN WITH EAGER, excited faces pull me to my feet, and hold me upright when I stumble. I can't understand why they are so pleased to see us, and then exhaustion hits me, and I am overcome with a peculiar trembling and singing in my ears. As the people clustered around nod and smile and chatter in answer to something Parker says, I don't register anything beyond a confused buzz of noise and the fact that my eyes, though burning hot, remain completely dry. Perhaps I am dehydrated; perhaps I am ill. It is irrelevant; Francis is alive, and we have found him. That is all that matters. I even find myself thanking God, in case long-rusted channels of communication are still open.

I think I succeed in controlling the upwelling of feeling in me when I see him. It has been over two weeks since he left home; he looks pale, his hair seems blacker than ever; and he is thin, a child's body beneath the sheets. It is as though my heart swells to bursting point, and threatens to choke me. I cannot speak, but lean forward to hold him and feel his sharp bones just under the skin. His arms tighten around my shoulders; I can smell him, which is almost more than I can bear. Then I have to pull back as I can no longer see him, and I need to see him. I stroke his hair, his face. I clasp his hands in mine. I can't stop touching him.

He looks at me, prepared for my presence, I have been led to believe, but still he seems surprised, and a ghost of a smile flits across his face.

"Mama. You came. How did you do that?"

"Francis, we have been so worried . . ."

I stroke his shoulders and arms, try to fight back the tears. I don't want to embarrass him. Besides, I don't need to cry anymore, ever again.

"You hate traveling."

We both laugh, shakily. I allow myself to think, for a moment, of how when we get home we will start again; how there will be no more closed doors, no more brooding silences. After this, we will be happy.

"Is Papa here, too?"

"Oh . . . he could not leave the farm. We thought it better if just one of us came."

Francis's gaze falls to the bedclothes. It sounds like the thin excuse it is. I wish I had thought of a more convincing lie, but his absence is more eloquent than any explanation of it. Francis does not draw his hands away from mine, but there is a slipping away, somehow. He is disappointed, in spite of everything.

"He will be so happy to see you."

"He'll be angry."

"No, don't be silly."

"How did you get here?"

"With a tracker called Mr. Parker. He kindly offered to bring me, and . . ."

Of course, he has no knowledge of the happenings in Dove River since he left. Of who Parker is, or might be.

"They think I killed Laurent Jammet. You know that, don't you?" His voice is flat.

"My dear, it's a mistake. I saw him . . . I know you didn't do that. Mr. Parker knew Monsieur Jammet. He has an idea . . ."

"You saw him?" He is looking at me, his eyes wide, with shock or sympathy, I can't tell. Of course he is surprised. I have thought of the moment I stood at the door of Jammet's cabin a thousand times a day, each day since, until the memory of that terrible sight has worn smooth. It no longer shocks me.

"I found him."

Francis narrows his eyes, as though a sudden burst of feeling seizes him. For a moment I think he is angry, though there is no reason why he should be.

"*I* found him."

The emphasis is delicate but unmistakable. As though he has to insist on it.

"I found him, and followed the man who did it, but then I lost him. Mr. Moody doesn't believe me."

"Francis, he will. We saw the footprints you were following. You must tell him everything you saw, and he will understand."

Francis sighs sharply—the contemptuous sigh he frequently uses at home when I betray my bottomless stupidity. "I *have* told him everything."

"If you . . . found him, why did you not tell us? Why follow the man alone? What if he had attacked you?"

Francis shrugs. "I thought if I waited, I would lose him."

I don't say—because he must be thinking it, too—that he lost him anyway.

"Does Papa think I did it?"

"Francis . . . of course not. How can you say such a thing?"

He smiles again—a twisted, unhappy smile. He is too young to smile like that, and I know that it is my fault. I failed to make his childhood happy, and now that he is grown up I cannot protect him from the sorrows and difficulties of the world.

I reach out a hand and lay it against the side of his face. "I'm sorry."

He doesn't even ask what I am apologizing for.

I make myself keep talking, about how I will speak to Mr. Moody and make him understand that he is wrong. About the future, and how there is nothing to worry about. But his eyes stray away to the ceiling; he is not listening to me, and although I keep hold of his hands in mine, I know that I have lost him. I smile, forcing my face and demeanor to be cheerful, prattling on about this and that, because what else can any of us do?

T HE BAY HAS BEEN QUIET today. All of yesterday, in the snowstorm, the roar of water smashing on rocks made an angry murmur that permeated the town. Knox has thought previously that there must be a peculiar configuration of the rocky coast that produces, under certain weather conditions, this low but interminable growling. As far as you could see through the swirling veil of snow—which wasn't very far—the bay was gray and white, its surface violently ripped and slashed by the wind. At such times one can understand why the first settlers had chosen to build their homes in Dove River, away from this massive, unpredictable presence.

There are few people about now, as dusk falls. The undrifted snow is eighteen inches deep, but wet, and settling into itself. Trampled routes crisscross the street, the most traveled making deep, dirty furrows in the whiteness. The least used are faint sketches, tentative. They go from house to store, from house to house. You can see who in Caulfield is popular, and who rarely goes out. He follows one of the fainter ones now, his feet getting wetter and colder at every step. What on earth possessed him to come out without his galoshes? He tries to remember the minutes before he left the house, to discover what he had been thinking of, but can find nothing. A black hole in his mind. He has had a few of those lately. He does not find this unduly disconcerting.

At the house, all is very quiet. He walks into the drawing room wondering where the usually noisy Susannah is, and is surprised to find Scott and Mackinley seated together on the sofa. There is no sign of his family. He has the impression they have been waiting for him.

"Gentlemen . . . Ah, John, I am sorry, we were not expecting company tonight."

Scott drops his gaze and looks uncomfortable, pursing his small mouth.

Mackinley speaks. His voice is now firm and sober. "It is not as company that we are here tonight."

Knox understands and shuts the door behind him. It occurs to him, briefly, to deny everything, to insist that Mackinley's drunkenness led him to hear things that were not real; but even as the idea comes to his mind he rejects it.

"A few days ago," Mackinley begins, "you said you had not been back to the warehouse, and that Adam and I were the last people to see the prisoner. Adam has been punished for leaving the lock unchained. Yet today, you told me that you had seen the prisoner with your own eyes after I had left him."

He leans back in his seat, exuding the satisfaction of a hunter who has set a precisely engineered trap. Knox glances at Scott, who meets his eyes for an instant before his gaze shies away. Knox feels that treacherous desire to laugh welling up in him again. Perhaps it is true after all that he is losing his mind. He wonders whether, if he starts to tell the truth now, he will ever be able to stop.

"What I actually said was that I had seen your idea of justice with my own eyes."

"You don't deny it then?"

"I saw it, and it disgusted me. So I took steps to avoid a travesty of justice. That is what you would have made."

Scott looks at him, as if he hadn't believed it before but now finds the courage to confront him. "Are you saying that you . . . let the prisoner go?" He sounds more indignant that anything.

Knox takes a deep breath. "Yes. I decided that was the best thing to do."

"Have you gone quite mad? You have no authority to do such a thing!" This from Scott, who is looking rather ill, as though he has eaten some green potatoes.

"I am still the magistrate here, I believe."

Mackinley makes a small noise in his throat. "It is a Company matter. I am in charge of it. You have deliberately perverted the course of justice."

"It is not a Company matter. You sought to make it so. But if the Company did have anything to do with it, then the justice should be even more impartial. That was not going to happen while you had that man locked up."

"I am going to report you for this." Mackinley's color is heightened, his breathing deep and fast. Knox studies a split in his left thumbnail as he answers, "Well, you must do as you see fit. I am not going anywhere. You, on the other hand . . . I think it is time you found alternative lodging in this town. I am sure Mr. Scott can help you with that matter, as with so many others. Good evening, gentlemen."

Knox stands up and holds the door open. The two men rise and walk past him, Mackinley with his eyes set on a fixed point out in the hallway, Scott following with his eyes on the floor.

Knox sees the front door close behind them and listens to the creaking silence of the house. He is vaguely aware of the two men pausing outside and talking in low voices, before they move away. He feels no regret about what he has done, no fear. Standing in his unlit hallway, Andrew Knox is aware of three things at once: a sort of trembling looseness, as though a life-long tether has been suddenly untied; a desire to see Thomas Sturrock, who at this moment seems the only man who could possibly understand him; and the fact that for the first time in weeks, the pain in his joints is entirely gone.

SNOW FALLS FOR THE NEXT two days without cease, and each day is colder than the last. Jacob and Parker go out one morning and return with three birds and a hare. God knows how they managed to see them in this weather. It's not much, but it is a good gesture, since the Norwegians have all these extra mouths to feed.

I spend the time sitting with Francis, although he sleeps a lot, or pretends to. I worry about him, and about the injury to his knee, which is swollen and obviously painful. Per, who claims to have some medical knowledge, says it is not broken, just badly sprained, and only needs time to heal. With patient questioning—Francis volunteers nothing—I manage to extract some sort of account of his journey, and I am amazed and moved that he managed to get so far. I wonder if Angus would be proud of him if he knew. Before I came, he was chiefly looked after by the woman whose name is Line, but now I have taken over these duties. She did not seem pleased when I arrived, and seems to avoid me, although I saw her talking with great intent to Parker in the barn opposite. I cannot imagine what they would have to say to each other. I have to confess that an uncharitable thought entered my mind: after all, she is the only woman here without a husband, albeit through no fault of her own. And she is, admittedly, rather good-looking, in a dark, foreign way. When we were introduced, she greeted me with a hostile look. I thanked her for taking such good care of Francis, and she demurred, in excellent English, but with a sullenness that I could not understand. Then I realized that by my arrival I had usurped her and sent her back to the common chores where, presumably by reason of her widowhood, she is ordered about by the married women. Francis says that she has been very kind and he is fond of her.

Either Moody, or more usually Jacob, sits on watch outside the door, as though they are waiting for me to scream that Francis is attacking me, whereupon they will rush in and save my life. I have revised my first opinion of Mr. Moody. In Dove River he seemed kind and diffident, an unwilling law enforcer. Now he has a peevish impatience about him. He has assumed the mantle of authority and wears it without grace. I have asked to speak to him in private. So far he has managed to avoid this, by claiming pressing work duties. But after two days of unrelenting snow everyone knows that there is nothing for him to do but wait, and I can see this in his eyes as he toys with the idea of trotting out another excuse.

"Very well, Mrs. Ross. Why don't we go to . . . ah, my room."

I follow him down the corridor, and the woman Line passes us, giving Moody a nasty look as she does so.

Moody's room has the same monastic quality as mine, only his belongings are strewn wildly on the furniture and floor as though he has just been burgled. He sweeps his clothes off the chairs and throws them on the bed. As I sit down I see on the desk beside me an envelope addressed to Miss S. Knox. I find this interesting. I am sure he did not intend me to see that, and this is confirmed a moment later when he scoops all the papers on the desk into an untidy heap. He fusses over the mess for a few moments, and I reflect that under different circumstances I could feel sorry for him. He is only a few years older than Francis, and has arrived in this country recently and alone.

He clears his throat a couple of times before speaking.

"Mrs. Ross, I fully understand your concern for Francis. It is only natural, as his mother, that you should feel that."

"And it is only natural that you should want to find a perpetrator for this terrible crime," I say, pleasantly enough, I think, but his face changes to a look of harried irritation. "Francis, too, wants to find the man responsible, as he has told you."

Moody composes his expression into one that suggests patience and tolerance under trying circumstances.

"Mrs. Ross, I cannot tell you all my reasons for holding your son as a suspect, but those reasons are very pressing. You have to believe me."

"I would have thought that, of all people, you should tell *me* what they are."

"It is a matter of justice, Mrs. Ross. There are very good reasons for my actions. Murder is a very serious crime."

"The footprints," I say. "The other trail. What about that?"

He sighs. "A coincidence. A trail that the . . . that your son followed to find a place of safety."

"Or the murderer's trail."

"I fully understand your wanting to believe your son is innocent. It is natural and right. But he fled Dove River after the murder with the dead man's money, and then lied about it. The facts point to one conclusion. I would be neglecting my duty not to act on it."

I hold my breath for a moment, trying not to show my surprise. Francis didn't tell me about any stolen money.

"It would surely be just as negligent not to pursue other possibilities. The trail may be the murderer's . . . or it may not. How can you find out if you don't follow it?"

Moody sighs through his nostrils, and then rubs the bridge of his nose where his spectacles wear two red dents. He has no desire to do anything at all about the other trail.

"In the current conditions, my duty is to get the suspect to a secure place. Further investigation will have to wait until the weather permits it."

He seems pleased at this speech, having put the onus on his duty, rather than on himself. He even allows himself a slight smile, as though he rather regrets having these matters taken out of his own hands. I smile, too, since that is the way things are going, but I no longer feel inclined to spend any sympathy on him, lonely young man or not.

"Mr. Moody, that is no excuse at all. We must follow that trail, because when the weather permits, as you put it, there will be nothing left to follow, and your duty is to find the truth, and nothing else. You can leave Francis in the care of the people here, or, if you don't trust them, then leave your colleague to watch him. Parker will follow the trail, and you and I will see where it leads."

Moody looks astonished and angry. "It is not for you, Mrs. Ross, to tell me how to do my duty."

"It is for anyone to point out a dereliction of duty in a case as important as this."

He stares at me, surprised at being spoken to like this. I can tell I am pressing on a nerve; perhaps he has already thought about the trail, and it bothers him. I suspect him of having a tidy mind, and those footsteps leading off into the wilderness are a nagging loose end.

"After all, if you are right . . ." I can't bring myself to say it. "If you are right, you will know that you have eliminated every possibility, and your conscience will be clear. Besides, if it comes to a court of law, the presence of the trail and the possibility that it gives rise to . . . well, it would throw your conclusions into question, at least, would it not?"

Moody stares hard at me, then his eyes go to the window. Even there he seems unable to find an answer.

When I ask Francis about the money, he simply refuses to talk. He sighs sharply, implying that the answer is obvious and I am a fool for not seeing it. I feel a surge of the old irritation with him.

"I am trying to help you. But I can't if you won't tell me what happened. Moody is convinced you stole it."

Francis looks at the ceiling, at the walls, anywhere but my eyes. "I did steal it."

"What? Why on earth?"

"Because I needed money if I was going on a journey. I might need help to find the killer. I might have to pay for it."

"You had help at home. Money at home. Why didn't you take that?"

"I told you why I couldn't come back."

"But . . . tracks don't disappear that quickly."

"So you think it was me, too?"

He is smiling, that bitter, old smile.

"No . . . of course I don't. But—I wish you would tell me why you were there in the middle of the night."

Francis stops smiling. He doesn't say anything for a long time, long enough that I think I will just get up and walk away.

"Laurent Jammet . . ." he pauses ". . . was the only person I could talk to. Now there's no one. I don't care if I never go back."

After some moments I realize I have stopped breathing. I tell myself that he is speaking without thinking, or that he wants to wound me. Francis has always been able to hurt me more than anyone else.

"I am sorry you lost a friend. And in such a way. I would give anything for you not to have seen that."

His anger comes leaping out at me, childish anger on the verge of tears.

"Is that all you can say? You wish I hadn't seen it? What does that matter? Why does no one think about Laurent? He was the one who was killed. Why don't you wish he hadn't been killed?"

He flings himself back on the pillows, dry-eyed, and the anger is gone as suddenly as it appeared.

"I'm sorry, my darling. I'm sorry. I do wish that, of course. No one should die like that. He was a nice man. He seemed to . . . love life."

I am reminded that I hardly knew him, but this seems a safe enough bet. But if I think I am comforting Francis, or saying what he wants to hear, I am, as usual, wrong. His voice is a low murmur.

"He wasn't nice. He was callous. He would find your weakness and use it to make jokes. Anything to make people laugh, no matter what it was. He didn't care."

This sudden about-face is more than I can follow. I have a sudden, dreadful fear that Francis is about to confess something to me. I stroke his forehead and say "shh," as if he were still a child, but I do not know what to think. And so I talk nonsense, saying anything, just to keep Francis from opening his mouth and saying something I will regret.

Parker is in a barn with Jacob and one of the Norwegians. They seem to have cut themselves off from the drama going on across the courtyard, and are discussing ringworm, as far as I can tell. I feel awkward asking Parker to speak to me alone, now that we are back in a sort of civilization. I catch a glimpse of the Norwegian looking at me, speculating, I am sure, about my marriage and my peculiar choice of companion. In the shadows of the barn I am reminded of the cold, dark warehouse. It seems a long time ago.

"Mr. Moody has no interest in following the other trail. We may have to go alone."

"It will be very hard. It would be better if you stayed here, with your son."

"But, there have to be . . . witnesses."

I think I've put it carefully—without stating that I don't trust him, but he is, in any case, not offended.

"You don't know that I would come back."

"Moody must be made to see . . . whatever we find. If only we could take Francis . . ."

Parker shrugs. "If your son was the killer, he would want to put the blame on someone else. Moody would not accept that."

I know Parker is right. For the first time, I have a sense of hopelessness, of utter weariness. I have been struggling to climb a steep and slippery slope, but I have done it. Now the ground is starting to slide away beneath me, and I do not know what to do. I do not know that I can count on Parker to help me. I do not know why he should. Looking into his eyes I can see no trace of compassion—no trace of anything I recognize. Still, if pleading is the price to pay, I will do it. And a lot more besides.

"You have to take me. I have to find proof that he is innocent. No one else cares whom they arrest as long as they have someone. I beg you."

"What if there is nothing to find? Have you thought of that?"

I have thought of that, but have no answer for it. I stare at his impassive face, at the eyes that seem to have no distinction between iris and pupil at all, but are all darkness, and feel a chill pass through me.

THERE IS NO INTOXICATING LIQUOR of any kind in the Fields of Heaven. The elect have no need for artificial stimulants, or for a road to oblivion. They are at all times happy and serene. After being harangued by Mrs. Ross, Donald speculates on just what he would give for a glass of the disgusting rum drunk in such quantities at Fort Edgar. Winter is drinking season; it smooths the flow of endless nights when warmth is a distant memory. It makes endurable the terrible jokes your companions tell and retell. It makes the companions themselves endurable. Donald has half a flask of whisky that he swore to himself he would save for the journey back, but he is sorely tempted. He has a feeling that he will not be going back anytime soon.

The snow has turned to rain. The temperature rises, and the snowflakes are heavy with water, no longer floating but falling to the ground. The nature of the lying snow changes, too: from being light and feathery like a quilt, it has become sodden and unstable. Loaded with moisture, the snow has no strength; large masses break away and slide off the roof opposite Donald's window, landing with a soft, heavy thump. The roofs are gradually revealed in their somber colors—rust red, mineral blue. The snow itself is no longer white but a translucent gray. Water drips continually from the eaves. The sound is inescapable—quiet but insistent, like conscience.

He sees the tall native, Parker, cross the yard. He seems to be packing up ready to leave. Donald knows in his bones that he will go with Parker and the woman. Just to make sure that there is nothing in this story. He wonders if this is bravery; the thought of setting out across that dreadful plain terrifies him. On the other hand, if he takes the boy back as his suspect and then turns out to have been wrong, he will be reprimanded, condemned, talked about in low voices in drinking rooms. Dereliction of duty will not be good for his career. When it comes to a choice between the wilderness and professional ignominy, he knows which frightens him most.

Parker told him the trading post is no more than six days' march from here—weather conditions allowing. It is an opportunity to meet the factor there—perhaps a man who can help him advance. He tells Jacob that he must stay and guard the boy. The prisoner will be safe here for the time being.

Jacob looks very serious. "Excuse me, but it would be better if I go with them. It will be hard traveling. I know what to look for."

There is nothing Donald would like more than to stay at Himmelvanger while Jacob trudges through the slush and ice to this godforsaken place, but it's no good.

"Thank you, Jacob, but I must go and decide what is to be done. And someone must stay here." He smiles at Jacob, who looks gravely back.

"It would be better if I came with you. I can . . . look after you."

Donald smiles, touched at his loyalty. Also at how Jacob seems to regard him, out there anyway, as a defenseless child.

"There is no need. Parker has to come back here in any case, to bring Mrs. Ross back. It will be interesting to see another Company post."

He forces himself to sound more cheerful than he feels. There is apprehension, and more than a little dread, in the prospect of the cold wilderness ahead. Jacob looks thoughtful, as if struggling with himself.

"But you see . . . I had a dream. You might think it stupid, but listen: I had a dream about you on your own. There was danger. I think I should go with you."

Donald quells the lurch in his stomach, and raises his voice further, to chase out the superstitions in Jacob, and in himself. Native nonsense—he didn't think Jacob was prey to such fancies.

"I'm not surprised you've been dreaming with that bloody goat's cheese they eat here: it's enough to give anyone nightmares!"

Jacob doesn't join him in laughter. He knows he has been reprimanded.

"It is important to keep an eye on the boy. He may . . . say something important. You should try to gain his confidence."

Jacob looks doubtful, but nods.

"Would you go and tell Mr. Parker that I will be accompanying them?"

When Jacob has gone, Donald has a sudden impulse to shout after him, to express his fervent gratitude for his concern, however misguided, and his friendship. Jacob is the only person here who cares in the slightest what happens to him. Then he stops himself; he is a grown man. He does not need a native servant to look after him, not even Jacob.

Donald reflects on the change that has taken place in their relationship. After the trip to Dove River and its grisly aftermath, there was a closeness between them that he must have treasured more than he knew, since now he regrets its absence. Donald attributes it to the fact that he is now the boss, whereas before, Mackinley treated them both with much the same sort of mild contempt, and they (or at least Donald) reflected that contempt back on him in a subtler form. Now he sees Mackinley in a different light, with more understanding of the complexities of command. Well, his father always told him that life was not a picnic, that is, not there to be enjoyed. As a child he used to find that an extraordinary, perverse idea, but now his father's words make sense. To be an adult is to rise to uncertain and alarming challenges, to eschew friendship in favor of responsibility. Sometimes you must forgo being liked in order to be respected. And something else occurs to him: something that chimes with his thoughts of Susannah. For only by being respected can a man truly win love, since for a woman, love must contain an element of awe.

He looks at his letters: love letters, he supposes, although they contain nothing of a very sentimental nature. It is too early for that, though one day, who knows . . . There are four, neatly folded and addressed, and these he will give to Per to send to Dove River when the weather allows. He is pleased with the letters, which he has copied out in his room, embellishing them with tortuous philosophical digressions, the composition of which took up two long, alcohol-free evenings. He imagines Susannah reading them and keeping them in a pocket, or wrapped in a scented handkerchief (the one he gave her?) in a drawer.

With a rush of feeling, he tries to conjure the image of her face at the precise moment she smiled at him in the library, but finds, to his consternation, that he can't quite fix her in his mind. He has a vague impression of her smile, the soft light brown hair, the pale, glowing skin and hazel eyes, but the parts keep shifting and fading, and refuse to coalesce into a recognizable human whole. For some reason he can remember the face of her sister Maria, and that of her father, in perfect, three-dimensional clarity, but Susannah's likeness is just beyond his reach.

He sits down to write a short note to her, to tell her of his forthcoming journey. He is torn between wanting to make it sound dangerous and daring, and not wanting to worry her unduly if she receives it before his return. In the end he makes light of it, saying he will probably be back in

Caulfield in about three weeks, and it will be a fine opportunity to represent the Company and meet another factor, while setting his mind at rest on the subject of Francis's guilt. He assures her of his best wishes, and asks, in a coda that slightly surprises him, to send his warm regards to her sister. He stares at the page for a moment, wondering if it looks odd, but there is no time to copy out the whole letter, and so he seals it in an envelope and places it with the others.

It is ten o'clock on a Thursday evening, three weeks since Laurent Jammet's body was found. Maria is staring out of the window of her father's study, even though there is nothing to see. She can make out lances of rain drumming into the mud of what is supposed to be the garden, but at the moment resembles a cattle pen. Beyond that, only a seething darkness, where occasional veils of water are swathed this way and that by the wind, picking up light from who knows where.

Inside the house it's not much better. After the events of the afternoon, Mrs. Knox lies prostrate in her bedroom under the influence of something Dr. Gray gave her an hour ago. She was less upset than Maria would have thought, but the doctor had been persuasive in talking of the dangers of delayed shock, so Maria had encouraged her mother to swallow the draft. Susannah was more overtly distressed, but that is Susannah's way—a sudden storm followed by clear skies. As yet, still stormy, although from down here Maria can hear nothing. The house is deathly quiet.

After some debate—very much debate, as the town elders could not agree and it was all so unprecedented—her father was taken into custody on a charge of perverting the course of justice. Because he is, after all, the supposed magistrate of this community and not some scruffy half-breed stranger, he has not been consigned to the warehouse, but it was decided that he should be detained at John Scott's leisure. This means that he is locked in the room next door to Mr. Sturrock and has his meals brought up to him. The room is very similar to Mr. Sturrock's lodgings and the fare is the same, but Maria's father does not have to pay for the privilege.

John Scott, together with Mr. Mackinley and Archie Spence, came and knocked on the door at half past five this evening. Maria answered, and then led them to the drawing room while she fetched her father. They talked behind closed doors for twenty minutes before her father came out to explain that he was, in effect, in custody. There was a slight smile playing around his mouth, as though he was enjoying a private joke. While his wife remonstrated, dry-eyed and furious, and Susannah wept, Maria stood by and could not think of anything to say. Her mother marched into the drawing room and coruscated the men there. They sat openmouthed and cowed as she withered them with her scorn. John Scott had clearly wavered in the plan to actually incarcerate her father in his house, but Mackinley stood firm, his eyes and mouth betraying his delight. Her father closed the argument by saying that he would be staying just along the road, only until the magistrate from St. Pierre could be brought to officiate. He asked without a hint of irony whether they would be setting bail. Obviously the men had forgotten all about such a thing. John Scott opened his mouth, but no sound came out. Mackinley cleared his throat, and said they would think on the matter overnight and set a figure tomorrow. The trouble was, they really needed to ask her father what to do.

Eventually Knox had put an end to it by suggesting that they go; it was dinnertime, he said, and they were keeping the cooks waiting. Of course, he was referring to Mary in their kitchen, but it sounded rather as though he was chiding his arresters for making him late for his supper, and Mackinley had frowned, although her father did not seem to notice. There was a lightness about his demeanor, Maria thought: it was almost as though he was pleased to be arrested, as though they had fallen into some trap of his own making. The three women watched as their husband and father led the other men out of the house, having asked if they wanted to borrow umbrellas or galoshes. Mackinley and the others declined, although it was by now raining heavily, and there were several spares.

STURROCK LISTENS TO THE SOUND of footsteps mounting the stairs. He has been resting on his bed, thinking about Mrs. Ross and whether she has caught up with her son—who undoubtedly, to his mind, has taken the bone tablet with him. The shambolic events of the last few days make him think he should not stay here any longer. Now the snow is melting, maybe it is time to make his escape. But any place he goes can only be farther from the object of his desire, and surely they must bring the boy back here when they have found him. He sighs; the whisky bottle that has been such good company for the past few days is nearly empty. It is the story of his life, to be so near and yet still so far from achieving anything of lasting worth, and to have run out of liquor.

At this point in his reflections he rouses himself to get up and find out what all the noise was about: a new neighbor, perhaps. He opens the door to see Mr. Mackinley from the Company and John Scott, together with another man he does not know. Scott comes toward him, having closed the door to the room opposite.

"Ah, Mr. Sturrock. I was just coming to tell you—"

"A new neighbor?" Sturrock asks with a smile, the possibility of some good conversation the cause for optimism.

"Not exactly." Sturrock notices the look of contempt Mackinley throws at the back of Scott's head. "No, we find ourselves in the awkward situation of, em, having to detain the magistrate, Mr. Knox . . . and since we cannot put him in the warehouse, ha-ha, it seemed this house would be as good a place as any, for the time being."

Scott pauses, a light sweat beading his forehead. The man looks under considerable strain, his face pinker than ever.

"I hope it will not inconvenience you, Mr. Sturrock." This from Mackinley.

"You mean you're locking Knox in that room there?" Sturrock asks, almost gaily. "What the hell has he done?"

The men all glance at one another, as if wondering whether Sturrock is entitled to such information.

"It turns out that the prisoner's escape was no accident. Knox released him, thus halting the wheels of justice."

Sturrock becomes aware that his eyebrows are trying to crawl up his forehead and join his hair. "Good God, is he mad?"

It suddenly occurs to him that Knox will be listening to every word—for he can hardly do otherwise. "I mean to say, what an extraordinary thing."

"Extraordinary, yes."

Mackinley makes to turn away, and Sturrock feels a surge of dislike.

"Well, well . . ."

"Quite."

Scott says, in a conversational tone of voice: "Dinner will be ready shortly, Mr. Sturrock."

"Ah, thank you. Thank you."

At Mackinley's signal the other men make to go downstairs, leaving Sturrock staring at the locked door. When the footsteps have died away, he calls out in a low voice, "Mr. Knox? Mr. Knox?"

"I hear you, Mr. Sturrock."

"Is this true?"

"Yes, it's true."

"Well . . . are you all right?"

"Quite comfortable, thank you. I think I will retire now."

"Well, good night. Give me a shout if you . . . well, if you want someone to talk to."

There is no further reply. Sturrock wonders whether this means his source of income has run dry.

Sturrock is downstairs by the stove in Scott's store, which becomes a bar after dark, when Maria Knox walks in. The rain has kept up its assault for several hours; the snow is entirely gone, and the citizens of Caulfield are wading in mud up to their ankles. It is late—he can't remember how late now, but presumably she has come to speak to her father. However, she comes straight toward him. He knows who she is although they have never spoken.

"Mr. Sturrock? I am Maria Knox."

He inclines his head gravely out of deference to her situation. The gravity is heightened by the five or so glasses of whisky he has drunk, and the memories he has been immersed in for the past hour.

"I know it is late, but I was hoping to speak to you."

"Speak to me?" He inclines his head again—really, he must be quite drunk—though this time gallantly. "That would be an undeserved pleasure."

"There is no need for flattery. I wanted to talk to someone . . . well, you are not one of us, and the town seems to have gone quite mad."

Her voice is low, although there is no one else within earshot. "You mean your father's . . . predicament."

She looks at him with a look that is both exasperated and calculating. "I don't quite know what I am doing here. I think it is because Mr. Moody, the Company man, spoke of you, and seemed to have formed a favorable impression, despite . . . everything. Heaven knows what I expected . . ."

He realizes—the drink is making him slow-witted—that she is on the verge of tears, and her exasperation is with herself. "I don't know who else I can talk to. I am very worried, very worried indeed. You are a man of experience, Mr. Sturrock, what would you do in my circumstances?"

"About your father? Is there anything you can do, other than wait? I believe they are sending for the magistrate from St. Pierre in the morning, or when the roads are passable."

"You think they are not passable?"

"Weather like this? I doubt it very much."

"I was thinking of going tonight, to be there first. There is no telling what they will say about him."

"My dear girl . . . you cannot mean it. To attempt the journey tonight, in this rain . . . it would be madness. Your father would be horrified. It would be the worst thing you could do to him."

"You think so? Perhaps you are right. In any case, the truth is I am too much of a coward to attempt such a journey on my own. Oh, God!" She hides her head in her hands, though only for a second. She does not dissolve into tears. Sturrock feels an admiration for her, and orders another drink for himself, and one for her.

"You knew Monsieur Jammet, did you not? What do you think happened to him?"

"I didn't know him all that well. But he was a man with many secrets, and men with secrets have, perhaps, more enemies than those without."

"What on earth are you talking about?"

"Erm, only that . . . well, I came to Caulfield—and am here still—because I wanted to buy an item that Jammet owned. He knew that. Only the item has vanished."

"Stolen?"

"It seems likely. Perhaps by Francis Ross. So I wait for his return."

"Do you think Francis killed him then?"

"I did not know him at all. So I cannot say."

"I did . . . I mean, I do."

"And what do you think?"

Maria pauses, staring into her glass—to her surprise already empty. "How can you know what people are capable of? I have thought I have judged people well in the past, only to be proved quite wrong."

T HE MORNING THE OTHERS ARE due to leave, Jacob walks in and stands by the bed. He speaks to Francis but looks at the wall.

"I don't suppose you're going anywhere, but if you do, I'll come after you and break the other leg. Do you understand?"

Francis nods, thinking of the knife scar Donald showed him.

"So I don't need to sit in here all day."

Francis shakes his head.

So he is surprised when Jacob comes back. Jacob has found a piece of wood in the store; it is straight and strong—the trunk of a young birch—and will be just the right length. He strips off the bark, whittles away any irregularities, and rounds off the forked top into a smooth Y. Francis watches his hands with reluctant fascination; it is amazing how fast the tree takes on the qualities associated with a crutch. Jacob pads the top with strips of old blanket, which he winds around the wood like a bandage.

"I should do this with leather, or it will get wet."

"During my escape, you mean."

At first, when Francis said reckless or stupid things, not caring what he thought of him, Jacob didn't seem sure whether Francis was joking or not; he would glance doubtfully at him, his face impassive. This time, though, he smiles. Francis thinks, he's not much older than I am.

It will be a relief—to both of them, he thinks—to be free of the tense and anxious Moody. And a relief to himself, although he feels guilty for admitting it, to be free of his mother. Whenever she is in the room, there is such a weight of unspoken words pressing on them both he can hardly breathe. It would take years to say them all, just to get them out of the way.

Just before leaving, his mother comes into his room and looks at Jacob, who gets up and leaves without a word. She sits by his bed and folds her hands together.

"We are leaving. We will follow the trail you followed—Mr. Parker knows where it goes. It's a pity you can't come, in case we see the man, but . . . at least we can look."

Francis nods. His mother's face is grim and determined, but she looks tired, and the lines around her eyes are more noticeable than usual. He feels a sudden surge of gratitude to her, for doing what he meant to do, when she is so afraid of the wilderness.

"Thank you. You're brave to do this."

She twitches her shoulders, as if annoyed. But she isn't; she's pleased. She touches her hand to his face, running her fingers along his jaw. Someone else did a very similar thing, from time to time. Francis tries not to think about that.

"Don't be silly. I'll be with Parker and Moody; there's nothing brave about it."

They share shy, wintry smiles. Francis fights an almost overwhelming urge to tell her the truth. It would be such a relief to tell someone, to put down the burden. But even in the second he allows himself to imagine such a luxury, he knows he will say nothing.

Then she says, to his surprise, "You know I love you, don't you?"

Francis is embarrassed. He nods, unable for some reason to meet her eyes.

"Your father loves you, too."

No, he doesn't, Francis thinks. You have no idea how much he hates me. But he says nothing.

"Is there nothing else you can tell me?"

Francis sighs. There are so many things she doesn't know.

"Mr. Moody thinks the bone tablet may be important. If it is valuable, it might have been a . . . reason. Will you let me take it?"

Francis doesn't want to give it up, but can't think of a good reason not to, so he hands his mother the leather bag with the tablet in it. She takes it out and looks at it. She has read a lot, and knows a lot, but she stares at the tiny angular markings with a frown of incomprehension.

"Be careful with it," he mumbles.

She gives him a look: she who is always careful with things.

The previous summer, before school broke up, which it did early to allow the boys to help shorthanded fathers, something unprecedented had happened to him. Never having thought too much about such things, Francis, like every other boy within a ten-mile radius, fell in love with Susannah Knox.

She was a year above him at school and was without doubt the outstanding beauty of that year: slender, rounded, happy, with a sweet, exquisite face. He dreamed of Susannah by night, and by day imagined her and him together—in various vague but romantic scenarios, such as rowing a boat on the bay, or his showing her his secret hiding places in the woods. The sight of her walking past the classroom, or laughing with friends in the school yard, would send an exquisite, thrilling shock through his body; skin prickled, breath caught, head thrummed with blood. He would turn his head away, feigning disinterest, and since he had no close friends, his secret was well hidden. He was well aware that he was not alone in this passion, and that she could take her pick of older and more popular candidates, but she did not seem to bestow special favors on any of them. It probably wouldn't have mattered if she had; it wasn't as though he actually expected anything to happen. It was enough that he could annex her in his dreams.

There was an occasion—the annual summer picnic, which took place every year at the end of term—when the entire school trekked down to a slim stretch of sandy beach on the bay. Under the indolent eyes of two bored teachers they ate sandwiches, drank ginger beer, and swam, shrieking and splashing, until it got dark. Francis, who generally hated such occasions of enforced jollity and had considered avoiding it, ended up going, because Susannah would be there, and as she was about to leave school, he did not know how he was going to catch the quick, sweet glimpses of her that fed his passion.

He found a spot not far from where Susannah and some of the other senior girls had sat down, only to be joined about a minute later by Ida Pretty. Ida was two years younger than Francis and his next-door neighbor. He liked her, alone of her large family; she was sharp-tongued and funny, but she could be something of a pain. She liked Francis and was always pestering him, had been watching him as assiduously (but not as covertly) as he was watching Susannah.

Now she sat down with her basket and shaded her eyes, looking over the water.

"I reckon it's gonna rain later. Look at that cloud. They coulda chosen a better day for it, doncha think?"

She sounded hopeful. A malcontent and a loner like him, she shared his horror of events that were supposed to be both communal and fun.

"I don't know. I guess."

Francis hoped that, if he didn't speak to her too much, Ida would take the hint and wander off. He debated the question of whether it was less desirable to be seen sitting moodily alone, or with an annoying junior member of the school, but from Susannah's intense whispered conversations with her girlfriends, it didn't seem likely that she would notice whatever he did. And there were various senior boys circling, ostentatiously minding their own business, but doing so within eyeshot of the senior girls; larking about, whooping and competing to throw stones farthest into the water.

As the sun beat down, levels of activity declined: sandwiches were eaten, flies were swatted, clothes shed. Susannah's group had split off into threesomes and twosomes, and she herself had gone for a walk with Marion Mackay. Francis lay back with his head against a slab of rock and pulled his hat over his eyes. The sun pierced the loose weave, dazzling him pleasantly. Ida had lapsed into a grumpy silence, and was pretending to read *Pudd'nhead Wilson*.

By turning his head minutely from side to side, he was making the sunlight flare into his eyes and disappear, when Ida said, "Whatcha think of Susannah Knox?"

"Huh?"

He had of course been thinking of her. Guiltily he tried to banish her from his mind.

"Susannah Knox. Whatcha think of her?"

"She's all right, I guess."

"Everyone in school seems to think she's about the prettiest girl they've ever seen."

"Do they?"

"Well, yeah."

He couldn't tell whether Ida was looking at him or not. His heart was thumping, but his voice sounded suitably bored.

"She's pretty enough."

"You think so?"

"I guess."

This was getting irritating. He pulled the hat from his face and squinted at her. She was sitting with her knees hunched up, shoulders around her ears. Her small face was scrunched up against the sun, and she looked miserable and angry.

"Why?"

"Does it matter?"

"Does what matter? That she's pretty?"

"Yeah."

"I don't know. Depends, I suppose."

"On what?"

"On who you're talking to you. I guess it matters to her. Geez, Ida."

He pulled the hat back over his eyes and a moment later heard her get up and walk huffily away. He must have fallen asleep, because he woke up when she sat down again, slightly startled and wondering where he was, and why he was so hot. The hat had slipped off his face, and he was dazzled, red rockets bursting in front of his eyes. The skin of his face felt tight and tender. He was going to have a sunburn.

"Do you mind if I sit here a minute?"

The voice was not Ida's. Francis pulled himself up, to see Susannah Knox smiling down at him. Shock slid down his spine like ice water.

"No. No, not at all."

He looked around. The beach seemed much emptier than before, the group of girls she had been sitting with nowhere in sight.

"Guess I was asleep."

"I'm sorry. I woke you up."

"It's okay. A good thing. Think I'm going to have a sunburn."

He touched his forehead gently. Susannah leaned toward him, peering at him from what seemed a very close distance. He could see each curved, individual eyelash; the tiny blond hairs on her cheek.

"Yeah, it looks a little red. It's not too bad, though. You're lucky, you've got that skin that, well, it's quite dark, you know what I mean? Me, I just get freckles and look like a beetroot."

She smiled her enchanting smile. The sun was partially behind her and cast a radiant halo around her head, her light brown hair turned to strands of gold and platinum. Francis was finding it difficult to breathe. At least if he blushed now, she wouldn't notice.

"So, are you having a good time?" he managed to say at last, having failed to think of anything cleverer.

"What, here? I guess it's okay. Some of those boys are being a pain.

Emlyn Pretty pushed Matthew into the water with all his clothes on and laughed for about an hour. It was kind of mean."

"Yeah?"

Francis was secretly exultant. He had an unfortunate past with Emlyn. Lucky it wasn't him pushed into the water.

Then, try as he might, he could not come up with anything else to say. He stared out at the water for a long time, praying for inspiration. Susannah didn't seem to mind; she picked at the ends of her hair, apparently deep in thought.

"Is Ida your girlfriend?"

This came so out of the blue that Francis could hardly speak for astonishment. Then he laughed. What an extraordinary idea. An extraordinary question.

"No! I mean, she's just a friend. She lives next door, you know. Just up-river. She's two years younger than me," he added, for good measure.

"Oh . . . You live next door to the Prettys, huh?"

She must have known, as everyone knew where everyone else lived. She busied herself even more with her hair. What she was doing to it, he couldn't tell; obviously something fiddly that required immense concentration.

"You know"—at last she tossed the piece of hair aside with a decisive movement, and shook it back from her face—"we're going to have a picnic next Saturday, just a few of us, up by the dipping pool. You can come, if you like. It'll just be Maria, you know, my sister, and Marion and Emma, maybe Joe . . ."

She was looking at him, finally, her eyes unreadable. Francis saw her as a dark shape blocking the sun, her features misty and dazzled, like a Sunday school angel.

"Saturday? Um . . ." He couldn't quite believe what was happening. But it appeared that Susannah—the one and only Susannah Knox—was inviting him to a picnic—an exclusive picnic, to which only her nearest friends were invited (and Joe Bell, but he was well known to go around with Emma Spence). Then suddenly it crossed his mind that maybe it was all a terrible joke. What if she had come to ask him to a picnic that didn't exist? If he turned up next Saturday, there would be no one there, or, worse, hordes of seniors watching and laughing their heads off at his presumption. She didn't look like she was joking, though. She was still looking at him, and then she let out a short, nervous laugh.

"Geez. Keep a girl waiting, why don't you!"

"Sorry. Um . . . it's just that, I'll have to speak to my dad, to see if he wants me to work . . . first. Thanks, though. It sounds nice."

His heart was hammering its consternation. Did he really just say that?

"Well, okay. Let me know, if you can, huh?" Uncertainly, she stood up.

"Yeah, I will. Thanks."

She looked more beautiful than usual at that moment, her face serious and lovely, smoothing down her hair. She gave a little smile and turned away. He thought she looked sad. He lay back and tipped the hat back over his eyes so that he could secretly watch her wander back over to another part of the beach, where she rejoined some other seniors. Suddenly he felt a sense of wonder sweep over him. She had asked him to a picnic. She, who had never spoken more than ten words to him before, ever: she had asked him to a picnic!

Francis watched some younger boys hurtling a piece of driftwood into the shallow water, spinning it across the surface dangerously close to one another's legs, skittering out of the way of the bright splashes. Their howls of laughter were strangely distant. He thought of the next Saturday. His father had long ago given up asking him to help out at weekends; he certainly wasn't expecting him to. He thought of the picnic by the dipping pool on the river, where oaks and willows dappled the sun on water the color of tea, and girls in light summer dresses would sit in pools of pale cotton.

And he knew he would not go.

The Winter
Partners

"I know it," I said.

"Ah, excellent. Well . . . so, you see, an illustration of that would be a . . . a lovelorn pose, with a crown of flowers and so on. You see what I mean?"

"I think so."

"It will be a great help to me with a monograph I am writing. The pictures will illustrate my thesis, particularly for people who have never been inside an asylum and find one difficult to imagine."

I nodded politely, and when he didn't elaborate, asked, "What is your thesis?"

He looked a little startled. "Oh. My thesis is, well . . . that there are certain patterns to madness, certain physical attitudes and movements that are common to different patients, indicative of their inner states. That, although every patient has an individual history, they fall into groups which share certain traits and attitudes. And also that"—he paused, apparently deep in thought—"by a repeated and concentrated study of these attitudes, we can discover more about ways to cure those poor unfortunates."

"Ah," I said, brightly, wondering what attitudes I, as one of those unfortunates, tended to strike. Several unsuitable pictures presented themselves.

"And," he went on, "perhaps you could join me for lunch on those days when you are so kind as to give me your time?"

My mouth watered at the thought. The food in the asylum was wholesome enough but bland, stodgy, and monotonous. I think there was a theory (maybe even a thesis) that certain tastes were dangerously stimulating, and too much meat, say, or anything overly rich or spicy would inflame already delicate sensibilities and cause a riot. I was already pleased at the prospect of being a model, but the promise of proper, interesting food would alone have persuaded me.

"Well," he smiled, and I realized that he was actually nervous, "does that sound . . . agreeable to you?"

I was intrigued that he was nervous—of me? Of the possibility that I would say no?—and nodded. I couldn't for the life of me see how staring at pictures of women covered in flowers would produce a cure for madness, but who was I to say so?

Besides, he was a handsome, kind, youngish man, and I was an orphan in a mental asylum with no one to sponsor me and little prospect of leaving. However unusual the events that came my way, they were unlikely to change my life for the worse.

And so it began. To start with I would go to his office perhaps once or twice a month. Watson would have gathered a number of costumes and props to create the scenario. The first one was to be called, apparently, Melancholia, which I felt more than qualified to portray. He had arranged a chair by a window, at which I was to sit, in a somber dress, holding a book and gazing longingly out, as though, as he put it, I was dreaming of my lost love. I could have told him that there are worse troubles in life than an errant suitor, but I held my tongue and stared out of the window, dreaming instead of braised venison with port sauce, curried chicken, and trifle with nutmeg.

The lunch, when it arrived, was every bit as good as the ones my imagination had come up with. I am afraid I ate with all the grace of a farmhand, and he watched me, smiling, as I had second and third helpings of a pear and cinnamon tart. I stuffed myself, not because I was so enormously hungry, but because I had been starved of tastes, of piquancy and subtlety. To taste spices and blue cheese and wine for the first time in four or five years (with the odd exception at Christmas) was heaven. I think I said as much, and he laughed, and seemed tremendously pleased. As he walked with me to the door of his study, he held my hand in both of his, and thanked me, looking deep into my eyes.

As I expected, I was summoned to the study with increasing frequency, and as we became more accustomed to each other, the poses became less formal. By which I mean I gradually wore less and less, ending up reclining against the fernery partially tangled in a diaphanous sheet of muslin. I think that fairly early on any pretense at contributing to the forward march of medical science was abandoned. Watson, or Paul, as I came to call him, made the studies it pleased him to make, sometimes guiltily, blinking and avoiding my gaze as though he were embarrassed at asking me to do such things.

He was kind and thoughtful, and was interested in my opinions, which many men who have known me outside the asylum have not been. I liked him, and was happy when he put his hand on mine, trembling, one day at the end of the meal. He was sweet, desperate, terrified at doing wrong, and apologized every time we met for taking advantage of me, and giving in to his base nature. I never minded. For me it was a thrilling secret, a sweet craving, although he was always nervous and jumpy when we consummated, swiftly, after another spectacular lunch, behind the locked study door.

And he smelled of the greenhouses, of tomato leaves and damp earth, sharp and satisfying. Even now, I cannot remember that smell without also thinking of fruit pies with cream or steak in brandy. Even the other night, years later, in a frozen tent in the forest, when I smelled that scent from Parker, it brought water to my mouth, and the recollection of a bitter chocolate tart.

What happened, I don't suppose I will ever now find out. Somehow Watson was disgraced. Not through me, as far as I know, and certainly nothing was ever said, but one morning it was announced by the head attendant that Dr. Watson had to leave suddenly, and that within days another superintendent would be taking his place. One day he was there, the next not. He must have taken the apparatus, and the pictures we made together. Some of them were beautiful: dark, silvery shadings on glass that shimmered as you tilted them to the light. I wonder if they still exist. When I feel melancholy, and that is quite often nowadays, I remind myself that he trembled when he touched me, that I was once someone's muse.

We have been walking across the plain for three days with no end or change in sight. The rain that brought the thaw persisted for two days and made progress very difficult. We waded ankle-deep in mud, and if that does not sound very much, I can only insist that it is bad enough. Each foot was weighted with a couple of pounds of clinging slime, and my skirt dragged, heavy with water. Parker and Moody, not burdened with skirts, trudged on ahead with the sled.

Late on the second day the rain stopped, and I was just thanking whatever gods are still sparing me a thought, when a wind got up that has been blowing ever since. It has dried the ground and made walking easier, but it comes from the northeast and is so cold that I experience the phenomenon, previously only heard of, of tears freezing in the corners of my eyes. After an hour my eyes are red raw.

Now Parker and the dogs wait for us to catch up. He stands on a slight rise, and when we finally stagger up to him, I see why he has waited: a few hundred yards away is a complex of buildings—the first man-created thing we have seen since leaving Himmelvanger.

"We are on the right road," says Parker, although road is hardly the word I would have chosen.

"What is that place?" Moody is peering through his spectacles. His eyes are bad, made worse by the dim gray light, which is all that struggles through the clouds.

"It was once a trading post."

I can see from here that there is something wrong with it; it has the sinister quality of a building in a nightmare.

"We should go and look. In case he has been there."

Closer to, I realize what has happened. The post has been burned to a skeleton; rafters stand gauntly against the sky, broken beams jut out at wrong, upsetting angles. Where walls remain they are charred black, and sag. But the strangest thing of all is that it was recently covered with snow, which melted by day then froze by night, layer on layer of meltwater congealing so that the bare bones are swollen and glazed with ice. It is an extraordinary sight: black, bulbous, glittering, the ice engulfing the buildings as though they have been swallowed by some amorphous creature. It inspires me, and Moody as well, I think, with a sort of horror.

I want, more than anything, to get away from here. Parker walks in between the walls, studying the ground.

"Someone has left clothes." He indicates a shapeless bundle on the ground in one corner. I don't ask him why anyone would do something like that. I have a hunch I don't want to know.

"This is Elbow Ridge. Have you heard of it?"

I shake my head, fairly sure this is something else I would be better off not knowing.

"It was built by the XY Company. The Hudson Bay Company didn't like the fact that they tried to set up a post here, so they burned it down."

"How can you know that?"

Parker shrugs. "Everyone knows. Things like that happened." I glance over toward Moody, thirty yards away through a vanished door, poking about by a jumble of wood that might once, a long time ago, have been a piano.

I look back at Parker to see if he intended any malice, but his face is blank. He has picked up the stiff, frozen cloth and stretches it out—the ice creaks and splinters in protest—to reveal a shirt that was probably once blue but is now so dirty it is hard to be sure. It has been soaked and stained and left here to rot. I suddenly, belatedly, realize the import of this.

"Is that blood?"

"I don't know. Maybe."

He pokes around some more, and lets out an exclamation of satisfaction. This time even I understand why—there are traces of a fire, black and sooty, close by a wall.

"Recent?"

"About a week old. So our man came through here, and stayed the night. We could do worse than copy him."

"Stay here? But it's early. We should go on, surely?"

"Look at the sky."

I look up; the clouds, sliced into quadrilaterals by the black beams, are low and dark. Storm-colored.

Moody, when told of the plan, is bullish. "But what is it—another two days to Hanover House? I think we should keep going."

Parker replies calmly, "There is going to be a storm. We will be glad of shelter."

I can see Moody's brain whirring, deciding whether or not it is worth arguing, whether Parker will yield to his authority. But the wind is getting up, and he loses his nerve; the sky has become ugly and oppressive. Despite the brooding strangeness of the abandoned post, it is a good deal better than nothing.

Accordingly, we pitch camp within the ruins. Parker constructs a large lean-to against one of the remaining walls, and reinforces it with blackened timbers. I am alarmed when I see how much sturdier this shelter is than any I have seen him build before, but I follow his instructions and unpack the sled. Over the past few days I have become much more adept at the tasks necessary for comfort and survival; I stack the food inside (does he really think we will be trapped for days?), while Moody collects wood—at least there is plenty of that around—and chips ice off the walls for water. We work quickly, infected with a dread of the darkening day and rapidly increasing wind.

By the time we finish our preparations, snow is whipping about us, stinging our faces like a swarm of bees. We crawl into the shelter; Parker lights a fire and boils water. Moody and I sit facing the entrance, which has been secured with large beams, but which has begun to twitch and heave as though desperate men are trying to get in. Over the next hour the wind rises in force and volume until we can hardly hear ourselves speak. It makes an eerie screeching noise, together with the sharp snapping of canvas and a horrible creaking of wall timbers. I wonder if they are going to withstand it, or will collapse under the force and the weight of ice on top of us. Parker seems unconcerned, though I would wager that Moody shares my fears; his eyes are wide behind his spectacles, and he jumps at any variation in the noises around us.

"Will the dogs be all right out there?" he asks.

"Yes. They will lie down together and keep each other warm."

"Ah. Good idea." Moody laughs shortly, glancing at me, then drops his eyes when I don't summon up a laugh to keep him company.

Moody swallows his tea and takes off his boots and socks, revealing feet covered in dried blood. I have watched him tend to his feet on previous evenings, but tonight I offer to do it for him. Perhaps it is the thought of Francis, that the age difference between them is not so great; perhaps it is the storm outside, and the thought that I need all the friends I can get. He leans back and stretches out one foot at a time for me to clean and bandage with strips of linen, which is all we have. I am not gentle, but he makes no sound as I clean the wounds with rubbing alcohol and bind them tightly. He has his eyes shut. From the corner of my eye Parker seems to be watching us, although what with the smoke from the fire and from his pipe, visibility in the tent is practically nil and I could be mistaken. When I have finished bandaging his feet, Moody digs out a hip flask and offers it to me. It is the first time I have seen it. I accept, gratefully; it is whisky, not particularly good, but bright and fiery as it burns down my throat, making my eyes water. He offers the flask to Parker, too, but he merely shakes his head. Come to think of it, I have never seen him touch liquor. Moody replaces the blood-soaked socks and boots—it is too cold to keep them off.

"Mrs. Ross, you must be a tough backwoods woman indeed if you can keep this up without blisters."

"I have moccasins," I point out. "They don't chafe the feet in the same way. You should try to acquire some when we get to Hanover House."

"Ah. Yes." He turns to Parker. "And when will that be, do you think, Mr. Parker? Will this storm blow itself out tonight?"

Parker shrugs. "It may. But even so, the snow will make the going harder. It may take more than two days."

"You've been there before?"

"Not for a long time."

"You seem to know the route well enough."

"Yes."

There is a short, hostile pause. I'm not sure where the hostility came from, but it is there.

"Do you know the factor there?"

"His name is Stewart."

I notice that this doesn't exactly answer the question.

"Stewart . . . Know his first name?"

"James Stewart."

"Ah, I wonder if that is the same one . . . I heard a story recently about a James Stewart, who was famous for making a long winter journey in terrible conditions. Quite a feat, I believe."

Parker's face is, as usual, unreadable. "I can't say for certain."

"Ah, well . . ." Moody sounds tremendously pleased. I suppose that if you know no one in a country, having heard of someone before meeting them is tantamount to having an old friend.

"So you do know him, then?" I ask Parker.

He gives me a look. "I met him when I worked for the Company. Years ago."

Somehow his tone warns me against making any further pleasantries. Moody, of course, doesn't notice.

"Well, well, won't that be splendid . . . A reunion."

I smile. There is really something rather endearing about Moody, crashing about like a bull in a china shop . . . Then I remember what he is trying to do, and the smile fades.

The snow does not stop, nor does the shrieking wind. By unspoken consensus, the canvas is not rigged into a curtain to give me privacy. I lie down between the two men, rolled in layers of blankets, feeling the heat from the embers scorching my face but not wanting to move. Then Moody lies down beside me, and finally Parker smothers the ashes and lies down, so close I can feel him and smell the scent of greenhouses that he carries with him. It is pitch-dark, but I do not think that I will close my eyes all night. What with the howling of the wind and the battering the tent is getting, it billows and trembles like a live thing. I am terrified that we will be buried in the snow, or that the walls will collapse and trap us underneath; I imagine all sorts of awful fates as I lie with racing heart and wide-stretched eyes. But I must have slept, because I dream, although I do not think I have dreamed in weeks.

Suddenly I awake to find—as I think—the tent has gone. The wind is screaming like a thousand banshees and the air is full of snow, blinding me. I cry out, I think, but the sound goes unheard in the maelstrom. Parker and Moody are both kneeling, fighting to close the mouth of the tent where it has been torn free. They eventually manage to secure it again, but snow has gathered in drifts inside the tent. There is snow on our clothes and in our hair. Moody lights the lamp; he is shaken. Even Parker looks slightly less composed than normal.

"Well." Moody shakes his head and brushes the snow off his legs. We are all wide awake and extremely cold. "I don't know about you, but I need something to drink."

He pulls out the hip flask and drinks from it before handing it to me. I give it to Parker, who hesitates and then accepts. Moody smiles as though this is some sort of personal triumph. Parker lights the fire for tea, and we are all grateful, huddling around it with scorching fingers. I am trembling, whether through cold or shock I do not know, and do not stop until I have drunk a mug of sweet tea. I watch the men smoking their pipes with envy; it is another warm and soothing thing and that would be welcome, as would a rosewood stem to clench between my chattering teeth.

"It looked deep out there," Moody says when the whisky is finished.

Parker nods. "The deeper it gets, the warmer it will be in here."

"Well, that is a nice thought," I say. "We will be warm and comfortable while we are smothered to death."

Parker smiles. "We can easily dig ourselves out."

I smile back at Parker, surprised to see him so amused, and then some little thing recalls to me the dream I was having when I awoke, and I bury my face in my cup. It is not that I remember what I was dreaming exactly; it is more that the feeling around it washes over me with a sudden, peculiar warmth and causes me to turn away, feigning a fit of coughing, so that the men cannot see my cheeks color in the darkness.

By late morning the storm has almost blown itself out. When I wake again it is light, and more snow has drifted into the corners of the shelter and into the spaces between us. Struggling out of the tent, I emerge into a day still gusty and gray, but seeming glorious after the night we have spent there. Our tent is half hidden in a drift three feet deep, and the whole place looks entirely different under its blanket of snow—better somehow, less foreboding. It takes me a few minutes to realize that, despite Parker's assurances, a section of the wall did blow down in the night, though without endangering us. I try not to think about what would have happened if we had made our shelter twenty feet to the east. We did not, and that is the main thing.

Initially I am afraid the dogs are gone, buried for good; as I look around there is no sign of them, whereas usually they are barking their heads off demanding food. Then Parker reappears from somewhere with a long stick of wood that he plunges into the drifts, calling to his dogs with the strange sharp cries he uses to communicate with them. Suddenly there is a sort of explosion by him, and Sisco erupts from a deep drift, followed by Lucie. They jump up at him, barking furiously and wagging their whole bodies, and Parker pets them briefly. He must be relieved to see them; normally he does not touch them at all, and yet now he is smiling, looking genuinely delighted. I have never seen him smile at me like that. Or anyone else, of course.

I go over to where Moody is clumsily packing up the tent material. "Let me do that."

"Oh, would you, Mrs. Ross? Thank you. You put me to shame. How are you this morning?"

"Relieved, thank you for asking."

"I also. That was an interesting night, was it not?"

He smiles, looking almost mischievous. He, too, seems in high spirits this morning. Perhaps we were all more frightened last night than we cared to admit.

And later, when we are walking northeast once more, even struggling as we are through a foot of driven snow, we walk closely together, Parker regulating his stride to ours, as though we are three people who find solace in one another's company.

WRESTLING WITH ESPEN'S CLOTHING IN the absolute dark of the cupboard, pressed against stacks of soap and something that feels like a broom, Line has a jolting, incoherent vision. It is as though the lack of light exonerates them. She cannot even tell who is in here with her. It must be the same for him—they could be any man and woman, anywhere. Toronto, for example. And then she knows what she will do.

Line prises her mouth from his skin long enough to say, "I cannot stay here. I am going to leave. As soon as I can."

Espen pulls back. She can hear his breathing but cannot see his face in this darkness.

"No, Line, I can't stand to be without you. We can be careful. No one will know."

Line feels the roll of money in her pocket, and is filled with its power. "I have money."

"What do you mean, you have money?"

Espen has never had money in his life, has always lived hand to mouth, until he came to build Himmelvanger, and stayed. Line smiles in secret.

"I have forty dollars. Yankee dollars."

"What?"

"No one knows about it except you."

"How did you come by that?"

"It's a secret!"

Espen's face breaks into an incredulous smile. Somehow she knows this. She can feel him tremble with laughter under her hands.

"We can take two of the horses. It'll only take us three days to get to Caulfield; we can wear all our clothes and take the children behind us. Then we can get a steamer to Toronto . . . or Chicago. Anywhere. I've got enough money to get a house while we look for work."

Espen sounds faintly alarmed. "But Line, it's the middle of winter. Wouldn't it be better if we waited till spring—what with the children?"

Line feels a flicker of impatience. "It's not even snowing—it's practically warm! What do you want to wait for?"

Espen sighs. "Besides, when you say 'the children,' you mean Torbin and Anna, don't you?"

Line has been waiting for this. It's all Merete's fault, really. If only she were dead. She's good for nothing and no one likes her, not even Per, who's supposed to like everybody.

"I know it's hard, my darling, but we can't take all the children away with us. Maybe later, when we've got a house, you can come and get them, huh?"

Privately she thinks this unlikely. She can't imagine Merete, or Per for that matter, letting Espen take the children away to live with his floozy. But Espen adores his three children.

"We can all be together again soon. But now . . . I have to go now. I can't stay."

"Why all this hurry?"

It is her trump card, and Line plays it carefully. "Well, I am almost sure . . . no, I am sure, that I am in the family way."

There is a total silence in the cupboard. For heaven's sake, Line thinks to herself, it's not as if he doesn't know how these things happen.

"How can that be? We were so careful!"

"Well . . . we weren't always careful." He not at all—it could have happened much sooner, she thinks, if he had had his way. "You're not angry, are you, Espen?"

"No, I love you. It's just rather—"

"I know. But that's why I can't stay until spring. Soon the others will begin to notice. Here . . ." She takes his hand and slips it under her waistband.

"Oh, Line . . ."

"So we should go then, shouldn't we, before the snow comes to stay? Otherwise . . ."

Otherwise, the alternative is unthinkable.

Late that afternoon Line goes to the boy's room. She waits until she sees Jacob walk out and disappear into the stables, then she goes in. The key is left in the outside of the door—now that Moody has gone, no one takes the locking of the door very seriously.

Francis looks up in surprise when she comes in. She hasn't been there, alone with him, since before his mother came: the day she tried to kiss him, and he gave her the money. It still brings blood to her cheeks to think about it. Francis is dressed in his own clothes and sitting in a chair by the window. He has a piece of wood and a knife in his hands—he is whittling something. Line is taken aback—she had pictured him still in bed, weak and pale.

"Oh," she says, before she can stop herself. "You're up."

"Yes, I'm much better. Jacob even trusts me with his knife." He gestures with it, and smiles at her. "You're quite safe."

"Can you walk now?"

"I can get about all right, with the crutch."

"That's good."

"Are you all right? Are things all right, I mean, beyond that door?" He sounds concerned.

"Yes . . . that is, no, not really. I came to ask you something—I need your help. About your journey from Caulfield . . . Will you promise not to say anything? Not even to Jacob?"

He stares in surprise. "Yes, all right."

"I'm going to leave. I have to go now, before the snow comes again. We're going to take horses and go south. I need you to tell me the way."

Francis looks astonished. "The way to Caulfield?"

She nods.

"But what if it snows when you're on the way?"

"Your mother did it. In the snow. On horseback it can't be so hard."

"You mean you and your children?"

"Yes." She holds her head up, feeling the blush spread up her neck and into her hair. Francis turns aside, looking for somewhere to put the wood and knife. And now I've embarrassed you again, she thinks, taking out the pencil and paper she has brought with her. Oh well, some things can't be helped. It's not as though you'll be jealous.

THE MAGISTRATE FROM ST. PIERRE sits opposite Knox in his bedroom-cum-prison and sighs. He is an elderly man, squat, at least seventy, with milky eyes caught behind pebble glasses that look too heavy for his frail nose.

"If I am to understand you correctly"—he glances at his notes—"you said that you 'could not agree with Mackinley's brutal attempts to force a confession out of William Parker,' so you let him go."

"We had no grounds to hold him."

"But Mr. Mackinley says Parker could not account for his whereabouts over the period in question."

"He accounted for them. There was no one to back them up, but that is hardly surprising in a trapper."

"Furthermore, Mr. Mackinley said that the prisoner attacked him. Any damage suffered by the prisoner was done in self-defense."

"There wasn't a scratch on Mackinley, and if he had been attacked, he would have told everyone. I saw the prisoner. It was a vicious attack. I knew he was telling the truth."

"Hmm. I am familiar with one William Parker. Perhaps you are aware that this same William Parker has something of a record for assaulting servants of the Hudson Bay Company?"

Knox thinks, Oh, no.

"It was some time ago, but he was suspected of a fairly serious attack. You see, if you had only waited a little longer, this could all have been brought to light."

"I still don't believe he is the murderer we seek. Just because a man has done one wrong thing—some time ago—does not mean that he has done another."

"True. But if it is in a man's nature to be violent, it is likely that this tendency will erupt again and again. The same man is not violent and then peaceable."

"I'm not sure I can agree with you there. Especially if the violence is committed in youth."

"No. Well. And there is another suspect still at large?"

"I don't know that I'd put it quite like that. I sent two men after a local youth who went missing around that time. They haven't returned yet."

And where the hell are they? he asks himself. It's been nearly two weeks.

"And, I believe, the boy's mother is also missing?"

"She has gone looking for her son."

"Quite so." He unhooks the spectacles, which have made shiny red dents in the bridge of his nose, and rubs the spot with finger and thumb. His look to Knox clearly says, "What an unholy mess you have made of this town."

"What do you intend to do with me?"

The magistrate from St. Pierre shakes his head. "It really is most irregular." His head goes on wagging gently as though, once started, the motion is self-perpetuating. "Most irregular. I am hard-pressed to know what to think, Mr. Knox. But I suppose, in the meantime, we can trust you to go home. As long as you don't—ha-ha—leave the country!"

"Ha-ha. No. I don't suppose I will attempt that." Knox stands up, refusing to return the man's mirthless smile. He finds that he towers over the other magistrate by at least a foot.

Free to go, Knox finds himself strangely reluctant to return home immediately. He pauses on the landing and, on impulse, knocks on the door of Sturrock's room. After a second the door opens.

"Mr. Knox! I am happy to see you at liberty again—I assume—or have you escaped?"

"No. I am at liberty, for the time being, at least. I feel like a new man."

Despite his smile and attempted jocular tone, he is not sure that Sturrock realizes he is joking. He never had much success with jokes, even as a youth—something to do with the severity of his features, he suspects. As a young lawyer he became aware that the emotion he most often inspired in people was alarm and a sort of preemptive guilt. It has had its uses.

"Come in." Sturrock ushers him inside as though Knox is the person he most wanted to see in the world. Knox allows himself to be flattered by this, and accepts a glass of whisky.

"Well, *slainthé*!"

"*Slainthé!* I am sorry it is not a malt, but there we are . . . Now tell me, how did you like your night behind bars?"

"Oh, well . . ."

"I wish I could say that I have never experienced the pleasure, but sadly that is not the case. A long time ago, in Illinois. But since most everyone is a criminal down there, I was in some very good company . . ."

They talk for some time, at ease with each other. The level in the bottle falls as the window darkens. Knox looks at the sky, and what he can see of it above the rooftops is dark and heavy, auguring more bad weather. Down below, a small figure hurries diagonally across the street into the store below. He can't tell who it is. He thinks it is probably going to snow again.

"You are staying here then, waiting for the boy's return?"

"I suppose I am, yes."

There is a long pause; the whisky is finished. They are both thinking the same thing.

"You must set great store by this . . . bone."

Sturrock looks at him sideways, a calculating look. "I suppose I must."

THEY HAVE FIRST SIGHT OF their destination on the evening of the sixth day. Donald lags behind—even Mrs. Ross can walk faster than he can with his lacerated feet. Impossible to abandon the purgatorial boots altogether, but even with his feet entirely bandaged, each step is agony. Also, and this he has kept secret from the others, his scar has begun hurting. Yesterday he became convinced it had opened again, and under the pretext of a private stop he unbuttoned his shirt to look. The scar was intact, but slightly swollen and weeping a little clear fluid. He touched it anxiously, to see where the fluid was coming from. Probably just the exhausting journey wearing him down; when they stopped, it would recover.

And so the sight, in the distance, of the trading post—whose very existence he has come in moments of stress to doubt—is cause for jubilation. At this moment, Donald can think of nothing more glorious than lying down on a bed for a very long time. Clearly the secret of happiness, he reflects quite cheerfully, is a variation on the general principle of banging your head against a wall, and then stopping.

Hanover House stands on a rise of land surrounded on three sides by a river. There are some trees huddled behind it, the first trees they have seen for days—bent, stunted birches and tamaracks, hardly higher than a man, granted, but still trees. The river is flat and slow but has not frozen—it's not quite cold enough for that yet—and is black against its snowy banks. When they are quite close and there is still no sign that anyone has seen them, Donald experiences a nagging fear that there is no one there at all.

The post is built along the same lines as Fort Edgar, but is clearly much older. The palisade leans; the buildings themselves are gray and woolly with the repeated assaults of weather. Overall, it has a frayed air—although attempts have been made to restore it, its appearance speaks of neglect. Donald is vaguely aware of the reason for this. By now they are deep in the Shield Country south of Hudson Bay. Once this area was a rich source of furs for the Company, but that was long ago. Hanover House is a relic of former glories, a vestigial limb. But outside the fence and pointing out over the plain is a circle of small guns, and someone has taken the trouble—since the snowstorm—to come outside and clear the snow off them. The squat black shapes, stark against the snow, are the only sign of human activity.

The gate in the palisade stands ajar, and there are human tracks here and there. And though the three of them and the dogsled must have been visible against the snow for at least an hour, no one comes to greet them.

"Are you sure this is the right place?" Donald says, and then finds that he is quite unable to stop himself sinking down on the ground and tearing off first one boot and then the other. He cannot bear the pain a single moment longer.

"Yes," Parker says.

"Perhaps it's been abandoned." Donald looks around at the desolate yard.

"No, not abandoned." Parker looks over at a thin coil of smoke rising from behind a low warehouse. The smoke is the same color as the sky. Donald heaves himself to his feet—superhuman effort—and staggers a few yards.

Then a man walks around the corner of a building and stops dead: a tall, dark-skinned man with powerful shoulders and long, wild hair. Despite the icy wind he wears only a loose flannel undershirt open to the waist. He stares at them with openmouthed and sullen incomprehension, his large body slack and apparently numb to the cold. Mrs. Ross is staring back at him as if she's seen a ghost. Parker starts to tell him that they have come a long way, that Donald is a Company man, but before he can finish the man turns and walks back the way he came, leaving Parker in midsentence. Parker looks at Mrs. Ross and shrugs. Donald hears her whisper to him, "I think that man is drunk," and smiles grimly to himself. Clearly she has little experience of winter pastimes at a quiet trading post.

The dogs, left outside the gate in their harness, are barking and working themselves into a frenzy. They seem incapable of standing still without breaking out into fights. Now, for instance, they seem to be trying to kill each other. Parker goes over to them and yells at them, lashing out with a stick, a tactic that is unpleasant to watch but effective. After another couple of minutes there are steps in the snow and another man comes around the corner. This, to Donald's relief, is a white man, possibly a little older than

Donald, with a pale, worried face and chaotic reddish hair. He looks harassed but sober.

"Good heavens," he says with obvious irritation. "So it's true . . ."

"Hello!" Donald is even more cheered to hear a Scottish accent.

"Well . . . welcome." The other man recovers a little. "Forgive me, it's such a long time since we had visitors, and in winter . . . extraordinary. I have quite forgotten my manners . . ."

"Donald Moody, Company accountant at Fort Edgar." Donald sticks out his hand, swaying.

"Ah, Mr. Moody. Er, Nesbit. Frank Nesbit, assistant factor."

Donald is momentarily troubled by the phrase "assistant factor," which is not a position he has ever heard of, but remembers himself enough to make a flourish toward Mrs. Ross. "This is Mrs. Ross, and that is"—Parker reappears in the gateway, a menacing figure with a large stick—"er, Parker, who has guided us here."

Nesbit shakes their hands, then gazes down at Donald's feet with horror. "My God, your feet . . . have you no boots?"

"Yes, but I have been in some discomfort, so I took them off, over there . . . It is nothing, though, really. Merely blisters, you know . . ."

Donald experiences a pleasantly light-headed sensation, and wonders if he is going to fall over. Nesbit shows no inclination to take them indoors, even though it is nearly dark and freezing hard. He seems nervous and jumpy, wondering out loud whether he can expect them to use the terribly neglected guest rooms, or whether he should turn himself out of his quarters . . . Eventually, after dithering for what seems to Donald like hours in which his feet, already cold, lose feeling altogether, he leads them around the corner and through a doorway. He leads them down an unlit corridor and opens the door of a large, unheated room.

"Perhaps you would be so good as to wait here for a moment. I will fetch someone to light the fire and bring you something hot. Excuse me . . ."

Nesbit withdraws, banging the door behind him. Donald hobbles over to the empty fireplace and sinks down into a chair beside it.

Parker disappears, claiming he has to see to the dogs. Donald thinks of Fort Edgar, where visitors are always a cause for celebration and treated like royalty. Perhaps half the staff here have deserted; he notices the fireplace is extremely dirty, before succumbing as the exhaustion that has been waiting to claim him closes his eyes like a velvet hand.

"Mr. Moody!"

Her voice is sharp, causing him to open his eyes again.

"Mm? Yes, Mrs. Ross?"

"Let us not say anything about why we are here, not tonight. Let us see how things are first. We do not want them to be on their guard."

"As you wish." He closes his eyes again. He cannot imagine holding a coherent conversation until he has had some sleep. Just to be out of the raw, cutting cold is bliss.

He shut his eyes for what felt like only a moment, but when he opens them again the fire is lit and Mrs. Ross is nowhere in sight. The window has turned black, and he has no idea of the time. But it is such a luxury to sit in this warmth that he cannot bring himself to move. Only if there were a bed; that would probably get him going. Then through his monumental tiredness he realizes there is someone else in the room. He turns to see a half-breed woman who has brought in a bowl of water and some bandages. She nods to him and sits on the floor by his feet, where she begins to unwrap the blood-crusted linen.

"Oh, thank you." Donald is somewhat embarrassed by this attention, and the disgusting state of the bandages. He tries and fails to stifle a jaw-cracking yawn. "My name is . . . Donald Moody, Company accountant at Fort Edgar. What is your name?"

"Elizabeth Bird."

She barely looks at him, but sets about cleaning the wounds on his feet. Donald allows his head to loll back against the chair, happy not to talk, or even think. His duties can wait until tomorrow. Before that, to the rhythm of the dark woman's hands wiping his feet, he can sleep and sleep and sleep.

THE COURTYARD IS COMPLETELY DARK, and I cannot hear dogs anywhere, which is odd. Normally, when dogs arrive at a place, there is a frenzied contest of barking and snarling, but when we came, there was silence. I call for Parker. A wind whips around me, and a few flakes of snow sting my face. There is no reply, and I experience a lurch of dread; perhaps now that we have arrived, he has gone on to wherever his business takes him. Just when I feel tears pricking at the back of my eyes, someone opens a door to my left and spills a rectangle of light onto the snow. There is a hurried, urgent argument, and I hear Nesbit's voice.

"You'd better not say anything about him if you don't want to feel my hand. In fact, it would be better if you just stayed out of the way altogether!"

The other voice is unclear—but it is a woman's voice, remonstrating with him. Without thinking clearly, I have moved deeper into the shadow of an overhanging eave. But nothing else is audible, until Nesbit finishes the argument, if that is what it is, with a querulous, "Oh, for God's sake, do as you like then. Just wait till he comes back!"

The door bangs shut and Nesbit starts across the courtyard, scrubbing one hand through his hair, which doesn't make it any tidier. I open and close the door behind me and step out into the courtyard to meet him, as though I had just that moment come outside.

"Oh, Mr. Nesbit, there you are . . ."

"Ah, Mrs. . . ." He stops dead, his hand groping in the air.

"Ross."

"Mrs. Ross, of course. Forgive me. I was just . . ." He gives a short laugh. "I apologize for abandoning you. Has no one lit the fire? You'll have to forgive us at the moment. We're a little short-staffed I'm afraid, and at this time of year . . ."

"There is no need to apologize. We have imposed rather suddenly on you."

"No imposition. No imposition at all. The Company prides itself on its hospitality and all that . . . More than welcome, I assure you." He smiles at me, although it seems to be something of an effort. "You must join me for dinner . . . and Mr. Moody and Mr. Parker as well, of course."

"Mr. Moody was asleep when I came out. I fear he has suffered a great deal with blisters."

"And you have not? I must say that is remarkable. Where did you say you have come from?"

"Why don't we go inside? It's so cold . . ."

I'm not sure how to broach this one. I wanted to talk to Parker about it, but Parker is nowhere to be seen. I follow Nesbit down another corridor— there seem to be any number of doors leading off it—into a small warm room where a fire burns in the grate. A Sutherland table sits in the center, with two chairs. Pinned to the walls are colored pictures of racehorses and prizefighters, cut from magazines.

"Please sit down, please. Yes. A bit warmer in here, eh? Nothing like a good fire in this god-awful place . . ."

He suddenly and without warning leaves the room, leaving me wondering what has just happened. I haven't opened my mouth.

Among the fighters and the horses are a couple of good prints, and I see that the furniture is also good—brought over, not country-made. The table is mahogany, burnished with use and age; the chairs fruitwood with lyre backs, possibly Italian. Above the fire is a small hunting scene in a rich gilded frame, dark and glowing with the red coats of the huntsmen. And there are glasses on the table of a heavy lead crystal, finely engraved with birds. There is a man here with taste and cultivation, and I suspect it isn't Nesbit.

Nesbit bursts back into the room with another chair. "Normally, you see"—he speaks as though he never left the room—"there are only the two of us—officers I mean, so we are very quiet. I have asked for some supper, so . . . Ah-ha, of course!" He springs up again, having just sat down. "You'd like a glass of brandy, I expect. We have some that is rather good. I brought it myself, from Kingston, summer before last."

"Just a small glass. I fear, any more, and I will fall asleep on the spot." This is the truth. The warmth is soaking into my limbs for the first time in days, making my eyes heavy.

He pours two glasses, taking considerable trouble to make sure the levels are the same in each, and hands me one of them.

"Well, *slainthé*. And what brings you and your friends here—this unexpected but welcome pleasure?"

I put down my glass carefully. It's annoying that we didn't have time to discuss our story before arriving; or rather, not that we didn't have time, since we had six days, but that somehow it never seemed the right time to bring it up. I run over my story one more time, testing it for weaknesses. I hope Moody doesn't wake up for a long time.

"We have come from Himmelvanger—do you know it?"

Nesbit stares at me with intense brown eyes. "No, no, I don't believe I do."

"It is home to a group of Lutherans. Norwegians. They are endeavoring to build a community where they can live good lives in the sight of God."

"Admirable."

The fingers of his right hand fidget ceaselessly with a stub of pencil, flicking it back and forth, twirling it around, drumming it faintly on the table; and something clicks into place. Laudanum, or perhaps strychnine. God knows what misfortune brought him all the way up here, far from druggists and doctors.

"We undertook this journey because . . ." I stop and sigh heavily. "This is painful to relate . . . my son ran away from home. He was last seen at Himmelvanger, and from there, there was a trail that led in this direction."

Nesbit's face, his eyes so intently on me it makes my skin crawl, relaxes a little. Perhaps he was waiting for something else after all.

"A trail in this direction? All the way here?"

"It seemed so, although after the snowstorm we could not be certain."

"No." He nods his head thoughtfully.

"But Mr. Parker thought this the most likely place. There are not many settlements in this part of the country, I believe—in fact, very few."

"No, we are quite isolated. Is he . . . very young, your son?"

"Seventeen." I drop my eyes. "You can understand how worried I am."

"Yes, of course. And Mr. Moody . . . ?"

"Mr. Moody kindly offered to accompany us since we were coming to a Company post. I believe he is anxious to meet your factor."

"Ah, yes. I am sure . . . Well, Mr. Stewart has gone on a short trip, but he should return in the next day or so."

"You have neighbors?"

"No, he has gone hunting. It is a keen interest of his."

Nesbit has already drained and refilled his glass. I sip mine slowly. "So . . . you have not seen or heard of any stranger?"

"Alas, no. No one at all. But perhaps he may have met an Indian band, or some trappers . . . All sorts of people do come and go. You'd be surprised, even in winter, how people gad about."

I sigh again, and look despondent, which is not difficult. He takes my glass and refills it.

The door opens, and a short, broad Indian woman of indeterminate age comes in with a tray.

"The other man, he wants to sleep," she says, with a baleful look at Nesbit.

"Yes, all right, Norah. Well, put it down . . . thank you. Could you see if you could possibly locate the other visitor?"

There is a trace of sarcasm in his voice. The woman dumps the tray on the table with a crash.

With clumsy panache Nesbit uncovers the tray and serves me a plate of moose steak and corn hash. The plate itself is good, English, but the steak is old and gristly, not much better than the stuff we have been eating on our journey. I have to struggle to keep my eyes open and my wits about me. Nesbit eats little but drinks steadily, so fortunately his perceptions are not the sharpest. I feel an urgent need to get him to talk now, tonight, while he still has no reason to suspect.

"So, who lives here? Are you a large company?"

"Lord, no! We are very small. This is not exactly the heart of fur country. Not anymore." He smiles bitterly, but not, I think, from any thwarted personal ambition. "There is Mr. Stewart, the factor, and he is one of the finest men you could hope to meet. Then there is your humble servant, general dogsbody . . . !" He sketches a sardonic bow. "And then there are several half-breed and native families around the place."

"So that woman who came in, Norah—she is the wife of one of your men?"

"That's right." Nesbit takes a swig of brandy.

"And what do the voyageurs do in winter?" I think of the half-dressed man in the courtyard. He could barely stand. Nesbit seems to read my thoughts.

"Ah, well, when there is little to do, like now, I'm afraid they are . . . prey to temptations. The winters are very long."

His eyes have lost their focus and look glassy and bloodshot, though whether from alcohol or something else, I don't know.

"But people travel around, even so . . ."

"Oh yes, there is hunting and so on, for the men—and Mr. Stewart . . . Not my cup of tea." He makes an elegant expression of distaste. "A little trapping, of course. We take what we can get."

"And has anyone from here come up from the southwest recently? I just wonder whether the trail we saw could be one of your men, and not my son. Then we would know to . . . look elsewhere." I try to keep my voice as neutral as possible, but tinged with sadness.

"One of ours . . . ?" He assumes a look of extreme vagueness, his brow almost comically furrowed. But then, he is drunk. "I can't think . . . no, not that I know of. I could ask . . ."

He smiles at me frankly. I think he's lying, but I'm so tired it's hard to be sure of anything. The longing to lie down and sleep has suddenly become as imperative as a physical pain. After another minute I can't fight it any longer.

"I am sorry, Mr. Nesbit, but I . . . have to retire."

Nesbit stands up and grips my arm, as though he thinks I am about to fall, or run away. Even the sudden chill in the corridor cannot rouse me.

Something wakes me. It is almost dark, and silent except for the wind. For an instant I think that there is someone else in the room, and I sit up with an exclamation I can't control. As my eyes grow accustomed to the near-dark, I realize there is no one there. It is not yet dawn. But something woke me, and I am alert, heart hammering, ears sensitive to the slightest sound. I slip out of bed and pull on the few clothes I took off before succumbing. I pick up the lamp but somehow don't want to light it. I tiptoe to the door. No one outside either.

Creaks and whines come from the roof timbers, the hum of wind slipping under shingles. And a strange crackling noise, very light and indistinct. I listen at each door for a long moment before turning the handle and peering inside. One is locked; most are empty, but through a window in one of the empty rooms I see a greenish shimmer outside, a flickering curtain of light in the north that perforates the darkness and gives me this dim sight.

I open one door and see Moody, his face young and vulnerable without his spectacles. I close it quickly. Parker, I think. I must find Parker. I need to talk to him. About what I am doing, and before I do something inconceivably stupid. But behind the next few doors I find nothing, then one gives me a shiver of shock. Nesbit is lying in a fathomless sleep, or stupor, and next to him lies the Indian woman who served dinner, one broad arm flung over his chest, dark against his milk-white skin. Their breathing is loud. I had formed the impression that she hated him, but here they are, and there is an innocence about their tainted sleep that is curiously touching. I look for longer than I mean to and then, not that they are going to wake all of a sudden, I close the door with especial care.

At last I find Parker, where I half expected: in the stables near the dogs. He is rolled into a blanket and sleeps facing the door. Suddenly at a loss, I light the lamp and sit down to wait. Although we have slept under the same few yards of canvas for many nights, under a wooden roof it seems improper that I should be watching him sleep, crouched in the straw beside him like this, like a thief.

After a few moments, the light wakes him.

"Mr. Parker, it is I, Mrs. Ross."

He seems to surface quickly, without experiencing the impenetrable fog that surrounds me on waking. His face is as unreadable as ever; apparently he is neither angry nor surprised to see me here.

"Has something happened?"

I shake my head. "Something woke me, but I couldn't find anything. Where did you go last night?"

"I saw to the dogs."

I wait for something else, but nothing comes.

"I had dinner with Nesbit. He asked what we were doing. I said we were looking for my son, who has run away, and was last seen at Himmelvanger. I asked him if anyone here has recently returned from a trip, and he said he didn't know. But I don't think he was entirely frank."

Parker leans against the stable wall and looks at me thoughtfully. "I spoke to a man and his wife. They said that no one had been away recently, but they were unhappy. When they spoke, they looked into the distance, or over my shoulder."

I don't know what to make of this. Then, very faint but distinct, as though from a great distance, I hear something that sends a cold prickling up my spine. An ethereal howling, mournful yet indifferent. A symphony of howls. The dogs wake, and a low growling comes from the corner of the stable. I glance at Parker, at his black eyes.

"Wolves?"

"Far away."

I know that we are surrounded by strong walls, and that those walls are armed with cannon, but still the sound chills my blood. I experience a nostalgia for the cramped quarters of the tent. I felt safer there. It is even possible that I shiver, and move closer to Parker.

"They are short of things here. The hunting is bad. There isn't much food."

"How can that be? This is a Company post."

He shakes his head. "There are posts that are badly run."

I think of Nesbit in his narcotic cradle. If he is in charge of administrating the post and its supplies, that is hardly surprising.

"Nesbit is an addict. Opium or something like that. And . . ." I look at the straw. "He . . . has a liaison with one of the Indian women."

I am certain that I am trying not to, but I find myself looking into Parker's eyes for a second that lengthens and grows into a minute. Neither of us says anything; it's as if we are mesmerized. I am suddenly aware that my breathing sounds very loud, and I am sure he can hear my heart beating. Even the wolves are silent, listening. I tear my eyes away at last, feeling light-headed.

"I had better go back. I just thought I should find you to . . . discuss what we should do in the morning. I thought it wise to conceal our true reason for being here. I said as much to Mr. Moody, though what he will want to do tomorrow I can't say."

"I don't think we will know more until Stewart comes back."

"What is it you know of him?"

After a pause, Parker shakes his head. "I won't know until I see him."

I wait for a moment, but I have run out of reasons to stay. As I make to stand up, my arm brushes against his leg in the straw. I didn't know his leg was there, I swear it, or whether he moved it to brush against me. I leap to my feet as if scalded, and pick up the lamp. In the sway of light and shadow, I cannot tell what is on his face.

"Well, good night then."

I walk out into the yard quickly, aware and hurt that he did not reply. The cold instantly cools my skin but can do nothing for my churning thoughts, chiefly an intense desire to go back into the stable and lie down in the straw next to him. To lose myself in his scent and his warmth. What is this—my fear and helplessness overtaking me? His body brushing against mine in the straw was a mistake. A mistake. A man has died; Francis needs my help; that is why I am here, no other reason.

The aurora shimmers in the North like a beautiful dream, and the wind has gone. The sky is vertiginously high and clear, and the deep cold is back—a taut, ringing cold that says there is nothing between me and the infinite depth of space. I crane skyward long after it sends me dizzy. I am aware that I am walking a precarious path, surrounded on all sides by uncertainty and the possibility of disaster. Nothing is within my control. The sky yawns above me like the abyss, and there is nothing at all to stop me from falling, nothing except the wild maze of stars.

DONALD WAKES TO DAYLIGHT OUTSIDE the window. For several moments he cannot remember where he is, and then it comes back to him: the end of the trail of footprints. A respite from that hellish journey. Every inch of his body aches as if he has suffered a severe beating.

God . . . did he really just fall unconscious last night—out like a light? That woman who tended to his feet . . . he sticks a foot out from under the covers and sees that it is freshly dressed, so she was real and not a dream. Did she undress him as well? He remembers nothing but feels a prickling shame wash over him. He is, without a doubt, thoroughly undressed. His scar has even been salved and bandaged. He fumbles around the bed until he locates his spectacles. With them back on his nose, he feels calmer, more in control. Inside: a small room, sparsely furnished like the guest quarters at Fort Edgar. Outside: bleak, not snowing, but soon will. And somewhere within the complex of buildings: Mrs. Ross and Parker, asking questions without him. Heaven knows what they will say to Mr. Stewart, left to their own devices. He struggles to get out of bed, and picks up his clothes, which have been laid neatly over a chair. He dresses, moving stiffly like an old man. Strange (and yet in a way fortunate) how much worse he feels now that they have finally arrived.

He shuffles out into the corridor and works his way around two sides of the inner courtyard without seeing a living soul. It is the strangest Company post; there is none of the bustle he is used to at Fort Edgar. He wonders where Stewart is, what sort of discipline he keeps. His watch has stopped, and he doesn't know what time it is, whether early or late. Finally, a door flies open farther down the corridor, and Nesbit emerges, slamming it behind him. He is unshaven and hollow-eyed, but dressed.

"Ah, Mr. Moody! I hope you are rested. How are your, ah, feet?"

"Much better. The . . . Elizabeth dressed them for me, very kindly. I fear I was too tired to thank her."

"Come and have breakfast. They should have managed to light a fire and get something under way by now. God knows it's hard enough to get the devils to do anything in winter. Do you have these problems at your place?"

"Fort Edgar?"

"Yes. Where is that?"

Donald is surprised that he doesn't know. "On Georgian Bay."

"How civilized. I dream of being posted somewhere within shouting distance of . . . well, somewhere people live. You must find us very poor in comparison."

Nesbit leads Donald into the room where they had been first brought, but now the fire is burning and a table and chairs have been brought from elsewhere; Donald can see drag marks in the dust on the floor. Housekeeping is clearly not the priority here. He is not sure what is.

"Are Mrs. Ross and Mr. Parker about?"

As Nesbit goes to the door, Mrs. Ross comes in. She has managed to do something to her clothes that makes them look halfway presentable, and her hair is neatly dressed. The slight thaw he detected after the snowstorm seems to have ended.

"Mr. Moody."

"Capital! You are here . . . And Mr. Parker?"

"I am not sure." She drops her eyes and Nesbit goes out, calling for the Indian woman. Mrs. Ross comes swiftly over to Donald, her face tense.

"We must talk before Nesbit comes back. Last night I told him we are here to look for my son who has run away, not to look for a murderer. We should not put them on their guard."

Donald gapes in astonishment. "My dear lady, I wish you had consulted me before inventing an untruth—"

"There was no time. Don't say anything else or he will be suspicious. It is best for us if they suspect nothing, you must agree with that?" Her jaw is tight, and her eyes hard as stones.

"And what if . . . ?" He breaks off his whisper as Nesbit comes back in, followed by Norah with a tray. They both smile at him, and Donald feels it must be obvious that they were whispering furtively. With any luck Nesbit will assume their secret is of a romantic nature . . . he finds himself blushing at the thought. Perhaps he has a touch of fever. As he sits at the table he reminds himself, with a conscious effort of will, of Susannah. Strange that he has not thought of her in a while.

Parker arrives, and when they are all eating grilled steaks and corn bread—Donald as if he hadn't eaten for days—Nesbit explains that Stewart is on a hunting trip with one of the men, and apologizes for the poor hospitality. However, he is very proud of one thing: he speaks sharply to Norah about the coffee she brought, and she silently takes it away and comes back with a pot of something entirely different. The smell precedes her into the room—the aroma of real coffee beans, such as none of them have smelled for weeks. And when Donald tastes it, he realizes that perhaps he has never drunk anything like this before. Nesbit leans back in his chair and smiles broadly.

"Beans from South America. I bought them in New York when I was on my way over. I only grind them for special occasions."

"How long have you been here, Mr. Nesbit?" This from Mrs. Ross.

"Four years and five months. You're from Edinburgh, are you not?"

"Originally." Somehow she makes one word sound like a reprimand.

"And you're from Perth, if I'm not mistaken?" Donald smiles at him, anxious to make amends. Then he glares at Mrs. Ross; if she does not want to arouse suspicions, she should be more gracious.

"Kincardine."

There is a silence. Mrs. Ross returns Donald's stare coolly.

"I'm sorry we can't help you with Mrs. Ross's errant son. That must be a worry."

"Ah. Yes." Donald nods, embarrassed; acting is not his forte. And angry with her for taking the initiative away from him, who should be leading in a matter to do with the Company. He feels at a loss to know how to proceed.

"So, you think . . ." Donald begins, but just then there is a rapid thudding in the corridor, and a shout from outside. Nesbit is suddenly alert, like an animal, senses straining, and he gets up with a jerky movement. He turns to them with a half smile, although it is more like a grimace.

"I think, my dears—that may be Mr. Stewart returning now."

He almost runs from the room. Donald and the others are left looking at one another. Donald feels slighted—why did Nesbit not invite them, or at least him, outside? He is aware of a nagging sense of wrongness, which leaves him floundering, without rules. After a moment's silence, Donald excuses himself with a murmur, and hesitantly follows Nesbit out into the courtyard.

Four or five men and women are gathered in a knot around a man with a sled and a tangle of dogs. More figures appear from different directions, some hanging back near the buildings, some going right up to the newcomer. Donald has time to wonder where they have all come from; most of them he has never seen before, although he recognizes the tall woman who washed his feet last night. The newcomer, stout with furs, his face hidden under a fur hood, is talking to the group, and then a silence falls. Donald alone keeps walking toward them, and a couple of faces turn to him, staring as if he were something outlandish. He stops, confused, and then the tall woman, who has been in the first group all the time, lets out a long, high-pitched wail. She sinks down in a heap on the snow, making a high, thin, otherworldly noise that is neither scream nor sob. It goes on and on. No one attempts to comfort her.

One of the men appears to remonstrate with Stewart, who shrugs him off and walks toward the buildings. Nesbit speaks sharply to the man and follows his superior. When he sees Donald, he glares at him, then recalls himself and beckons him to come back inside. His face is the same color as the dirty snow.

"What's going on?" Donald mutters when they are out of earshot of the men in the yard.

Nesbit's mouth is pressed into a hard line. "Most unfortunate. Nepapanees has met with an accident. Fatal. His wife was outside there."

He sounds more angry than anything else. As if he is thinking: what now?

"You mean the woman on the ground . . . Elizabeth? Her husband is dead?"

Nesbit nods. "Sometimes I think we are cursed."

It is muttered, half to himself. Then Nesbit abruptly turns around, effectively blocking the way down the corridor to Donald. However, he attempts to smile.

"This is most unfortunate, but . . . why don't you rejoin the others? Enjoy your breakfast . . . I need to speak to Mr. Stewart now, under the circumstances. We will join you later."

Donald feels he has no option but to nod, and watches Nesbit's back disappear around a corner. He hovers in the corridor, puzzled and disturbed. There was something almost obscene about the way Nesbit, and Stewart himself, brushed aside the grief of the others, as though they wanted nothing to do with it.

Instead of going back to the breakfast room, he returns to the courtyard, where snow has started to fall in a concentrated silence, as if to say, this is winter now; this is no joke. Its flakes are tiny and quick, and seem to come at him from every direction, blurring visibility over a few yards. Only the bereaved woman is still outside where she sits, rocking back and forth. The others are nowhere to be seen. Donald is angry with them for leaving her alone. The woman is not even wearing outdoor clothes, for heaven's sake, just her indoor dress, which leaves her arms bare below the elbow. He goes up to her.

She is half kneeling, rocking, silent now, her eyes wide but fixed on nothing, tearing her hair. She does not look at him. He is horrified to see the bare flesh above her moccasin mottled against the snow.

"Excuse me . . . Mrs. Bird." He feels awkward, but can think of no other way to address her. "You will freeze out here. Please come inside."

She gives no indication that she has heard him.

"Elizabeth. You were kind to me last night . . . Please come in. I know you are stricken. Allow me to help you."

He puts out a hand, hoping she will take it, but nothing happens. Snowflakes cling to her lashes and hair, melt on her arms. She does not brush them away. Donald is struck, looking at her, by her thin face, her fine, almost English features. But then some half-breeds are like that, more white than Indian.

"Please . . ." He puts a hand on her arm, and suddenly the thin keening wail rises again. He draws back in alarm—such a strange, ghostly noise, like an animal. He loses courage. After all, what does he know about her, or her dead husband? What can he say to alleviate her pain?

Donald looks around, for assistance, or witnesses. There is no sign of movement through the dizzying snow, although, at a window opposite, he sees an indistinct figure, who seems to be watching.

He stands up—he has been squatting—and decides to find someone else. Perhaps a woman friend can persuade her to come inside; he does not feel it is his place to force or carry her. He is sure Jacob would know what to do, but Jacob is not here. He brushes the snow off his trousers and walks away from the widow, though he cannot go without glancing back at her. She is a black shape half hidden by the snow, like a demented figure in a Japanese print. He has a happy idea: he will bring some of that coffee out to her—it is the least Nesbit can do. He is sure she will not drink it, but perhaps she will be glad he did so.

LINE LIES AWAKE, FULLY DRESSED, staring at the curtainless window. Torbin and Anna are asleep beside her. She has said nothing to them, not trusting them to keep such a secret. Shortly she will wake them and get them dressed, making it seem like an adventure. They know nothing of her plans. She won't tell them until they are well away from Himmelvanger. She wishes they had made the rendezvous earlier—everyone has been asleep for over an hour. An hour of travel wasted. She is uncomfortably hot, as she has put on layers of petticoats under two skirts, and all her shirts, one on top of another, until her arms look like tightly packed sausages. Espen will be doing the same. A good thing it is winter. She glances at the clock again, turns the hands to suit herself; she can't wait any longer. She leans over and wakes her children.

"Listen, we are going on a holiday. But it's very important to keep really, really quiet. All right?"

Anna blinks sullenly. "I want to sleep."

"You can sleep later. Now we are having an adventure. Come on, put these on, quick as you can."

"Where are we going?" Torbin seems more excited. "It's dark outside."

"It's nearly dawn, look—five o'clock. You've been asleep for hours and hours. We have to start early if we're going to get there today."

She tugs Anna's dress over her head.

"I want to stay."

"Ach, Anna." Barely five years old; where did she get to be so stubborn? "Put this dress on on top of that one. It's going to be cold. And this way, there will be less to carry."

"Where are we going?"

"South. Where it's warmer."

"Can Elke come?" Elke is Torbin's best friend and Britta's daughter.

"Maybe later. Maybe some other people will come, too."

"I'm hungry." Anna is not happy and wants everyone to know it. Line gives her and Torbin a cookie each, stolen for just this occasion, to buy their silence.

At ten to, she swears them to silence and listens in the corridor for a whole minute before pulling them after her. She closes the door on the room that has been their home for the past three years. All is quiet. The heavy bag containing food and the few personal items she cannot bear to leave bumps against her back. They cross the courtyard to the stable. It is black dark without a moon, and she stumbles, cursing. Torbin gasps at the word she uses, but there is no time to worry about that. Line feels a thousand eyes on her back, the fear making her grip their hands too tight, until Anna whimpers.

"I'm sorry, darling. Here we are, look." She opens the door to the stable. Even darker, but warmer, with the sounds of the horses stomping in their hay. She pauses, listening for him.

"Espen?"

He's not here yet, but they are a few minutes early. She hopes he does not cut it too fine. They could have been riding away from here for the past hour, getting farther from Himmelvanger with every step. She sits the children down in an empty stall.

Only a few minutes more, and Espen will be here.

She owns no watch, but has a fair idea of time passing by the numbness of her fingers and toes, and her fingers are like ice. The children fidgeted for a while, but now Anna has curled up and gone to sleep, and Torbin leans against her in a half-waking doze. It must be at least an hour since they came, and no one has come into the stable. At first she told herself: he's always late. He can't help it. Then she began to think, maybe he thought it was two o'clock, maybe he made a mistake. Then, as the hour crawled past and still no one came, she imagined that Merete had not been able to sleep, and that, what with the baby or an illness or something, had made it impossible for him to leave. Maybe he was lying awake, cursing and worrying about her.

And then, maybe he never intended to come at all.

She contemplates this bleak possibility. No. He would not let her down like that. Would not. Will not.

She will give him another chance—or shame him in front of them all. She shakes the children awake, more roughly than is necessary.

"Listen. There has been a delay. It turns out we cannot leave tonight after all. We will have to go tomorrow night. I'm sorry . . ." She cuts off their predictable complaints. "I'm sorry, but that's just the way it is."

She remembers using that phrase when telling them their father was never going to come back and they had to go and live in the middle of nowhere. "There's no point complaining. That's just the way it is."

She swears them to secrecy—if they tell anyone about this, they won't be able to go on holiday at all, and she has painted a picture of the warm south that appeals to both of them. Hopefully one day they might even be able to go there.

As she stands up and starts to usher them back to their bedroom—at least it is still dark—there is a movement near the door. She freezes, and the children freeze, too, infected by her sudden fear. Then a voice:

"Is someone there?"

For a moment—the shortest fragment of a second—she believes it is Espen, and her heart leaps. Then she realizes the voice was not his. They have been discovered.

The man walks toward them. Line is immobile with the shock. What can she possibly say? It takes her another second to realize that he spoke English, not Norwegian. It is the half-breed, Jacob. She isn't lost, not yet. He lights a lamp and holds it in the air between them.

"Oh, Mrs. . . ." Then he realizes that he doesn't know, or can't pronounce, her name. "Hello, Torbin. Hello, Anna."

"I'm sorry if we have disturbed you," Line says stiffly. What is he doing here? Does he sleep in the stable?

"No, not at all."

"Well, then. Good night." She smiles and walks past him; then, when the children are walking in front of her across the yard, she turns back.

"Please, it is most important to say nothing of this, to anyone. Anyone at all. I beg you . . . or my life is not worth living, I cannot stress this too much. Can I trust you?"

Jacob has put out the lantern, as if appreciating the need for secrecy. "Yes." he says simply. He does not even sound curious. "You can trust me."

Line helps the children undress and watches as they fall asleep. She is too agitated to sleep. She pushes the bag behind a chair. She cannot bear to unpack; it seems too much like an admission of failure. In the morning she will have to strew clothes around to disguise it; hopefully that will fool anyone who chooses to look in. Oh, to go somewhere where she has her own house, with doors you can lock. She detests this lack of privacy; it chafes like a bridle.

At breakfast she is wary, showing her bland and cheerful mask to the community. She does not even glance toward Espen until halfway through the meal, and then his head is bowed. He does not look in her direction. She tries to assess whether he or Merete looks particularly tired, but it is hard to tell. The baby is crying, so perhaps it has colic. She will have to bide her time.

It is afternoon when she gets her chance. He comes to her when she is feeding the chickens. One minute he is there, although she did not see him arrive. She waits for him to speak.

"Line, I'm sorry. I'm so sorry. I don't know what to tell you . . . Merete couldn't sleep for hours, and I didn't know what to do." He is fidgeting, restless, his eyes everywhere but on her. Line sighs.

"Well, it's all right. I made up some story for the children. We will go tonight. One o'clock."

He is silent for a moment.

"Have you changed your mind?"

He sighs. She finds she is trembling.

"Because if you have, I won't go without you. I will stay, and I will tell everyone that I am carrying your child. I will shame you in front of everyone. In front of your wife and children. If Per turns me out, I don't care. We might freeze to death. Your child will die, and I will die. And you will be responsible. Are you prepared for that?"

Espen's face goes pale. "Line, don't say such things! That's awful . . . I wasn't going to say I wouldn't come. It's just hard, that's all. What I have to leave behind . . . you don't have to leave anything behind."

"Do you love her?"

"Who? Merete? You know I don't. I love you."

"Tonight at one, then. If Merete can't sleep you will just have to think of an excuse."

His face is resigned. It is going to be all right. It is just that he is a man who needs to be led, as many do.

* * *

Still, Line does not know how she gets through the remaining hours of the day. She cannot sit still, and observing her restless fidgeting as they sew their quilts, Britta says, "What's the matter, girl? Ants in your pants?" It is all Line can do to smile.

But finally, of course, finally it is one o'clock and they are on their way to the stables. As soon as they push the door closed, she can feel that Espen is there. His voice whispers her name in the dark.

"It is us," she replies.

He lights a lamp and smiles at the children, who look at him with a doubtful, suspicious shyness.

"Are you looking forward to your holiday?"

"Why do we have to go in the middle of the night? Are we running away?" This from sharp Torbin.

"Of course not. We need to leave early, so that we can cover a good distance before it gets dark again. This is the way people travel in winter."

"Hurry up, no more chatter. You'll see when we get there." Line is worried, and her voice is sharp.

Espen straps their bags behind the saddles—he has already made the horses ready. Line feels a surge of fondness for the stout, slow-moving creatures; they do whatever is asked of them, without fuss or argument, even at one o'clock in the morning. They lead them outside, where the yard is so muddy their hooves make no noise. There are no lights in the whole of Himmelvanger, but they lead the horses to a copse of scrub birch, out of view of any windows, before Espen helps the children and Line onto the horses' backs and then springs into the saddle behind Torbin. Line has a stolen compass in her hand.

"We go southeast to start with." She looks up at the sky. "Look, there are stars. They will help us. We are going toward that one there, see?"

"Aren't you going to ask God to bless our journey?" Torbin squirms around to look at his mother. He can be a pedantic boy at times, always wanting to be correct, and he has lived at Himmelvanger for three years, where you barely move without saying a quick prayer.

"Of course. I was just about to."

Espen reins in his mount, and drops his head. Mutters quickly, as though Per's pious ears can pick up a prayer for miles around, "May the Lord God who is King of all there is in heaven and on earth, who sees and protects all, watch over us in our journey, guide us safe from dangers, and keep us on the right path. Amen."

Line digs her heels into her horse's sides. The dark mass of Himmelvanger grows smaller and smaller behind them. With the clear sky, it has gotten cold. Much colder than the night before. They have left just in time.

EVER SINCE HER FATHER CAME home after his incarceration, he has seemed a different man. He sits alone in his study, not reading or writing letters or in other ways occupying himself, but staring out the window for long periods without moving. Maria knows this because she has peered in through the study keyhole, having been forbidden to disturb him. It is not like him to cut himself off from her, and she is worried.

Susannah is also worried, but for different reasons. Of course she is concerned for her father and his peculiar behavior, but he still takes all his meals with the family, and is cheerful enough. It's not as though, as she says to her sister, he can go on with his magisterial duties at the moment; so what else should he be doing? No, Susannah has decided to become passionately concerned for Donald. He and Jacob have been gone for three weeks, which is not particularly long, although they did expect to be back sooner. Maria and Susannah have speculated on the reason. The most obvious answer is that they have not found Francis Ross. If he were dead, they would have returned. Likewise if they had found him nearby.

"But what if they found Francis, and he killed them to escape justice?" Susannah asks with rounded eyes, on the verge of tears.

Maria is scornful. "Can you really see Francis Ross killing Mr. Moody and Jacob, when they are both armed? Besides, he wouldn't have the strength. He's no taller than you. Really, that's about the most absurd thing I've ever heard."

"Maria . . ." her mother remonstrates from the chair where she does her sewing.

Susannah shrugs, irritated. "I just think they would have sent a message before now."

"If there are no people to carry messages, it's impossible."

"Oh, it's not as though they are in the middle of . . . Outer Mongolia."

"Actually, Mongolia is far more densely populated than Canada," Maria can't stop herself from saying.

"If that is supposed to reassure me, well . . . it doesn't!" Susannah gets up and walks out of the sitting room, slamming the door.

"You could be kinder," says Mrs. Knox, mildly. "She is worried."

Maria bites back a rejoinder. She may be worried, too, but as usual everyone is more concerned for Susannah's emotional state than her own.

"The fact is, it is worrying. One would have expected to get some sort of message by now. In a way I'm surprised the Company hasn't sent someone to look for them."

"Well, in my experience"—Mrs. Knox bites off a thread with a snap—"bad news always travels fastest."

The atmosphere in the house is stifling, what with her father sitting like a sphinx in his study, and Susannah's tears, and her mother's weird calm. Maria decides she needs to get away from them all. The truth is, she was slightly disturbed by her own reaction to the discussion about Moody. She, too, has been wondering what has happened to them, and hoping that he is all right, just as you would be concerned about any friend you haven't heard from in a while. It doesn't mean anything. But she has been thinking about his face, surprised at the detail that has remained with her: the freckles high on his cheekbones, the way his spectacles slip down his nose, and the humorous smile whenever he is asked a question, as though he doubts his ability to answer it, but is prepared to have a go anyway.

She reaches the store with a few inches of icy mud clinging to her boots and skirt. Mrs. Scott is behind the counter, and lifts her head only a fraction when Maria comes in. When she greets her, Maria catches sight of a swollen, yellowing bruise high on her left cheekbone, spoiling the perfect symmetry of her face. Mrs. Scott—or Rachel Spence, as she was once known—played the Virgin Mary in the school nativity. Older townspeople still remind her of it, but it is a long time since they inquired after one of the frequent accidents she seems to suffer nowadays.

Mr. Sturrock is in his room. Maria waits by the stove downstairs, not certain that he will see her, but he comes down a minute later.

"Miss Knox. To what do I owe the pleasure?"

"Mr. Sturrock. Boredom, I'm afraid."

He shrugs elegantly, taking it in the spirit in which it was meant. "I am glad of it, if it brings you here."

There is something about his expression that makes her slightly self-conscious. If he were a younger man, she would suspect him of making love to her. Perhaps he is. She thinks it would be typical if the only male interest she elicits is from a man older than her father.

Sturrock calls for coffee and then says, "Would you think it very improper if I were to invite you up to my room? Only there is something I would very much like to show you."

"No, I would not think it improper." And, the strange thing is, despite her suspicions, she doesn't.

His room is musty, but clean. He clears the table by the window of a pile of papers, and arranges the two chairs. Maria sits down, enjoying his attentions. He must have been a remarkably handsome man when young, and indeed is still so, with his thick silver hair and clear blue eyes. She smiles at herself for her foolishness.

The view from the window is of the street in front of the store, excellent for a watcher of human traffic. Everyone in Caulfield comes to the store sooner or later. Even her own house is partially visible in the distance, and obliquely beyond, the expanse of gray water brooding under low cloud.

"Hardly palatial, but I find it serves."

"Are you working here?"

"In a manner of speaking." He sits down, and pushes a piece of paper toward her. "What do you think of that?"

Maria picks up the page, torn, not freshly, from a notebook. It has pencil marks on it, but at first she cannot decide which way up it is meant to go. There are small angular marks—mainly lines in various configurations: diagonals, parallels, and so on. Around these marks are sketched a few small stick figures, but in no discernible pattern. She studies it carefully.

"I am sorry to disappoint you, but I can make nothing of it. Is it complete?"

"Yes—as far as I know. It is copied from a whole piece, but there may of course be others."

"Copied from what? It's not Babylonian, is it, although in some ways it looks rather like cuneiform writing."

"That was my first thought also. But it isn't Babylonian, or hieroglyphics, or Linear Greek. Nor is it Sanskrit, or Hebrew, or Aramaic, or Arabic."

Maria smiles; he is setting her a puzzle, and she likes puzzles. "Well, it isn't

Chinese or Japanese. I don't know, I don't recognize it—these figures . . . Is it an African language of some sort?"

He shakes his head. "I would be impressed if you could. This is something that I have taken to museums and universities and shown to many experts on languages, and none of them had any idea what it was."

"And something makes you think that it is more than a . . . an abstract pattern? I mean, these figures look quite childish."

"I fear that is more to do with my lack of skill at reproducing them. The originals have a definite presence. As you said, this is only part of it. But yes, I do think it is more than a few scratches."

"Scratches?"

"The original is cut into a piece of bone, and colored with some black pigment, possibly a soot mixture. It is very carefully done. There are these figures all around the outside, in a chain. I think the marks are a language and record an event of some sort, and the figures illustrate it."

"Really? You deduced all that? Where is the original?"

"I wish I knew. It was promised to me by the man who owned it, but . . ." He shrugs. Maria watches him closely.

"This man . . . was it Jammet?"

"Well done."

She feels a thrill of satisfaction. "So then it will be with his effects, won't it?"

"It has gone."

"Gone? You mean, stolen?"

"I cannot say. It was either stolen, or he sold it or gave it to someone else. But I think the last two are unlikely; he said he would keep it for me."

"So . . . are you waiting to see if Mr. Moody brings it back?"

"It may be a vain hope, but, yes."

Maria looks at the paper again. "You know, it does remind me of something . . . or rather, the figures do. I'm not sure what, though. I can't remember."

"I would be grateful if you would try."

"Please, Mr. Sturrock, put me out of my misery. What is it?"

"I regret I cannot. I do not know."

"But you have an idea."

"Yes. This may sound fantastical, but . . . I have a—well, I suppose hope is the best word. I have a hope that it is an Indian language."

"You mean . . . American Indian? But there are no written Indian languages—everyone knows that."

"Perhaps there were once."

Maria absorbs what he has said. He looks entirely serious.

"How old is the original?"

"Well—I would need to have it to find out."

"Do you know where it came from?"

"No, and it will be hard to find out, now."

"So . . ." She considers her words carefully, not wanting to offend him. "Of course, you have thought of the possibility that it could be a fake?"

"I have. But fakes are generally only made where there is something to be gained by it. Where there is a market for such artifacts. Why would anyone go to the quite considerable trouble of making something that has no value?"

"But it is the reason you are here, in Caulfield, isn't it? So you must believe in it."

"I am not rich." He smiles, self-mocking. "But there is always the possibility—however slight—that it is genuine."

Maria smiles again, unsure what she thinks. Her natural skepticism is a barrier put up to protect herself from ridicule, and it is her way to play devil's advocate. But she is afraid that he is following a false trail.

"Those figures . . . they do remind me of Indian drawings I have seen. Calendars, and so on, you know."

"You are not convinced."

"I don't know. Perhaps if I saw the original . . ."

"Of course, you would need that. You are right, that is why I am here. It is an interest of mine, Indian affairs and history. I used to write articles. I was known for it, in a small way. I do believe"—he pauses, glances out of the window—"I do believe that if the Indians had a written culture, their treatment at our hands would have been different."

"You may be right."

"I had a friend, an Indian friend, who used to talk of such a possibility. You see, it is not entirely unheard of."

If Sturrock is disappointed by her response, he does not show it. Feeling as though she has been harsh, she reaches for it.

"May I copy it? If you would allow—I could take it away and . . . try some things."

"What sort of things?"

"Writing is a code, isn't it? And any code may be broken." She shrugs, disclaiming any expertise in that area. Sturrock smiles and pushes it over to her.

"Of course, you are more than welcome. I have tried myself, but with no success to speak of."

Maria is very doubtful that she will be of any use, but it is, at the least, something to take her mind off the frustrations and concerns that surround her on every side.

He IS OF MIDDLE AGE and height, with striking blue eyes in a weathered face, and close-cut hair that is halfway in turning from fair to gray. Apart from the eyes his appearance is unremarkable, but the overall impression is modest, attractive, trustworthy. I can imagine him as a country lawyer or doctor, some sort of public servant who has channeled his intelligence to the greater good—except perhaps for those eyes, which are piercing, far-sighted, bright yet dreamy. The eyes of a prophet. I am surprised, even charmed. For some reason I was expecting a monster.

"Mrs. Ross. Delighted to meet you." Stewart takes my hand and bows slightly. I nod.

"And you must be Moody. Delighted to make your acquaintance. Frank tells me you are based at Georgian Bay. A beautiful part of the country."

"Yes, it is," says Moody, smiling and shaking his hand. "And I am delighted to meet you, sir. I have heard much about you."

"Oh, well . . ." Stewart shakes his head with a smile, seeming embarrassed. "Mr. Parker. I believe thanks are in order for guiding these people on such a difficult journey."

Parker hesitates for a fraction of a second and then shakes the proffered hand. There is not a trace of recognition on Stewart's face as far as I can see.

"Mr. Stewart. I am pleased to meet you again."

"Again?" Stewart has a look of slightly apologetic puzzlement. "I am sorry, I don't recall . . ."

"William Parker. Clear Lake. Fifteen years ago."

"Clear Lake? You'll have to forgive me, Mr. Parker, my memory isn't what it used to be." His face is smiling pleasantly. Parker doesn't smile.

"Perhaps if you roll up your left sleeve, it will help."

Stewart's face changes and for a moment I can't read it. Then he bursts out laughing, and claps Parker on the shoulder.

"My God! How could I have forgotten? William! Yes, of course. Ah well, a long time ago, as you say." Then his face grows serious again. "I am sorry I couldn't come to meet you as soon as I arrived. There has been a tragic accident, I am sure you heard."

We nod, like children with their headmaster.

"Nepapanees was one of my best men. We were hunting on a river not far from here." His voice tails off, and I think, although I'm not sure, that I see the gleam of tears in his eyes. "We were following some tracks and . . . I can still hardly believe what happened. Nepapanees was a very experienced tracker: a skillful hunter. No one knew more than he did about the bush. But as he was following a track that led out along the river, he stepped on a spot of weak ice and went through."

He stops, his eyes focused on something not in the room. I notice that his face, which on first impression inspires such confidence, is also creased and tired. He could be forty. He could be fifteen years older. I can't tell.

"One minute he was there, the next he had gone. He went through, and though I crawled out as far as I could, I saw no sign of him. I even put my head under, but it was no good. I keep asking myself—perhaps I could have done more?"

He shakes his head. "You can do the same thing a thousand times, and think nothing of it. Like walking on ice. You get to know it, how thick it is, whether the current is strong or weak. And then the next time you set foot on it, after all those times when you knew it was safe, you make a mistake, and it does not bear your weight."

Moody nods his head in sympathy. Parker is watching Stewart with minute attention, scrutinizing him with the same look I saw on his face when he was studying the ground, looking for the trail. I don't know what he finds so enigmatic; Stewart exhibits nothing but regret and sadness.

"That was his wife out there?" I ask.

"Poor Elizabeth. Yes. They have four children, too—four children without a father. A terrible business. I saw you went out to her." He speaks to Moody now. "Perhaps you thought us callous to leave her alone, but that is the way with these people. They believe that no one can say anything at such a time. They have to grieve in their own way."

"But surely, they could tell her she was not alone? And in this weather . . ."

"But in her particular grief, she is alone, is she not? He only had one wife, and she only one husband." He turns his startling blue eyes on me, and I cannot disagree. "It is particularly hard for her that I could not bring back his body. For Indians, you know, drowning is unlucky. They believe that the spirit cannot go free. At least she is baptized, so perhaps she will find some comfort. And the children, too. That is a blessing."

Instead of a dozen Company officials, there are now only Stewart and Nesbit. The only other member of staff who lives in the main building is the chief interpreter, Olivier, a boy no older than Francis. Stewart calls him to meet us, and if he is grief-stricken he hides it well. He is a quick-witted youth who seems eager to please, and Stewart tells us proudly that he is proficient in four languages, having the natural advantage of one French-speaking parent and one English-speaking, each from a different native tribe.

"Olivier will go far in the Company," Stewart says, and Olivier beams with shy pleasure. I wonder if that is true; how far can a brown-skinned boy go in a company owned by foreigners? But then, perhaps he is not so badly off. He has a job and a talent, and, in Stewart, a mentor of some sort.

From the third wing of the fort, made up of offices, Stewart takes us to the storehouse where the goods are stocked. They have shipped out most of their furs over the summer, he explains, so stocks are low. Trappers spend the winter hunting, and it is in spring that they bring the results to the post to sell. Donald asks questions about outfits and yields, and Stewart answers him with interest, flattering him. I glance at Parker, to gauge his reaction, but he doesn't return my look. I feel snubbed. Ignored by the others, something catches my eye. I lean down and pick up a square of paper. Written on it are some numbers and letters: 66HBPH, followed by the names of animals. It reminds me that I still have the scrap of paper that Jammet had, perhaps, so carefully hidden in his cabin.

"What is this?" I pass the paper to Stewart.

"That is a pack marker. When we pack the furs"—he is addressing me alone, the only one who doesn't know Company practice—"a list of contents goes on top so we know if we lose anything. The code at the top refers to the outfit—here the year to May last, the company, of course, the district, which is Missinaibi, designated by the letter P, and the post—Hanover, H. So every pack is identified with where it came from and when."

I nod. I can't remember the letters on Jammet's scrap, only that it was from some years ago, perhaps when he worked there last. As an explanation this leaves a lot to be desired.

Beyond the storehouses are the stables, empty except for the dogs and a couple of squat ponies. And beyond that, the seven or eight wooden huts where the voyageurs live with their families, and the chapel.

"Normally I would take you to meet everyone, but today . . . It is a close community, especially now that we are not so many. There is much grieving. Please feel free," he turns, and again seems to address me more than the others, "to go into the chapel whenever you choose. It is always open."

"Mr. Stewart, I know you have many things on your mind at the moment, but you know that we are here for a reason?" I don't care if it isn't the right time to bring it up, I don't want Moody getting there first.

"Of course, yes. Frank mentioned something . . . You are looking for someone, is that right?"

"My son. We have followed his trail. It led us here . . . or near here, at least. You haven't seen any strangers recently? He is a youth of seventeen, black hair . . ."

"No, I'm so sorry. We have had no one here, until you came. I'm afraid it had quite gone out of my mind, what with all this . . . I will ask the others. But no one has been here that I am aware."

So that is it for the time being. Moody looks most unhappy with me, but that is the least of my problems.

Stewart leaves us to see to some Company business, and I turn to Parker and Moody. We have been left in Stewart's sitting room, where a fire makes it relatively comfortable, and there is an oil painting above it, of angels.

"Last night, just after we got here, I heard Nesbit threatening a woman. He said she would feel his hand if she didn't keep quiet 'about him.' That's what he said—'about him.' She was arguing; she refused, I think. And then he said something would happen to her when 'he' came back. That must have been Stewart."

"Who was this?" asks Moody.

"I don't know. I didn't see her, and she was speaking more quietly than him."

I hesitate over whether to tell Moody about Nesbit and Norah. Something makes me think it was her; she looks the type to argue. But then the door opens and Olivier, the young interpreter, comes in. It seems that he has been sent to entertain us. But it feels to me as though someone wants us watched.

SHE ONCE HEARD OF A woman who was in trouble because her husband threatened to kill her. She went to the nearest Company post and stood outside the gate, with all her belongings in a heap in front of her. First she set fire to the belongings. Then she put the match to a bag hanging round her neck. It was full of gunpowder, and exploded, blinding her and burning her face and chest. Inexplicably alive, she took a rope and tried to hang herself from a tree branch. Still she lived, so then she took a long needle and stuck it into her right ear. Even with the needle all the way inside her head, she didn't die. It wasn't her time, and her spirit wouldn't let her go. So she gave up and went off to make a new life somewhere else, where she prospered. Her name was Bird-that-flies-in-the-sun.

Strange that she remembers the story in such detail. The woman's name, the right ear. The name perhaps because it is a little like her own: Bird. She knows nothing else about the woman, except that she, too, knows what it is to want to die. Were it not for her children she thinks she would try to hang herself. Alec would be all right, thirteen and clever and already working, apprenticed to Olivier as interpreter. Josiah and William are younger but with less imagination to scare and confuse them. But Amy is only little, and girls need more help in this world, so she will have to stay in it a while longer at least, until it is her time. But without her husband by her side it will always be winter.

Without being aware of looking out the window, she sees the visitors come and stand a few yards from the house, looking in her direction. She can feel them talking about her; he will be talking about her husband, spinning his tale of how he died. She doesn't trust him anymore; when he talks to you, he makes you keep secrets. He made her husband keep secrets, which he didn't like, although he shrugged them off, dropped them outside the house when he came back from their hunting trips.

That morning—she was expecting him to come back as soon as she woke up, and Amy asked if Papa would be back today, and she said yes—

she walked out to the western gate, hearing the distant dogs barking, smiling to herself. She could hear so well she was sure she could hear the hush of runners on snow. She still smiled when he came back from a trip, even though they had been married for such a long time. She heard the dogs and walked up to the bump from where you could see over the fence. And saw that there was only one man with the sled. She stayed there watching until he reached the palisade, then went down to the yard to hear what he had to say, although she already knew. Others, William and George and Kenowas and Mary, had seen that he was alone and came to find out, but he had spoken straight to her, laying his eyes on her like a blue spell, so that she could not speak. She did not remember anything else until the visitor, the moonias with the knife wound and the bad feet, came out and tried to talk to her, but his voice sounded like the humming of bees and she did not know what he said. Then a little while later he brought out a cup of coffee, and put it in the snow beside her. She didn't remember asking for it, but maybe she had; it smelled good, better than any coffee she had ever drunk, and she watched tiny snowflakes land and vanish on its oily black surface. Land and melt, so they were gone forever. And then all she could think of was the face of her husband trying to speak to her, but she couldn't hear him because he was trapped under a thick layer of river ice, and he was drowning.

She picked up the cup of coffee and poured it onto the skin on the underside of her forearm. It was hot, but not hot enough. The skin went pink, that was all, and her arm smoked like meat in the cold air.

They brought her back to the house, and Mary stayed with her, stoking the fire and bringing food for the children. She stays now, as if she is afraid Elizabeth will throw herself on the fire if she leaves her alone. Alec came and put his arms around her, and told her not to cry, although she wasn't crying. Her eyes are as dry as a stick of wood. Amy doesn't cry either, but that is because she is too young to understand. The other boys cry until they fall asleep exhausted. Mary sits by her and doesn't say anything; she knows better than that. George came in once and said he will pray for her husband's soul: George is a Christian and very devout. Mary shooed him away; she and Elizabeth are both Christians, but Nepapanees was not. He was Chippewa, without a drop of white blood in his veins. He went to church and heard a preacher a couple of times, but said it wasn't for him. Elizabeth nodded at George; she knew he meant to help. And maybe it will;

who is to say Our Heavenly Father cannot intervene in her husband's fate? Perhaps there is a reciprocal agreement.

"Mary," says Elizabeth now, her voice rasping like a key in a rusty lock. "Tell me if it is snowing."

Mary looks up. She is cradling Amy on her lap, and for a moment Elizabeth has the fantasy that Mary is the mother, and Amy a child she doesn't know.

"No, it stopped an hour ago. But now it's getting dark. It will have to be tomorrow."

Elizabeth nods. The snow has stopped for one reason only, and she knows what she will do in the morning. Would have done it earlier but for the snow, which fell to make them stop and think for a while. So that they would act with thoughtfulness. In the morning they will go back to the river and find him, and bring him back.

Amy wakes up and stares at her mother. She is hers, after all, with her gray-brown eyes and pale skin. They'd wanted another girl. Nepapanees joked that he wanted a girl who was like him, instead of like her.

There will not be another girl now. Her spirit, if what Nepapanees believed is true, will have to wait to be born in another place, at another time.

The trouble is, she doesn't believe in anything anymore.

Donald RETIRES AFTER DINNER TO write to Susannah. More snow fell as they ate; if Stewart is right, this storm could last days, and there will be no chance of traveling before it is over. But he has more than one reason to be grateful for this. He is alarmingly tired. His feet, even in moccasins, hurt like hell, and the wound on his stomach is red and weeping. He waited for a moment in the dining room when he could draw Stewart aside, and quietly mentioned that he might need some medical attention. Stewart nodded to him and promised to send someone with some expertise. Then he had, rather unexpectedly, winked.

Anyhow, he doesn't feel too bad now, sitting at the rickety table that he requested, with his packet of paper and some defrosted ink. He tries, before he starts, to fix Susannah's oval face in his mind's eye, but once again finds it hard to grasp. Again, Maria's face comes to him with absolute clarity, and he reflects that it would be interesting to write to her and discuss the complexities of their situation, which he feels sure would bore her sister. Not to mention the upsetting business with the widow. Somehow he thinks he would like to know what Maria would have to say about it all. Tomorrow, or the day after, there is no real hurry, he will have to make some proper inquiries, he supposes. But for now, he can put his duties out of his mind.

"Dear Susannah," he writes, confidently enough. But after that, he pauses. Why should he not write to both sisters? After all, he knows both of them. He taps the pen on the table a few times, then takes a fresh sheet of paper and writes "Dear Maria."

After an hour or so there is a soft tap on the door. "Come in," he says, still writing away.

The door opens and a young Indian girl slips noiselessly inside. She was pointed out to him earlier; her name is Nancy Eagles, the wife of the youngest voyageur. She can be no more than twenty, has a face of arresting loveliness, and speaks with a voice so soft he has to strain to catch it.

"Oh, Nancy, isn't it? Thank you . . ." he says, surprised and pleased.

"Mr. Stewart says you are hurt." Her voice is quiet and toneless, as though she is speaking to herself. She holds up a bowl of water and some strips of cloth—she has clearly come to tend to him. Without speaking again she indicates that he should take off his shirt, and sets the bowl on the floor. Donald covers the letter with some blotting paper and unbuttons his shirt, suddenly aware of his meager white torso.

"It's nothing serious, but . . . here, you see, I received a wound two . . . three months ago, that has not healed properly." He peels off the dressing, pink and damp with fluid.

Nancy puts out a hand and pushes his chest lightly, making him sit down on the bed. "That was a knife." She states it flatly, not asking him.

"Yes. But it was an accident . . ." Donald laughs, and begins to tell her the long, rambling story of the rugby game.

Nancy kneels in front of him, uninterested in the wound's origin. When she sponges the wound, he takes a sharp breath in, and stops talking, his explanation of a diving tackle left unsaid. Nancy leans forward and sniffs the wound. Donald feels a heat in his cheeks and holds his breath, acutely aware that her head is almost in his lap. Her hair is blue-black, fine and silky, not coarse as he had assumed. Her skin is silky, too, of a very pale, creamy brown: a silky girl, lithe and innocent of artifice. He wonders if she is aware of her beauty. He pictures her husband, Peter—a tall, strongly built voyageur—walking in at this moment, and blanches at the thought. Nancy seems unperturbed. She makes a clean dressing and applies some smelly herbal paste before indicating that he should lift his arms, and binding it on so tightly Donald is afraid he might suffocate during the night.

"Thank you. That is very kind . . ." He wonders if there is something he can give her, and mentally ransacks the few belongings he brought with him. He cannot come up with anything suitable.

Nancy gives him the ghost of a smile, her fine black eyes for the first time looking into his own. He notices how her eyebrows have the elegant arch of a gull's wing, and then, to his complete and total astonishment, she picks up his hand and presses it to her breast. Before he can utter a word or pull it away, she fastens her lips on his, and her other hand grasps the not indifferent organ between his legs. He gasps something out—he cannot be sure what—and after a moment in which his senses are so overloaded he doesn't know what is going on, he pushes her firmly away. (Be honest, Moody—how long was that moment? Long enough.)

"No! I . . . I'm sorry. Not that. No."

His heart is thundering, the sound of his pulse crashing like waves against his eardrums. Nancy looks at him, her blunt, almond-colored lips parted. It has never before occurred to him that native women could be as beautiful as white women, but he cannot imagine anything more beautiful than the girl in front of him. Donald shuts his eyes, to take away the sight of her. Her fingers are still on his arms where he holds them away from him, as though they are dance partners frozen in the midst of a step.

"I can't. You're beautiful, but . . . no, I can't."

She glances down at his trousers, which seem to disagree with him.

"Your husband . . ."

She shrugs. "Doesn't matter."

"It matters to me. I'm sorry."

He manages to turn away, half expecting her to launch another attack. But nothing comes. When he glances back at her, she is gathering up the bowl of dirty water, the cloths, and the used dressing.

"Thank you, Nancy. Please don't be . . . offended."

Nancy looks at him swiftly but says nothing. Donald sighs and she goes out as quietly as she came in. He looks at the closed door, cursing. Cursing himself and her and the whole ramshackle, godforsaken place. The letter on the table reproaches him. The cool, well-constructed sentences, the humorous asides . . . why is he writing to Maria anyway? He picks up the letter and crumples it into a ball, regretting it instantly. Then he picks up his spare shirt and flings it on the floor, just for the sake of throwing something (but something that won't break). The floor is filthy. Why is he so angry when he did the right thing? (Regret, possibly? Because he is a milk-and-water, lily-livered coward who hasn't the courage to take what he wants when it is offered to him?)

Damn, damn, damn.

SHORTLY AFTER MOODY MAKES HIS excuses and leaves the table, Parker also gets up and begs leave to retire. After he's gone I wonder if they are both up to something, although Moody looks so exhausted it is possible that he really has gone to sleep. About Parker I'm less sure. I hope he is working some mysterious miracle of deduction, which as yet I cannot guess at. Stewart suggests Nesbit take me to the sitting room for a glass of something. He, he says, will join us in a few minutes—in such a way that I immediately wonder what he is doing. It is all very well having a suspicious cast of mind, but I can't say it has so far led to any useful discoveries.

Nesbit pours two glasses of malt whisky and hands one to me. We clink glasses. He has been strained and edgy tonight; his eyes are fervid, his hands twisting constantly or drumming on the table. He ate next to nothing. Then, before coffee, he excused himself. Stewart responded in some appropriate way, but his eyes were hard. He knows, I thought. Norah served us throughout, and though I watched her carefully, I could not discern any of the same tension in her. Now that Stewart is here she is far more docile, showing none of the sullenness of the first night. When Nesbit came back ten or fifteen minutes later, his demeanor had changed; his movements were languorous, his eyes sleepy. Parker and Moody gave no sign of noticing anything amiss.

I go to the window and part the curtains. It is not snowing, but it lies several inches deep.

"Do you think there is more snow on the way, Mr. Nesbit?"

"I don't claim to understand the weather here, but it seems likely, wouldn't you say?"

"I was only wondering when we might leave again. If we have to go on looking . . ."

"Ah, of course. Not the best time of year for it." He seems unconcerned about the fate of my seventeen-year-old son out in the wilderness on his own. Or perhaps he is sharper than I give him credit for.

"Frightful place, this. Perfect for convicts, I've always thought, instead of sending them to Tasmania, which as far as I can make out is jolly pleasant. Rather like the Lake District."

"But here is not so isolated. Or so far from home."

"Feels isolated enough. Do you know, a few years ago, a bunch of employees—foreigners, I think—tried to make a run for it from Moose Factory. In January! Of course, none of them were ever seen again. Froze to death in the middle of nowhere, poor bastards." He laughs softly, bitterly. "Excuse my language, Mrs. Ross. It has been so long since I've been in the company of a lady, I have forgotten how to talk."

I demur, something along the lines of having heard worse.

He looks at me in a speculative way I don't like. He's not drunk tonight, but his pupils are very small, even in the dim light. His hands are calm and relaxed now, soothed. I know you, I think. I know how it feels.

"Disappeared, you say? How awful."

"Yes. Don't get too upset—as I said, they were foreigners. Krauts or something."

"You don't like foreigners?"

"Not particularly. Give me a Scot any day."

"Like Mr. Stewart?"

"Exactly. Like Mr. Stewart."

I drain my glass. Dutch courage, but better than none at all.

When Stewart comes in, my face is warm from the whisky, but my head is still clear. Nesbit pours a glass for Stewart and we talk easily for a few minutes. Then Stewart turns to me.

"I was thinking about your Mr. Parker. You know, I can't believe I didn't recall the name immediately, but then it was a long time ago. Tell me, how did you meet?"

"We only met recently. He was in Caulfield and when we needed a guide, someone suggested him."

"So you do not know him well?"

"Not particularly well. Why?"

Stewart smiles the smile of someone with interesting news to impart. "Oh . . . He is, or at least was, a rather colorful character. There were certain incidents at Clear Lake . . . Let's say some of our voyageurs are rather wild, and . . . he was one such."

"How fascinating! Do go on." I smile, as though it is no more than so much gossip.

"It is not really so fascinating. Some rather ugly incidents. William was prone to fighting when younger. We went on a journey together—I'm talking more than fifteen years ago, you understand—a journey in winter. There were other men there, too, but . . . it was a hard journey and quarrels blew up. Over whether to go on, or turn back, that sort of thing. Food was running low and so on. Anyway, we came to blows."

"Blows! Good heavens!" I lean forward in my chair, giving him an encouraging smile.

"You may recall what he said, and indeed, he gave me something to remember him by." Stewart rolls up his left sleeve. Running down his forearm is a long white scar, a good quarter of an inch wide.

There is nothing feigned about my shock.

"Sometimes these half-breeds, give them half a bottle of rum and they turn into a dervish. We had an argument and he went for me with a knife. In the middle of nowhere, too; that was no joke, I can tell you."

He rolls the sleeve down again. Right now I can't think of anything to say.

"I'm sorry, maybe I shouldn't have shown you. Some ladies find scars distressing."

"Oh, no . . ." I shake my head. Nesbit refills my glass. It's not the scar that disturbs me, but the last picture of Jammet I will ever have flashing up in my mind. And the first sight of Parker: the artificial man searching the cabin; a savage, alien, terrifying figure.

"It is not the sight of your scar," says Nesbit happily, "more the thought that her guide is such a handy fellow with a knife!"

"He has seemed nothing of the kind these past weeks. He is the model guide. Perhaps, as you say, his violence was the result of rum. He does not drink now."

Stewart could be lying, I tell myself. I look into his eyes, trying to read his soul. But he looks only kind, sincere, a little wistful, thinking of old times.

"It is good to hear that some men can learn from their mistakes, eh, Frank?"

"Indeed so," I murmur. "If only more of us did."

Later, in my room, I remain dressed and sit in the chair to prevent myself falling asleep. I would like nothing more than to lie down and succumb to oblivion. But I can't, and I'm not sure oblivion would have me; I am troubled, it would be fair to say. I want to ask Parker about Stewart, about their past, but I am reluctant to go and wake him again. Reluctant, or afraid. The picture that came back to me earlier gave me a shock. I had forgotten how the sight of Parker had sent shivers down my spine, how brutal and alien he appeared. I had not forgotten his appearance, of course, but I had forgotten the effect it first had on me. Strange how that can happen, when you come to know someone.

But I do not know him. In his defense, he made no attempt to hide the fact that they had met before, but perhaps he was only preempting the inevitable, a double bluff.

My eyes are long accustomed to the dark, and the snow gives off its dull, directionless light, enough to make my way when I come out into the corridor again. I knock on his door very softly, and then let myself in, closing the door behind me. I think I have been very quiet, but he sits bolt upright in the bed with an exclamation.

"My God . . . No! Go away!" He sounds terrified and angry.

"Mr. Moody, it is I, Mrs. Ross."

"What? What the devil?" He fumbles with matches and lights the candle by his bed. When his face blooms out of the darkness, he is already wearing his spectacles, and his eyes are starting out of their sockets.

"I'm sorry, I didn't mean to alarm you."

"What the devil do you mean by coming in here in the middle of the night?"

I was expecting surprise and irritation, not white-knuckle fury. "I had to talk to someone. Please . . . it won't take long."

"I thought you talked to Parker."

There is something in his tone, but I'm not sure what it is. I sit on the single chair, squashing some of his clothes in the process.

"I don't know what to think, and we need to discuss it."

"It can't wait until morning?"

"They don't want us to be alone all together. Didn't you feel that?"

"No."

"Well . . . I was telling you what I overheard Nesbit say, and then Olivier came in and we couldn't talk about it further."

"So?" His voice is still bright with anger, but he is less scared than when I came in. As though he had been afraid I was someone else.

"Doesn't that seem to indicate that there are things going on here they don't want us to know? And since we are on the trail of a murderer, those things might be connected."

He looks at me, disgruntled. But he doesn't throw me out. "Stewart said no one strange had come to the fort recently."

"Maybe it wasn't someone strange."

"You're suggesting it is someone who lives here?" He sounds shocked that I'm impugning a member of the Company.

"It's possible. Someone whom Nesbit knows. Perhaps Stewart knows nothing about it."

Moody stares into the corner behind my left ear. "I think the whole thing would have been much better dealt with on the straight. If we'd told them the truth about why we are here, not your absurd story."

"But someone already suspects us. I think merely the fact that we mentioned we were following a trail put them on their guard. Nesbit was threatening a woman—Norah, I think—not to talk about someone. Why would he do that?"

"There could be any number of reasons. I thought you had no idea who it was."

"It's true I didn't see her, but Norah . . . Norah and Nesbit are having a . . . liaison."

"What? The serving woman?" Moody looks startled. But more because it is the squat, unlovely Norah than because Nesbit is committing an impropriety. Such things go on all the time. He compresses his mouth; it is possible that he is thinking of filing a report. "How do you know?"

"I saw them." I don't want to say I saw them when I was sneaking around the fort at night, and luckily he doesn't ask.

"Well . . . she is a widow."

"Is she?"

"One of the voyageurs here. Sad business."

"I didn't know." I ponder that being a Company servant is a dangerous profession. "What I was going to say is, we will have to ask people questions . . . without them knowing."

Even as I say this, I wonder how on earth we are going to manage it. Moody looks less than impressed. I have to admit it's not a brilliant plan, but it's the best I can do.

"Well, if there's nothing else . . ." He shoots a meaningful glance at the door. I think of Stewart's arm and telling Moody about it, but he doesn't trust Parker as it is, and may well start asking questions about how Parker came to be in Dove River. Questions I don't think I want to answer at the moment. "I really must get some sleep. If you don't mind."

"Of course. Thank you." I stand up. He somehow looks smaller huddled beneath the bedclothes. Younger and more vulnerable. "You look exhausted. Have you got someone to look at your blisters? I am sure there is someone with medical knowledge here . . ."

Moody grips the covers and pulls them around his chin, as though I have advanced on him with an axe. "Yes. Please just go! All I need is some sleep, for heaven's sake . . ."

As it turns out, plans to talk to the staff the next day are postponed, because by the time we get up, most of them have left. George Cummings, Peter Eagles, William Blackfeather, and Kenowas—in other words, all the adult, nonwhite males who live and work at Hanover House, with the single exception of Olivier—have gone to search for Nepapanees's body. They left before dawn, silently, on foot. Even the man we saw on that first afternoon, the cataleptically drunk Arnaud (who is, it turns out, the watchman), even he has been sobered by grief and joined the search party.

The widow and her thirteen-year-old son have gone with them.

A WEEK AFTER FRANCIS REJECTED SUSANNAH'S overtures, he went to Jammet's cabin on an errand for his father. He still thought of Susannah Knox, but now school had closed for the summer and the day on the beach seemed like a hazy, unsteady memory. He had not gone to the picnic, nor had he sent any message. He had not known what to say. If he wondered at himself for spurning what he had for so long dreamed of, he did not do so often, or with any self-reproach. It was somehow that, having held her for so long an unattainable ideal, he could not imagine her being anything else.

That day, it was late in the afternoon and Laurent was inside brewing tea when Francis whistled outside the front door.

"*Salut, François,*" he called, and Francis pushed the door open. "You want some?"

Francis nodded. He liked the Frenchman's cabin, which was shambolic and utterly unlike his parents' house. Things were held together with string and nails; the teapot had no lid but was kept on because it still managed its job of holding tea; he kept his clothes in tea chests. When Francis had asked him why he didn't build a chest of drawers, as he was perfectly capable of doing, he replied that one wooden box was as good as another, no?

They sat down on two chairs inside the door, which Laurent wedged open, and Francis smelled brandy on the Frenchman's breath. Sometimes he drank during the day, although Francis had never seen him the worse for it. The cabin faced due west and the low sun struck them both in the face, forcing Francis to shut his eyes and tilt his head back. When he glanced at Laurent again, he found the older man looking at him, the sun mining golden lights in the depths of his eyes.

"*Quel visage,*" he murmured, as if to himself. Francis didn't ask him what it meant, as he didn't think it was for him.

There was a wonderful stillness in the air—the sound of crickets the loudest thing. Laurent produced the brandy bottle and tipped some, unasked, into Francis's tea. Francis drank it, feeling agreeably reckless: his parents would yell at him if they found out, and he said so.

"Ah well, we cannot please our parents all our lives."

"I don't think I please them any of the time."

"You're growing up. Soon you will leave, no? Get married, get your own place, all the rest."

"I don't know." This seemed unlikely, dizzyingly distant from crickets and brandy and the low, blinking sun.

"You got a sweetheart? That little dark girl—is she your sweetheart?"

"Oh . . . Ida? No, she's just a friend—we walk home from school some days." God! Did everyone in the county think Ida was his girlfriend? "No, I . . ."

For some reason, he found he wanted to talk to Laurent about it. "There was a girl I liked. Everyone likes her actually; she's real pretty, and real nice, too . . . At the end of term she asked me to a picnic. She'd never really spoken to me before . . . and I was really flattered. But I didn't go."

There was the longest silence after that. Francis felt uncomfortable and began to wish he had not spoken of it.

"Don't know what's the matter with me!" He tried to laugh it off, not altogether successfully. Laurent put out a hand and patted him on the leg.

"Nothing is the matter with you, *mon ami*. My God, nothing at all."

Francis looked at Laurent then. The Frenchman's face looked very serious, almost sad. Was it him? Did he make people sad? Maybe that was it. Ida always seemed to be sad around him lately. As for his parents, well . . . they were gloomy beyond belief. Francis tried smiling, to cheer him up. And then things changed. They got very slow—or was it very fast? He realized that Laurent's hand was still on his leg, only not patting him now; now it was stroking his thigh with strong, rhythmic movements. He couldn't stop looking into the golden-brown eyes. There was a smell of brandy and tobacco and sweat, and he seemed to be glued to the chair, his limbs heavy and immovable as if filled with a warm, viscous liquid. More than that, he was being drawn toward Laurent, and no power on earth could have stopped him.

At some point Laurent got up and went to the still-open door to close it, then turned to Francis. "You know, you can go, if you want."

Francis stared at him, breathless and suddenly horrified. He didn't think he could speak, so he shook his head, just once, and Laurent kicked the door shut.

* * *

Afterward, Francis realized he would, at some point, have to go home again. He even remembered the tool he had come for, although it seemed an inconceivable length of time ago. He was scared of leaving in case things went back to normal. What if the next time he saw Laurent he behaved as though nothing had happened? He seemed perfectly relaxed now, pulling his shirt on, with his pipe clenched between his teeth and clouds of smoke swirling around his head, as though this were a normal, everyday thing, as though the earth had not shifted on its axis. Francis was scared of going home, of having to look at his parents with these eyes, wondering, from now on, if they knew.

He stood in the doorway with the flaying tool, uncertain how to leave. Laurent came over to him, smiling his wicked smile.

"S-so . . ." Francis stuttered. He had never stuttered in his life. "Shall I come . . . tomorrow?"

Laurent put his hands on Francis's face. Rough and tender, the thumbs traced his cheekbones. Their eyes were absolutely on a level. He kissed him, and his mouth felt like the center of life itself.

"If you like."

Francis walked up the path toward home, in ecstasy and in terror. How ludicrous: the path, the trees, the crickets, the fading sky, the rising moon, everything looked just the same as before. As if it didn't know, as if it didn't matter. And he thought, as he walked, "Oh God, is this what I am?"

In ecstasy and in terror: "Is this what I am?"

Susannah was forgotten. School and the concerns of schoolboys faded into a distant past. That summer, for a few weeks, he was happy. He walked through the forest, strong, powerful, a man with secrets. He went with Laurent on hunting and fishing trips, although he neither hunted nor fished. When they met anyone in the forest, Francis would nod to them, grunt curtly, his eyes on the end of the fishing line, or scanning the trees for signs of movement, and Laurent would hint that he was becoming a tremendous shot, eagle-eyed and ruthless. But the best times were when they were alone at the end of the day, in the forest or at the cabin, and Laurent would become serious. Usually he was drunk as well, and he would take Francis's face in his hands, looking and looking as if he couldn't get enough.

Looking back, there weren't so many times like that—Laurent insisted that he should not stay at the cabin too often, or people might suspect. He had to spend a reasonable amount of time at home, too, with his parents. He found it difficult—ever since that first evening, when he had walked in to find them sitting down to dinner. He held up the tool.

"Had to wait for him to come back."

His father nodded briefly. His mother turned around. "You were so long. Your father wanted to get it done before dinner. What were you doing?"

"Told you, I had to wait." He put the tool on the table and walked upstairs, ignoring his mother's weary cries about dinner.

Trembling with shivery joy.

Since relations with his parents were rudimentary at the best of times, they did not seem to notice a difference if he was silent or distracted. He spent the time between visits to Laurent's going for walks, lying on his bed, carrying out his chores with impatience and bad grace. Waiting. And then there would be another night at the cabin, or a trip to a fishing lake, when he could be truly himself. Seized moments, intense and sharply flavored, when time could dawdle like Sunday afternoon, or rush like a speeding torrent. If he counted the number of nights he had ever spent at Laurent's cabin, what would it come to?

Maybe twenty. Twenty-five.

Too few.

Francis is jolted from his past by Jacob walking into his room. He is grateful for the interruption. Jacob looks more agitated than he has ever seen him. Francis rubs his hand over his face as if he has been asleep, hoping Jacob will not see the tears.

"What is it?" Jacob has opened his mouth, but nothing has yet come out.

"A strange thing. The woman Line and her children, and the carpenter—they have left in the night. The carpenter's wife is threatening to kill herself."

Francis gapes. The carpenter, whom he has never met, has been spirited away by his nurse. (So why did she kiss him?)

Jacob paces. "It is going to snow. It is not a good time for travel, not with children. And I saw her, the night before last, in the stables. She asked me not to say anything. So I did not."

Francis takes a deep breath. "They are adults. They can do what they like."

"But if they don't know the country . . . they don't know how to travel in winter . . ."

"How long before it snows?"

"What?"

"How long before the snow? A day? A week?"

"A day or two. Soon. Why?"

"I think I know where they might have gone. She spoke to me; she asked about Caulfield."

Jacob follows his thinking. "Well, they might make it. If they are lucky."

AN HOUR AGO THEY CAME to the first trees, small and sparse to be sure, but still trees, and Line felt a rush of joy. They really are going to get away. Here is the forest, and the forest goes all the way to the lakeshore. It is almost as though they are already there. Her piece of paper tells them to go southeast until they hit a small river, and then follow it downstream. Torbin is sitting on the saddle in front of her, and she has been telling him a story about a dog she used to have as a child in Norway. She makes him sound like the dog in the fairy story with the soldier, with eyes as big as dinner plates.

"You can have a dog, too, when we find somewhere to live. How would you like that, huh?" It slips out before she can bite her tongue.

"Somewhere to live?" echoes Torbin. "You said we were going on holiday. We're not, are we?"

Line sighs. "No, we're going to go and live somewhere else, somewhere nicer, where it's warm."

Torbin squirms around in the saddle to look her in the eye, a dangerous look on his face, closed and taut. "Why did you lie?"

"It wasn't really a lie, darling. It was complicated, and we couldn't explain it all to you, not at Himmelvanger. It was important that no one there knew or they wouldn't let us go."

"You lied to us." His eyes are hard and confused. Per and the red-roofed church have made him a pedantic little boy. "Lying is a sin."

"It wasn't a sin in this case. Don't argue, Torbin. There are some things you can't understand, you're too young. I'm sorry we had to do it this way but there it is."

"I am not too young!" He is angry, his cheeks red with cold and excitement. He is wriggling around now.

"Sit still, young man, or I'll give you a smack. Believe me, this is not the time for arguments!"

But somehow in his wriggling he manages to stick his elbow hard into her stomach, causing her to gasp and feel a surge of anger. "Enough!" She takes her hand off the reins and whacks him on the leg.

"You're a liar! Liar! I wouldn't have come!" he screams, and wriggles out from between her arms and slithers to the ground. His ankle buckles beneath him momentarily, then he picks himself up and starts to run off, back in the direction they have come.

"Torbin! Torbin! Espen!" Line shrieks, her voice a shrill cry, yanking on the reins to try to turn her horse around, which it doesn't seem to understand. It stops still, then doesn't move, like a train arrived at a station. Espen, up ahead with Anna, pulls his mount around, and sees Torbin darting between the trees.

"Torbin!" He jumps off, with Anna in his arms, and gives her to Line, who has dismounted, leaving her horse where it is.

"Stay here, I'll get him! Don't move!"

He runs off after Torbin, dodging around trees and stumbling over fallen boughs. In a frighteningly short time, they are out of sight. Anna looks at Line with her solemn blue eyes and starts to cry.

"It's all right, darling; your brother's just being silly. They'll be back in a moment." On impulse she bends down and puts her arms around her daughter, shuts her eyes against her cold, greasy hair.

It is probably no more than a few minutes before they reappear between the trees. Espen's face is set hard and he drags a cowed Torbin by the hand. But by then Line has realized that something far worse has happened.

She and Anna have been searching, at first thinking, we'll find it right away: a round, hard, steel object like a compass doesn't belong here, it will stick out like a sore thumb. Line turns it into a game for Anna, with a reward for the one who finds it. The game soon palls: the ground here is particularly treacherous: humps of rock, ankle-twisting hollows, hidden rabbit holes and tangles of roots, crisscrossed with dead and rotting boughs. She can't remember if she dropped it when Torbin hit her, or after, or when she was trying to pull the horse behind her. The tortured ground gives no sign of where they have been.

She tells Espen she can't find it, and Torbin sees the fear in their faces and shuts up. He knows it is his fault. All four of them start to look, treading in stoop-backed circles around the indifferent horses, pulling aside lichen and rotten leaves, sticking their hands into dark, clammy holes. Every direction looks mockingly the same: scrub pines growing and dying where they grew, falling and leaning in each other's arms, weaving around them a matted, deadwood trap.

Anna is the first to notice. "Mama, it's snowing."

Line straightens, her back aching. Snow. Silent, dry flakes float around her. Espen sees the look on her face.

"We'll keep looking for another half hour, then we'll go on. We can work out the direction pretty well anyway. It was more important to know the direction to reach the forest. This is the easy part."

Once Torbin gives a cry and pounces, but it turns out to be a round gray stone. Line is secretly relieved when Espen calls a halt. She loves him for the way he takes command, gathering them together for a little talk, and picking the direction to go in. He points out that lichen gathers on the north sides of the tree trunks, so that is what they have to keep an eye on: where the lichen gathers. To Line the lichen looks evenly distributed, but she shuts this thought away, slams and locks the door. Espen will know; he is their protector. She is only a woman.

Espen takes Torbin on his horse, and they move off silently. The snow muffles everything, even the clink of bridles.

I GO TO THE STABLES FOR no good reason, other than that I am think-ing about talking to the women, but, to tell the truth, I am afraid of them. They look tough and alien and contemptuous, tempered by grief. Who am I to question them, I, who have never been overburdened with charity and kindness, or even curiosity about my fellow men? The dogs at least are pleased to see me, crazy with the boredom of confinement. Lucie rushes up, tail wagging, her jaws stretched wide in that happy-dog smile. I feel an absurd rush of fondness for her, feeling her rough head under my hand, her tongue like hot sand. Then Parker is there. I wonder if he has been watching for me.

This is the first time he has come to find me. The first time, that is, since he knocked on my door in the middle of the night and we made our bar-gain. Yesterday I would have been pleased; today I'm not sure. My voice comes out shriller than I would have liked.

"Have you got what you wanted?"

"What do you mean?"

"Why you came. It was nothing to do with Francis or Jammet. You wanted to see Stewart again. Because of something that happened fifteen years ago. Because of a stupid fight."

Parker speaks without looking at me. Carefully. "That's not so. Jammet was my friend. And your son . . . well, he loved Jammet. I think they loved each other, didn't they?"

"Really!" I utter a strangled sort of laugh. "What a strange way of putting it. You make it sound . . ."

Parker says nothing. Lucie goes on licking my hand, and I forget to move it away.

"Really, I . . ." Parker seems to have his hand on my arm, and although a part of me wants to fling it off, I don't. "Really, I don't . . ."

I can't believe I didn't know. "What are you saying?" My voice crackles like dry leaves.

"Jammet was . . . Well, he had been married, but sometimes he also had . . . friends. Young men, handsome, like your son."

Somehow he has guided me away from the door, over to the dark corner stacked with bales of hay, and I am sitting on one of them.

"The last time I saw him alive—it was in the spring—you know, he mentioned someone who lived nearby. He knew I didn't judge him, not that he cared about that."

There is a half smile on his face. He begins to light his pipe, unhurried. "He cared about him deeply."

I smooth my hair into place. There are some loose strands that have slipped out of the knot, and I can see in the long light from the doorway that a couple of the hairs are white. I have to face facts. I am getting old, and my head is full of thoughts I cannot bear. I cannot bear the thought I did not realize what was happening. I cannot bear the thought that Angus hated him for it, for I realize now that he knew. I cannot bear the thought of Francis's grief, which must have been—must be—extreme, secretive, unbearably lonely. And I cannot bear the thought that when I saw him, I did not comfort him nearly enough.

"Oh God. I should have stayed with him."

"You are a brave woman."

This almost makes me laugh. "I am a stupid one."

"You came all this way for your son. Hating it. He knows that."

"And it has done no good. We haven't found the man who made the trail."

Parker doesn't jump in and deny this. He smokes for a minute in silence. "Stewart showed you the scar?"

I nod. "He says you did it in a fight while you were on a journey."

"Not on the journey. After it. I'll tell you a couple of things he probably didn't say, and then you can make up your own mind. Stewart was promising. Everyone said he would go far. He was the right sort. One winter at Clear Lake he made a group of us go on a journey to another post. Three hundred miles. The snow was three feet deep before the drifts. The weather was terrible. You don't travel in the middle of winter unless you have to. He did it to prove that he could."

"Was this the famous journey Mr. Moody spoke of?"

"It was famous, but not for the reasons he gave. There were five of us, to start with. Stewart, another Company man called Rae, Rae's nephew, who was seventeen. The boy didn't work for the Company; he was visiting the country. Then there was myself and another guide, Laurent Jammet.

"As I said, the weather was bad: deep snow and storms. Then it got worse. There was a blizzard, and by some luck we found a cabin, a hundred miles from anywhere. The blizzard went on and on. We kept waiting for it to blow itself out, but it was one of those January storms that go on for weeks. We ran low on food. The only thing we had plenty of was liquor. Jammet and I decided to go and get help. It seemed like the only chance. We told the other three we would come back as soon as possible, left all the food there was, and set out. We were lucky. After two days we found an Indian village, then the weather got worse, and we couldn't go back for another three days.

"When we did eventually get back, something had happened. We found Stewart and Rae in a drunken stupor. The boy was dead, lying on the floor, suffocated on his own vomit. They never made much sense, but what I think had happened was this: Stewart had talked of what he called 'going out in a blaze of glory.' He joked about it. I think, when we didn't come back right away, he gave up. He decided they should drink themselves to death. Rae and he didn't make it, but the boy died."

"How do you know it was his idea?" I am shuddering inside at the thought. The boy was the same age as Francis.

"That was the way he thought." His voice is flat with disgust.

"And then what? Didn't they sack him?"

"How could they prove it? It was just a tragedy. A misjudgment. That's bad enough. Rae went back to Scotland, Stewart moved on, and the boy's under the ground. I left the Company. I haven't seen him since."

"And the scar?"

"I heard him criticizing the boy. Saying he was weak and scared, and wanted to die. I drank then." He shrugs, without regret.

There is a pause for the longest time. All the same, I know that he hasn't finished.

"The other thing?"

"Yeah. Five or six years ago the Company was short of men, so they brought men over from Norway. Convicts. Stewart was chief at Moose Factory, and they had a group of these men. Norwegians joined up in Canada, too. The widow at Himmelvanger, the one who looked after your son—her husband was one of them."

I think of the widow—young, pretty, with an impatience and a hunger in her. Perhaps that explained it.

"I wasn't there, so this is hearsay. Some Norwegians mutinied and took off. Somehow they managed to take a lot of valuable furs. They set off across country, blizzards came up, they vanished. Stewart got into trouble that time, both for the mutiny and for losing so much valuable stock. Someone in the stores must have been in on it."

"Stewart?"

"I don't know. People exaggerated, of course, saying there was a fortune in furs to be had for the man who found them. Dozens of silver and black fox."

"That doesn't sound as though it was worth so much trouble."

"You know how much a silver fox pelt is worth?"

I shake my head.

"In London, more than its weight in gold."

I am shocked. And I feel sorry for the animals. I may not be good for much, but at least I'm worth more alive than dead.

"Stewart was sent out here. There are no furs here now. Nothing but hares. Worth nothing. I'm not sure why they bother to keep Hanover going. For an ambitious man, it was an insult. You don't get promoted from a place like this. It was punishment for what he might have done."

"What has this to do with Jammet?" I am impatient to get to the end of this.

"Uh. Last year . . ." He pauses here to fiddle with the tobacco in his pipe—deliberately, it seems to me. "Last winter . . . I found the furs."

"The silver and black fox?"

"Yes." There is a hint of amusement in his voice, or perhaps it is defensiveness.

"And were they worth a fortune?" I feel—I apologize to Francis for it—a thrill of excitement. Treasure comes in many forms, however gruesome, and it always makes a shallow heart like mine beat faster.

Parker makes a sort of grimace. "Not as much as people said, but . . . enough."

"And . . . the Norwegians?"

"I didn't find them. But any traces would be long gone. They were out in the open."

"You mean wolves?" I can't stop myself asking.

"Maybe."

"But I thought you said they would . . . leave parts."

"Over the years, all sort of creatures would come: birds, foxes . . . Maybe they had gone on. All I'm saying is, I didn't see anything. The furs were cached as though they intended to come back. But they never did.

"So I told Laurent. He was going to arrange buyers in the States. But he could never keep his mouth shut when he'd been drinking. He boasted. Word must have got out, and got back to Stewart here. That's why he died."

"What makes you think it was Stewart?"

"Stewart wanted those furs more than anyone. Because he lost them. If he got them back, he would be a hero. The Company would take him back."

"Or he could make himself rich."

Parker shakes his head. "I don't think the money matters. With him it's pride."

"It could have been someone else—anyone—who had heard Jammet talk and wanted the money."

He turns his eyes on me. "But the trail led here."

I think about this for a moment. It's true. It's true, but it's not enough.

"It led us here, but now it's gone. And if we can't find the man . . ."

Suddenly I think of something, and go hot with excitement.

"Here, I found this at Jammet's . . ." I pull the scrap of paper out of my pocket and hand it to Parker. He peers at it, slanted toward the door, dim even so.

"Sixty-one, that's the outfit, isn't it?"

"Yes. Yes it is. You found this?"

"In his flour bin."

Parker smiles. I feel flushed with pride—for a second—and then it fades. It doesn't prove anything, other than that Jammet was interested in the furs in some way. It doesn't help.

"I gave that to him, with a silver fox pelt. It made him laugh, so he kept it. Sold the pelt, of course."

"Keep it," I say. "Perhaps you will think of some use for it." I don't even ask myself what I mean by that. Parker doesn't ask either, but the paper has disappeared. I still don't know what to do. Of course it is Moody who needs to be convinced.

"Will you tell Moody all this? Perhaps then he will see it."

"It's not proof, like you say. Moody likes Stewart; Stewart was always good at making men like him. Besides, Stewart didn't go to Dove River. There is someone else."

"Why would anyone kill for someone else?"

"Lots of reasons. Money. Fear. When we know who it is, we'll know why."

"It could be one of the men here. Perhaps it was Nepapanees, and then he . . . he threatened to talk, and Stewart killed him."

"I was thinking, I wonder if they'll ever find his body."

"Meaning what?"

"Meaning, they went in the direction Stewart told them to go. The snow will have covered the tracks. They've got only his word for how it happened."

The silence is so intense that even the dogs' whining cannot break it.

THEY COME TO THE PLACE Stewart told them about toward evening. The light has seeped out of the sky, and everything is gray: pearlescent gray clouds, pale gray snow. The smoothness of snow on river ice gives it away, a wide road curving through the plain six or seven feet below ground level. The river has worn its way deeper into the earth's rind ever since it began to flow.

There are signs of someone having been here recently, veiled by the new snow. A roughened, much-trodden place where the ground slopes down onto a sort of beach. From above, the skin of ice on the river is a flat and even white, except for a patch, farther up, where it is darker, shadowy, meaning it was broken and new ice has formed, thinner and only lightly dusted with snow. That must be the place.

Alec has been walking beside his mother, sometimes putting his hand in hers, sometimes not. It is hard for him; Elizabeth wondered whether to let him come at all, but there was a look in his eye that reminded her of Nepapanees. He was resolute and serious. Only yesterday he was still a boy with a father to test himself against. Now he has to be a man.

The men leave the sleds up on the bank, and go down to the river. Elizabeth takes Alec by the hand. It will not be his place to pull his father's body from the water. The men walk out cautiously, jabbing the ice with long poles, testing its strength. When it breaks, near the shadow, the water beneath is black. One man exclaims—the water is shallower than they thought. They study the current, discussing how to go about it. From their higher point on the bank, Elizabeth looks downstream, at the white curving road. Somewhere down there, Nepapanees is waiting.

"Stay here," she tells Alec, knowing he will obey. She strides off downstream without looking back. The men watch her nervously.

What she has seen: an interruption in the white smoothness of the river, a rough place where branches have snagged on a sunken bar and held, forming a weir. Anything carried downstream with the current would come to rest here for the winter until the spring floods washed it all away.

Elizabeth slides and scrambles down the bank above the weir. Part of her mind wonders why Stewart didn't think to look here, but the snow is virgin. The ice is strong beneath her feet. She kneels down and scrapes the snow away with her mittens, throwing it aside, revealing the ice beneath. Glare ice, clear as glass. The river's darkness leers up at her, brown-black and full of rotted matter under its icy shield. She claws at the ice with her hands, breaking the edges where it is pierced and spoiled by the branches, punching and cracking it, until . . .

There . . . there deep down, caught in the morass, she can see something, something both light and dark, something large and wrong and trapped in the watery darkness.

There are shouts, and some of the men scramble down the bank behind her, but she is not aware of them, nor of her breath coming in great hissing gasps between her teeth, nor of her hands, bare now, bleeding and blue with cold, scrabbling at the jagged ice edge. Then they are beside her with their sticks and axes, smashing at the ice, chopping it into great foaming chunks. Hands try to pull her away from the hole, but she takes them by surprise, lunges forward, diving in headfirst, her hands reaching out to take hold of her husband's body and drag him free. In the sudden shock of dead cold, even with her eyes open she sees nothing but blackness in the depths, and green-gray light above; until the something breaks free of its bonds and comes to her outstretched arms like a nightmare lover.

The carcass of a deer is swimming toward her, its rotting eyes wide and empty, black lips eaten back from grinning teeth, skull gleaming coy and white through sodden fur. The skin floats around it like a tattered shroud.

When they pull her out again they think for a moment she is dead. Her eyes are shut and water runs out of her mouth. Peter Eagles strikes her chest and she coughs, vomiting river. Her eyes open. They are already carrying her up the bank, pulling off her wet skins, chafing her flesh. Someone has made a fire. Someone else brings a blanket. Alec is crying. He isn't ready to lose another parent.

Elizabeth tastes the river in her mouth, the taste trapped behind her teeth, cold and dead.

"He isn't there," she says, when her teeth have stopped chattering.

George Cummings is rubbing her hands with a piece of blanket.

"There's a long stretch to look in; we will smash every piece of ice until we find him."

She shakes her head, still seeing the pale dead deer face smiling in triumph at her. "He isn't there."

Later they sit around the fire eating pemmican and tea. Normally they would fish, but no one wants to fish in this river; no one even suggests it. Alec sits up against Elizabeth, so that she can feel the warmth of his side and thigh.

They have made their camp on another beach, out of sight of the destruction they caused, protected by high banks from the wind. But it is surprisingly still, and the smoke from their fire rises straight up in the air until it disappears.

William Blackfeather speaks in a low voice, to no one in particular. "Tomorrow, at first light, we'll look, upriver as well as down. Between us we can cover a lot of ground."

Nodding. Then Peter: "Strange how shallow the water is. You would have thought it would be hard to get swept away. The current isn't so fast."

George nods toward Elizabeth, warningly. She, however, doesn't seem to be listening. Kenowas drops his voice when he speaks.

"There was new ice, where it was broken. What was there before wasn't thick, half as thick as the new ice."

There is silence, in which they all think their own thoughts. Kenowas speaks his out loud.

"I wouldn't have gone onto that ice, no matter what I was following."

"What are you saying?" Arnaud is gruff and belligerent, even when sober. Kenowas turns to him. There is a long-standing dislike between them.

"I can't see Nepapanees going out on it either. Even an idiot like you would think twice."

No one laughs, even though it's meant as a joke. There is truth in what he says, and Nepapanees was the keenest tracker, the most experienced among them.

What no one says, although most of them think it, is that the guiding spirit of Nepapanees was a deer. He was not baptized, so instead of a baby looking after him, he had the deer-spirit. A strong, fast, brave spirit that knew the woods and plains. Better than a baby for him, he said. How could a human baby, born long ago in a hot, sandy country, know how to survive in the cold wilderness? What could it teach him? Then Elizabeth, baptized with a special saint for company and with white blood in her veins, shook her head and tutted if she was angry, or teased him and pulled his hair if she was not. When she became a convert in adulthood, she had liked the thought of St. Francis, with his kindness and his way of communing with the birds and other creatures. He was almost like a Chippewa in this, and for this reason was very popular—four children and two adults in their village alone had chosen him for confirmation.

Now St. Francis seems far away and irrelevant, a stranger who could not possibly understand this death, her icy grief. Elizabeth cannot shake the sight of the deer's head from her mind. In the river she had felt strongly that her husband was not there at all, was nowhere near, but perhaps she was wrong. Perhaps her husband's faith has been the right one all along, and what she saw was his spirit, come back to taunt her for her unbelief.

She feels distant, frozen by more than cold, utterly apart from the men and the food and the fire. Even from the snow and the silence and the bottomlessly hollow sky. The only thing that connects her to this world at all is the gentle pressure of her son's body, a thin thread of human warmth, easily broken.

THE TEMPERATURE CONTINUES TO DROP. In this cold, the air feels as though it is being tightened in a vice. It takes your breath away, sucks moisture from your skin, burns like fire. There is a deep, almost conscious silence in the yard, in which feet crunch the snow with startling loudness.

That's what wakes Donald: the press and squeak of new snow underfoot.

He has stayed in bed all day, pleading a slight fever, and slept into the late afternoon, a chair wedged under the door handle, dozing pleasantly as the light faded. There is nothing unusual about the footsteps—there are still people around to make them—only they have a peculiar, uneven pattern, which jolts him out of his comfortable daze. Unwillingly he finds himself listening as the person walks, stops, then walks a little farther. Then stops again. He waits—dammit!—for their next move. At length he is forced to push himself up on his elbows and peer out into the darkening courtyard. A couple of squares of light spill from rooms farther along: the offices, perhaps. At first he doesn't see the person, but that is because he is keeping to the shadows; presumably he assumes that Donald's room, because dark, is empty. Then he sees him: a man dressed in furs, with long dark hair. Donald wonders if the search party has returned. He does not recognize this man, and after a few moments realizes that he is not from any search party. He is furtive, looking around him with exaggerated care, and moving in a sort of pantomime of stealth. He is colossally drunk. Donald watches with mounting amusement as the man stumbles over something in the darkness, and swears. Then, when there is no response to the noise, he moves off toward the stores and out of sight. Someone too drunk to be any use in searching. Donald sinks back into his cocoon, pulling the blankets around his chin.

There are men at Fort Edgar who spend months inebriated, who are good for nothing all winter. It is sad when they get to that stage, and means their working life will be short. Drunkenness is a progressive disease, and Donald was initially shocked that the Company elders took no steps to counteract it, allowing the voyageurs unlimited access to their poor-quality liquor. When he tentatively pressed Jacob on the subject, Jacob hung his head; it had been alcohol that caused him to stick a knife in Donald's belly. As far as Donald knew, Jacob had not touched a drop since. Only once had Donald brought up the subject with Mackinley, to have Mackinley turn his pale eyes on him with amusement, if not downright scorn. "This is the way the world works," was what Mackinley's argument boiled down to. All the traders lure trappers and staff with liquor; if the Company didn't provide it, it would lose out to rival outfits with fewer scruples and less regard for the welfare of those who work for them. To act any other way would be naive. Donald felt there was something amiss with this argument, but did not dare say so.

After a while he gets to thinking about what Mrs. Ross told him last night. Nesbit is a young man like him, fairly recently arrived from Scotland. A man of education and some breeding. A junior clerk, but with the intelligence to advance in the Company. The similarities alarm Donald; or rather, once those similarities are taken into account, the differences begin to alarm him. Nesbit's nervous tics, his bitter laugh, the flagrant hatred for his life. He has been in the country more than twice as long as Donald, and though he is clearly miserable, he seems to assume that he will never leave. A slight shudder runs through Donald as he contemplates the prospect of Norah, with her wide, mistrustful face and insolent speech, in whose broad arms Nesbit has apparently found comfort. In the past he has been aware of mixed liaisons—even at Fort Edgar they were common—but Donald held himself aloof from the idea that this would ever happen to him. He felt he was destined to marry (somehow; the details were obscure) a nice, white English-speaking girl—a girl like Susannah, in fact, only he had never dared dream of someone as pretty. In his first eighteen months at Fort Edgar, such a prospect began to seem increasingly remote. But looking at the native women who abounded at the fort, he still drew back, even when the men teased him about this or that girl who had giggled in his presence. But he has never seen a native woman as beautiful as Nancy Eagles. He can still feel the warmth of her soft flesh, the thrilling boldness of her hand— that is, if he allows himself to think about it. Which he won't. Hard to imagine Norah having the same galvanizing effect on Nesbit, somehow. Still.

The letter to Maria is on the desk. Last night, after his private outburst, he picked up the balled paper, smoothed it out, and pressed it as well as he could under some spare sheets, weighted down with his boots, but he fears it will not be enough. Perhaps it was unwise of him to write to her anyway. Perhaps crumpling it up into a ball was a blessing in disguise. It is Susannah he should be thinking of, and he does, trying to grasp her elusive image, to hear her light, silvery voice in his head.

As the last of the light drains from the sky, Donald dresses. He is hungry, which he seizes on as a sign of returning vigor, and wanders out into the deserted corridors. He finds Nesbit in his office—the beacon of light he saw from across the courtyard. There is no sign of Stewart, Mrs. Ross, or anyone else.

Nesbit leans back from his desk with a grimace, unkinking the hunch in his back. He yawns hugely, revealing blackened molars. "Fucking accounts. Bane of my life. Well, one of them. Used to have an accountant here once— Archie Murray. Funny little chap—mousy sort of fellow. But since he went I've had to do it myself, and it's not my forte, I don't mind telling you. Not my forte at all."

Donald toys with the idea of offering his help, but decides he isn't feeling that vigorous.

"Not that we've got such a huge turnover to deal with. More outgoing than incoming, if you know what I mean. How's tricks at your place?"

"Fairly good, I suppose. But then we are more of a way station than a source. I suppose once—years ago, before there were so many men—the whole country was full of furs."

"I'm not sure that there was ever much of anything around here." Nesbit looks gloomy. "Do you know what the natives call this neck of the woods? Starvation Country. Even the bloody foxes can't find anything to eat—and they're all red, of course. Time for a drink."

From his slumped sitting position, Nesbit lurches past Donald and pulls a bottle of malt whisky from behind some ledgers. "Come on."

Donald follows Nesbit into his sitting room—the small, bare room next to his office that contains a couple of overstuffed armchairs and some pictorial relief of a questionable nature.

"Where is Mr. Stewart this evening?" Donald asks, as he accepts a large glass of malt. Fortunately it is of a better quality than the rum at Fort Edgar. Donald wonders fleetingly how it is that—at the back of beyond, when decent food and housekeeping seem beyond them—the inhabitants of Hanover House drink like kings.

"Oh, around and about," Nesbit says vaguely. "Around and about. You know . . ." He leans forward in his chair, staring at Donald with disconcerting intensity. "That man . . . That man is a saint. An absolute saint."

"Mm," says Donald, carefully.

"Running this place is a thankless task, believe me, but he never complains. You never hear him grumble about it, unlike yours truly. And he's a man who could have done anything—the highest caliber. The very highest."

"Yes, he seems very able," Donald says, a little stiffly.

Nesbit gives him a calculating look. "I daresay you may think that anyone who gets sent out to a hellhole like this must be second-rate, and it may be true in my case, but not in his."

Donald inclines—and then shakes—his head politely, hoping his agreement and disagreement will be attributed to the right things.

"The natives love him. They don't think much of yours truly, and it's mutual, so that's fair enough, but him . . . they treat him as a sort of minor deity. He's out there now, talking to them. For a moment, when he came back with the news about Nepapanees, I thought things might turn ugly, but he went out there and had them eating out of his hand in two shakes."

"Ah. Mm. Admirable," murmurs Donald, wondering whether Jacob would ever eat out of anyone's hand. It seems unlikely. He also pictures—vividly—the widow left in the snow as Stewart and Nesbit walked inside. But strangely enough, although Donald prides himself on having the independence of mind to take such a eulogy with a pinch of salt, it is only too easy to believe that Stewart inspires devotion. He finds himself drawn to Stewart almost as much as he is repelled by Nesbit.

"I know I am second-rate. I may not know much, but I know that." Nesbit stares into the amber lights in his glass. Donald wonders if he is a little unhinged; for a moment he has a horrible suspicion that Nesbit is about to cry. But then he smiles instead, the bitter, cynical expression that has become familiar. "How about you, Moody, where do you fit into the scheme of things?"

"I'm not sure that I understand you."

"I mean, are you second-rate? Or are you first-rate?"

Donald laughs uneasily.

"Or perhaps you don't know yet."

"I er . . . I'm not sure that I agree that it is a helpful distinction."

"I didn't say that it was helpful. But it is self-evident. That is, if you have the courage to see it."

"I don't think so. You may claim that it is courageous to accept your assessment of yourself, but I could suggest that to do so is a way of abdicating the responsibilities of life. Such cynicism gives you a license to give up and make no effort. All failures are excused in advance."

Nesbit smiles unpleasantly. Donald could enjoy this sort of half-serious discussion, which he has come across before—usually at the back end of a long winter evening—but his wound is starting to throb.

"You think I am a failure?"

Donald has a sudden, disturbing image of Nesbit clamped in Norah's mahogany embrace, and feels guilty at his knowledge of the other man. Almost at the same moment, Susannah's face crystallizes in his mind in sharp and wonderful clarity; after all this time grasping at fog, each element slots into place, and there she is: whole, precise, lovely. And at the same instant, he realizes with a shock of detachment that his feelings for her are finite, and comprise mainly admiration and awe. He experiences a strong urge to rush back to his room to finish the letter to Maria. Subtle, unpredictable Maria. How strange. How strange and yet freeing, this realization. How wonderful! He suppresses a smile at the thought.

"I said, do you?"

Donald has to make a momentary intense effort to remember what the question was.

"No, not at all. But I can imagine the frustrations of a place like this. I am sure I would feel the same. A man needs company, and variety. I know how long the winters become, and I have experienced only one so far. One companion is not enough, however first-rate."

"Bravo. I say, did you hear something?" Nesbit drains his glass and pauses in the act of refilling it, head cocked to one side. Donald listens, assuming it was footsteps in the corridor, but as usual, there is no one there. Nesbit shakes his head and sloshes more whisky into Donald's glass, although he has not yet finished.

"You are a capital fellow, Moody. I wish we had you here. You might even be able to unravel the accounts that I have been scrambling into a knot of Gordian proportions for the last two years." Nesbit smiles broadly, his bitterness mysteriously vanished.

"I saw one of your fellows outside earlier," Donald says, apropos of not much. "He clearly hasn't gone with the search party, but then he seemed so inebriated I daresay he would have been more hindrance than help."

"Ah." A faraway look overcomes Nesbit. "Yes. That is a problem we have in winter, as I am sure you know only too well."

"Is he a voyageur?" Donald wants to ask right out who it is, but feels that would be too blunt.

"I've no idea to whom you're referring, old chap. As far as I know all the men, except Olivier, have gone upriver. Maybe it was him you saw."

"No, no, it was definitely an older man. Heavier, you know. And long-haired."

"This dim light can play tricks on you. Why, I once looked out of the window—it was last winter and I was sitting at my desk next door—and nearly had a heart attack. There was a moose standing right outside—seven feet tall if it was an inch—staring at me. I gave a frightful bellow and ran out of the door, but when I got to the yard, there was no sign of it. And no footprints. Of course there was no way it could have got in over the palisade, but I would have sworn on a stack of Bibles that it was there. Imagine that!"

You were probably drunk, Donald thinks sourly. Donald knows perfectly well that the man in the courtyard wasn't Olivier, and is increasingly aware—really, it is as though his brain has been asleep for the last couple of days—that an unidentified man should be of some interest to them.

So much so that he makes an excuse to slip out when he can, some time later, to investigate the snow outside his window. Which is when he finds that for some reason standards of housekeeping have suddenly been raised, and the yard has been swept clear of snow.

AFTER HER VISIT TO STURROCK, Maria shut herself in her room with her copy of the markings, and managed to forget the state of her family while she puzzled over its contents. First she tried breaking down the lines into groups as they seemed to arrange themselves—though this assumed Sturrock had copied them down accurately in the first place. From an article in the *Edinburgh Review,* and from her own sense, she was from the beginning aware that each mark or group of marks might not stand for a letter in the Roman alphabet, but might represent a word, or a sound. After she had arranged and rearranged the clusters and substituted numbers of sounds and letters, all of which produced meaningless jumbles of sounds (da-ya-no-ji-te! ba-lo-re-ya-no?), she put it aside with rather less hope than she had started with. There were no grounds at all for expecting Maria Knox to be able to solve their riddles—an uneducated country girl with a few journal subscriptions and just one article on deciphering the Rosetta stone as a starting point. But the little angular marks swirled around her head, invaded her dreams, taunting her with a meaning that they dangled just out of her reach. She had an unhealthy desire to see the original tablet, and her mind turned to the North, where Francis, possibly, and Mr. Moody as well, held the key.

She pushes the remains of her breakfast around the plate. Congealed egg and the juices of a steak make a bilious abstract on the willow pattern.

"If you don't mind"—she scrapes her chair getting up—"I'd like to take a bit of a walk."

Mrs. Knox frowns at her eldest daughter. "All right. Be careful, won't you?"

"Yes, Mother." Maria is already halfway to the door. It is really quite comical how her mother thinks that anywhere outside Caulfield is a den of iniquity, crawling with white slavers. She'll have to get used to the idea if Maria is to move to Toronto, which she is definitely going to do, she has decided, next summer.

Outside the hotel, Maria takes a right, toward the waterfront. Straggled along the shore of the lake is a sprawl of wharves and warehouses, gathering points for goods from all over the North. Sault St. Marie is exciting, the thrum of commerce, of business; dirty and loud and somehow real in a way that Caulfield and John Scott's store are not. She has been warned away from just this part of town, which is part of its attraction. Men walk past her, keeping urgent appointments with steamer arrivals, stock prices, labor meetings. To a sheltered country girl it feels like being in the heart of things.

There are some hotels and boardinghouses in this end of town, too: less salubrious than the Victoria and Albert, farther removed from the opera house. She sees a man and woman come out of one and watches them idly for a moment before realizing, with a sudden quiver of shock, that the man is Angus Ross, the farmer from Dove River. Francis's father. When he turns his head, she gets a clear sight of his face; the blunt profile, the sandy hair. The shock is because the woman he is with is not Mrs. Ross. Mrs. Ross has not been seen for weeks. Maria feels herself flush with a shame that is not hers. There is something not quite right, even though Mr. Ross and the woman are only walking across the street. He has not seen her, and she instinctively shrinks back and turns to study the window of the shop nearest her. It displays nothing but a list of things that make no sense in her confusion.

She waits until the pair are safely out of sight. She has never seen an impropriety before, but she is somehow sure that is what it was. And where, after all, is Mrs. Ross? They have only her husband's word that she set off after her son. It suddenly occurs to Maria, who has read some lurid novels along with the improving ones, that perhaps Mr. Ross has done away with his wife. And what about Francis? Mr. Moody and his friend went haring off after him, but perhaps never found him. Perhaps that is why they have not returned. Perhaps Mr. Ross killed Mr. Jammet as well . . .

Maria reins herself in here, telling herself that she is not prey to wild fancies. But still, she feels shaken. Perhaps she should have finished her breakfast after all. Perhaps—she looks around, to see if anyone is watching her—perhaps, due to exceptional circumstances, she will go and have A Drink.

Buoyed up with daring, Maria chooses a quiet-looking bar set back from the waterfront and goes inside. She takes a deep breath, but there is no one here other than the barkeep and a man sitting at one of the tables, eating, with his back to the door.

She orders a glass of sherry and a piece of salmonberry pie, and sits at a table near the back, just in case anyone she knows should happen by. Like Mr. Ross. Her heart beats faster at the thought. She has never had a reason to either especially like or dislike Mrs. Ross before—the woman is rather distant—but now she feels sorry for her. It occurs to her that of all people, she and Mrs. Ross might have things in common.

Her order arrives, and, to give her eyes something to do, she takes out the papers with her attempts to break the code. She is aware that the other customer has noticed her, and she worries that he might try to join her. She sees what she did not notice before: that he is an Indian of rather disreputable appearance, and resolves not to look in his direction again. Soon she has taken out a pencil and begun annotating her efforts, which consist of a long line of nonsense words and syllables. She becomes so absorbed that she does not notice the barkeep standing beside her until he clears his throat.

"Excuse me, ma'am. Would you like another?" He holds the sherry bottle in his hand.

"Oh. Thank you, yes. The pie was very good." To her surprise, it had been.

"Thank you. Are you doing a puzzle?"

"In a way." He has nice eyes, the barkeep, and very long, drooping brown whiskers. He has an unexpected air of intelligence. "I am trying to understand a code. But it is hopeless, I think, as I do not know which language it is written in."

"You mean like French, or Italian?"

"Yes . . . although I think it is an Indian language, and there are so many."

"Ah. Then you need some help."

"Yes. From someone who is fluent in all of them." She shrugs and smiles, as this is unlikely.

"Ma'am, if I may make a suggestion? You see the gentleman sitting over there? He knows many Indian languages. If you like, I could introduce you."

He sees her doubtful glance at the hunched shoulder and greasy hair curling over the collar. "He is perfectly . . . pleasant." He smiles, as though he hasn't managed quite the right word, but decides it will have to do. Maria feels a blush threatening. This is what comes of walking into disreputable establishments; she is impaled on the sword of her own daring. She looks at her papers and feels like a silly schoolgirl.

"Of course, you would rather not. Forget I said it. It was impertinent."

Maria draws herself upright. If she is to be a scholar, a thinker, she cannot shirk from the path of knowledge because of a greasy collar.

"No, that would be very . . . nice. Thank you. If he doesn't mind the bother, that is."

The barkeep goes over to the other table and speaks to the man. Maria catches a glimpse of bloodshot eyes and has second and third thoughts about her decision. But he gets up and comes over to her table, carrying his glass. She smiles at him briefly; professionally, she hopes.

"Hello. I'm Miss Knox. You are Mr. . . . ?"

He sits down. "Joe."

"Ah. Yes. Thank you for—"

"Fredo says you want someone who knows Indian tongues."

"Yes, I have here part of a code, and, um, a friend of mine thinks it might be for an Indian language. I have been trying to decipher it, but since I don't know what language it represents . . ."

She smiles too much, giving a slight shrug, even more scared now that they are face-to-face. The man is older than she first thought, with streaks of gray in his hair. The skin below his eyes is pouchy, the cheeks slack. There are red threads in the whites of his eyes. He smells of rum.

But still, a keen face, or was once.

"There are no written native languages, so why would your friend think that?"

"I know, but, well . . . he has researched it. And these little figures—you see, this is just a copy, but they are like Indian drawings I have seen."

For some reason she is pushing her copy toward him, repellent though he is. She wants him at least to take her seriously.

He studies the paper for a long time but says nothing. Maria wishes she were back at the hotel.

"What is it a copy of?"

"A bone tablet."

He picks up her other papers, the ones with her tentative workings out. "What are these names?"

"Oh, they're not names; they're what I got from trying out certain letters and sounds, you know, substituting for the marks here . . ."

He studies the sheets, holding them up in the light to focus better. His finger stabs the paper. "Deganawida. Ochinaway. You think this is what it says?"

His manner has become more aggressive. Maria lifts her chin defiantly. There is nothing wrong with her method. She learned it from the *Edinburgh Review*.

"Well, I was guessing. You have to make certain assumptions about which sounds the marks might mean, and try them out. I tried many, many things. This is what came out with one . . . one combination of . . ."

The man leans back in his seat and smiles at her: a sneering, hostile grimace. "Lady, is this some kind of joke? Who told you I was here?"

"No, of course not. I had no idea . . . I don't know who you are!" She looks around, nervously, for Fredo, but he is serving some newcomers.

"Who was it? Was it that fat bastard McGee? Huh? Or Andy Jensen? Was it Andy?"

"I don't know what you're talking about. I don't know what you're implying; this is quite uncalled for!"

Now Fredo has heard the tone in her voice; he glances toward her . . . he is coming over, at last.

"What's your friend's name, lady?" insists Joe.

"Ma'am, I'm so sorry. Joe, you'll have to leave."

"I just want to know his name."

"Mr. . . . Joe seems to think I am playing some sort of trick on him."

"Joe, apologize to the lady. Come on now."

Joe shuts his eyes and bows his head: an oddly ethereal mannerism that restores to his ruined face a delicacy that has been blurred by time and alcohol.

"I'm sorry. I'd just like to know the name of your friend who has this . . . whatever you called it."

Maria feels braver with Fredo standing over her. And something in the man's face when he closed his eyes, something endlessly long-suffering and pained, sad even, makes her want to answer.

"Well, his name is Mr. Sturrock, since you ask. And it is no trick. I do not play tricks."

"Sturrock?" Joe looks serious. His whole demeanor sharpens, as though his connecting threads have been pulled together, transforming him. "Tom Sturrock. The searcher?"

"Yes . . . he was. Do you know him?"

"Did once. Well, I wish you luck, lady, and tell your friend Kahon'wes said hello."

Maria frowns, struggling with the word. "Ga-hoo' ways?"

The man, whatever his name is, gets up and walks out of the bar. Maria looks at Fredo for an explanation. But he is as surprised as she is.

"I am so sorry, ma'am, I didn't know he would be like that. Normally he is so quiet, he just comes in and drinks, but is perfectly pleasant. Let me get you another sherry, or a piece of—"

"No, thank you. I really must be going. My father will be waiting. How much do I . . . ?"

"No, no, I cannot let you pay."

After some minutes' insisting on both sides, Maria prevails, feeling it would not be a good precedent to become obliged to a stranger. She leaves with a flurry of papers and thank-yous, and keeps her gaze rigidly fixed ahead as she hurries away from the waterfront.

The morning has been more of an adventure than she bargained for, the path of knowledge a rocky and alarming one. But at the very least she will have something to tell Mr. Sturrock, and perhaps something to rouse her father from his lethargy as well. With a sense of relief at having left the docks behind, Maria slows down to compose her story and, as she rearranges her adventure into a suspense-laden narrative with an intrepid heroine, almost manages to convince herself that she was not afraid at all.

THE LIGHT IS DIM UNDER the trees, and it goes early, so they stop, because the children are whining so badly. Espen tries to hide his fear, but he has no real idea how to build a snow shelter, nor how to light a fire when the snow is this deep. He clears a bare patch on the forest floor, manages after some time to light a fire with damp wood, but before their water has boiled, the surrounding snow banks have melted and doused the flames. The children look on through tears of disappointment and cold. Line keeps talking and encouraging, her throat dry with thirst, lips cracked with cold. She has never talked so much in her life; she is determined not to give in, not to look scared, not to cry.

When Torbin and Anna have finally fallen into an exhausted sleep, she says, "We're bound to hit the river tomorrow. The snow has slowed us down, but we'll get there."

Espen does not speak for a while. She has never seen him look this unhappy.

"Line, we have been going around in circles. I can't tell what direction we're going in. Without the compass, or seeing the sun, I have no idea."

"Wait. We went wrong." She needs to take him in hand, steady him, let him know that she is still in charge of things. "So we went wrong once. It probably wasn't a big circle. We are not going around in circles. The forest has been changing. The trees are changing, getting taller, so we must be getting farther south. I have noticed that, very particularly. We just need to keep going. I am sure that tomorrow we will find the river."

He doesn't look as though he believes her. He looks down, like a mutinous child who doesn't want to give in, but has nowhere else to go. She takes his face in her mittened hands—it is too cold to attempt greater intimacy.

"Espen . . . my darling. Don't give up now. We're so close. When we get to Caulfield, and we can get some rooms, we'll be sitting in front of a roaring fire and we'll laugh about this. Such an adventure to start our life together!"

"And if we don't get to Caulfield? My horse is ill. They haven't got nearly enough to eat—or drink either. It's been eating bark, and I'm sure they're not supposed to."

"We'll get there. We'll get somewhere. It's only three days to cross the forest. Tomorrow we might come to the lake! Then you'll feel foolish."

She kisses him. This makes him laugh.

"You are a vargamor. Unbelievable. No wonder you always get what you want."

"Ha." Line smiles, but thinks this unfair, as well as wrong. Did she want Janni to disappear into the wilderness? Did she want to go and live in Himmelvanger? Still, at least he is more cheerful, and that is the main thing. If she can keep him going, keep them all going, then they'll be all right.

As they lie together under their pitiful shelter, clasping the children between them, Line hears things through her tiredness: the pistol crack of freezing sap, the sough of snow slipping off the branches. And once, very far away, she thinks she hears wolves, howling into the empty night, and her skin prickles with sweat, despite the cold.

The next morning, after they have been walking for about an hour, a loud crack resounds among the trees. It's so loud Anna flinches and nearly falls over. They all stare at one another.

"A hunter!" Espen exclaims in excitement.

"Are you sure it wasn't just sap freezing?" Line asks, because someone should.

"It was too loud, and it's different. It's a rifle. Someone is hunting around here."

He sounds so sure. The children whoop with such delight and relief that Line is won over. Human beings are here. Civilization is suddenly within reach.

"I'll see if I can find him . . . Just to check we're on the right path," Espen adds hastily.

"How will you get back?" Line says sharply.

"Light a fire. I won't be long. He must be very near." Espen starts to shout in English. "Hello! Hey. Who's there? Hello!"

Without waiting for a reply he turns back to them. "I think it came from over there. I won't be long. If I don't find him, I'll come straight back, I promise."

Espen gives them all a big, confident grin, and walks off between the trees. His footsteps vanish into the silence. One of the horses, Jutta, emits a long equine sigh.

I T IS INTERESTING TO NOTE the ebb and flow of personnel at the post. The way people divide up, or are drawn together. Just from my own observation, it is evident that Olivier is not popular with the other employees. He sticks close to Stewart, runs errands for him, even apes some of his mannerisms. From the others, there is a sense of distance between white and nonwhite, and it is as though Olivier is a turncoat who has gone over to the other side. Initially I thought they respected Stewart, and were even fond of him. Now I'm not so sure. There is respect, but it is of a wary sort, the kind with which you might regard a potentially dangerous animal. Norah hates him, and while she presumably cares for Nesbit, she is equally rude to both. She treats Stewart with such insolence it makes me wonder if she holds some sort of power—otherwise, I cannot imagine how she is allowed to get away with it. And a few times I have seen the pretty one—Nancy—in the corridor here. Since she does not appear to clean or serve, I wonder what she has been doing. Cooking, perhaps.

I am waiting for something to happen. Two hours have passed since the search party returned. I have been hovering between my room, the kitchen, and the dining room—I keep finding petty things that need to be addressed, a lack of kindling (because I have thrown it outside), or spilled coffee. I am very unpopular with Norah as a result, but just after six o'clock I am rewarded by the sound of shouting from Stewart's office. The raised voice belongs to Nesbit; it has a hysterical note.

"For God's sake, I keep telling you I don't know! But it's gone, there's no doubt about it."

Low murmuring from Stewart.

"Christ, I don't care. You promised! You've got to help me!"

Some more muttering—something about "carelessness."

I am in the corridor, tiptoeing closer, praying to the god of creaking floorboards.

"It has to be one of them. Who else would do that? And there's some-thing else . . . Half man—you've got to keep better control of him."

The murmuring gets even lower. For some reason, this chills me more than anything. I don't dare go closer. What does Nesbit mean by "half a man?" Is he insulting Stewart? Or someone else?

Heavy footsteps approach the door. I scuttle past, and make the dining room door safely before anyone comes out. From his chair by the fire, Moody looks up as I come in.

"Mrs. Ross. There is something I would like to discuss with you . . ."

"Just a moment . . ." I put the coffeepot down. Outside, all seems to be quiet. "I'm sorry, Mr. Moody, I seem to have forgotten something. Excuse me a moment."

His face droops in the narrowing rectangle as I close the door.

I walk back down the empty corridor. Stewart's door is shut. I knock on it.

"What is it?" Nesbit's voice. Very bad-tempered.

"Oh, it is I, Mrs. Ross. May I come in?"

"I am rather busy right now."

I open the door anyway. Nesbit looks up from the desk—I have the im-pression that he had just been sprawled forward over it; his face is sweaty and pale, his hair more disheveled than ever. I feel a stirring of sympathy. I remember what it is like.

"I said—"

"I know, I am sorry. It is just that I feel terrible. I have broken the milk jug, I am so very sorry."

Nesbit looks at me with a frown of mixed incomprehension and irritation. "For goodness' sake, it really doesn't matter. If you don't mind . . ."

I take another step inside the room and close the door behind me. Nesbit flinches. There is a murderous look in his eye: a cornered animal.

"Have you lost something? I know how vexing that can be. Perhaps I can help you?"

"You? What are you talking about?"

But almost as soon as I closed the door, he got the idea. I have his full at-tention now.

"Why would you assume I had lost anything?"

"He keeps it for you, doesn't he? He makes you beg."

It is as though I have torn away a mask; his face is so white it is almost blue. His fists clench; he wants to strike me but he dares not.

"Where is it? What have you done with it? Give it to me."

"I will give it back, if you tell me something."

He frowns, but it gives him hope. He stands up and takes a step toward me, but doesn't come too close.

"Tell me who needs to be controlled. Who must not be spoken of?"

"What?"

"The first night, I heard you telling a woman not to speak of him. Who were you talking about? Just now, you told Stewart to keep better control of him. You said he was half a man. Who? Tell me who it is, and I will give it back."

He deflates. His head turns this way and that. He half smiles. Something in him seems relieved.

"Oh. We didn't want Moody to find out. If it gets back to the Company . . . One of our men has gone mad. It's Nepapanees. Stewart is trying to protect him, because of his family . . ."

"Nepapanees? You mean he isn't dead?"

Nesbit shakes his head.

"He lives on his own, like a wild man. He was all right until a few weeks ago, but now he's quite crazy. Maybe dangerous. It would mean terrible shame for his family. Stewart thought it better if they believed him dead." He shakes his head. "That's all. Ha . . . ! I mean, it's terrible."

"And he's been away . . . hasn't he, recently?"

"He comes and goes."

"Three weeks ago . . ."

"I don't know where he goes. He returned about ten days ago."

I don't know what else to say. Or ask. He looks furtively at me. "Can I have it?"

For I moment I consider smashing the bottle on the floor, because something has gone wrong, and I can't put my finger on it.

"Please." He takes another step toward me.

I pull it out of my pocket and hold it out: the bottle I took from beneath his mattress yesterday while he was with Moody. He grabs it, checks it to see if I've stolen any—a reflex, momentary action—then turns away and drinks from it. A remnant of dignity wanting to preserve some privacy. It takes a while for it to work that way, but perhaps he has no other. He remains in that position, staring at the curtains.

"And where is he now?"

"I don't know. Far from here, I hope."

"Is this true?"

"Yes."

I can just see the bottle in his hand. What would I not give to take it from him, and drink?

He doesn't look at me again. His voice is low, already composed again. It brings me back to myself. I leave him standing by the desk, his back to me, but with shoulders squared and defiant.

I walk back to the dining room. Nepapanees a madman. Nepapanees Jammet's insane killer? This is, it seems, what I wanted to find. But I feel no triumph. No satisfaction. I don't know what to think, but I can't keep from my mind the picture of Elizabeth Bird, sitting in the snow, deliberately scalding her flesh out of grief.

STEWART COMES TO HER HOUSE when they get back. He looks concerned, like a father with a wayward child—ready to be indulgent, but only up to a point.

"Elizabeth, I am so sorry."

She nods. It is easier than speaking.

"I have been trying to think what might have happened. You found the place?"

She nods again.

"I am sure his spirit will be at peace, wherever he is."

Now she doesn't nod. Murdered men do not lie in peace.

"If you were worried . . . Of course you can stay here. You need not worry about your future. You will always have a home here, as long as you want."

She is aware, without looking straight at him, of his horrid blue eyes, like the glinting bodies of flies that feed on carrion. He is looking intently at her, trying to sap her strength, trying to bend her to his will. Well, she won't look at him, she won't make it easy. She makes a sideways movement of her head, hoping he will go away.

"I'll leave you. If you want anything at all, please come and ask."

She nods for the third time.

She thinks: in hell.

Outside, she hears English voices: Stewart telling the moonias, "I'd leave her if I were you. She is still in shock."

The voices start to move away. Elizabeth jumps up, from sheer contrariness, and goes outside.

"Mr. Moody . . . Please come in, if you wish."

The two men turn, startled. Moody's face is a question. Elizabeth, unsure why she rushed out like that, feels foolish.

Moody insists on sitting on the floor, like her, although his movements are a little stiff.

"Are you all right? Is it better?" Her gaze goes to his midriff, where she bandaged his wound four nights ago. A lifetime ago, when she was still a man's wife. "It was a bad wound. Did someone try to kill you?"

"No." He laughs. "Or, well, it was a moment of passion, deeply regretted. A long story. And I came to see how you were. If there is anything I can do to help . . ."

"Thank you. You were kind, the other day."

"No . . ."

Elizabeth pours tea into enamel mugs. She tastes again the river water, bitter with treachery. Perhaps the deer was a sign: I am killed. And you have to find me.

If only she could pray for guidance, but she cannot go to the wooden church. That is Stewart's church, and she has an aversion to it. She never thought about her faith much, before. She assumed it was there under the surface, carrying on without conscious effort, the way her lungs breathed. Perhaps she neglected it too much. Now that she needs it, it seems to have withered away.

"Do you pray?"

Moody looks at her in surprise. He considers his answer. He doesn't just say what he thinks he should, but really seems to give it thought. She likes that, along with the way he doesn't rush to fill every little silence.

"Yes, I do. Not as often as I should. Not nearly."

Just then, her little girl stumbles in through the front door. She has only just learned to walk.

"Amy, go back to Mary. I'm talking."

The child gazes at Donald before toddling back outside.

"I suppose we only . . ." His voice trails off. "I mean to say, we turn to God only when in trouble or need, and I have never been in great trouble or need. Not yet, thank God."

He smiles. He looks troubled now, puzzled. His words slower, as if he's having difficulty ordering them. Something has happened.

"I cannot."

He looks at her, questioning.

"Pray."

"Were you born a Christian?"

She smiles. "I was baptized by the missionaries when I was twenty."

"So you knew . . . other gods. Do you pray to them?"

"I don't know. I never really prayed, before. You are right. I never had the need."

Moody puts his tea down and folds his long wrists across his knees. "When I was a young boy, I became terribly lost, in the hills near my home. I was lost for a day and a night. I was afraid I was going to wander in the hills until I starved. I prayed then. I prayed that God would show me the way home."

"And?"

"My father found me."

"So your prayers were answered."

"Yes. I suppose there are some prayers that cannot be answered."

"I would not pray for my husband to be brought back to life. I would only pray for justice."

"Justice?" His eyes widen, fixed on her, as though she has a smut on her face. He seems fascinated, as if she's suddenly said something of intense and vital interest.

Elizabeth puts down her cup. Neither of them speaks for a long minute, staring into the fire, which pops and hisses.

"Amy. That's a pretty name."

"She doesn't understand why her father isn't here."

Moody sighs sharply, then smiles. "I am sorry. You must think me impertinent. I have just had the most amazing thought. Please tell me if I am wrong, but I cannot keep it in." He laughs awkwardly, without taking his eyes off her. "I know the time is not right. But I can't help thinking . . . Your daughter's name. And your . . . I don't know how to say this . . . Were you ever . . . were you once a Seton?"

Elizabeth stares into the flames, and a loud singing in her ears drowns the next thing he says. A surge of something like laughter threatens to choke her.

His mouth is moving; he is apologizing, she thinks from a distance. Things she thought long forgotten are suddenly clear as glass. A father. A sister. A mother. No, not her sister. She never forgot her sister.

Slowly his voice becomes audible again. "Are you Amy Seton?" Moody leans forward, flushed with excitement, with the thrill of an imminent and momentous discovery. "I won't tell anyone, if you don't want me to. I promise on my honor to keep it a secret. You have your life here, your children . . . I would just like to know."

She doesn't want to give him this pleasure. It is not his to take. She is not a bounty to be found and claimed.

"Mr. Moody, I don't know what you mean. My name is Elizabeth Bird. My husband was deliberately killed. What am I to do? What are you going to do?"

"Deliberately? What makes you say that?"

She sees him lurch, with difficulty, from one sort of excitement to another. It disagrees with him; he cannot take it. She seems to watch from a great distance as he gasps and clutches at his stomach, his face knotted up in anguish. His face is red. He should not have asked such a personal question. At length he recovers himself, panting like a dog.

"What are you saying? That . . . Stewart killed your husband?"

"Yes."

"Why would he?"

"I don't know why."

She stares at him. He must know something; she can see him calculating behind his eyes. Then he opens his mouth.

"Excuse me for asking . . . Was your husband mad?"

Elizabeth stares, and feels very small and weak. She is crumbling, dissolving.

"Did he say that?" Tears are running down her face, whether from anger or grief, she doesn't know, but suddenly her face is wet. "He was not mad. That is a lie. Ask anyone here. Half Man is the only mad one."

"Half Man? Who is Half Man?"

"The one he doesn't want us to talk about!" Elizabeth gets up. It's too much, all at once. She walks in circles around and around the fire. "If you're so clever, if you can see so much, why don't you open your eyes?"

"IF THE WEATHER ALLOWS, TOMORROW I will leave."

I stare at Parker with my mouth open. There is an immediate strong pressure around my chest, as when you suffer from croup: an unpleasant stricture that makes it impossible to draw a breath. My breathing has been short since he knocked on the door of my room and I let him in, wondering what he wanted.

"You can't! It isn't finished."

He stares back at me for an instant, challenged but not surprised. He must know me better than that now.

"I think it is the only way to finish it."

I did not know what I meant when I spoke, but now I do. We have all been relying on Parker to show us the way, from when we first met in Dove River until now. Moody, too, however much he dislikes the fact.

"How can you finish it?"

Parker pauses. His face seems different now: softer, less composed, or perhaps it is just the faintness of the lamplight.

"In the morning I will somehow show Stewart the marker you gave me. Then he will know, if he did not already, that I was in with Jammet. I will tell him I am leaving, and if I am right . . ." Here he pauses. "And if he is the man I think he is, he will not be able to resist following, in case I lead him to the furs."

"But if he had Jammet killed . . . he may kill you, too."

"I will be ready."

"It's too dangerous. You cannot go alone. He will not be alone—he will have this . . . Half Man with him."

Parker shrugs. "You think I should take Moody?" He smiles at the unlikelihood of this. "He needs to stay. He needs to see that Stewart follows me. Then he will know."

"But, but you are . . ."

I am trying to reorder the facts again. Proof . . . what proof could there be, other than Stewart confessing?

"You can't go alone. I will come with you. I can be another pair of eyes. I can . . . You need a witness. A witness who can corroborate what you say. You should not go alone!"

My cheeks are burning. Parker smiles again, but gently. His hand reaches out, almost to my face, but stops short of touching it. I can feel tears in my eyes, threatening to wash away my composure, my dignity, everything.

"You should stay here. Moody needs you. He is lost."

And what about me? I think. The words seem so loud I am not sure I did not speak them, but Parker shows no sign of having heard. I try to keep my voice steady.

"I don't know what proof you think Stewart will provide, other than by killing you. That would probably be conclusive. And . . . and what if he sends someone else to kill you instead—how then could we link it to him? If you go on your own, and do not return, I do not think that will satisfy Mr. Moody. That will not prove anything."

"Well"—Parker looks down, a hint of impatience coming into his voice—"we will see tomorrow morning. Perhaps Stewart will tell us everything. Good night, Mrs. Ross."

I bite my tongue, hurt and angry. Parker may be unaware of it, but there are two people in this room who do not give up on a thing until it is finished.

"Good night, Mr. Parker."

He goes, closing the door silently after him. For several minutes I remain rooted to the spot, wondering, among all the things I could or should be wondering, whether he knows my first name.

That night, I dream.

I dream, in a way that is vague yet disturbing, of Angus. I turn my head from side to side, wanting to turn away from my husband. He does not reproach me. He cannot.

I wake up in the depths of the night, in a silence so heavy I feel I could not get out of the bed if I tried. There are tears drying on my face, cold, making my skin itch.

I wondered for so long why he had become so distant from me. I assumed it was something I had done. And then, when Parker told me about Jammet, I thought it was because of Francis, because he knew and hated it.

In truth, it had begun a long time before that.

I bury my face in the pillow that smells of must and damp. Its cotton slip is as cold as marble. It is only here, alone and in the dark, that I can allow those thoughts some rein. Thoughts that come from nowhere, from dreams, taking me delirious hostage. I long for sleep again, because only in sleep can I slip the bonds of what is possible and right.

But as I have found so often in life, what you truly long for eludes you.

DONALD PRESSES A HAND TO the window pane. It melts the frost that has formed on the inside overnight, leaving a clear print: the cold is getting stronger. The season moves on; they must leave soon, or become snowed in at Hanover House.

Yesterday he finished the letter to Maria. This morning he reads it over; he thinks it strikes the right note: it says nothing overly affectionate, but after laying out his thoughts—such a relief to be able to say what he thinks—he expresses the warm wish to see her and resume their interesting conversations. He folds it into an envelope, but leaves it blank. He has a horror of other people reading his letters. He is sure Mrs. Ross, on one of her nosy and importunate visits to his room, noticed an earlier one to Susannah.

Susannah. Well . . . not having been in this situation before, Donald is unsure how to proceed. He has an idea that she will not be heartbroken—after all, he tells himself, nothing was said, not really. Nothing that was a promise. He feels uncomfortable, because on the face of it it is not admirable behavior, and Donald does so want to be admirable. But he sees, more clearly from a distance than he did in Caulfield, that Susannah is a robust creature. Even as he knows this, he chastises himself for taking solace in it. Perhaps he will not allow his letters to her to be delivered. Perhaps he should rewrite them yet again, to rinse them clean of any redundant yearning.

At this juncture, with Donald still sitting at the table surrounded by missives to the Knox sisters, there is a knock at the door. It is Parker.

Stewart is in his office, a pot of coffee on his desk, the fire lit but losing the battle with the metallic cold that advances from window, door, and even through the walls.

Donald, feeling it is his place to lead, and having said as much to Parker and Mrs. Ross, clears his throat rather aggressively.

"Mr. Stewart, please forgive the early hour. We need to have a talk with you."

Stewart hears the grave tone in his voice, but he still smiles as he invites them in. He orders more cups—this time it is Nancy who answers the bell and goes to fetch them. Donald keeps his eyes on the floor while she is in the room, hoping the warmth in his face is invisible. No one looks at him anyway.

Donald begins, "I think you should know the real reason for our being here." He ignores Mrs. Ross's look. He cannot see Parker's expression, as he sits beside Stewart in front of the window, and is thrown thereby into shadow. "We followed a trail. It led north from Dove River, and we have good reason to believe it led here."

"You mean it was not Mrs. Ross's son?"

"No. At least, not this far. And there are men here whose presence has been kept from us."

Stewart nods, his face serious, his eyes downcast. "I believe some things have been said that misled you. I apologize for it. Let me tell you what I know; perhaps you can then fill in some of the gaps. What I said was true— Nepapanees was one of my best men. A good worker, a skilled steersman, a great tracker. But over a year ago, something happened to him. It's usually drink, as I'm sure you must have seen . . ." He glances at Donald, but some- how includes them all. "But not in his case. At least not at first. I don't know what it was, but his mind became deranged. He did not know his wife. He did not know his own children. This spring he walked out of the fort, and it seemed he was living wild. Occasionally he came back, but it was better when he stayed away. He was away for a long time some weeks ago. I had a feeling he had done something. I had that feeling more strongly when you came. But by then . . ." He shrugs, letting his shoulders fall.

"I did not want to bring any more disgrace on his wife and family. I wanted to spare them that. Nesbit and I agreed to . . . cover it up. To pretend that he was dead. It was foolish, I know." He lifts his eyes, and they seem to be shining with tears. "In a way, I wish he were. He is a poor wretch who has caused much suffering to those who loved him."

"But how could you tell his wife he was dead? How could you make her suffer so?" Mrs. Ross is leaning forward, her eyes boring into Stewart's, her face pale and taut, some emotion, anger probably, radiating from her like a magnetic force.

"Believe me, Mrs. Ross, I thought about that a great deal. I decided that his death would bring less pain to her and the children than he ultimately would, alive."

"But how did you think you could keep his presence from her? He was seen here two days ago!"

Stewart goes very still for a moment, before he looks up, revealing his awkwardness. "It was foolhardy. I allowed myself to . . . Sometimes, over the past few years, in winter especially, I have felt that I am losing my judgment. But if you had seen him with his children . . . staring at them as they ran up to him, screaming the foulest abuse, full of hatred and fear . . . God knows what demons he thought they were. It was terrible to see their faces."

Stewart's eyes are haunted, as though he can see them still. Donald feels a surge of sympathy. God knows, he can imagine the strain of one endless winter after another.

Mrs. Ross looks at Parker, and then back at Stewart. Almost as though Donald is not there.

"Who is Half Man?"

Stewart smiles a pained smile. "Ah. There you see . . ." He looks up, this time directly at Mrs. Ross. "Half Man is another unfortunate. A regular drunk. He is Norah's husband, so we give him food now and again. He is a trapper, but not a very useful one."

There is a nakedness about his face that makes Donald uncomfortable. What right have they to force this man to reveal his troubles?

"I must apologize again for deceiving you. One wants to be thought— especially in a Company like this . . ." He glances at Donald again, which makes Donald drop his eyes in embarrassment. "One wants to be thought of as a good leader, a father, in some ways, to those under one's responsibility. I have not been a good father to these people. It has been difficult, but that is no excuse."

Mrs. Ross is leaning back in her chair, a confused, distant look on her face. Parker's is obscure, in his own shadow. Donald breaks in.

"It happens everywhere. There is drunkenness, and there is madness. It does not reflect on your leadership that some men go astray."

Stewart bows his head. "You are kind to say that, but it is not so. Anyway, what concerns you now is the man you followed . . . I assume because of something he did. Some . . . crime?"

Donald nods. "We will need to find him and question him, no matter what state he is in."

"I don't know exactly where he is, but we could probably find him. But if you are looking for a criminal, you will not find one. He does not know what he does."

While Stewart is speaking, Parker takes pipe and tobacco out of his pocket. As he does so, a scrap of paper falls onto the floor between his chair and Stewart's. Parker does not notice, teasing strands of tobacco out of the pouch and firming them into the bowl. Stewart sees it and bends down to pick it up. He pauses fractionally with his hand on the floor, then hands it back to Parker, all without looking at his face.

"I will arrange for a couple of the men to search for him. They should be able to follow his tracks."

Parker puts the fragment of paper back in his pocket with barely a break in the ritual of filling the bowl. The whole incident has taken perhaps three seconds. The two men have sat side by side during the whole conversation without exchanging so much as a glance.

NEAR THE END OF THE corridor, Parker turns to me. "I am going to get ready."

"You are going?"

I assumed his questions were answered. Foolish of me; of course he would not believe anything Stewart said.

"He never said he did not send Nepapanees to Dove River."

His certainty irritates me, so I do not reply. He is looking at me with that peculiar blank intensity of his, which speaks of great concentration while giving no clue as to its subject, or even its tenor. But it is only the habitual lines of his face that make you assume anger and violence are behind it; now I know that it is not so. Or perhaps I have lulled myself into a false sense of security.

"You still have the shirt from Elbow Ridge?"

"Of course I have. It is rolled at the bottom of my bag, underneath my fur-lined coat."

"Fetch it."

Halfway across the open ground behind the stores, the sun breaks through a gap in the cloud. A shaft of light, solid as a staircase, strikes the plain beyond the palisade, illuminating a stand of scrub willow, skeined with snow and glittering with icicles. Its brightness is piercing; its whiteness hurts the eyes. As suddenly as a smile, the sun causes beauty to break out on this sullen plain. Beyond a range of a hundred yards, all imperfections are hidden. Beyond the palisade lies a perfect landscape like a sculpture carved in salt, crystalline and pure. Meanwhile we trudge through roiled slush and dirt, trampled and stained with the effluent of dogs.

The widow is in her hut with one of her sons, a solemn-looking boy of about eight. She is boiling meat over the fire, squatting beside it. She looks, to my eye, thinner and more ragged than when I last saw her, and somehow more native, although with her fine features she is, of all of them, the most clearly a half-breed.

She looks up without expression as Parker enters without knocking and says something I don't catch. She replies in another language. My reaction to this—a sudden and violent jealousy—takes my breath away.

"Sit down," she says listlessly.

We do so, on the blankets around the fire. The boy stares at me steadily—winter petticoats do not make sitting on the floor an elegant task, but I do my best. Parker starts in a roundabout way, asking about the children and giving his condolences, to which I murmur agreement. Eventually he gets to the point.

"Did your husband ever talk about the Norwegians' furs?"

Elizabeth looks at him, then at me. It seems to raise no recognition in her.

"No. He did not tell me everything."

"And the last trip he made—what was the purpose of it?"

"Stewart wanted to hunt. He usually took my husband with him, because he was the best tracker." There is a quiet pride in her voice.

"Mrs. Bird, I am sorry to ask you this, but was your husband ill?"

"Ill?" She looks up sharply. "My husband was never ill. He was as strong as a horse. Who is saying that? Is that what Stewart says, huh? Is that why he walked on ice he would never have walked on?"

"He says he was sick and did not know his own children." Parker keeps his voice low, not wanting to include the boy. Elizabeth's face literally contorts with feeling—disgust, or contempt, or rage, or all of them—and she leans forward, her face a livid orange from the fire.

"That is a wicked lie! He was always the best of fathers." There is something frightening about her: hard and implacable but also, it seems to me, true.

"When was the last time you saw your husband?"

"Nine days ago, when he left with Stewart."

"And when was the last time he had been away before that?"

"The summer. The last voyage they made was to Cedar Lake at the end of the season."

"He was here October, the beginning of November?"

"Yes. All the time. Why are you asking this?"

I look at Parker. There is just one more thing left to do.

"Mrs. Bird, I apologize for asking this, but have you one of your husband's shirts? We would like to look at it."

She glares at Parker as if this is insurmountable insolence. Nevertheless, she gets up with a jerky movement and goes to the back of the hut, behind a curtain.

She comes back with a blue shirt folded in her hand. Parker takes it and unfolds it, spreading it out on the floor. I take out the dirty roll, wrapped in calico; I spread it out, stiff and fouled, the dark stains giving off a rank odor. The boy watches us solemnly. Elizabeth stands with her arms folded, looking down on us with hard, angry eyes.

Instantly I see that the clean shirt is smaller than the other. It seems incontrovertible to say that they could not belong to the same man.

"Thank you, Mrs. Bird." Parker hands her back her husband's shirt.

"It's no good to me. There is no one to wear it now." She keeps her arms folded. "You wanted it, you keep it."

There is an unpleasant twist to her mouth. Parker is disconcerted. It's a novel and refreshing experience for me—seeing him not know what to do.

I speak for the first time. "Thank you, Mrs. Bird. I'm sorry we had to ask you, but you have helped greatly. You have proved that what Stewart says is a lie."

"What do I care? I don't give a shit for helping you! Is it going to bring my husband back?"

I stand and pick up the soiled shirt. Parker is still holding the other.

"I'm so sorry." On a level with her, only two feet away, I look into her eyes, which are a clear gray-brown, set in a mask of fury and despair. I feel withered by it. "I really am. We are going to . . ."

I wait for Parker to break in and explain what we are going to do. Any time now would be fine. He is on his feet, too, but seems happy to let me do the talking.

"We are going to find justice."

"Justice!" She laughs, but it's more like a snarl. "What about my husband? Stewart killed my husband. What about him?"

"For him, too." I am backing toward the door, more anxious to leave than to stay and find out why she is so convinced of this.

Elizabeth Bird grimaces—a rictus that looks like a smile, but isn't. It emphasizes the skull beneath the skin, and gives her the appearance of a death's-head, animated but not alive: wan, bloodless, radiant with hate.

Walking back to the main building, Parker gives me the clean shirt, as if he doesn't want the taint of holding it anymore. He feels guilty for upsetting her.

"We'll show Moody these," I say. "Then he will see."

Parker shakes his head slightly. "It's not enough. That shirt could have been there a few months."

"You don't believe it was! And you believe her, too—about her husband's death, don't you?"

Parker glances at me briefly. "I don't know."

"You're going, then."

Parker assents without speaking. I feel that familiar crushing weight on my chest, and my breath seems stuck in my throat, although we have walked only a few dozen yards.

"If he killed his guide it would be madness for you to go alone. I will borrow a rifle. If you don't take me with you, I will follow your trail, and that's all there is to it."

Parker does not speak for a moment, then looks at me again, a little ironically, I think.

"Don't you think that people will talk if they see us leave together?"

There is a great leap in my chest as the weight takes wing. Suddenly even the compound looks beautiful to me, the sun painting the dirty drifts by the fence a glowing white-blue. Momentarily I am sure that no matter the danger, armed with right, we cannot do other than prevail.

The feeling lasts almost until I reach my bedroom door.

LAURENT WAS OFTEN AWAY ON business. Francis knew as much, and therefore as little, as anyone else about his mysterious absences. In summer the wolves disappeared from the forest thereabouts, so this was when Laurent carried on his trading. That summer he seemed particularly busy—or perhaps it was just the first time that Francis had cared whether he was there or not—and made trips to Toronto and the Sault. When Francis asked him about his time away, Laurent was casual or downright evasive. He made jokes about lying drunk in bars, or visiting prostitutes. Or perhaps they weren't jokes. The first time he mentioned a whorehouse, Francis stared at him with dumbstruck horror, feeling an intense and dreadful pain around his heart. Laurent took his shoulders and laughed, shaking him roughly, until Francis lost his temper and shouted hurtful things he couldn't later remember. Laurent laughed at him, and then, suddenly, lost his temper, too. They hurled insults at each other, until there was a sudden hiatus in the shouting and they stared at each other, mesmerized and reeling. Francis was hurt and hurtful; Laurent had a cutting, cruel way of putting him down, but when, afterward, he apologized, he was so serious and sweet and beseeching—that first time he went down on his knees until Francis had to laugh and enthusiastically forgive him. It made Francis feel old—even older than Laurent.

Then there were the men who came to see Laurent at home. Sometimes when Francis went down and whistled outside the cabin, there would be no reply. That meant Laurent had someone with him, and often they would stay the night before shouldering their packs and trudging off, dogs at their heels. Francis discovered in himself a deep and terrible capacity for jealousy. On more than one occasion he would come back early in the morning and conceal himself in the bushes behind the cabin, waiting until the men left, studying their faces for clues, finding nothing. Most of the men were French or Indian; long-distance, disreputable-looking men more used to sleeping under the sky than a roof. They brought Laurent furs, tobacco, and ammunition, and they left the way they had come. Sometimes they didn't seem to bring or leave with anything. Once, after a particularly hysterical argument, Laurent told him that men came to him because they were setting up something, a trading company, and it had to be a secret because they would bring down the wrath of the Hudson Bay Company if anyone found out, and that was something well worth avoiding. Francis was delirious with relief, and made up for it with an excess of high spirits, whereupon Laurent picked up his fiddle and played it, chasing him around the cabin until Francis burst out of the front door, gasping with laughter. There was a figure on the path, quite far away, and he bolted back inside. He saw it only for a moment, but he thought it was his mother. After that he lived in a terror of uncertainty for days, but nothing changed at home. If she had seen anything, she could not have thought anything of it.

Autumn came, and with it school, and then winter. He could not see Laurent so often, but occasionally he would creep down the path after his parents had gone to bed, and whistle. And sometimes he would hear an answering whistle, and sometimes he would not. As time went on it seemed to him that the frequency with which his whistle was answered grew less and less.

Sometime in spring, after Laurent had been away, again, to some unspecified destination, he started dropping hints that something big was going to happen. That he was going to make his fortune. Francis was confused and disturbed by these vague, usually drunken allusions. Was Laurent going to leave Dove River? What would happen to him, Francis? If he tried to lead him (cleverly, he thought) into clarifying his plans, Laurent would tease him, and his teasing could be blunt and cruel. He frequently alluded to Francis's future wife and family, or to whoring, or living south of the border.

There was one occasion, the first of many; they had both been drinking. It was early summer, and the evenings were getting just warm enough to sit outside. The first bees had emerged from wherever they had spent the cold months and buzzed around the apple blossom. Only seven months ago.

"Of course, by then," Laurent was alluding to his unspecified future riches again, "you'll be married on some little farm somewhere, with a handful of kids, and you'll have forgotten all about me."

"I expect so." Francis had learned to play along with these dreary little scenarios. If he protested, it just tended to egg Laurent on.

"I guess when you leave school, you're not going to stay here, huh? Nothing much for you here, is there?"

"Nah . . . 'Spect I'll go to Toronto. Maybe I'll come and visit you in your bath chair once in a while."

Laurent grunted and drained his glass. It occurred to Francis that he was drinking more than he used to. Then he sighed. "I'm serious, *p'tit ami*. You shouldn't stay here. It's a nothing place. You should get out as soon as you can. I'm just an old country fool."

"You? You're going to be rich, remember? You can go anywhere you want. You could move to Toronto—"

"Oh shut up! You shouldn't be here! You certainly shouldn't be here with me. It's no good. I am no good."

"What do you mean?" Francis tried to still the tremor in his voice. "Don't be ridiculous. You're drunk, that's all."

Laurent turned to him, forming the words with alarming clarity. "I'm a fucking idiot. You're a fucking idiot. And you should just fuck off back to your mama and papa." His face was mean, his eyes narrow with drink. "Go on! What are you waiting for? Fuck off!"

Francis stood up, in agony. He didn't want Laurent to see him cry. But he couldn't just walk away either, not like this.

"You don't mean that," he said, as calmly as he could. "I know you don't. And you don't mean it either when you talk about going to whorehouses and having kids all over the place, and . . . all that. I see how you look at me—"

"Ah, *mon Dieu*! Who wouldn't look at you like that? You're the most beautiful thing I've ever seen. But you're a fucking stupid kid. I'm bored with you. And I'm married."

Francis stood in stunned disbelief, unable to reply to this. "You're lying," he said at last. Laurent looked up at him, wearily, as if telling him had relieved something.

"No, it's true, *mon ami*."

Francis felt as though his chest was being ripped apart. He wondered why he did not fall, or faint, since the pain was so dreadful. He turned and walked away from the cabin, and kept walking through one of his father's fields and into the forest. He began to run, his breath so ragged it disguised the sobs tearing through him. After a time he stopped running and went down on his knees in front of a huge pine, and rammed his head into the tree's bark. He didn't know how long he was there; perhaps he had dazed himself, glad of the pain that crowded out the other, more terrible, torment.

Laurent found him just before dark. He tracked him down like one of his stricken wolves, following his erratic progress through the bush. He bent down and cradled him in his arms, his fingers discovering the wound on his forehead, tears gleaming on his cheek, whispering that he was sorry.

Briefly, Francis thought that after that night, he had won. So what if Laurent had been married, so what if he had a son; that was all in the past: it didn't matter now, to them. But still Laurent resisted his attempts to pin him down, to find things out. The truth was, he didn't want Francis to change anything about his life, didn't want Francis as anything other than an occasional diversion. Francis, his voice uneven and thick, accused Laurent of not caring about him. Laurent, brutally, agreed.

And on, and on. The same conversation repeated with slight, pointless variations over many summer nights. Francis wondered how much longer he could stand this exquisite torture, but he could not stop submitting himself to it. He tried to be casual and lighthearted in Laurent's presence, but hadn't had much practice. He knew, in his heart of hearts, that sooner or later Laurent would push him away altogether. But like a moth drawn to a candle flame, he could not stop himself from going down to the cabin, although Laurent was increasingly absent. He didn't understand how Laurent's feelings could have changed so much, when his had intensified.

And then, somehow, his father found out.

It wasn't a cataclysmic event. It was more as though his father had been putting together pieces of a puzzle, patiently watching and accumulating the fragments, until finally the picture had come clear. There were the times when Francis had not returned until after his parents had got up, and he had muttered unconvincing comments about early-morning walks. Then there was the time that his father had arrived at Laurent's cabin and Francis was there, and he pretended to be taking a wood-carving lesson. Perhaps that was when he knew, although he gave no outward sign of it. Or there was another time, ill advised, when he claimed he had stayed the night at Ida's. His father had raised his eyebrow very slightly, but said nothing. Then Francis, panicking, had to find an excuse to rush over to the Prettys' house and find Ida. He wasn't sure what to say to her either, but concocted a story about having gotten drunk in Caulfield and having to hide it from his parents. Her face was stony and set, and, though she nodded agreement, she looked at him with wounded eyes and he felt ashamed.

However it had happened, his father, who for some time had found it hard to talk to Francis—and they were never that close—became intolerable. He never said anything directly, but would not look him in the eye when speaking to him, and only did so to order him to carry out some chore or mend his behavior. He seemed to regard his son with a cold, withering contempt; it felt as though he could hardly bear to be in the house with him. Sometimes Francis, sitting at the table in the frigid zone between his mother and father, felt a nausea welling up in his throat that threatened to overwhelm him. Once, while speaking to his mother about something, he caught his father's eye on him, unguarded, and saw in it nothing but cold, implacable rage.

One thing that surprised him was that he must have kept it from his mother. She clearly felt the coldness between father and son, and it saddened her, but she did not regard him any differently; that is, she was the same impatient, unhappy woman she had been for as long as he could remember.

It was the end of October. Francis had vowed to himself many times not to go back to Laurent's, a vow he found impossible to keep. This particular evening he found him in, and after a while they began a long, bitter argument, saying the same things they had said before, over and over again. Francis hated himself at such moments, but he was quite unable to stop. Occasionally, when alone, he could picture himself walking away with dignity, head high, but when he was standing in Laurent's kitchen, facing the man himself—shambolic, unshaven, crude—then he was seized with a mad desire to throw himself at his feet, to beg him in tears; to kill himself; anything to end this torture. To kill Laurent.

"I didn't come to you, remember?" Francis shouted hoarsely, as he had done many times before. "I didn't ask for this! You made me like this . . . You!"

"And I wish I'd never set eyes on you. Christ, you make me sick!" And then Laurent said, "Anyway, it doesn't matter. I'm going away. For a long time. I don't know when I will come back."

Francis stared at him, not believing it for a moment.

"Fine. Say what you like."

"I leave next week."

The anger had drained out of Laurent's face, and Francis had a cold, sick feeling that it was true. Laurent turned away, busying himself with something.

"Maybe then you'll get over it, huh? Find a nice girl."

Francis felt tears threaten. His whole body felt weak, as if he was coming down with a fever. Laurent was leaving. It was over. He did not understand how it was possible to feel such pain and go on living.

"Hey, it's not so bad. You're a good kid really." Laurent had seen his face, and was trying to be kind. This was worse than any obscenities or cutting remarks.

"Please . . ." Francis did not know what he was going to say. "Please, don't say that now. Just go, sometime, but don't say that now. Let's go on, until . . ."

Maybe Laurent, too, was tired of fighting, and that's why he shrugged and smiled. Francis went to him, and put his arms around him. Laurent patted him on the back, more like a father than anything else. Francis clung to him, wishing he could walk away, wishing more that it was the summer of the previous year, gone for good.

My love, who is sick to death of me.

He stayed that night but lay awake throughout it, listening to Laurent breathe beside him. He managed to rise and dress without waking him, although before he left, he leaned over and kissed him softly on the cheek. Laurent didn't wake, or chose not to.

And then, two weeks later, he was standing in the dark cabin, looking at the warm empty shell that lay on the bed.

And God help him if the second thought he had was not: *Oh, oh my love, you cannot leave me now.*

The Sickness of
Long Thinking

Y EARS AGO, WHEN HE WAS searching for Amy and Eve Seton, Sturrock sat in a barroom very like this, drinking whisky punch with a young man he had just been introduced to. He had heard of Kahon'wes before, and was flattered by the younger man's desire to meet him. Kahon'wes proved to be a tall, striking Mohawk who was trying to make his way in journalism. Though articulate and intelligent, he was caught between two worlds and did not seem to know quite where to place himself. This was evident from his dress, which on that occasion was entirely that of a young man of fashion—cutaway coat, top hat, button boots, and so on. He was even something of a dandy. But on subsequent meetings, he was dressed in buckskins, or in a strange hybrid of the two styles. His language also wavered between a fluent and educated English—as at the first meeting—and a more stilted way of speaking that he seemed to feel was more "Indian"; it all depended on whom he was with. Sturrock was happy to talk about journalism, but he was also hoping that the man could be useful to him in his search. Kahon'wes had a wide range of contacts, as he was always traveling, talking to people, and generally being what the governors in Toronto called a troublemaker. Since Sturrock was also a troublemaker, they got on well.

Sturrock told him of the search for the girls. He had already been working on it for the best part of a year, and by then had little hope of success. Kahon'wes, like most people in Upper Canada, had heard of the case.

"Ah . . . the two girls who were spirited away by wicked Indians."

"Or eaten by wolves, I am beginning to believe. Still, the father will leave no stone unturned in the whole of North America."

He told Kahon'wes he had visited bands on both sides of the border, going to the contacts and men of influence who had helped him before. But he had heard nothing of any use.

Kahon'wes paused before saying that he would ask those he met: as Sturrock must be well aware, there are times when an answer (like his own manner of speech and dress) depends on who sits on the other side of the table.

Several months later, Sturrock had word from the journalist. He was passing through Forest Lake, and was told that Kahon'wes was only a few miles away. On this occasion he was dressed in the Indian style, and his speech was altered. He was frustrated by his attempts to get articles published in the white press. Sturrock had the impression of a volatile character who, without the right encouragement, could become lost. He offered to read some of his articles and give advice, but Kahon'wes now seemed uninterested in his help.

This was the occasion on which the two men spoke of an ancient Indian civilization, greater and more sophisticated than the one that came after. Kahon'wes was passionate in describing such a thing, and though Sturrock did not believe in it for a moment, he could not help but be beguiled by his vision. He saw Kahon'wes only once after that, some months later outside Kingston, when they did not speak for long, and Sturrock got the impression he was drinking heavily. However, at that last meeting he did have news. He had spoken to the chief of a Chippewa band living around Burke's Falls, who had news of a white woman living with Indians. That was all, but it was no worse a lead than many Sturrock had followed in his line of business.

Some weeks later, Seton and he journeyed to a small village from where, after much negotiation, they were taken to an Indian camp to meet the girl. It was more than six years since the girls had vanished, three since Mrs. Seton had died of a mysterious ailment, commonly said to be a broken heart. Sturrock had always felt sorry for Charles Seton, his distress ever present, like a terrible wound under the thinnest of scar tissue. But this anticipation was worse, if anything could be worse. Seton had said barely a word since they set out from the village, his face white as paper. He looked like a sick man. Beforehand, he had seemed most taken up with not knowing which of his daughters this was supposed to be: Eve would now be seventeen, Amy nineteen, but no one seemed to know how old this girl was. There was no suggestion of a name: or rather, she now had an Indian name.

Sturrock tried to keep Seton talking, reminding him that the girl, if indeed she was his daughter, would be very changed. Seton insisted he would know her, no matter what.

"I could not forget the slightest detail of their faces, as long as I live," he said, staring straight ahead.

Sturrock persisted, gently. "But it is remarkable how changed some of them become. I have seen parents not recognize their own children, even after a short period with the Indians. It is not just a matter of the face . . . it is everything. How they speak, how they move, how they are."

"All the same, I would know them," Seton said.

They dismounted outside the teepees and left their horses grazing. Their guide went and spoke at the largest teepee, and a grizzled old man came out, listening as he spoke in the Chippewa language. The guide translated the reply:

"He says the girl came with them of her own free will. She is one of them now. He wants to know if you have come to take her away?"

Sturrock intervened before Seton could speak. "We are not going to force her to do anything she doesn't want to, but if she is this man's daughter, he wishes to talk to her. He has searched for many years."

The old man nodded, and led them to another teepee. After a moment, he beckoned Sturrock and Seton to follow him in.

For several moments, as they sat down, it was impossible to discern anything. The interior was close, dark, and smoky, and it was only gradually that they became aware of two figures sitting opposite them: a Chippewa man and woman. Charles Seton gave a little gasp, almost a mewing noise, and stared at the woman, who was barely more than a girl.

The skin of her face was dark, with dark eyes, and her hair was long and black, and glinted with grease. She wore a skin tunic and was wrapped in a striped blanket, although the day was warm, and she stared at the ground. At first glance, Sturrock would not have taken her for anything other than a Chippewa girl. He assumed the young man at her side was her husband, although they were not introduced. After that first exclamation Seton made no other sound. It was as though he was choking on words, his mouth open but his throat closed.

"Thank you for agreeing to see us," Sturrock began. He thought he had never in his life seen anything so cruel as the pain on Charles Seton's face at that moment. "Could you look up please, so that Mr. Seton can see your face properly?"

He smiled encouragingly at the young couple opposite. The man stared back, impassive, then rapped the girl on the hand. She lifted her head, although not her eyes. Seton's breathing sounded loud in the confined space. Sturrock looked from one to the other, waiting for one to recognize the other. Perhaps it was all a wild-goose chase. A minute crept by, and then another. It was agonizing. Then, at last, Seton took a breath.

"I don't know which one she is. She is my daughter . . . if I could see her eyes . . ."

Sturrock was startled. He looked at the girl, still as a graven image, and used her Indian name.

"Wah'tanakee, what color are your eyes?"

At last she looked up, at Seton. He looked into her eyes, which, as far as Sturrock could tell in the murky light, were brown.

Seton drew another painful breath. "Eve." There was a catch in his voice, and a tear slid silently down his cheek. But it was a statement. After six years of searching, he had found one of his missing daughters.

The girl stared at him for a moment, then dropped her eyes again. It could have been a nod.

"Eve . . ."

Seton wanted to lean over to her, to gather her in his arms, Sturrock could feel it, but the girl was so still and forbidding Seton did not move. He merely said her name again, one or two times, and then struggled to calm himself.

"What . . . I don't know how . . . Are you well?"

She moved her head in that single up-and-down movement. Now the old man spoke again, and the interpreter, who was also crammed into the teepee behind them, translated.

"This man is her husband. The old man is his uncle. He has brought her up in his own family since they found her."

"Found her? Where? When was this? With Amy? Where is Amy? Is she here? Do you know?"

The old man made some remark that Sturrock recognized as a curse. Then Eve herself began to speak, and all the time her eyes looked past them, at a spot on the floor.

"It was five, six, seven years ago. I don't remember. It seems very long ago. Another time. After we went for a walk we got lost. The other girl went first. She went off without us. We walked and walked. Then we were so tired we lay down to sleep. When I woke up, I was alone. I didn't know where I was, where anyone was. I was frightened, and I thought I would die. And then Uncle was there, and took me with him and gave me food and shelter."

"And Amy? What happened to her?"

Eve did not look toward him. "I don't know what happened. I thought she had left me. I thought she was angry and had gone home without me."

Seton shook his head. "No. No. We did not know what had happened to either of you. Cathy Sloan came back, but there was no trace of you, or Amy. We looked and looked. I have never stopped looking for you since that day; you must believe that."

"It is true," Sturrock said into the silence. "Your father has spent every waking minute, and everything he has, in the search for you and your sister."

Seton swallowed—it sounded loud in the little tent. "I have to tell you, I am sorry to say, that your mother passed away three years ago this April. She never recovered from your disappearance. She could not bear it."

The girl looked up, and Sturrock thought he saw the first—and last—trace of feeling on her face. "Mamma is dead." She digested this, and shared a glance with her husband, although what it meant Sturrock could not guess. Although it sounds callous to say it, it was unfortunate—the presence, even at a distance, of Mrs. Seton, could have made a difference to what happened next.

Seton wiped a tear from his face. There was a moment when Sturrock thought he would start to make small talk, start to release the terrible tension he had been holding, and then there would be a way forward. He was wondering how long he should leave it before bringing the meeting to an end, before anyone got irritated. And then it was too late.

Seton's voice seemed harsh and too loud in the confined tent:

"I don't mind what took place, but I must know what happened to Amy. I must know! Please tell me."

"I told you, I don't know. I never saw her alive again."

The phrasing sounded odd, even to Sturrock.

"You mean . . . you saw her dead?" Seton's voice was strained but controlled.

"No! I never saw her again at all. That's what I meant." Now the girl was sullen, on the defensive. Sturrock wished Seton would leave the ques-

tion of Amy alone; harping on about her to the other daughter would
hardly help.

"You will come back with me. You must. We must carry on looking." Seton's eyes had a faraway, glazed appearance. Sturrock leaned toward him
and put a hand on his arm to calm him. He didn't think Seton even noticed.

"Please, I think we should . . . Excuse me . . ." He was talking to everyone
now. "It's the strain. You cannot imagine how hard it has been for him all
these years. He does not know what he is saying—"

"Good God, man, of course I know what I am saying!" Seton threw his
hand off with a violent movement. "She must come back. She is my daughter. There is no other course . . ."

Then he reached toward the girl across the fire, and she flinched backward. With that movement, she revealed what the striped blanket had so far
hidden—that she was heavily pregnant. The young man was on his feet,
barring the way to Seton.

"You should leave now." His English was perfect, but then he switched to
his own language, addressing the interpreter.

Seton was gasping and crying all at once, shocked, but determined.
"Eve! It doesn't matter. I forgive you! Just come with me. Come back with
me! My dearest! You must—"

Sturrock and the interpreter manhandled Seton out of the teepee and
over to the horses. They managed to get him into the saddle. Somehow, although Sturrock's memory is vague on this matter, they persuaded him to
leave. Seton never stopped calling out to his daughter.

A year later, at the age of fifty-two, Seton was dead of a stroke. He never
saw Eve again, and despite further searching, they never found the slightest
trace of Amy. At times Sturrock doubted she had ever existed. He was
ashamed of his own part in it: he wanted to stop the search, because Seton's
obsession was unanswerable; the meeting with Eve had taught him that.
And yet he couldn't bring himself to walk away—the man had suffered too
much already. So Sturrock carried on, unwillingly, without being much use
or comfort. He should, he thought afterward, have got someone else to take
his place. But the afternoon at Burke's Falls had somehow bound the two
men into a confederacy of silence, for the strangest thing of all was this:
Seton refused to admit that they had found Eve; he let out that it had been
another false alarm, another girl. He persuaded Sturrock to keep it quiet

also, and Sturrock reluctantly complied. Only Andrew Knox had been let in on the secret, and that inadvertently.

Once or twice Seton mentioned going back to Burke's Falls and trying to persuade Eve to come away, but he seemed halfhearted. Sturrock suspected he wouldn't have gone through with it. Without telling Seton, Sturrock went back a week later to speak to her alone, but he could not find them anywhere. He doubted it would have done much good if he had.

THE WAY NORTHWARD ALONG THE river exerts its pull on all of them. Now more men, it is rumored, are getting ready to set off. Searchers after searchers. She will not be included, of course. But she feels the pull just the same—that is why she is here. A sharp wind cuts into Maria's face as she follows the path beside the river. The trees are bare now, the fallen leaves muddied, the snow spoiled. She sees the smooth lump of Horsehead Bluff up ahead, below which the water swirls in its self-scoured basin. In summer she and Susannah used to come swimming here, but that all stopped years ago. Maria has never swum since the day she saw the thing in the water.

She wasn't one of the ones who found it—they were a group of younger boys who had come fishing, but their shouts attracted the attention of Maria and her best friend at the time, David Bell. David was the one person at school who sought her out; they weren't sweethearts, but outcasts united in opposition to the rest of the world. They rambled in the woods, smoking and discussing politics, books, and the shortcomings of their peers. Maria didn't much like the smoking but liked doing something that was forbidden, so she forced herself.

When they heard the urgent cries, they ran up the riverbank, and saw the boys staring down into the water. They were laughing, which jarred with the alarm in their initial yells. One boy turned, addressing David, "Come'n see! You ain't seen nothing like this!"

They stepped up to the bank, smiles already forming on their faces in anticipation, and then they saw what was in the water.

Maria put her hands to her face in shock.

The river was playing a joke on them. The hands rotated slowly, reaching up out of the brown depths. They were bleached and slightly bloated. Then she saw the head below, now facing toward them, now turning away. The face is as clear in her memory now as it was then, and yet she could not describe it if she tried—whether the eyes were open or shut, or how the mouth was set. There was a peculiar horror in the lazy motion of the body caught in the eddy; by some freak chance it was twirling upright in one spot, hands above its head as if it were dancing a reel, and she could not stop watching any more than the others could. She knew the man was dead, but did not recognize him. Even afterward, when told that it was Doctor Wade, she could not reconcile the face in the water with what she remembered of the elderly Scotsman.

Even now, all these years later, she has to force herself to peer into the depths of the dark pool. Just to be sure that it's empty.

When they left the river, David held her hand on the way home. He was silent, unusually for him, and before they came out of the woods, he pulled her behind a tree trunk and kissed her. There was a desperate look in his eyes that scared her; she didn't know what it meant. Frozen, unable to respond, and somehow repelled, she pulled away and walked home ahead of him. Their friendship was never quite as easy as it had been after that, and the following summer his family moved back east. He was the only boy who ever wanted to kiss her, until Robert Fisher.

After nearly an hour she comes to Jammet's cabin and dismounts. She walks through the crust of rotten snow around to the front door. The unwarmed roof still has snow on it, and the cabin looks small and dejected. Maybe a murder will be enough to put off prospective buyers, where a drowning was not.

There are various footprints circling the cabin, mostly of children playing dare. But in front of the door the ground is smooth—no one has been inside recently. Maria marches firmly across it. A wire on the door holds it shut. She takes this off, tearing the skin on her thumb. She has never been inside; Jammet was not thought a suitable acquaintance for girls of good family. She finds herself murmuring an apology to his spirit, or something like it, for the intrusion. What she is doing, she tells herself, is just checking to make sure that the bone tablet was not overlooked in a corner. A little thing like a bone tablet could easily have been missed. She is also forcing herself to do something she is afraid of, although exactly what she fears, she is not sure.

Only a weak light seeps through the buckskin windowpanes, and the whole place has the queer feeling of being under a shroud. It is very quiet. There is nothing inside, other than a couple of tea chests and the stove, waiting for new hands to bring it back to life. And dust, like a thin layer of snowflakes on the floor. Her feet print a trail in it.

Even an empty house, it turns out, has plenty to offer when you start to look: old kitchen implements, pieces of newspaper, a handful of nails, wadded dark hair (she shudders), a bootlace . . . All the things that people don't bother to remove, because they're not worth anything; because no one would want such things, even the person who lived there.

We leave so little.

There is no way of knowing what Laurent Jammet was like now, not for her. Upstairs, where she ventures at length, there are a couple of half-empty wooden boxes. Nothing like a bone tablet in either, but she unearths something else, something tucked into the gap between the door frame and the wall (and what made her look there?).

A piece of brown paper, such as you might find wrapping a purchase from Scott's store, has been used as a makeshift artist's pad, on which someone has drawn a pencil sketch of Laurent Jammet. Maria's cheeks burn: in the drawing, Jammet lies on the bed, apparently asleep, naked. It must have been summer, for a sheet is tangled around his feet, as though he has kicked it off in the night. The artist was unskilled, but there is grace, and a palpable sense of intimacy. Maria feels not only a searing embarrassment at seeing this representation of a naked man, but also shame, as though she has blundered into the most private, most hidden recesses of someone's mind. Because the artist, whoever she was, loved him; of that she is sure. Then she sees a signature of sorts, scrawled into the scribbled lines that make up the sheet. It looks like François. No "e," she is sure. Not Françoise.

And instantly she thinks of Francis Ross.

She stands there holding the piece of paper, barely aware that it is almost dusk. She sees to her horror that a smear of her blood has stained it. Her first coherent thought is that she must burn it, in case anyone else should ever see it and reach the same conclusion. Then she realizes, with a guilty lurch of the heart, that she will have to give the drawing to Francis, because if it were hers (if only her cheeks would stop burning), she would want it back. She feels strangely, intimately disturbed by it, and folds the paper carefully, the drawing to the inside, before putting it in her pocket. Then she removes it from her pocket, picturing, for some reason, her sister plunging a hand in and finding it. Instead, she tucks it into her bodice, where no one but she will go. There, next to her heart, it burns like a hot coal, causing a warm flush to climb over her throat. In the end she tucks it impatiently down the side of her boot, but even from there it sends filaments of heat stealing up her leg as she rides back to Caulfield through the falling dark.

LINE BUSIES HERSELF BUILDING A fire. After that one rifle crack, there was nothing. They wait, at first chattering, excited, cheerful, then silent, huddling a little closer to the fire. The light starts to fail too soon; darkness comes stealing out of its daytime lairs in root hollows and rotten stumps. Line boils water and adds sugar, and makes them all drink it while it's scalding, so that it burns their mouths. She makes a stew of oatmeal, berries, and dried pork, which they eat silently, waiting for the sound of footsteps and a body pushing through the branches. Espen's share bakes hard in the kettle. Still he doesn't come.

Line fends off the children's questions and sends them to gather more wood to bank up the fire, so that it will be bright and he will be able to see it from a long way off. Then she rigs a shelter for them to sleep. Then they stop asking questions.

But, after Anna has curled in a warm comma around Line's right thigh, Torbin, on her other side, speaks in a whisper. He has been quiet these last couple of days, since they lost the compass. Not at all his usual unquenchable self.

"Mamma, I'm sorry," he whispers, his voice tremulous. She strokes his hair with her mittened hand.

"Shh. Go to sleep."

"I'm sorry I tried to run away. If I hadn't, we wouldn't be lost, would we? And Espen wouldn't have gone off like that. And now he's lost, too . . ." He cries quietly. "It's all my fault."

"Don't be silly." Line speaks without looking at him. "That's just the way it is. Go to sleep."

But her lips press themselves in an unbecoming line: the truth is, it *is* his fault they lost the compass. It is his fault they are lost in the cold forest; his fault that, once again, she has lost her man. Her hand strokes mechanically, and she does not notice that Torbin has gone rigid; does not notice that she is hurting him, but that he does not dare ask her to stop.

* * *

She cannot sleep, so she sits in the mouth of their shelter with the children curled around her back and legs, staring into the fire. She tries so hard not to think. It's easy when Torbin and Anna are awake and she has to reassure them, but alone, like this, with no one but her fears for company, it's hard to keep them from overwhelming her. Despite being lost, freezing, deep in the forest, surrounded by snowdrifts and God knows what else, her greatest fear is that Espen has left her. When she sat in the stable at Himmelvanger, she knew she could force him to do what she wanted, however unwilling. Now it occurs to her that he seized on the rifle shot as an excuse, that he has run off, not intending to return; and this time she does not know where to find him.

Nearby, the two horses stand nose to tail, heads down. At some point, when she is very cold, one of them starts, spooked at something in the trees. It flattens its ears along its skull, weaving its head from side to side as if it detects a threat but does not know exactly where it is. The other horse—the sick one—barely moves. Line, after the initial, heart-wrenching shock, strains into the darkness, hoping to hear Espen, but knowing that Jutta would not react that way if it were him. She hears nothing. Eventually, she can wait, or fend off sleep, no more, and curls up beside her children, wrapping her shawl over her face.

She dreams, almost instantly, of Janni. Janni is in trouble and seems to be calling for her. He is somewhere dark and far away, and cold. He says he is sorry for his foolishness, for thinking he could make money this way, by theft and mutiny. Now he is paying with his life. She can see him from an immense distance, and he seems to be lying in the snow, a tiny dark speck in a vast field of white, and he cannot move. She yearns with all her being to go to him, but she cannot. Then it all changes and he is right there with her, so close she can feel his warm, moist breath on her face. In the dream she closes her eyes and smiles. His breath smells rank, but it is warm and it is his. She doesn't dream of Espen at all.

She wakes before it is fully light. The fire is out, a sodden charred mess; the air is wet and smells of thaw. She looks around. She cannot see the horses; they must have moved off behind the shelter, foraging for food. No sign of Espen—but then, she didn't really think there would be. She pushes herself onto her elbows, her eyes becoming used to the grayness. And then she sees the trampled and stained snow only twenty yards away.

At first she refuses to accept that the dark red stains are blood, then detail piles on vile detail: a spray of red arcs across the snow there; here a smear of red, and a staccato of hoof prints, stabbed into a deep drift. She makes no sound at all. The children must not see this, or they will panic . . . Then she looks down.

Between her elbows, pressed into the only untouched patch of snow that remains outside the shelter, is a paw print. Just one. It is at least four inches across, with the prick holes of claws ranged in front of it. A dark-red stain colors two of the holes.

With a sick jolt, she is reminded of what Espen called her: a vargamor—a woman who consorts with wolves. She tastes bile, remembering the warm stinking breath from her dream, and how she reveled in it. The wolf must have stood right over her, leaning into the shelter, panting into her face as she slept.

Line gets up as quietly as she can. She kicks snow over the worst of the traces, scattering clods of snow over the parabola of blood. She can see the trail as Bengi tried to get away, followed by the wolves—there must have been more than one. Fortunately it leads back in the direction they came from; they will not have to see where, or with what, it ends.

She sees another trail and stares at it: a boot print crisply outlined near the bole of a cedar. It takes her a long moment to realize that this is Espen's boot print, from yesterday. He was heading almost due west, whereas their path lies south. No more snow has fallen since he left, nothing to cover his traces. He could have followed his own trail back to them, but for some reason did not.

Line jumps, heart pumping painfully, as Jutta ambles through the trees toward her, and then sighs with trembling relief as the horse sticks her nose in Line's armpit. The relief seems to be mutual.

"We're all right," Line tells the horse fiercely. "We're all right. We're all right."

She holds on to the horse's mane until she stops trembling, then goes to rouse the children, to tell them they must go on.

DONALD WATCHES PARKER AND MRS. Ross leave the post. They walk out of the gate and head into the northwest without a backward glance. Nesbit and Stewart wish them a good journey and go back to their offices. Nesbit manages to give Donald an unpleasant, meaningful look as he does so, defaming both Mrs. Ross and Parker, and somehow Donald himself, in the process. Donald bears it, but it riles him. He thought Parker a fool when he had explained his reasoning, and worse when he said Mrs. Ross was going with him, although it seemed to be Mrs. Ross's wish also. He pulled her aside and told her his opinion. Was it his imagination, or was she amused by him? Both Parker and she impressed upon him the importance of watching Stewart's movements, and though he thinks there is little point, he supposes he will do it.

He watches Stewart walk over to the village to inquire after Elizabeth. Despite her sullen hostility, Stewart does not cease to take an interest in her. As for himself, he cannot restrain the urge to visit her again. He has developed an overpowering curiosity about her since conceiving the notion that she is one of the Seton girls, albeit based as it is, somewhat tenuously, on the name of her daughter. No, not just that: on her features, which are undoubtedly white, and which to his mind bear a faint but discernible resemblance to those of Mrs. Knox. He finds himself outside her hut after Stewart has gone back to his office, waiting for a signal to go in.

The fire stings his eyes, and he breathes through his mouth to acclimatize himself to the smoke and smell of unwashed bodies. Elizabeth squats by the hearth, wiping the face of the little girl, who has been crying. She flings Donald a brief, dismissive glance, and then picks up the squalling child and hands her to him.

"Take her. She's giving me the devil of a time."

Elizabeth walks behind the partition that divides the room from the sleeping quarters, leaving Donald with the girl, who squirms and wriggles in his arms. Nervously, he jiggles her up and down, and she stares at him, affronted.

"Amy, don't cry. There, there."

Were it not for his experiences with Jacob's children, this would be the first time he had ever held a small child. He holds her as if she were an unpredictable small animal with sharp teeth. However, by some miracle she stops crying.

When Elizabeth comes back, Amy has discovered Donald's tie and, enchanted by its strangeness, is playing with it. Elizabeth watches for a moment.

"What made you think of the Setons?" she asks suddenly. "Was it just the name?"

Donald looks up, caught off guard. He had been about to ask her about Stewart.

"I suppose so. But the story was in my mind, you see, because recently I was told it by someone who was very close to it."

"Oh." If she has a more than passing interest, she hides it well.

"I recently made the acquaintance of the family of Andrew Knox. His wife was, well, she is . . ." He is watching her now, while the child gives his tie a sharp tug, almost throttling him. "She is the sister of Mrs. Seton, the girls' mother."

"Oh," she says again.

"She is a delightful, kind person. One can tell that even after so many years, she finds the memory of the disappearance deeply distressing."

There is a long silence in the hut, punctuated by noises from the fire.

"What did she say about it?"

"Well, that it . . . it broke the parents' hearts. That they never got over it."

Donald tries to read her face, but she looks angry more than anything.

"They—the Setons—are both dead now."

She nods briefly. Donald finds he has been holding his breath, and exhales.

"Tell me about Aunt Alice." She says it very quietly, with a sort of sigh. Donald feels a great leap inside him. He tries not to show it, or to look at her too hard. She stares at her daughter, avoiding his eye.

"Well, they live in Caulfield, on Georgian Bay. Mr. Knox is the magistrate there, a very fine man, and they have two daughters, Susannah and Maria." Emboldened, he adds, "Do you remember them?"

"Of course. I was eleven years old, not a baby."

Donald struggles to keep the excitement out of his voice, but it makes him squeeze the child more tightly. She pushes her fist into his spectacles in retaliation.

"Susannah . . . I can't remember which was which. The last time we saw them, one was only a baby. The other was no more than two or three."

"Maria would have been about two," he says, with a warm feeling at saying her name.

She stares into the shadows, and he has no idea what she is thinking. He removes the child's surprisingly strong fingers from his mouth.

"They are all well, and . . . they are a charming family. All of them. They have been very kind to me. I wish you could meet them. They would be so happy to see you . . . you cannot imagine!"

She smiles queerly. "I suppose you will tell them about me."

"Only if you wish it."

She turns her face away, but when she speaks her voice is unchanged. "I have to think of my children."

"Of course. Think about it. I know they would not force you into anything you did not want."

"I have to think of my children," she says again. "Now, without a father . . ."

Donald manages with difficulty to extract his handkerchief from under the child's body. But when Elizabeth turns back, her eyes are dry.

"Did they tell you my father found me?"

"What? They said you were never found!"

Her face flickers with something—pain? disbelief? "He said that?"

Donald doesn't know what to say.

"I refused to go back with him. I was not long married. He kept asking about Amy. He seemed to blame me for her not being there, too."

Donald can't keep the shock from his face.

"Can't you understand that? They lost their daughters, but I lost everything! My family, my home, my past . . . I had to learn to speak again! I couldn't break from everything I knew . . . again."

"But . . ." He doesn't know what to say.

"There was horror on his face when he saw me. He never came back after that one time. He could have. It was Amy he was hoping for. She was always his favorite."

Donald looks at the unconcerned child; it keeps the wave of pity from overwhelming him.

"He was in shock . . . You can't blame him for asking. He did nothing but go on searching until he died."

She shakes her head, eyes hard: you see?

"You were the"—he struggles on, trying to make it better—"the great mystery of the age! You were famous, everybody knew about you. People wrote from all over North America, pretending to be you—or to have seen you. Someone even wrote from New Zealand."

"Oh."

"I don't suppose you remember what happened."

"Does it matter, now?"

"Doesn't it always matter, finding the truth?" He thinks of Laurent Jammet, of their supposed quest for truth—all those events tumbling one into another like a trail of dominoes—all leading him across the snow-covered plains to this little hut. Elizabeth gives a sort of shudder, as if a draft bothers her.

"I remember . . . I don't know what you heard, but we had gone for a walk. Collecting berries, I think. We argued about where to stop; the other girl, what was her name, Cathy?—she didn't want to go far; she was worried about burning her face because it was so hot. Really, she was scared of the bush."

Her eyes are fixed on a point just over Donald's shoulder. He hardly dares move, in case he breaks her thread.

"I was scared, too. Scared of Indians." She gives a tiny smile. "Then I argued with Amy. She wanted to go farther, and I was worried about dis-obeying our parents. But I went along because I didn't want to be alone. It got dark, and we couldn't find the path. Amy kept telling me not to be silly. Then we gave up and fell asleep. At least, I think . . . And then . . ."

There is a long silence, filling the hut with ghosts. Elizabeth seems to be looking past him at one of them.

Donald finds he is holding his breath.

"She wasn't there anymore."

Her eyes refocus, find his. "I thought she'd found the way home and left me in the forest because she was angry with me. And no one came to find me . . . until my uncle—my Indian uncle—found me. I thought they had left me there to die."

"They were your parents. They loved you. They never stopped looking."

She shrugs. "I didn't know. I waited for such a long time. No one came. Then, when I saw my father again, I thought, now you come, when I'm happy, when it's too late. And he kept asking about Amy." Her voice is thin and husky, stretched to breaking point.

"So Amy . . . disappeared into the forest?"

"I thought she'd gone home. I thought she'd left me." Elizabeth—despite everything, he can't think of her as Eve—looks at him and a tear runs down her cheek. "I don't know what happened to her. I was . . . exhausted. I went to sleep. I thought I heard wolves, but I might have been dreaming. I was too scared to open my eyes. I would remember if I'd heard screams or cries, but there was nothing. I don't know. I don't know."

Her voice has trailed away into nothing.

"Thank you for telling me."

"I lost her, too."

She drops her face until it is hidden in shadow. Donald feels ashamed of himself. Her parents had been the object of so much sympathy; everyone was in awe of their loss. But the lost grieve, too.

"She may be alive somewhere. Just because we don't know, doesn't mean she is dead."

Elizabeth doesn't speak, or lift her head.

Donald has only one sibling, an elder brother he has never really liked; the prospect of his vanishing forever into a forest is rather appealing. He becomes aware that his right leg has gone to sleep and shifts it, painfully. He makes his voice jovial. "And here is Amy . . ." The child on his lap is unconcernedly pulling off her stockings. "I'm sorry. Forgive me for making you speak of it."

Elizabeth picks up her daughter, shakes her head. She paces for a few moments.

"I want you to tell them about me." She kisses Amy, pressing her face into her neck.

Outside the hut, two women are in heated discussion. One of them is Norah. Donald turns to Elizabeth.

"Please, one more favor. Can you tell me what they are saying?"

Elizabeth gives him a sardonic smile. "Norah is worried about Half Man. He is going somewhere with Stewart. Norah told him to refuse, but he won't."

Donald stares toward the main building, his heart suddenly in his throat. Is it happening now?

"Does she say where, or why? It's important."

Elizabeth shakes her head. "On a trip. Maybe hunting . . . though he's usually too drunk to shoot straight."

"Stewart said he was going to find your husband."

She doesn't bother to answer this. He calculates rapidly. "I am going to follow them. I have to see where they go. If I don't come back, you will know what you said is true."

Elizabeth looks surprised—the first time he has seen this expression. "It's dangerous. You can't go."

Donald tries to ignore the mocking amusement in her voice. "I have to. I need proof. The Company needs proof."

Just then Alec, her eldest son, walks out of a neighbor's hut with another boy, and the two women move away, Norah back to the main building. Elizabeth calls out to the boy, and he veers toward her. She speaks to him briefly in their language.

"Alec will go with you. Otherwise you will lose yourself."

Donald's mouth drops open. The boy's head barely reaches his shoulder.

"No, I couldn't . . . I am sure I will be all right. It will be easy to follow the trail . . ."

"He will go with you," she says simply, with finality. "It is his wish also."

"But I cannot . . ." He doesn't know how to say it—he feels unqualified to look after anyone in this climate: not even himself, let alone a child. He lowers his voice. "I couldn't take responsibility for him, too. What if something happened? I can't allow him to come." He feels hot with shame and uselessness.

Elizabeth says simply, "He is a man now."

Donald looks at the boy, who lifts his eyes to his and nods. Donald can see nothing of Elizabeth in him: his skin is dark, his face flat, his eyes almond-shaped under heavy lids. He must be like his father.

Later, when he is going back to his room to pack, Donald turns around again and sees Elizabeth framed in her doorway, watching him.

"Your father only wanted an answer. You do know that, don't you? It wasn't that he didn't love you. It's only human to want an answer."

She stares at him, her eyes slitted by the setting sun out of a sky like polished steel. Stares at him but says nothing.

SOMETHING STRANGE HAS HAPPENED TO the weather. It is nearly Christmas, and yet, though we walk across frozen snow, the sky is as brilliant as a sunny day in July. Despite the scarf wrapped around my face, my eyes burn with the brightness of it. The dogs are delighted to be on the go again, and in some ways I can understand. Outside the palisade there is no treachery or confusion. There is only space and light; miles done and miles ahead. Things seem simple.

And yet they are not; it is only numbness that makes me think so.

When the sun goes down, I find out what my stupidity has led to. First I fall over one of the dogs, managing in the process to tear my skirt and set off a cacophony of barking. Then, having set down the pannikin of snow water, I cannot find it again. Quelling a flutter of fear I call Parker, who examines my eyes. Even without his telling me, I know they are red and weeping. Flashes of red and purple cross my dull vision. There is a throbbing pain behind my eyes. I know I should have covered them on leaving yesterday, but I did not think of it; I was so happy to be going with him, and the wide white plain was so good to look at after the soiled surroundings of Hanover.

Parker makes a poultice of the tea leaves wrapped in calico and cooled in snow, and makes me press it to my eyes. It is some relief, though not as good as a few drops of Perry Davis's Painkiller. Perhaps it is as well we do not have any. I think of Nesbit in the office—cornered and feral—how once that was me.

"How far are we from this . . . place?"

It is habit that makes me lower the poultice, impolite not to look at someone when you are talking to them.

"Keep it on," he says. And when I have replaced it, "We will get there the day after tomorrow."

"And what is there?"

"A lake, with a cabin."

"What is its name?"

"It has no name that I know."

"And why there?"

Parker hesitates for a long minute, so that I peer at him from behind the poultice. He is staring into the distance and doesn't seem to notice. "Because that is where the furs are."

"The furs? You mean the Norwegians' furs?"

"Yes."

Now I drop the poultice and look at him in earnest. "Why do you want to lead him to them? That is exactly what he wants!"

"That is why we are doing it. Keep it on."

"Couldn't we . . . pretend they are somewhere else?"

"I think he already knows where they are. If we went in another direction, I don't think he would follow. He came this way before—he and Nepapanees."

I think about what this means: Nepapanees, who did not come back, so must be there still. And fear steals through me, creeping into my bone marrow, making itself at home. It is easy to hide my reaction behind the sodden poultice, not so easy to pretend I am brave enough for this.

"This way, when he comes, it will be sure."

And then what? I think, but don't dare say out loud. Another voice in my head—the annoying one—says, You could have stayed behind. You've made your bed. Now lie in it.

Then, after another pause, Parker says, "Open your mouth."

"I beg your pardon?" Can he read my mind? Shame rushes through me, just about obliterating the fear.

"Open your mouth." His voice is lighter now, amused at something. I open it a little way, feeling childish. Something angular and hard meets my lips, forcing them wider, and into my mouth slips a jagged piece of what feels like lake ice—flat and deliquescent. His thumb or forefinger brushes against my lips, rough as sandpaper. Or perhaps it is his glove.

I close my mouth around the object, and as it warms and melts, it explodes with dark, smoky sweetness, causing a dizzying rush of water to my mouth. I am smiling: maple sugar. Where he got such a thing I have no idea.

"Good?" he asks, and from his voice I can tell he is smiling, too. I tilt my head to one side as if considering my answer.

"Hm." I say lightly, still secure behind the poultice. It makes me reckless. "Is this supposed to make my eyes better?"

"No. It is supposed to taste good."

I take a deep breath—scented with autumnal smoke and sweetness, an undertow of bitter char. "I am afraid."

"I know."

I wait behind my mask for Parker's soothing words of reassurance. He is thinking about them, choosing them carefully, it seems.

They don't come.

THERE ARE FIVE VOLUNTEERS IN the search party: Mackinley; a native guide, Sammy; a local youth called Matthew Fox, intent on proving his backwoods worth; Ross, the man with the missing son and wife; and Thomas Sturrock, ex-searcher. Of all of them, Sturrock is aware that he is there on sufferance; to the rest he must seem an old man, and no one is quite sure what he is doing in Caulfield anyway. It was only his considerable charm that bought his place on the party—that and a long evening buttering up the fox-faced Mackinley and reminding him of his past triumphs. He even talked up his tracking skills, but fortunately Sammy has had no need of help; in the pristine dazzle of the new snow, Sturrock has no idea whether they are following previous tracks or not. But he is here, every step taking him closer to Francis Ross and the object of his journey.

Since Maria Knox came back from the Sault with her extraordinary account of meeting Kahon'wes, he has been fired with an excitement he thought he had lost forever. In his mind he has turned it over many times— could Kahon'wes have known that he was behind it? Could the names he said have been pure coincidence? Impossible. He has decided that the tablet is written in an Iroquoian language and records the confederacy of the Five Nations. Who knows, it might even have been written at the time. Whether it was or not, the greater implications are not lost on him: the effect such a discovery would have on Indian policy; the embarrassment it would cause the governments above and below the border; the weight it would lend to native calls for autonomy. What man does not long to do good, and profit by the doing at the same time?

Those were his thoughts for the first couple of hours. Then he started to think—because he is nothing if not a pragmatist—of the possibility that Maria was right, and the thing is a clever fake. In the deepest recesses of his mind he knows it will make no difference. He will persuade Kahon'wes to back him up; that shouldn't be difficult. If he presents the thing with enough conviction and cleverness (no problem there), the initial splash will make his name, and any subsequent controversy can only be good publicity. As for the matter of not knowing where the tablet is, he refuses to let it worry him. He is confident that Francis Ross did take it, and that as soon as they catch up with him, he will be able to talk it into his own hands. He has rehearsed the lines he will use, many times . . .

He stumbles on something uneven, his snowshoe catches on the crust, and he goes down on his knees. Last in the line, he pauses, one gloved hand flat on the snow, while he recovers the breath jolted from his body. His joints ache with cold. Years since he has traveled this way; he has forgotten how it takes its toll. Hopefully it will be the last time. The next man to him, Ross, notices he has fallen behind and turns to wait for him. Thank God he doesn't walk back and offer him a hand; that would be too humiliating.

Maria had described seeing Ross at the Sault with another woman, and speculated as to whether his wife's disappearance was as innocent as was generally supposed. Sturrock was amused, because Maria seemed like the last person to entertain such a lurid notion. But as Maria pointed out, it was hardly more lurid than the widely accepted theory that Mrs. Ross had run off with the escaped prisoner (and her husband not turned a hair!). Sturrock finds the man interesting. Nothing shows in his face; if he is worried about the fate of his wife or son, he does not reveal it. This does not endear him to the other men of the party. Ross has so far resisted Sturrock's attempts to engage him in conversation, but, undaunted, Sturrock puts on a spurt to catch up with him.

"You seem easy in this country, Mr. Ross," he says, trying to still his laboring breath. "I would wager you have done a fair bit of this sort of travel."

"Not really," Ross grunted, and then, relenting perhaps at the older man's wheezing breath, "just hunting trips and so on. Nothing like you."

"Oh . . ." Sturrock allows himself to be modestly flattered. "You must be worried about your family."

Ross trudges for a moment in silence, his eyes fixed on the ground. "Some seem to think not worried enough."

"One doesn't have to make a public display to feel concern."

"No." He sounds sarcastic, but Sturrock is too taken up with placing his snowshoes in the imprints made by the youth ahead of him to look at his companion's face.

And after a moment, Ross says, "The other day I was in the Sault. I went to a friend of my wife's, just to see if she had heard from her. While I was there I saw the elder Knox girl. She saw me and gave such a start—I suppose word has got all over town that I have a fancy woman."

Sturrock smiles, guilty but relieved. He is glad Mrs. Ross has someone who cares about her. Ross casts him a dry look. "Aye, I thought so."

On the second day out from Dove River, Sammy stops and holds up his hand for silence. Everyone pauses in midstride. The guide confers with Mackinley at the front, who then turns to the others. He is about to speak when there is a cry from the trees on their left, and the sound of crashing branches. All the men turn in panic; Mackinley and Sammy raise their rifles in case it is a bear. Sturrock hears a high-pitched cry and realizes that it is a human—a woman.

He and Angus Ross, being nearest, start forward, plunging into deep, drifted snow and hampered by brushwood and hidden obstacles. The going is so difficult that it is some moments before they can see who is calling them. Glimpses through the trees: Sturrock thinks there is more than one figure—but a woman? A number of women . . . out here in the middle of winter?

And then he catches her in plain sight: a thin dark-haired woman struggling toward him, her shawl trailing behind her, her mouth open in a cry of exhaustion and relief vying with terror that they might, all these men, be just a figment of her imagination. She plunges through the brush toward Sturrock, collapsing in a heap just a few yards away, as Ross catches a child in his arms. Another figure darts through the trees behind them. Sturrock reaches her and goes down on one knee in an awkward parody of romance, his snowshoes getting in the way. The woman's face is sharp with exhaustion and fear, her eyes haunted as if she is afraid of him.

"There now, it's all right. You are safe now. Hush . . ."

He's not sure she understands him. Now a young boy has come up behind her and stands with one hand protectively on her shoulder, staring at Sturrock with dark, suspicious eyes. Sturrock never knows what to say to children, and this one doesn't look friendly.

"Hello. Where have you come from?"

The boy mutters some words he cannot understand, and the woman answers him in the same strange tongue—not French, which he knows, nor is it German.

"Do you speak English? Can you understand me?"

The others have joined them and crowd around, staring in amazement. There is the woman, the young boy, maybe seven or eight years old, and a little girl, even younger. They all exhibit the early symptoms of exposure and cold. None of them says a word anyone can understand.

It is decided that they will pitch camp, even though it is barely two o'clock. Sammy and Matthew build a shelter behind an uprooted tree and collect wood for a large fire, while Angus Ross prepares hot tea and food. Mackenzie walks back into the forest where the woman points and reappears leading a malnourished mare that is now draped in blankets, eating oatmeal. The woman and children huddle by the fire. After they have had a quiet conversation, she stands up and comes to Sturrock. She indicates she wants to talk in private, so they go a little way away from the camp.

"Where are we?" she asks, without preamble. He notices her English is almost without accent.

"We are a day and a half out from Dove River, to the south. Where have you come from?"

She stares at him, and her eyes flick toward the others. "Who are you?"

"My name is Thomas Sturrock, of Toronto. The other men are from Dove River, apart from the man with short brown hair—that is Mackinley, a servant of the Hudson Bay Company, and a guide."

"What are you doing here? Where are you going?" If her questions seem ungrateful, she gives no sign of being aware of it.

"We are following a trail north. Some people have gone missing." No way to explain this complicated scenario simply, so he does not try.

"And where does this trail lead?"

Sturrock smiles. "We will not know that until we come to the end of it."

The woman breathes out then, and seems to release a little of her pent-up suspicion and fear. "We were making for Dove River. We lost our compass and the other horse. There was someone else with us. He went off to . . ." Her face changes with hope. "Have any of you fired rifles in the last few days?"

"No."

She droops again. "We became separated; we don't know where he is now."

At last her face crumples. "There were wolves. They killed one of the horses. They could have killed us. Maybe . . ."

She gives in to sobbing, but quietly, and without tears. Sturrock pats her on the shoulder.

"Hush. You are quite all right now. It must have been terrible, but it's over. There's no need to be frightened anymore."

The woman lifts her eyes to his, and he notices how fine they are: clear light brown in a smooth oval face.

"Thank you. I don't know what we would have done . . . We owe you our lives."

Sturrock himself treats the woman's frostbitten hands. Mackinley calls an impromptu meeting and decides that Sammy and he will go and look for the missing man—there are clear tracks to follow—while the others stay in the camp. If they have not found him by the following evening, Matthew and Sturrock will escort the woman and her children to Dove River. Sturrock is not entirely happy with this arrangement, but he can see the sense of allowing the three hardened travelers to go on as swiftly as possible. Besides, a part of him is flattered by the woman's preference for him; she has spoken privately to no one else, and keeps close to him, even favoring him with a particularly sweet smile from time to time. ('So, you are from Toronto . . . ?') He tells himself that it is his age that makes him less threatening, but he knows that is not the whole reason.

Mackinley and Sammy leave while there is light, gathering from the woman's rather confused story that her husband may be hurt. They are swallowed up in the gloom beneath the trees and Ross doles out nips of brandy to everyone. The woman cheers up noticeably.

"So who are the people you are following?" she asks, when the children have fallen into a fathomless sleep.

Ross sighs and says nothing; Matthew looks from Ross to Sturrock, who takes this as his cue.

"It is rather peculiar, and not easy to tell. Mr. Ross, perhaps . . . No? Well, a few weeks ago there was an unfortunate incident, you see, and a man died. Mr. Ross's son went missing from Dove River at the same time—possibly he was following someone. Then two Hudson's Bay men went to look for him as part of their inquiries. They have been gone some time and no one has heard from them."

"And"—Matthew leans forward eagerly, encouraged by the woman's interest—"that's not all! There was another man, arrested for the murder—a half-breed and an evil-looking fellow—and then he escaped, well, no, actually someone released him, and he went missing with Francis's mother . . . and they haven't been seen since!"

Matthew stops and blushes deeply, realizing too late what he has said, and throws a scared glance at Ross.

"It is not known that they were together, or that either of them came this way," Sturrock reminds him, with a wary look at Ross, who seems unmoved. "But that, in short, is why we are here—to find whomever we can, to see that they are . . . safe."

The woman leans in to the fire, her eyes very wide and shining; she is quite transformed from the terrified creature in the forest of a few hours before. She takes a breath and puts her head on one side.

"You have been so kind to us. We owe you our lives. So I feel I must say to you, Mr. Ross, that I have seen your son, and your wife, and they are both quite well. They are all quite well."

Ross turns to her for the first time, and stares at her. Sturrock would never have believed, had he not seen it, how that granite face could melt.

FRANCIS WAKES UP TO BRILLIANT sunshine for the first time in weeks. There is an uncanny silence all around—none of the usual noises from the corridor or the yard. He dresses and goes to the door. It is open; things have got rather lax since Moody left. He wonders what will happen if he goes out on his own; perhaps someone will panic and take a shot at him. Unlikely, since the Elect are people of God and don't tend to carry arms. There is nowhere he could go, anyway, without leaving his distinctive limping print behind him in the snow. He hops out into the corridor, leaning on the crutch. No one comes running, and, indeed, there are few sounds of life. Francis thinks quickly—is it Sunday? No, there was one only a few days ago (it is difficult to keep track of the days here). He fantasizes that everyone has left. He negotiates the corridor stretching out in front of him. He has no idea where any of the doors lead, as he has not left his room since he was brought here. No sign of his jailer, Jacob. He finds at last a door that leads to the outside, and goes through it.

The shock of the fresh air is as cold as it is sweet. The sun is blinding; the cold makes his face sting, but he sucks great drafts of it into his lungs, savoring the ache. How could he have put up with lying in that room for so long? He is revolted by himself. He practices moving faster, hopping back and forth outside the door, getting used to the crutch. And then he hears a cry. He follows the sound around the corner of the stables, and sees, a hundred yards away, a knot of people. Despite his first impulse to duck back out of sight, they do not seem very interested in him, so he hops nearer. Jacob is one of them; he notices Francis and comes toward him.

"What is happening? Why is everyone out here?"

Jacob glances over his shoulder. "You know I told you Line and the carpenter had left? Well . . . the man has come back."

Francis hops slowly toward the gaggle of Norwegians: several of the women are crying; Per is intoning what sounds like a prayer. In the midst of them, he sees the man Jacob must mean—a hollow-eyed, unshaven creature, his nose and cheeks flayed red with frostbite, his beard and mustache white with rime. So this is the carpenter he has never seen, whom Line stole away. Someone seems to be questioning him, but he looks dazed. Francis chastises himself for being slow on the uptake, then staggers toward him, his anger growing.

"What have you done with her?" he shouts, not knowing if the man even speaks English. "Where is Line? Have you left her out there? And her children?"

The carpenter turns toward him in amazement—understandable, since he has never seen him before.

"Where is she?" demands Francis, fierce and afraid.

"She . . . I don't know." The man falters. "One night . . . we got to a village, and I couldn't bear it. I knew I was doing wrong. I wanted to come back. So I left her . . . at the village."

There is a sharp-featured woman beside him, clinging to him, in tears. Francis guesses she is the abandoned wife.

"What village is this? How far away?"

The man's eyes flicker. "I don't know its name. It was on a river . . . a small river."

"How many days away?"

"Uh . . . Three days."

"You're lying. There is no village three days from here, not if you went south."

The man blanches, even behind his pallor. "We lost the compass . . ."

"Where did you leave her?"

The carpenter starts to cry. At last, half in Norwegian and half in English, he explains.

"It was awful . . . We were lost. I heard a shot, and I thought I could find the hunter and he would show us the way. But I couldn't find him . . . There were wolves. When I went back, I found blood, and they were . . . gone."

He sobs wretchedly. The thin-featured woman draws away from him, as if in disgust. The others look at Francis with openmouthed curiosity—half of them have not seen him since he was brought in half dead. Francis feels tears threaten; his throat has closed up, choking him.

Per holds up his hand in a command for attention. "I think we all had better go inside. Espen needs treatment, and food. Then we will find out what happened and send men out to look for them."

He speaks in his own tongue, and gradually, they all turn and walk back to the buildings.

Jacob falls into step with Francis. He doesn't speak until they are nearly inside.

"Listen. I don't know, but . . . it is strange that wolves attack and kill three people. Maybe that is not what happened."

Francis looks at him. He wipes his nose on his sleeve.

At the door of his room, Per hails them. "Jacob . . . Francis . . . you don't need to go back in there. Come to the dining room with everyone else."

Surprised, and touched, Francis follows Jacob to the refectory.

They eat bread and cheese and drink coffee. There is a hushed murmur as people speak, but only just above a whisper, awed by the occasion. Francis thinks of Line's kindnesses to him, her yearning to leave. But she is tough, too. Maybe it didn't happen like that. He won't think of it, not yet.

No one in this room seems to look at him with suspicion. He would go with them and search for Line, if he could, but his knee is throbbing with the unaccustomed exercise, and he feels as weak as water. It has been weeks that he has lain up in the white room, his muscles softening and his skin growing pale like rhubarb under a pot. Weeks since . . .

With a shock, he realizes that he has not thought of Laurent for at least an hour, not since he saw the crowd of people bunched on the white field; not even, if he is truthful, since he opened the outside door and tasted the sweet, cold air. He has not thought of Laurent for that long, and he feels as though he has been unfaithful.

From the rise behind the cabin that night, a long time ago, Francis saw a light through the parchment window. He started down the bank, quietly, in case Laurent had visitors. He often does—did—and Francis stayed out of the way if that was the case. He didn't want another telling-off from that vicious tongue. He heard the door open and saw a man with long black hair come out into the yard. He held something in one hand—Francis couldn't see what it was—that he tucked carefully into his pouch, looking about him, or rather listening, with the alert stillness of a tracker. Francis stayed still and quiet. It was midnight and quite dark, but he knew it was no one from Dove River—he knows the way they all walk, move, breathe. This one was different. The man spat on the ground, turning toward the open door, and Francis caught a swift impression of dark, reflective skin, greasy hair curling around his shoulders, a stony, closed face. Not young. He moved back into the cabin, disappearing from view. Then the light in the cabin went out. The man left, muttering something under his breath, and moved off toward the river, northward. His tread was silent. Francis breathed a sigh of relief—if a trader was around, he would have to keep out of the way. But this man was not staying.

Francis crept down the bank and padded around to the front of the cabin. He could hear no sound within. At the door he paused before opening it.

"Laurent?" he whispered, ashamed of himself for whispering. "Laurent?"

There was every chance Laurent would be angry with him—it was only a day and a half since their last argument. Or—a chill strikes his heart at the thought—what if he has already left on his mysterious final journey, giving him the slip? He might have chosen to go earlier than he said, to avoid him, to avoid a scene. That would be like him.

Francis pushed the door open. Inside there was silence and darkness, but also warmth from the stove. Francis felt his way over to where a lamp usually stood, and found it. He opened the stove door and lit a rush, touched it to the lamp wick, and blinked in the sudden light. There was no response to his entrance; Laurent has gone, but for how long? He could be out tracking. He might not have left for good, for surely he would not have left the stove burning? He could be . . .

There were only seconds of his old life left, and Francis squandered them thoughtlessly, fiddling with the lamp wick. When he turned around, he would see Laurent lying on his bed. Would see instantly the curious red patch in his hair; would then move swiftly to where he would see his face, his neck, the fatal wound.

Would see that his eyes were still moist.

Would feel that he was still warm.

Francis blinks away the tears. Jacob is speaking: he says he is going outside—he doesn't like sitting for long periods. Jacob puts a hand on his shoulder—everyone is being nice to him today; he can hardly bear it—will Francis be all right here for a while? He no longer needs to threaten him not to run away . . . ha!

Francis assents, somehow, and his expression is taken for grief at Line's imagined fate.

After he had seen Laurent's body, after he had stood in shock for heaven knows how long, Francis decided he must follow the killer. He could not think of anything else to do. He could not go home, knowing what he knew. Did not want to stay in Dove River a moment longer without Laurent to make it bearable. He found Laurent's satchel and packed it with a blanket, food, a hunting knife—bigger and sharper than his own. He looked around the cabin, seeking a sign, a last message from Laurent to himself. There was no trace of Laurent's rifle—had the man been carrying one? He tried to picture him; suddenly he realized what the man had tucked so carefully into his pouch and felt his gorge rise.

Keeping his eyes from the bed, Francis prized up the loose floorboard and felt for Laurent's money bag. There wasn't much in it, just a small roll of notes and the funny piece of engraved bone Laurent thought was valuable, so he took that as well. After all, Laurent had tried to give it to him, months ago, when he was in a good mood.

Finally he put on Laurent's wolfskin coat, the one with the fur on the inside. He would need it, at night.

He said good-bye in his mind. And walked away in the same direction the stranger had taken, not knowing what he would do if he ever found him.

I REMEMBER A TIME ONCE, WHEN I set out on a long journey, and I suppose it has stayed in my mind so vividly because it marked the end of one period of my life and the beginning of another. I am sure the same is true of a great many people in the New World, but I am not referring to the voyage across the Atlantic, unspeakable though that was. My journey was from the gates of the public asylum in Edinburgh to a great crumbling house in the Western Highlands. I was accompanied by the man who was to become my husband, but of course I had no idea of that then. And I had no idea of the significance of the journey, but once begun, my whole life began to change absolutely and forever. I would never have guessed it, but I never returned to Edinburgh, and indeed, as the carriage left the asylum behind on its long curved drive, certain ties were severed—from my past, from my parents, from my relatively comfortable background, from my class, even—that would never be reconnected.

I liked to think of that journey, afterward, imagining the hand of fate at work, snipping the threads behind me, as I sat in stupefied ignorance in that jolting box, wondering whether I was mad (so to speak) to have left the asylum and its relative comforts. And I wondered, how often are we aware of irreversible forces at work while they are in operation? Of course I was not. And conversely, I suppose, how often do we imagine that something is of great significance, only for it to evaporate like morning mist, leaving no trace?

Whatever my musings, we have arrived at last. The end of this journey, which feels so important. But perhaps it is just the fear of violence that makes it seem so.

We walk across the frozen lake. The sun shines coldly out of the West; the sky is a wash of perfect cerulean blue, the trees a charcoal sketch against the snow. I try to imagine we are here for another reason, a good reason, but the truth is, there could be no other reason for me to be here with Parker. We have nothing in common except the death that ties us together:

that and a desire for justice of some sort. And when that is done—whatever is done—there will be nothing tying us together at all. And that is something I cannot bear to think about.

So that is why I force myself to look, however much my eyes burn. I have to see. I have to remember this.

The snow is thinner on the ground under the trees. The derelict cabin has become so weathered that it is invisible until you are right up against it. The door is ajar, drooping from rotten hinges, and snow has found its way inside, forming a partial barrier. Parker climbs over this, and I follow, pulling my scarf from my face. There is only one shuttered window, and it is blessedly dark. The interior holds nothing that indicates it might once have been a habitation, just a heap of bundles, whitened with drift.

"What is this place?"

"Trapper's cabin. Could be a hundred years old."

The cabin, sagging and dilapidated, its timbers silver with weather, really could be that old. I'm fascinated by the thought. The oldest building in Dove River has been on this earth exactly thirteen years.

I stumble over something on the floor. "Are these the furs?" I point to the bundles. Parker nods, and goes to one, slicing a binding with his knife. He pulls out a dark, grayish pelt.

"Ever seen one of these before?"

I take it, and in my hands it is supple, cold, and unbelievably soft. I have seen one before, in Toronto, I think, wrapped around the wattled throat of a rich old woman. A silver fox fur. People were commenting on it, how it was worth a hundred guineas, or some such extraordinary sum. It is silvery, and heavy, and as slippery and smooth as silk. It is all those things. But worth all this?

I feel disappointed in Parker. I don't know what I expected, but somehow, at the end of all this, I hate to admit that he has come all this way for the same thing as Stewart.

We set up camp in the cabin without speaking. Parker works silently, but it is a different sort of silence, not the usual total absorption in whatever he is doing. I can tell he is preoccupied with something else.

"How long do you think it will take?"

"Not long."

Neither of us specifies what we mean, but we both know it is not the task at hand. I keep peering out of the cabin door, which faces south, so you cannot see the route we took. The light outside is dazzling; every glance sends a stabbing pain deep into my skull. But I can't stay in the cabin; I have to be alone.

I keep within the trees that line the west shore, moving up to the black, unfrozen part of the lake, drawn by the falls at its head, which move but are uncannily silent. When I see them, I pick up dead branches in a desultory way, for firewood. Will we even have a fire, if we are waiting for Stewart? There is a sour, metallic taste in my mouth that I have come to know well. The taste of my cowardice.

It is only a hundred yards to the head of the lake, so you would think it would be impossible to get lost. But that is exactly what I do. I stay close to the edge of the lake, but even walking back along the shore, I cannot see the cabin anywhere. Initially I don't panic. I retrace my steps to the falls, where the water is dark, smoking, ringed with progressively paler ice. I feel that urge—as the walker on the cliff is impelled to go ever closer to the edge—to walk out onto the ice, from white to gray, to see how strong it is. To walk as far as I can, and then a little farther.

I turn back, keeping the setting sun and its fiery flashes to my right, and walk into the trees again. The trunks break the sunlight into pulsing waves that streak and smear across my sight, making me dizzy. I shut my eyes, but when I open them I can see nothing at all—a burning blankness wipes over everything, and the pain makes me cry out. Despite what I know, I have the sudden fear that my eyes will not recover. Rare for snow blindness to become permanent, but it has been known. And then I think, would that be so bad? It would mean Parker's would be the last face I ever saw.

I am on my hands and knees, tripped by what seems to be a mound of churned snow. I pat the ground with my hands: the lair of some animal, perhaps. The earth is dark and loose beneath the snow. A flicker of fresh alarm ignites in me; it must be a very large animal to have dug up so much earth, and so recently—it seems friable and fresh, yielding under my hand. I start to push myself up and my hand meets something just under the earth that makes me stagger back with a yell before I can stop myself. It is soft and cold, with the unmistakable give of cloth or . . . or . . .

"Mrs. Ross?"

Somehow he is next to me before I hear him approach. The blankness dissolves a little and I can see his dark shape, but my eyes are playing tricks on me; red and violet shapes blur with branches and patches of white snow. He takes my arm and says, "Shh, there's no one here."

"Over there . . . something in the ground. I touched it."

A wave of nausea fills me and then recedes. I can no longer see the earth mound, but Parker scouts around and finds it. I stand where I am, wiping the tears that run ceaselessly (for no reason, as I am not crying) from my eyes. If I don't wipe them away immediately, they freeze onto my cheek in little pearls.

"It's one of them, isn't it? One of the Norwegians." I can't get the feeling of it off my hand, which is unaccountably bare.

Parker is squatting now, scraping earth and snow away. "It isn't one of the Norwegians."

I heave a sigh of relief. So an animal after all. I pick up handfuls of snow and scour my hands to clean them of that terrible feeling.

"It's Nepapanees."

I take a few steps toward him, unsteady, as my eyes cannot be relied on to tell the truth. Parker on the ground flickers and burns before me like a Guy on the fifth of November.

"Stay back."

I can't see much anyway, and my feet keep moving closer of their own accord. Then Parker is on his feet and holding me by the arms, blocking me from the thing in the ground.

"What happened to him?"

"He was shot."

"Let me see."

After a moment he steps aside, but keeps hold of my arm as I kneel beside the shallow grave. By keeping my eyes almost closed I can make out what's on the ground. Parker has scraped away enough snow and earth to uncover a man's head and torso. The body lies facedown, its braided hair soiled, but the red and yellow thread binding the braids is still bright.

I don't have to turn him over. He didn't go through the ice and drown. There is a wound in his back the size of my fist.

It isn't until we get back to the cabin that I notice my latest imbecility. I must have lost my mittens somewhere in the trees, and the skin on my fingers is white and numb. Two cardinal sins in as many days; I deserve to be shot.

"I'm sorry, stupid of me . . ." Apologizing again. Useless, stupid, helpless burden.

"They're not too bad."

The sun has gone for the night, the sky is a tender blue-green. A fire burns inside the cabin, and Parker has heaped up a fortune in furs as a bed.

This is only the second time I have let this happen to me; the other was during my first winter here, and I learned my lesson then. I seem to have forgotten much in the last few weeks. Like how to protect myself. In all sorts of ways.

Parker chafes my hands with snow. The feeling in my fingers is creeping back, and they have started to burn.

"So Stewart was here—he knows about the furs."

Parker nods.

"I am worried I won't be able to use the gun."

Parker grunts. "Maybe it won't be necessary."

"It would probably be best if you took them both. I can just . . ."

I was going to be another pair of eyes. Look out for him. Protect him. Now I can't even do that.

"I'm sorry. I am no help." I smother a bitter laugh. It seems inappropriate.

"I am glad you're here."

I can't see his expression—if I look straight at him, bright flares fill the center of my vision; I can see him only in glimpses, from the corners of my eyes.

He is glad I am here.

"You found Nepapanees."

I pull my hands away. "Thank you. I can do that now."

"No, wait." Parker unbuttons his blue shirt. He takes back my left hand and guides it inside, to where his right arm meets his body, where he traps it in his warm flesh. I reach my right hand into the other armpit, and so we are locked like that, an arm's length apart, face-to-face. I put my head on his chest, because I do not want him staring at my face, with its red, weeping eyes. And its burning cheeks. And its smile.

With my ear against a sliver of bare skin I can hear Parker's heart beating. Is it fast? I do not know if this is normal. My heart is fast, I know that. My hands are searing, coming back to life with the warmth of skin I have never seen. Parker pushes the bundled silver pelt under my head; a hundred-guinea pillow that is soft and cool. The weight of his arm rests on my back. When, some time later, I move a little, I find that he is holding the hair that has come loose, twisted into a rope in his hand. He strokes it, absently, like stroking one of his dogs. Possibly. Or perhaps not. We don't speak. There is nothing that can be said. No sound but our breathing, and the hiss of the fire. And the unsteady beat of his heart.

To be honest, if I could be granted one wish, I would wish that this night would never end. I am selfish, I know. I do not pretend otherwise. And very probably wicked. I do not seem to care for the men who have lost their lives, not if it means that in the end I get to lie here like this, with my lips close to a triangle of warm skin, so that he can feel my breath come and go.

I do not deserve to have my wishes granted, but then, I remind myself, whether I do or not, it makes no difference.

Somewhere out there, Stewart is coming.

I AM WOKEN BY A LIGHT touch on the shoulder. Parker crouches beside me, rifle in hand. Instantly I know we are not alone. He hands me his hunting knife.

"Take this. I'm going to take both guns. Stay inside and keep listening."

"They are here?"

He doesn't need to answer.

There is no noise from outside. No wind. The clear, icy weather continues, the stars and a waning moon lending a soft almost-light to the snow. No birdsong. No sound of beast or man.

But they are here.

Parker positions himself beside the makeshift door and peers out through the cracks. I shuffle over to the wall behind the door, clutching the knife. I can't imagine what I could do with it.

"It's nearly dawn. They know we're here."

I've always hated waiting. I don't have the gift that all hunters have, of letting time pass without worrying at every moment. I strain to hear the slightest sound, and am beginning to think that Parker may be mistaken, when there is a light scraping outside, on the very wall of the cabin, it seems. The blood seems to go slack in my veins, and I make a sudden involuntary movement—I swear I can't help it—and the blade of the knife knocks against the wall. Whoever is outside must hear it, too. There is an intensifying of the silence, then the softest sound of footsteps in snow, retreating.

I don't feel like apologizing anymore, so I say nothing. Then there are more foot sounds, as though whoever owns the feet has decided it's not worth the effort of being quiet.

"What can you see?"

I speak so softly it is less than a breath. Parker shakes his head: nothing. Or I'm to shut my mouth. On the whole I would have to agree with him.

After another endless clump of time—a minute? twenty?—there comes a voice: "William? I know you're there."

It's Stewart's voice, of course. Out in front of the cabin. It takes me a moment to realize he's speaking to Parker.

"I know you want those furs, William. But they are Company property, and I'm going to have to return them to their rightful owners. You know that."

Parker looks at me quickly.

"I have men out here." He sounds confident, unworried. Bored.

"What happened with Nepapanees? Did he find out about Laurent?"

Silence. I wish Parker hadn't said that. If Stewart knows we have found the grave, he will never let us go alive. Then the voice comes again.

"He was greedy. He wanted the furs for himself. He was going to kill me."

"You shot him from behind."

I swear I can hear a sigh, as though he is running low on patience. "Accidents happen. You know that, William—you of all people. It wasn't . . . intended. I'm going to have to insist that you come out."

A long gap now. I see Parker's grip on the rifle tighten. My eyes still burn, but I can see. I have to see. The other rifle is slung crosswise across his back. The sky is lighter. Dawn is coming.

William Parker, you are my love.

It hits me like a runaway horse. Tears fill my eyes at the thought of him walking out of that door.

"We can make a deal. You can take some of the furs, and go."

Parker says, "Why don't you come in and talk?"

"You come out. It's dark in there."

"Don't go out! You don't know how many men he's got." My teeth are clenched on the words. I'm praying with every tattered remnant of faith I ever had that he will be spared.

"Please . . . !"

"It's all right." He says it very softly. He's looking at me. And now there is enough light to see his face in sharp relief. And I can see every detail of his face, each curving line that I once thought savage and cruel, each furrow, indescribably dear.

"Come out into the open first. Let me see you're not armed."

"No!"

It is I who says that, but under my breath. There is some noise outside, and then Parker pulls the makeshift door, and steps outside into a gray twilight. He closes the door behind him. I squeeze my eyes shut, waiting for the bullet.

It doesn't come. I position myself behind the door so I can see through the cracks. I can see a figure that must be Stewart, but not where Parker is; perhaps he is too close to the cabin.

"I don't want a fight. I just want to take the furs back where they belong."

"You didn't have to kill Laurent. He didn't even know where they were." His voice comes from somewhere to my right.

"That was a mistake. I didn't want that to happen."

"Two mistakes?" Parker's voice again, moving farther away.

I cannot see Stewart's expression from where I am, but I can feel the anger in his voice, like something hard and rigid stressed to breaking point. "What do you want, William?"

Having spoken, Stewart moves suddenly, disappearing from my field of vision. A shot rings out, and a flash, bursting from somewhere in the trees behind him, and something thuds into the cabin wall at the far end, to my right. There is no other sound. I don't know where Parker is. The powder flash seared my eyeballs like a white-hot needle stabbed into my brain. My breath comes in loud ragged gasps that I can't quiet. I want to cry out to Parker. I can't seem to get my breath. Now no one is in sight. There is some sound to my left, then I hear cursing. Stewart.

Cursing because Parker got away?

Footsteps outside, very near. I grip the handle of the knife as tightly as my numb fingers can manage; I'm poised behind the door, ready . . .

When he kicks the door in, it's very simple. It slams into my forehead, knocking me over, and I drop the knife.

For a moment nothing else happens, perhaps because his eyes take a moment to adjust to the darkness. Then he sees me groveling on the floor at his feet. I scrabble for the knife; by some miracle it has fallen underneath me, and I seize it by the blade and manage to get it into my pocket before he grabs my other arm and jerks me roughly to my feet. Then he pushes me, in front of him, out of the door.

W HEN DONALD HEARS THE SHOT, he starts to run. He knows this is probably not the wisest thing to do, but somehow, perhaps because he is a tall man, the message doesn't get to his feet in time. He is aware of Alec hissing something behind him, but not what it is he says.

He is near the end of the lake; the noise came from the trees on the far shore. He keeps thinking, they were right. They were right—and now Half Man is killing them. He knows he is extremely, foolishly, visible, a running figure against the ice, but he knows also that Stewart would not shoot him. Some simple solution can be reached; they can talk, like two reasonable men both in the employ of the great Company. Stewart is a reasonable man.

"Stewart!" he shouts as he runs. "Stewart! Wait!"

He doesn't know what else he is going to say. He thinks of Mrs. Ross— bleeding to death, perhaps. And how he did not save her.

He has almost reached the trees at the foot of a large hillock when there is a movement up ahead. The first sign of life he has seen.

"Don't shoot, please. It is I, Moody . . . Don't shoot . . ." He is holding his rifle by the barrel, waving it to show his peaceful intentions.

There is a flash of light from under the trees, and something strikes him with tremendous force in the midriff, knocking him over backward. The branch, or whatever it was he ran into, seemed to hit him just over his scar, not helping matters.

Winded, he tries to get up, but can't, so he lies for a few moments, trying to get his breath. His spectacles have fallen off; really they are not the thing for Canada, always frosting or steaming up at the wrong moments, and now . . . he gropes around him in the snow for them, encounters nothing but coldness everywhere. Surely someone could think of something more con- venient.

Eventually he finds the rifle, and picks it up. At this point, because the stock is slippery and warm, he becomes aware of the blood. Raising his head with a great effort, he sees blood on his coat. He is annoyed; in fact, he is furious. What a bloody fool he is, charging into trouble like that. Now Alec will be in danger, too, and it is all his fault. He thinks of calling out to the boy, but something, some greater sense from somewhere, stops him. He concentrates on getting the rifle into position; at least he can fire a shot, not roll over and die without a murmur. He will not be entirely useless; what would his father say?

But there is silence, as though he is, once again, the only person for miles around. He will have to wait until he can see something. Well, the person who fired, whoever it was, obviously doesn't think he needs to come and finish off the job. Fool.

Then, at some later point, he looks up and sees a face above him. It is a face he distantly remembers from Hanover House: the face of a drunk, impassive and empty, closed somehow, like the stone that blocks a burrow. It is not drunken now, but there is no curiosity or fear, nor even triumph, there. It is the face, he realizes, of Laurent Jammet's killer. The man whose footprints in the snow have drawn them all here. It is what he came for—to know him, and to find him. And now he has. And it is too late. Typical, thinks Donald, for him to be so slow on the uptake, just like his father always said. And with a rush of heat to his eyes he thinks, Oh, to hear my father's voice chastising me now.

Donald starts to think it would be a good idea to aim the rifle at the face, but by the time he's thought it, the face has gone again, and his rifle has gone, too. He is so tired. Tired and cold. Perhaps he will just lay his head back on the soft snow, rest awhile.

Outside the cabin, I can see no one, not even Stewart, who holds my left arm twisted so tight behind my back I can take only shallow breaths for fear my shoulder will come out of its socket. No sign, at least, of Parker lying wounded, or worse, in the snow. No sign of Half Man, if that is who it is. Stewart brandishes his rifle in front of me. I am his shield. There is some movement, but all behind the cabin; a sound—inconclusive. He inches me toward the end wall, to where the sun is starting to burn the horizon. Of course, I have no scarf to protect my eyes. And my hands are bare.

"Careless," he says, as though reading my mind. "And your eyes, too. He shouldn't have brought you here." He sounds mildly disappointed.

"He didn't bring me," I say through gritted teeth. "When you had Jammet killed, you brought me."

"Really? Well, well, I had no idea. I thought you and Parker . . ."

It hurts to talk, but it pours out of me; I am molten with anger. "You have no idea how many people you have hurt. Not just the ones you killed, but—"

"Shut up," he says calmly. He is listening. A crackle in the trees. From far to our left, there is a deafening crack—a rifle. It sounds different from before.

"Parker!"

I can't help it. A split second later I could bite my tongue off; I don't want him to think it is a cry for help and come running.

"I'm all right!" I shout with my next breath. "Please don't shoot. He'll do a deal. We'll go away. Just let us go, please—"

"Shut up!"

Stewart puts a hand over my mouth, squeezing it so tight it feels as though his fingers will break my jaw. We move like some ungainly four-legged creature to the end of the cabin, but again there is no one in sight.

Another shot splits the silence in two—to our left, beyond the cabin now. And after it, this time, a noise. A human moan.

I gasp, the breath catching in my throat like tar.

Stewart shouts in a strange language. A command? A question? If Half Man is listening, he does not answer. Stewart shouts again, the pitch of his voice taut, his head whipping back and forth, unsure of himself. Now I have to act, I tell myself; now while he is uncertain. He lets go his grip on my mouth so that he can point the rifle one-handed. I grasp the knife in my pocket, working it around until the handle is snug in my palm. I start to pull it out, inch by inch.

And then a voice comes from somewhere in the trees, but surely not the voice of Half Man. A young voice answers, in the same language. Stewart is disconcerted; he doesn't know the voice. This is not part of his plan. I swing the knife across my body and into his side, as hard as I can. Although at the last moment he seems to realize what is happening and flinches away, the blade meets yielding resistance, and he howls with pain. I have a glimpse of his face, and his eyes catch mine—they are reproachful, bluer than sky; but he seems to have a half smile on his face, even as he swings the rifle toward me.

I run. Another rifle crack, deafening me, somewhere very close, but I feel nothing.

ALEC WATCHES DONALD RUN ACROSS the frozen lake, despite his shouts, and then his curses. He shouts to him to stop, but he does not stop. Alec feels an ugly fear clutch at his insides, is afraid he might vomit, and so turns away. Then he tells himself not to be a baby; he must do as his father would have done, and sets off after him.

Alec is a hundred yards behind when the flash comes—he would later swear he heard nothing—and Donald falls. Alec throws himself down behind some reeds that poke through the ice. He holds George's rifle cocked in front of him, grinding his teeth in his anger and his fear. They shouldn't have shot Donald. Donald was kind to his mother. Donald told him about his beautiful, clever aunts who live on a huge lake like the sea. Donald hurt no one.

His breath hisses through his teeth, too loud. He scans the trees—they have the advantage of cover—then gets up and runs, half crying, bent double; he throws himself flat in the snow and crawls to the top of a hummock to look. He has reached the first of the trees, and it is possible they haven't seen him. Up ahead, there is another rifle shot, and then silence. He couldn't see the flash. It was not aimed at him. He darts from one tree trunk to the next, pausing, looking right and left, everywhere. His breathing sounds like sobbing, is so loud it must give him away. He thinks of the others—the white lady and the tall man—to give himself courage.

This rifle is heavier than the one he is used to, the barrel longer. It is a good rifle, but he has had little practice. He knows he will have to get close to have a chance. He works his way closer to the source of the shot. To his right there is the hump of rock that interrupts the smooth flow of the lake, and ahead, among the trees, he glimpses a building of some sort. A little closer, and he sees two figures outside it—the man who killed his father hiding behind the white lady.

"They don't know I'm here," he tells himself, so he will be brave.

Stewart's voice, shouting out in Cree: "Half Man? What was that?"

Silence.

"Half Man? Answer me—if you can."

No answer. Alec moves forward from tree to tree, until he is fifty feet away, his body protected by the trunk of a spruce. He raises the rifle and sights it. He wishes he were closer, but doesn't dare move. Stewart calls out, impatient, but Half Man does not answer him. And so Alec answers, from his hiding place, in his father's tongue.

"Your man is dead, murderer."

Stewart whips around, seeking him, and then something happens: the lady lunges at him and breaks away; Stewart emits a howl like a fox, and takes his rifle to the only target he can see—her. Alec holds his breath; he has one chance to save her, they are so close. He squeezes the trigger; there is an almighty kick and a cloud of smoke engulfs the barrel.

One shot. One shot only.

He steps forward, cautious in case Half Man is hiding somewhere, waiting. As the smoke disperses, the clearing in front of the cabin seems to be empty. He reloads the gun and waits, then darts to a nearer shelter.

Stewart is lying in the clearing, spread-eagled, with one arm flung over his head as though reaching for something he wanted. One side of his face is gone. Alec drops to his knees and vomits. And that is where Parker and the woman find him.

I am so relieved to see Parker behind the cabin that I throw my arms around him for a moment, without thinking or caring. There is the briefest answering pressure, and, though his face doesn't change, his voice is rough.

"Are you all right?"

I nod.

"Stewart . . ."

I glance behind me, and Parker goes to the corner and peers around. Then he steps out; no danger. I follow him, and see a body lying in the middle of the clearing. It is Stewart—I recognize the brown coat; there is nothing else to recognize. A few yards away, a young boy kneels in the snow like a statue. I think I am hallucinating, and then I recognize Elizabeth Bird's eldest son.

He looks up at us, and says one word: "Donald."

We find Moody alive, but fading. He has been shot in the stomach, and has bled too much. I tear off strips of skirt to staunch the wound, and make a pillow for his head, but there is not much we can do with the bullet still in him. I kneel beside him and rub his hands, which are freezing cold.

"You're going to be all right, Mr. Moody. We got them. We know the truth. Stewart shot Nepapanees in the back and buried him in the woods."

"Mrs. Ross . . ."

"Shh. Don't worry. We'll look after you."

"So glad you are . . . all right."

He smiles weakly, trying, even now, to be polite.

"Donald . . . you're going to be all right." I'm trying to smile, but all I can think is, He is only a few years older than Francis, and I was never very nice to him. "Parker is making you some tea, and . . . we'll take you back to the post; we'll look after you. I'll look after you . . ."

"You've changed," he accuses me, which I suppose is hardly surprising, since my hair is loose and wild, my eyes weep without cease, and a large lump has risen on my forehead.

Suddenly he grips my hand with surprising strength. "I want you to do something for me . . ."

"Yes?"

"I have discovered . . . something extraordinary."

His breath is getting horribly short. His eyes, without his spectacles, are gray and distant, wandering. I notice the spectacles on the ground near my foot and pick them up.

"Here . . ." I try to put them on for him, but he moves his head slightly, pushing them away. "Better . . . without."

"All right. You've discovered . . . what?"

"Something extraordinary." He smiles slightly, happily.

"What? You mean Stewart and the furs?"

He frowns, surprised. His voice is fainter, as though it's leaving him. "Not what I meant at all. I . . . love."

I lean nearer and nearer, until my ear is an inch from his mouth.

T HE WORDS FADE AWAY.

Mrs. Ross leaning over him sways like a reed in the wind. Donald can't get over how she has changed—her face, even half hidden by her hair, is softer, kinder; and her eyes shine, all dazzling color like bright water, as though the pupils have contracted to nothing.

He stops himself from saying the name "Maria." Maybe, he thinks, it is better that she doesn't know. That she doesn't have that tug of loss, of regret, of possibility snuffed out, always nagging at the back of her mind.

But now, in front of Donald a tunnel opens up, an immensely long tunnel, and it is like looking down the wrong end of a telescope, through which everything is very tiny, but very sharp.

A tunnel of years.

He looks on with astonishment; through the tunnel he sees the life he would have had with Maria: their marriage, their children, their quarrels, their petty disagreements. The arguments about his career. The moving to the city. The touch of her flesh.

The way he would smooth out the little crease in her forehead with his thumb. Her taking him to task. Her smile.

He smiles back at her, remembering how she took off her shawl to staunch his wound at the rugby match, the day they first met, all those years ago. His blood on her shawl, binding them.

The life whirrs before him like a riffled deck of cards in the hands of a dealer, each picture glowing and complete in every detail. He can see himself when old, and Maria, also old, still full of energy. Arguing, writing, reading between the lines, having the last word.

Having no regrets.

It doesn't look like a bad life.

Maria Knox will never know the life she might have had, but Donald knows it. He knows, and he is glad.

Mrs. Ross is looking down at him, her face in a mist, dazzling and moist, beautiful. She is very near and very far away. She seems to be asking him something, but for some reason he can't hear her anymore.

But everything is clear.

And so Donald doesn't say Maria's name, or anything else at all.

THE WORST THING OF ALL was taking Alec to see the body of his father. He insisted we bring it back to Hanover House, as we will Donald, and bury them there. Stewart we decided to bury in the shallow grave he dug himself. That seems fair enough.

Half Man was badly wounded by Parker's bullet, but when we went back to the cabin, he had gone. His trail led off north, and Parker followed it for a while, then came back. He was shot in the neck and probably wouldn't last long. To the north of the lake there is nothing except snow and ice.

"Let the wolves take care of him," is what he said.

We wrapped Donald and Nepapanees in furs—Alec found a deerskin for his father, which seemed important to him. Donald we wrapped in fox and marten, soft and warm. Parker made a bundle of the most valuable furs and loaded it onto the sled. Jammet had a son: they are for him, and for Elizabeth and her family. As for the rest, I suppose Parker will come back for them someday. I do not ask. He does not say.

We did all this by noon of that day.

And now we are walking back to Hanover House. The dogs pull the sled with the bodies on it. Alec walks beside it. Parker drives the dogs, and I walk behind him. We are following our own outward trail, and that of our pursuers, printed deep into the snow. I find that I have learned, without realizing it, to identify tracks. Every so often I see a print that I know is mine, and I step on it, to rub it out. This country is scored with such marks: slender traces of human desire. But these trails, like this bitter path, are fragile, winterworn, and when the snow falls again, or when it thaws in spring, all trace of our passing will vanish.

Even so, three of these tracks have outlasted the men who made them.

I find, when it occurs to me to look, that I have lost the bone tablet. It was still in my pocket when I left Hanover House, but now it has gone. I tell

Parker this, and he shrugs. He says, if it is important, it will be found again. And in a way—although I feel sorry for poor Mr. Sturrock, who seemed to hanker for it—I am glad not to have something that other people want so much. No good seems to come of such things.

I have been thinking of course, and dreaming when I sleep, of Parker. And this much I know: he thinks of me. But we are a conundrum to which there is no answer. After so much horror, we cannot go on—if I am honest, never could have.

And yet, whenever we stop, I cannot take my eyes from his face. The prospect of leaving him is like the prospect of losing my eyesight. I think of all the things he has been to me: stranger, fugitive, guide.

Love. Lodestone. My true north. I turn always to him.

He will take me back to Himmelvanger and then go on—back to wherever he came from. I do not know if he is married; I suppose he is. I never asked, and will not now. I know almost nothing about him. And he—he does not even know my first name.

Some things could make you laugh, if you felt like laughing. A while after I think this, Parker turns to me. Alec is several paces ahead.

"Mrs. Ross?"

I smile at him. As I have said, I cannot help myself. He smiles back in that way he has: a knife in my heart that I would not remove for all the world.

"You have never told me your name."

It is lucky the wind is so cold, as it freezes the tears before they fall. I shake my head, and smile. "You have used it often enough."

He looks at me then, so hard that, for once, I drop my gaze first. His eyes do have a light in them after all.

I force my mind to turn to Francis, and Dove River. Angus. The pieces I have to put back together.

I force myself to feel the Sickness of Long Thinking.

And then Parker turns back to the dogs and the sled, and keeps walking, and so do I.

For what else can any of us do?

About the Author

STEF PENNEY is a screenwriter. She was born and grew up in Edinburgh. This is her first novel.